SILENT ABDUCTION

OTHER BOOKS BY AL LACY

Journeys of the Stranger series:

Legacy (Book One)

Battles of Destiny (Civil War series):

Beloved Enemy (Battle of First Bull Run)

A Heart Divided (Battle of Mobile Bay)

A Promise Unbroken (Battle of Rich Mountain)

Shadowed Memories (Battle of Shiloh)

SILENT ABDUCTION

AL LACY

MULTNOMAH
Sisters, Oregon 97759

This book is a work of fiction. With the exception of recognized historical figures, the characters in this novel are fictional. Any resemblance to actual persons, living or dead, is purely coincidental.

published by Multnomah Books
a part of the Questar publishing family

Edited by Rodney L. Morris
Cover design by Multnomah Graphics
Cover illustration by Bill Farnsworth

International Standard Book Number: 0-88070-674-0

Printed in the United States of America.

For information:
Questar Publishers, Inc.
Post Office Box 1720
Sisters, Oregon 97759

94 95 96 97 98 99 00 01 02 03— 10 9 8 7 6 5 4 3 2 1

To Rod Morris, my editor, friend, and brother in the Lord.

Behind every author there is that unseen person who spends many long and tedious hours reading, rereading, checking details, and refining a manuscript in a sincere effort to make it the best it can be.

Every one of my Questar novels is a successful combination of my storytelling and your hard work of editing. Thank you, Rod.

CHAPTER ONE

The gusting wind whipped along the broad main street of Prairie Centre, lancing through Dawson Hawes's heavy sheepskin coat. The horse beneath him nickered and shook its head, finding the cold wind as distasteful as it was to its owner.

Only a few people were on the street, and they paid Hawes no mind as they tugged at their coat collars and bent their heads into the wind. Hauling up in front of the Western Union office, Hawes slid from the saddle, tugged his hat tighter on his hoary head, and glanced dismally toward the lowering, gray sky. It was late March, but it was evident that spring wouldn't be showing up on the Nebraska plains any time soon. The aging farmer wrapped the reins around the hitch rail, crossed the boardwalk, and entered the telegraph office.

Agent Willie Hackett looked up from his desk, adjusted the green visor on his head, and smiled. "Howdy, Dawson."

Hackett was in his late twenties, but was already balding. He was so rail-thin, he looked as if there was a famine in the land.

"Howdy to yourself," nodded Hawes, tilting his hat to the back of his head and moving to the potbellied stove in the middle of the small office. Holding his palms toward the welcome heat,

Hawes said, "I don't suppose there's been any response to my wire."

Hackett knew Dawson Hawes was carrying a heavy load since his wife had died with pneumonia two winters previously. Hackett was also aware that even more than the loss of his wife, Hawes was carrying the grief laid on him by his two wayward sons.

"I've had two wires come in today from Hastings, Dawson, but nothing for you."

Hawes nodded dejectedly. "I was afraid he'd be gone from Hastings by the time my wire got there. He'd already been in Hastings a week before I got wind of it. Whatever business he had there wouldn't keep him long. I was sure of that. I...I just hoped my wire would catch him before he left town."

Hackett laid his pencil down, pushed the chair back from the desk, and stood up. Rubbing the back of his neck, he moved to the potbellied stove, stood beside the farmer, and opened his palms toward the heat. "I didn't want to push you too hard about this mysterious friend of yours when you came in and sent the wire to him at Hastings, Dawson, but you've got my curiosity up. I've been thinking about this for two days, now. This guy's name is really John Stranger?"

Hawes unbuttoned his coat. "You got any coffee? I could use some to warm up my blood before I ride for him."

"I can sure fix some in a hurry," grinned Hackett, hastening across the room to a cabinet. Next to the cabinet stood a small table that held a water bucket and a tin pitcher. The telegraph operator quickly produced coffee, an old tin coffeepot, and a pair of tin cups. While putting the coffee into the pot and pouring water in behind it, he said over his shoulder, "You haven't answered my question, Dawson."

Dawson pulled off his coat, hung it on the clothestree next to the front door, and replied while he removed his hat, "That's the only name I know for him, Willie. He never told me more than that. The man came along when I really needed him. I wasn't about to insult him by telling him that couldn't possibly be his name."

Willie carried the coffeepot to the potbellied stove, set it on top, and began stuffing some cut wood into its blazing bowels. "There," he said, banging the hot door shut, "coffee'll be ready in about ten minutes."

Both men sat down, facing each other as they had many times before. Willie started to say something when the telegraph key began to click. Jumping to his feet, he said, "Maybe this'll be your reply from Mr. Stranger."

Dawson did not know Morse code, so he had no idea the content of the message as Hackett penciled it down at his desk. When the clicking stopped, Willie stood and said, "Sorry, Dawson. This is for Barth Matterly. I've got to run it over to him. Be right back." Willie slipped into his coat, donned a hat on top of his visor, and hurried out the door.

Dawson Hawes reached into his pocket and pulled out the silver medallion he had found on his kitchen table the day John Stranger left his house nearly a year ago. The tall, dark, quiet-spoken man had come to his rescue when a bad crop had just about wiped them out. The bank in Kearney—some twelve miles south—was about to foreclose on the farm because Hawes could not meet his semiannual payment on the loan.

John Stranger had shown up out of the blue and made the payment for him. A good crop last summer had gotten him back on his feet financially. Hawes was also especially appreciative that while he was here, Stranger had given young Donnie a good talking to, and Donnie had seemed to respond. It wasn't Stranger's fault that Donnie decided to go ahead and follow his older brother's footsteps. Donnie, who was now nineteen, idolized Denvil, who was six years older. Denvil was just plain bad and had been a disciplinary problem from the time he was an adolescent.

Denvil had become an outlaw at twenty. Dawson was sure that one reason his wife had not lived through her bout with pneumonia was that Denvil's shameful life had destroyed her will to live.

Reports had come to Dawson that Denvil not only was a robber and a thief, but had also turned killer. He was now leading his own gang, and had a price on his head. To Dawson's dismay, Donnie had left home and joined up with his brother.

Dawson Hawes was finding the shame of it all more than he could bear. Some of the people in Prairie Centre were blaming him for the way his sons had turned out, and were shunning him as if he were part of Denvil's gang.

Dawson had tried to bring his boys up right. He and Martha had given them a Christian home. Though there was no church in the area, Dawson had regularly led his wife and sons in worship in their home, and taught them from the Bible.

Dawson was fingering the medallion when Willie Hackett came through the door, gasping for breath. "It's getting colder out there," he said, closing the door. As he was peeling out of his coat and removing his hat, he noted the medallion. "So you're still carrying that silver piece with you!"

"Yep," nodded Hawes. "Reminds me that there are still some decent people in this world."

Willie drew up, looked down at the medallion in a squint, and asked, "What does it say on there? Something from the Bible, isn't it?"

"Yes," replied Dawson, holding it up so Willie could see it. "It says, *THE STRANGER THAT SHALL COME FROM A FAR LAND—Deuteronomy 29:22.*"

"Got any idea what that means?"

"Not in the least. All I know is that I was about to lose my farm when from out of nowhere, this man dressed like a preacher showed up at my front door with a receipt from the bank, showing he had made my loan payment...principal and interest."

"I can't remember...did he tell you why? Or how he even knew you were in financial trouble?"

"Not really. When I asked him how he knew about it, he never did give me a direct answer. Just said something about my plight had been made known to him by an interested party. When I asked him why, even then, he would make such a payment for someone he didn't know at all, he said it was part of his job. So, of course, I asked him exactly what his job was and who he worked for. All he would say was the person he served had invested him with a high calling, and it was his duty and privilege to carry it out. And that's all I could get out of him."

Willie cocked his head. "Do you suppose this person he serves is God?"

"I have a feeling that's who he meant."

"But where would he get the money to go around paying people's debts?"

"I have no idea. I don't think the Lord has a mint in heaven and a chute by which He sends the money to earth. The man's a mystery to me. He leaves you with a lot of questions. Like even this medallion. I told him about Denvil, and that he was leading his little brother astray. Mr. Stranger had a long talk with Donnie. Read to him from the Bible, and even prayed with him. Well, the next morning I got up extra early to fix him breakfast so's he could leave at sunrise as he had planned...and he was already gone. That's when I found this medallion on the kitchen table."

Willie was at the stove, testing the coffee. "Some kind of mystery man. I'll say that for him."

Willie poured coffee for both of them, then sat down, facing his friend. "So...if you don't mind my asking, Dawson, why are you trying to reach this John Stranger?"

Dawson's face went pale. "I'd rather not say, Willie. Let's just leave it that...that, well, I've got some serious trouble, and he's the only person I know who can help me. I need to talk to him real bad."

Willie was quiet for a moment, then offered, "I'll bet Mr. Stranger is a preacher, Dawson. You know, one of those circuit riding kind. His travels and all the experiences he's been through have probably put all that wisdom in his head. But from what I know about Donnie, apparently this John Stranger's talk with him didn't do any good. I guess you know what people in town are saying."

"You mean about me not having brought my boys up right?"

"Yeah. And that every robbery they pull is your fault. And that you ought to personally pay back every dollar they've taken."

"Yes, I've heard that. Makes it almost impossible for me to come into town. I'd leave my farm and go elsewhere, but I have hopes that one day Donnie will see how wrong it is to follow his brother, and come home. I want him to have a home to come to. I want him to take the farm when I die, and continue to work it."

"That's only natural," nodded Willie, "a man wanting his son to follow his steps in life." He paused, then said, "I guess you've not given up on Donnie, like you have on Denvil."

"Denvil's past reclaiming, Willie. He's a murderer. One of these days, the law will catch up to him and hang him. I can only hope—yes, and pray—that it will happen before he makes a killer out of Donnie." Dawson's voice broke on those last words, and tears filled his eyes.

"Just this morning I heard some folks say..." Willie caught himself and glanced nervously at Dawson.

"Well, what did you hear?" demanded Hawes.

"If you haven't heard it, I guess it's better that you hear it from me," Willie said shakily. He cleared his throat. "Some folks are saying that *you* are responsible for every person Denvil has shot down. That *you* should be hanged as well as him."

The words hit Dawson Hawes like a battering ram. Rising, he moved slowly toward the cupboard and set his cup down.

Turning, he went to the clothestree and began shouldering into his coat.

"Dawson, I'm sorry for what people are saying...and I'm sorry I had to tell you," Willie said.

"Don't blame yourself, Willie. You can't help what they're saying. And you're right. I'd rather have heard it from you." He donned his hat, and added with a deep sigh, "Guess I'm just a miserable shame to the whole community."

Willie's heart went out to the man. "Aw, now, Dawson," he said tenderly, "it isn't that way at all. It's just that people—"

Willie's words were cut off as Dawson moved through the door quickly and closed it behind him.

Sleet was beginning to fall, slowly at first, like fine gravel falling from a shelf. Then it was seized by the relentless wind and whipped one way and another.

Dawson Hawes mounted his horse and rode out of town. He tried to pray as he rode toward home with the sleet pelting his body and stinging his face, but it seemed that the Lord was too far away, and probably felt toward him like the people in town did. Somehow, he had failed God, his community, and his sons.

Hawes wished for John Stranger. If he could only talk to the one man he had ever met who seemed to understand life's difficulties.

But John Stranger was far away, also.

When Dawson arrived at the farm, the sleet was letting up, but the wind was still fierce. He put the horse in the barn, along with the draft horses, made sure they had water, grain, and hay, and trudged his way to the house. The wind was whining around the eaves, and the house was cold. The fire had gone out in both the kitchen stove and the potbellied stove in the parlor.

Dawson did not bother to build a fire. Throwing his hat on a chair in the parlor, he opened a cabinet drawer, took out a .44 caliber revolver, and carried it to his roll-top desk. The top was already rolled back.

Sitting down, still wearing his coat, he laid the revolver on the desk, took out a sheet of paper, and picked up a pencil. The weight of the world was on him, and the room was filled with gloom as he began to scratch out a message:

> To whoever finds my body—
>
> My Martha has been gone for two years, now, and though I've coped with her loss by the Lord's help, seems I let Him down in bringing up my two sons. So He's turned His back on me. Since Denvil's turned out to be a killer and a robber, and it looks like Donnie's going to be just like him, my failure as a father is more than I can bear. There's nothing left for me on this earth.
>
> If Donnie somehow straightens out, I'd like for him to have the farm. But if he doesn't, just sell it and use the money to build a church in Prairie Centre, or even in Kearney. This community needs a good Bible-preaching church. Find one of those gospel-preaching kind of preachers and give him my blessing.
>
> Please see that my saddle horse and my draft horses find a good home. And thank you, whoever you are.
>
> Dawson Hawes

Leaving the note lying on the desk face-up, Dawson picked up the revolver and looked at it a moment. Then biting his lips, he cocked the hammer, then put the muzzle to his temple. Closing his eyes, he said through clenched teeth, "If You're listening at all, Lord...please forgive me."

There was a sudden break in the howl of the wind, and in that brief space of time, Dawson Hawes heard a horse blow, outside. Swinging his gaze toward the front of the house, he looked through the window and saw a rider clad in black dismounting from a coal-black horse.

"John Stranger!" he breathed.

Easing the hammer down, Hawes laid the gun on the desk and dashed to the door. Yanking it open, he smiled as he saw the tall man coming across the porch, head bent into the wind. "Mr. Stranger!" exclaimed Hawes. "Come in!"

Ducking his head as he passed through the doorway, John Stranger removed his black, flat-crowned hat and said in a low, soft voice, "I had left Hastings, Dawson, but just happened to pass back through late yesterday afternoon. The telegraph operator saw me on the street and hurried out to tell me about your wire. He tried to get a message through to the Western Union office in Prairie Centre for me, but apparently the line was down somewhere. Probably the wind. Anyway, I figured if you wanted to see me, it must be important. So, here I am."

As he spoke, Stranger's eyes wandered to the desk, where he saw the revolver lying next to the sheet of paper.

Hawes grabbed Stranger's hand, shook it vigorously, saying, "You're right, my friend! It *is* important! I—"

Stranger slipped his hand from Hawes's grip and moved toward the desk. "What's this?"

Hawes knew it was too late to stop him. Stranger was going to learn that he had been about to take his own life.

The tall man glanced at his friend as he picked up the note, then began reading it. Hawes stood a few feet away and looked at the floor.

Stranger read the note quickly, then turned to Hawes and said in an even tone, "Dawson, suicide isn't the answer."

Without looking up, Hawes said dismally, "It was the only answer I could come up with."

Stranger laid the note down, placed his hat over the revolver, and took off his overcoat, laying it on a nearby overstuffed couch. Hawes raised his eyes and looked at him. John Stranger towered over him, standing six-six, or better, in his shiny black high-heeled boots. Beneath his overcoat, he wore a black, broadcloth frock coat, with white shirt and black string tie. On his right hip, he wore a low-slung, tied-down Colt Peacemaker .45 in a black-belted holster. The handle grips on the .45 were bone-white.

"How about building a fire and let's talk about this?" said Stranger.

"A fire? Oh, sure. Right away."

While the farmer built a fire in the potbellied stove, Stranger said, "I'm sorry Donnie has decided to follow his brother's steps, Dawson. I thought maybe the talk he and I had would steer him away from it."

"It's not your fault," replied Hawes, speaking over his shoulder. "You tried, like I've tried with both boys for years, but Donnie's got a mind of his own. Trouble is, Denvil seems to have power over it."

"I explained to Donnie that day," said Stranger, "that until he let Jesus take control of his life, his brother's bad influence would win out. He said he knew I was right, but wouldn't submit to the Lord. All he would say was that he'd stay home and walk straight...and think about his spiritual condition."

"Well, that's all he did," sighed Dawson. "Just *thought* about it. And now, he's out there somewhere learning how to rob and steal from his wicked brother. He's joined Denvil's gang." A shudder went over him, as he added, "Won't be long till Donnie will be a killer, just like Denvil."

"You have any idea where they are now?" queried Stranger.

"No, sir," Dawson replied, closing the iron door on the stove. "They could be anywhere. Let's sit down."

As they sat opposite each other in the parlor, Stranger asked Dawson to tell him why he wanted to commit suicide. Hawes told him about the talk in Prairie Centre, and how the people of the community were saying he was responsible for every dollar his sons were stealing and for every person Denvil had killed, because he had failed to raise the boys correctly.

"The more I thought about it," he concluded, "the more I figured they're right. I failed miserably somewhere along the line. I failed my sons, and in so doing, I failed God. Denvil and Donnie are outlaws. I can't look people in the eye anymore. There's nothing to live for. I tried to get a hold of you because you're the best friend I've got. I knew if there was anybody on earth who could help me, it'd be you. But when I didn't hear back from my wire, I figured you were long gone. I just decided to end it all."

Stranger rubbed his fingertips over the twin jagged scars on his right cheekbone and said with conviction, "You didn't fail God and your sons. Donnie admitted to me that you were a good father and a godly example. No, Dawson. You did not fail the Lord, nor your sons. Have you ever noticed in the Bible how many godly men had sons who turned out bad?"

"Well, I—"

"How about King Hezekiah? He walked with the Lord in truth, yet his son Manasseh was as evil as they come. Manasseh's son, Amon, was as wicked, if not more so, than his father, yet from Amon's loins came one of the godliest men in the Bible—Josiah. Yet, when Josiah was killed in battle, his son Jehoahaz followed as king, and was as evil as his grandfather and great-grandfather. And so it goes in the Bible, Dawson. These godly men loved the Lord and raised their sons to be the same way. But as you said a little while ago, Donnie—like Denvil—has a mind of his own. Each person has to make up his or her mind whether they will live for God and serve Him, or go the other way."

"I know, but—"

"Let me ask you something. Is God a perfect Father?"

"Of course."

"Do any of His children ever go astray?"

Dawson Hawes met Stranger's iron-gray gaze, blinked, and after a few seconds, smiled and said, "Thank you, Mr. Stranger."

"Something else, too, Dawson."

"Yes, sir?"

"In that note you wrote, you said the Lord has turned His

back on you. I thought you believed the Bible to be the Word of God?"

"I do."

"Then why don't you believe Him when He says in Joshua 1:5, *Be strong and of a good courage; be not afraid, neither be thou dismayed: for the Lord thy God is with thee withersoever thou goest?* And why don't you believe Him when He tells David to write in Psalm 37:28, *The LORD forsaketh not his saints?* Why don't you believe Him?"

"Well, I—"

"And why don't you believe Him when He says in Hebrews 13:5, *I will never leave thee, nor forsake thee?*"

Dawson Hawes bit his lower lip and shook his head. "Mr. Stranger, I've been an unbelieving fool. I see that now. I just needed you to come along and preach to me a little. Of course the Lord hasn't turned his back on me."

"Good," grinned the tall, dark man. "I'm sure you and Martha made some mistakes as parents, Dawson, but don't whip yourself for what those boys have turned out to be. If I ever get a chance to talk to Donnie again, I'll try to help him see the error of his ways. In fact, if I should ever run onto Denvil, I'll work on him, too."

"You're a real friend, Mr. Stranger," breathed Hawes.

"I try to be. Is this the trouble you were trying to get a hold of me to talk about?"

"Yes, sir. And you've been more help than I even imagined."

Stranger thought a moment. "This gang of Denvil's. You have any idea how many are in it?"

"From what I could squeeze out of Donnie, about eight or nine. Fact is, Denvil's younger than about half of them. He's just got a way about him that men will follow. From what Donnie said, the oldest fella in the gang used to be a gang leader. Name's Gavin Cold."

"Gavin Cold? His gang got shot to pieces down in Kansas

about six months ago. Robbed a bank in a little town called Concordia. Posse chased them north across the Nebraska border. Caught up to them a mile or two inside the border. I did hear that somehow Cold got away. So he's joined up with Denvil, eh? Cold is exactly like his name. He's a cold-hearted, cold-blooded killer."

"You know him?"

"No. We've never met. I've just heard about him. Too bad Denvil has hooked up with him."

Dawson shook his head sadly. "I'm afraid Denvil's gone, Mr. Stranger. My only hope now is for Donnie. But running with the likes of Denvil and Cold and the rest of that bunch will ruin him for sure."

"Wish I knew where the gang is," said Stranger, rising to his feet. "Well, I've got to be going."

Dawson stood up. "Wish you could stay longer."

"Me too, my friend, but duty calls. Don't let what's being said by the gossips in town get to you. Experience has taught me that usually that kind of talk is coming from a small minority. You'll probably find it so in this case, too."

As Stranger was buttoning his coat, Dawson tilted his head, squinted, and asked, "*Are* you a preacher, Mr. Stranger?"

"Sometimes."

Pulling the silver medallion from his pocket, Hawes flashed it at the man and said, "What far country are you from?"

Stranger grinned as he finished the top button. "Now, Dawson, that has to remain my secret."

The wind was still whipping around the house when John Stranger opened the door and moved outside. Dawson Hawes stood in the open doorway and watched him step off the porch. The big black gelding nickered at its master.

"You don't like this wind any better than I, do you, Ebony?" Stranger said as he swung into the saddle.

"Will I ever see you again?" Dawson asked.

"Hard to say. Don't rule it out, though."

"I won't. If you're ever in the area, please stop in."

"Will do. God bless you, Dawson."

Tears welled up in the farmer's eyes. "God bless you, too, John Stranger. God bless you real good."

Stranger wheeled Ebony about, looked over his shoulder, waved, and put the big black into a gallop.

Dawson Hawes watched horse and rider until they were a tiny speck on the horizon. Stepping inside, he closed the door, went to the couch, fell on his knees, and poured out his heart to the Lord.

CHAPTER TWO

The mid-morning sun was shining in a clear Nebraska sky, but there was an arctic viciousness to the wind as it drove straight down from the north over the Great Plains.

Fourteen-year-old Jimmy Dell gripped the metal framework atop North Platte's windmill tower, turtling his head deep in his coat collar. His eyes were fixed on two riders coming from due south. When they came close enough that he could identify them, he shouted to the group on the ground, "It's them! Sheriff Purdum got 'im!"

There was a cheer from the men, women, and children on the ground. From his high perch, Jimmy looked at the shadeless, wind-bitten main street of North Platte, where people milled about, holding onto their hats.

"C'mon down, Jimmy!" called his father from the ground. "Let's join the welcoming committee!"

There was a rousing cheer on Main Street as the crowd gathered to welcome Lincoln County Sheriff Bo Purdum, who had gone after his man and caught him.

Everyone in southern Nebraska knew and hated the name of Denvil Hawes. He and his gang had robbed, plundered, and killed all over southern Nebraska and northern Kansas. For some unknown reason, Hawes had shown up alone in North Platte the previous afternoon and entered the Rusty Gun Saloon. While drinking, Hawes got into an argument with Clarence Buford, one of North Platte's leading citizens. Buford was owner of the North Platte Mercantile Company, and had often given goods to people of the area who were in financial straits.

Bartender Ralph Newman and six other North Platte citizens had witnessed the argument, which Hawes had instigated, and watched the outlaw gun down the unarmed Buford in cold blood.

Hawes had darted out of the saloon, jumped on his horse, and headed south. Sheriff Purdum was summoned quickly. He took one look at Buford's lifeless body, heard the testimonies of the eye-witnesses, and within five minutes was on his speedy horse after the killer. Though Purdum had just turned sixty-five, the townspeople knew he would give it all he had to run down the killer and bring him to justice. Purdum had not disappointed them.

Denvil Hawes, with his hands shackled behind his back, rode on a horse led by Purdum. He glowered with deep-seated hatred at the sheriff and at the crowd who pressed close as they hauled up in front of the Lincoln County Sheriff's Office and Jail. As Purdum swung stiffly from the saddle, George Dell—Jimmy's father—said, "Good for you, Sheriff! We checked the gallows out earlier this morning. It's working fine."

"Yeah!" shouted an elderly man. "Hang the dirty killer!"

The crowd loudly voiced its agreement. Denvil Hawes's grim face lost color.

"He'll get his trial first," spoke up Purdum.

"Well, let's get on with it and string him up!" came an unidentified male voice.

Sheriff Purdum moved to Hawes's horse and helped the outlaw down. Purdum nodded toward the office door across the boardwalk and said, "Inside, Hawes."

Several townsmen followed the lawman and the outlaw into the office, including George Dell. The group of men waited until Purdum had locked Hawes in a cell behind the office and returned with a large key ring in his hand.

"How'd you get him?" asked one of the men.

Purdum tossed the key ring on his desk, then sat down behind it with a weary grunt. "Little bit of ingenuity and a whole lot of luck."

"Well, tell us about it," said another.

"As you gentlemen know," replied Purdum, "I keep a fast horse under me at all times. I had that killer in sight before he reached Red Willow Creek. I was inchin' up on him when his horse did me a favor and took a spill. Hawes was stunned from hittin' the ground pretty hard, so I skidded to a stop and had him disarmed before he could see straight. Had to shoot his animal. Broke a leg. Made Hawes walk in front of me while I rode and directed him into Thornburgh with my gun trained on him. Cussed me all the way, he did."

I don't doubt that," said Dell. "But weren't you afraid his gang might be somewhere near? I mean if you'd run into them, we'd be burying you beside poor ol' Clarence."

"I thought about that," admitted Purdum, "but I wasn't about to let my fear of the gang keep me from gettin' their leader if I could. After all, he's got a price on his head...and besides, he killed one of my best friends."

"I'll check with Judge Blaine soon's I leave here," spoke up Harold Smith, who was mayor of North Platte. "We'll hold the trial whenever he says."

"What about the gang, Bo?" asked another man. "You got any idea where they might be?"

"I suspect they're somewhere south. Probably close to Culbertson. Might be camped along the Republican River. He was beelinin' that direction, which makes me believe they're right there somewhere. He kept lookin' behind us on the return trip, like he was maybe expectin' that they'd show up. Seven or eight times while we were ridin' in this mornin', he told me his boys would come lookin' for him...and that when they did, I was a dead man. Just said it again, when I locked him up."

Well, we'd best get the trial over and hang the dirty scum before they show up," Smith said. Heading toward the door, he called over his shoulder, "I'll talk to Judge Blaine right now. Be back shortly."

North Platte's barber, Howie Fletcher, asked, "Hawes tell you why he came to town yesterday, Bo?"

"Nope. I pressed him on that, and why he would be ridin' alone, but he kept a tight lip. I think he was casin' the town. No doubt was gonna bring his gang in and rob one of our banks."

"Or both of 'em," piped up one of the group.

Purdum nodded. "Yeah. Possible."

"So where'd you spend the night, Bo?" asked another.

"Well, the marshal over at Thornburgh is an acquaintance of mine—Paul Stedham. When I asked him if he'd lock up my prisoner for the night, he invited me to stay at his house. So I did. Got the local hostler out of bed at dawn so's I could buy a nag for Hawes to ride. I'd have made him walk all the way, but it'd take too long. You say you tested the gallows, George?"

"Yes, sir. Used that hundred-pound sack of sand you always test it with. Lever's working perfectly, as is the trap door."

Purdum grinned. "You must've been pretty sure I'd bring 'im back."

"I've seen you go after them and bring them in before. You may be sixty-five, but you're still the best lawman I know."

All eyes turned toward Harold Smith as he came through the door and quickly closed it behind him. "Judge Blaine says the trial will be at nine o'clock tomorrow morning. I tried to get him to make it today, but he said he's too busy."

"Well," said Purdum, "it ain't gonna take very long. We can

no doubt still have the hangin' before Clarence's funeral at two o'clock."

There were rapid footsteps on the boardwalk, and the office door swung open. Everybody recognized a local farmer named Will Fixx. His face was ashen, and his entire body was trembling. Moving past the group to Purdum, he said breathlessly, "Sheriff, we've got trouble. Real trouble."

"What kind of trouble?"

"Well, I headed for home in my supply wagon shortly after you came riding in with Denvil Hawes. I was about two miles out when these tough-looking riders came toward me from due south and signaled for me to stop. From the looks of 'em, I didn't really want to, but I figured if I didn't, they'd gun me down."

"Denvil's men?"

"Yessir! This real mean lookin' one cocked his pistol, aimed it square between my eyes and asked if I'd just been in North Platte. When I said I had, he asked if I knew anything about Denvil Hawes bein' in town. Well, I wasn't about to lie with that muzzle starin' me in the face, so I told him what I knew. When he heard that you'd captured Denvil, he got beet-red. Boy, he's a mean-lookin' dude!"

"That'd be Gavin Cold," commented Purdum. "So what'd he say?"

Fixx swallowed hard, eyes bulging. "He said he was goin' to go latch onto some more men and come to town. I was to tell you that if they didn't meet Denvil ridin' toward 'em, they'd come in here and bust him outta jail, and while they were doin' it, they'd kill you and anybody else who stood in their way...and they'd burn the town!"

Purdum's fist banged the desk. "Well, I'll show Cold a thing or two! We'll just arm ourselves and meet 'em with hot lead when they come. If he thinks he's gonna scare me into freein' Hawes, he'd better think again!"

Fear showed on the faces of the other men as Fixx said,

"Sheriff, when I pulled up outside, those folks out there asked me why I was lookin' so scared. When I told 'em, they got nervous and said to tell you they want to talk to you."

Purdum glanced toward the window and noted that the crowd was pressing close to the boardwalk just outside the door. "How many did Cold have ridin' with him?" he asked.

"Seven, includin' one who is a younger version of Denvil."

"That's his little brother, Donnie," commented Purdum. "Seven, eh? Did Cold give you any idea how many more men he'd bring with him?"

"No, but if they'll ride with him, they'll be plenty tough. I think those folks outside want you to let Hawes go."

"Let him go? Never!" Purdum shoved his chair back and started around the desk.

"Bo!" called Harold Smith.

The sheriff halted. "Yes?"

Smith's features were etched with fear, and his breathing was irregular. "Maybe...maybe we'd better think this over. We all feel bad about Hawes killing Clarence, but getting yourself and a bunch of citizens killed and the town burned to the ground won't bring Clarence back."

"He's right, Bo," spoke up another man. "Who knows how many killers this guy Cold might bring with him. It ain't worth it. I say let Hawes go."

Before Purdum could react, a loud male voice called from the street, "Sheriff! We want to talk to you out here!"

"The mayor's right, Bo," said another. "I say let Hawes go."

The others were nodding in agreement, fear visible in their eyes.

"I can't believe what I'm hearin'," Purdum hissed. Even as he spoke, he stomped to the door, yanked it open, and stepped outside.

Purdum knew what he was going to hear, but he asked the

question anyway as he scanned the faces of the crowd. "What do you want?"

Edgar Whitmore, the town's undertaker, spoke up. "Sheriff, if that gang of Hawes's brings a bunch like 'em in here, it's gonna get bloody. We don't want our town torched, either. We're all in agreement out here. Let Hawes go!"

"Wait a minute!" Purdum gusted. "They aren't gonna bring *that* many! We'll still outnumber 'em. I'll talk to Judge Blaine right now and tell him we've got to have the trial immediately. It won't take twenty minutes to hear the testimonies and get him convicted. I'll tell the judge to set the hangin' for thirty minutes after the trial. We'll have justice for Clarence Buford's murder and we'll have Hawes danglin' at the end of a rope within an hour. Then we can arm every man in town, set up barricades, and be ready for Cold and his bunch when they show up."

The silence that came over the crowd spoke loudly to Lincoln County's sheriff. The men of North Platte were not of a mind to back him. The group who had been in his office was now in a semicircle on the boardwalk behind him. George Dell moved close, facing the crowd, and said in a low tone, "Bo, I'm with you, but the two of us will be no match for the Hawes gang and whoever else they bring with them. You and I both know Cold will carry out his threat. They'll tear the jail apart and they'll turn this town into an ash heap. I'll back you if you decide to face the gang, but this county will be looking for a new sheriff if you do...and my wife will be looking for a new husband."

Encouraged by Dell's offer to back him, Purdum raised his voice so all could hear. "George Dell has just told me he'll stand with me and fight. Now, how many more will do the same? I believe there are enough real men in this town who'll meet the gang head-on. Now, let's hear it. How many of you are willing to stand and fight?"

The silence was deafening. Purdum had thought that Dell's move would stir other men to join him. But it did not.

"Sheriff," came the voice of a man in the street, "if we stand and fight, some of us will get killed. Is it worth even one life just to hang Denvil Hawes? I agree he oughtta hang, but not at the expense of more men dying. Our fighting the gang won't give Clarence's widow her husband back, but it will make widows of some of North Platte's women. I say let Hawes go."

"When I first took my oath of office seventeen years ago," Purdum said, "I swore to uphold the law in Lincoln County and to protect life, limb, and property. I meant it! If I let Hawes walk out of that jail and go free, I'm turnin' him loose to kill again. And that he will do! If you cowards won't stand and fight beside me, then go on home!"

A quivering male voice came from the crowd. "But we won't have our homes if the Hawes gang burns this town, Bo! I'm tellin' you...let him go!"

"You want me to break my oath, Jasper? Is that it? A man that takes an oath then breaks it isn't a man! Like I said, go home! George and I will face the gang by ourselves!"

George Dell's wife—who had joined the crowd only moments before—elbowed her way through, stepped onto the boardwalk beside her husband, and faced the crowd. "I can't believe this! I thought we had some men in this town. The sheriff's right—you're all a bunch of cowards! What have we got, here? A hundred and fifty of you who call yourselves men? How many can this Gavin Cold possibly bring with him? Certainly not more than twenty-five or thirty at the most. If you will all join together, you can make a trap for them and capture every one of them."

There was a buzzing in the crowd as men and women discussed how to force the sheriff to free Denvil Hawes before the gang showed up to wreak havoc on North Platte. No one had noticed the lone rider on the black gelding who had ridden in just before Sheriff Purdum left his office to face the crowd. Even then, the tall man-in-black remained aloof from the crowd near the hitch rail some sixty feet away.

North Platte's main thoroughfare ran east and west, but from where he stood, John Stranger could see down one of the north-south streets all the way to the south edge of town and onto the plains. On the southern horizon, he could see a small dust cloud rising and growing. It no doubt was the Hawes gang and whatever new recruits they had gathered.

Suddenly Jimmy Dell appeared, running along the boardwalk toward his parents. He was carrying a double-barreled 12-gauge shotgun in each hand. Drawing up, he said, "Here, Pa! I...brought your shotgun and mine. I'll stand with you and Sheriff Purdum...against those dirty outlaws when they come!"

George looked down at his fourteen-year-old son, smiled, and said, "You're a brave boy, Jimmy, but I want you to take your mother and go home. I don't want either of you here when the gang shows up."

Purdum saw the disappointment on Jimmy's face. He looked at the frightened townsmen and said, "Too bad you so-called grown men have to be shown up by a teenage boy."

There was a thick silence over the crowd.

Suddenly a man with terror in his eyes pushed himself to the front of the crowd, whipped out his revolver, and leveled it on Purdum. "Get your hands up, Bo! This situation has gone on long enough!" Keeping his eyes on the sheriff, he shouted for all to hear, "Go on inside and let Hawes out of the jail, men! I'll keep my gun on the sheriff." Waving his gun threateningly at George Dell, he growled, "Drop the shotgun, George, and get your hands in the air, too!"

Like everyone in the crowd, Sheriff Purdum was shocked at the move by North Platte's hostler, Hank Pardee. Eyeing him coldly, he said, "Hank, you're not thinkin' straight. Don't you know you can go to prison for twenty years for throwin' a gun on a lawman?"

"Or get your head blown off!" came an icy voice from behind Pardee as John Stranger placed the muzzle of his Colt .45

Peacemaker against the back of Pardee's neck. Pardee was paralyzed with shock and stood stiff. His eyes darted from side to side.

The voice that had spoken was unfamiliar. It spoke again. "Hand me your gun, mister."

Slowly and reluctantly, Pardee passed the gun over his shoulder to Stranger. The tall man then lowered his own weapon and eased the hammer into place. Moving past Pardee, he stepped up to Purdum and spoke so the crowd could hear. "Sheriff, I suggest you tell these people to clear the street. There's a band of riders coming this way from the south even as I speak. They'll be here in a few minutes. I have no doubt it's Gavin Cold leading the Hawes bunch."

Purdum licked his lips. Eyes wide, he asked, "Who are you, mister?"

"No time to answer questions. Get these people off the street. Fast!"

"You heard the man! All of you disappear...now! For your own good!"

"I'm sticking with you, Bo," said George Dell.

"Take your wife and son, sir," said Stranger. "The sheriff and I will handle the situation. Please don't argue with me. There isn't time. May I borrow your shotgun?"

There was something about the strange man's steel-gray eyes that made Dell give in without arguing. "Sure," he nodded, handing it to him. Then the Dells hurried away with Jimmy still carrying his shotgun.

"Sheriff, I know about this Gavin Cold," Stranger said. "He's as deadly as they come." As he spoke, he broke the shotgun open, checked the loads, and snapped it shut. "It looked to me like Cold is coming with about twenty men. I realize you don't know me, but I'm asking you to trust me. Will you do as I ask?"

Purdum was dumbfounded. This man had come from out of nowhere, yet he apparently had knowledge of the man who was now leading the Hawes gang...and he seemed to know exactly what was going on in North Platte.

Blinking, he asked, "Are you a U.S. marshal?"

"There's no time to answer questions, but if you'll work with me, we'll keep Denvil Hawes in jail and spare your town the wrath of his gang."

Looking down the street, Stranger noted a wagon in front of the general store. The bed was loaded, and a canvas tarp covered its cargo. The team was tied to a hitching post. "All right, Sheriff," he said hastily, "here's what we're going to do..."

Gavin Cold rode in the lead at a full gallop with an old friend he had run into in Culbertson—near the Kansas border—beside him. Cass Forker was a small-time thief and robber who had been born and raised in Culbertson. Cold had persuaded Forker to gather up some of his pals to ride with him and the Hawes gang into North Platte to break their leader out of jail. When offered a substantial sum for their services, Forker and his friends had agreed to help.

Trailing the twenty-one galloping riders was young Donnie Hawes, who led a saddled but riderless horse for his brother to ride once they broke him out of jail.

When they were within two hundred yards of North Platte, Cold signaled for them to stop and gather around. While the horses blew and snorted, he said, "We'll ride right up in front of the sheriff's office like I told you before, boys. Stay in your saddles and in close formation. We'll look more formidable that way. I have no doubt that farmer made a beeline for the sheriff to warn him about us, so keep your eyes peeled for snipers on the rooftops. People tremble before the Hawes gang all over these parts, and no doubt they're already shakin' in their boots. A little intimidation goes a long way."

"Do I understand correctly, Gavin," spoke up one of Forker's friends, "that if anybody makes a hostile move, we're to take 'im out?"

"Correct," nodded Cold. "We don't put up with no nonsense. Anybody looks cross-eyed at us gets it. Cass and I will handle the sheriff. We'll get Denvil out as fast as possible, and we'll be on our way. It'll be up to you boys to keep the townsmen in check. Got it?"

"Got it," came a chorus of voices.

"Okay," grinned Cold, "let's go."

Sheriff Purdum stood in the open door of his office with butterflies assaulting his stomach. He wore his sidearm, but according to the stranger's instructions, held no shotgun in his hands. The man who dressed like a preacher feared that the presence of a shotgun might get Purdum killed.

The sheriff had not returned to the cellblock to look in on his prized prisoner. He could barely hear Denvil Hawes screaming from his cell, demanding the removal of the handcuffs. *Scream your head off,* he thought. *If this strange man's plan works, you'll be facin' the noose tomorrow.*

Purdum rested his hand on the butt of his revolver and tried to quiet the drumming of his heart as he ran his gaze the length and breadth of the wide, dusty street. Though there was no one in sight, the sheriff knew that most of North Platte's citizens had not gone home. They were watching from inside stores and behind buildings. He hoped they would rally and show some spunk once the outlaws were disarmed...if the stranger's plan worked.

Suddenly the sheriff could hear the rumble of hooves from the south side of town. Sure enough. Gavin Cold had recruited more men and was coming to break his boss out of jail.

Purdum's mouth went dry. He wanted to draw his gun and be ready to start shooting, but the stranger had told him to stay calm and not to pull his gun unless forced to.

Looking toward the wagon that was now parked a few feet

from where he stood, he said, "Hey, mister! Can you hear 'em comin'?"

From beneath the canvas that covered the wagon bed, John Stranger answered, "Yes. I'm looking through the crack between the boards. I'll be able to see them as soon as they turn onto Main Street. You okay?"

Purdum cleared his throat. "Yeah."

"Get ready," said Stranger, his voice muffled by the canvas. "They're here."

CHAPTER THREE

The bold riders thundered onto Main Street less than a half-block away, and holding themselves in close formation, headed for the sheriff's office.

Bo Purdum closed the door behind him and slowly moved to the edge of the boardwalk to meet them. His heart was jumping. Tension stretched his nerves as the horsemen drew up with Gavin Cold in the lead and Cass Forker on his left, near the wagon where John Stranger lay motionless beneath the canvas tarp.

The riders noted that the street was empty, and scrutinized the rooftops as Cold set steady eyes on Purdum and rasped, "We didn't meet Denvil ridin' out of town, Sheriff. Which tells me you've still got him in the jail. Now, I'm a patient man, but my patience has a limit. I'll give you exactly one minute to go in there and turn him loose."

"Can't do it," Purdum said, masking his nervousness. "He's gonna stand trial for a murder he committed right here in this town. Since I'm Lincoln County sheriff, and he committed his crime under my jurisdiction, he's legally my prisoner. I assume you're Gavin Cold."

"You assume right. Am I to assume that you're fool enough

to stand in our way when you know you haven't got a chance to stop us from goin' in there and breakin' Denvil out? And if you play such a fool, Sheriff, we'll not only kill you, we'll burn this stinkin' town to the ground."

Purdum's voice was firm as he retorted, "You won't be doin' any such thing. Now, the best thing for you to do is turn around and get outta my county before you do somethin' that'll force my hand against you."

Gavin Cold looked around at his men and laughed. "You hear that, boys? Grandpa, here, is tryin' to scare us! Looks like he's gonna have to learn the hard way. We came here to get Denvil outta this one-horse jail, and that's what we're gonna do!"

Suddenly the canvas tarp in the back of the nearby wagon flew off and the tall man-in-black came to his feet in the wagon bed with a double-barreled shotgun aimed at Cold's head. Both hammers were cocked.

"Best you do what the sheriff suggested, Cold!" he blared. "Get out of this town right now, and never come back!"

The outlaws froze in their saddles. Not one of them had pulled a gun as yet. They had been cock-sure of having the upper hand against one lone lawman. Cold was stunned to find himself suddenly at a disadvantage, looking into the twin black bores of the shotgun. With effort he forced his line of sight down the length of the double barrels and into the chilling gray eyes of the man who held the shotgun.

At the backside of the mounted group, nineteen-year-old Donnie Hawes looked on with gaping mouth and widened eyes. He recognized the man who stood in the wagon bed.

Gavin Cold was experiencing blood-curdling fear and white-hot fury. This man who held the deadly 12-gauge on him meant business. He was going to foil Cold's attempt to free Denvil...maybe even blow his head off.

Cass Forker's gunhand was on the side away from the wagon. Slowly, cautiously, he moved his hand toward his revolver and closed steady fingers around the butt.

Cold blinked and said, "You've got me, mister. We'll leave as you say."

"And never come back?" queried Stranger.

"Yeah. And never come back."

The men on horseback sat rigidly in their saddles, realizing that a false move on their part could get Cold killed. Only three or four of them could see Forker slowly going for his gun.

"All right, mister, ease up on those triggers," Cold said. "We're going." Without taking his eyes off the twin bores, he choked, "Let's go, boys. Nice and easy."

Cold had just begun to tug on the reins to back his horse away when Stranger lowered slightly the muzzles of the shotgun. Forker whipped his gun out of its holster. Stranger swung the shotgun on Forker and dropped one hammer. The roar of the shotgun filled North Platte's main street with clattering thunder, reverberating along the clapboard buildings.

The blast caught Forker square in the chest, its impact flipping him out of the saddle. He was dead when he hit the ground.

As the breeze carried the smoke away, all eyes were fixed on the man in the wagon. One man cursed and shouted, "Let's take him, Gavin! He's only got one barrel, now!"

"Shut up, Max!" hissed Cold, throwing him a piercing glance.

Max Worley was a true and loyal follower of Denvil Hawes. Leaving Hawes behind to be hanged grated on him. There was sand in his voice as he said, "Gavin, we can't just ride away and leave Denvil to the hangman! We can drop the sheriff where he stands, and at best, this dude with the shotgun can only get off one more shot! We'll blast him, then get Denvil outta that jail!"

"Would you like to be the one to take that shot?" boomed Stranger, swinging the twin bores on Worley.

Max's face went rigid. His throat was suddenly constricted, and he could not speak.

"I can't hear you," Stranger said levelly. "Did you say something?"

Worley silently shook his head in tiny jerks.

Lining the shotgun back on Cold, Stranger said, "Tell them all to take their guns out of their holsters with their fingertips and drop them on the ground. Then I want the rifles taken from the saddleboots and on the ground, too. They'd better do as I say, or you will be lying down there beside your fool of a partner."

Looking around at his followers, Cold said, "Do as he says."

As the guns were plopping into the dust of Main Street, Sheriff Purdum saw townsmen coming through doors along the street and from around the corners of buildings. Every one of them had a revolver or a rifle in his hands. The stranger's bold move against the gang had put something in their backbones, and they had decided to appear in force.

When Cold saw the townsmen, he figured they had been there ready to open fire all the time. He thanked his lucky stars that he hadn't decided to shoot the sheriff down earlier.

Relieved that the incident was over, and the only blood shed was that of the dead outlaw on the ground, Purdum stepped up to where Cold sat his horse and said, "Take the fool's body with you, Cold. I don't want this town to have to pay for buryin' him."

Cold commanded two men to dismount and drape Forker's body over his own saddle. While they were doing so, Stranger said, "You're all leaving except Donnie Hawes."

Cold started to speak, but before he could get a word out, Stranger turned to young Hawes and said, "Get off your horse, Donnie. You're staying here."

Donnie's face blanched. "How come?"

"Because I told your pa the last time I saw him I'd do some talking to you if I ever ran into you again. Besides...don't you want to see your brother before they hang him?"

Donnie did not answer, but slid from his horse and led both animals to the hitch rail.

Forker's body was now draped over his horse's back, and the two men who had picked it up were swinging into their saddles. Still holding the shotgun on Cold, Stranger said, "All right, mister. Take your cronies and ride. I think you'd better not come back here with retaliation in mind. Denvil will be dead, anyhow, and you just might get yourselves shot to shreds."

Cold looked hard at the tall man with the twin scars on his right cheek and said, "I may not come back here with these men, mister, but I promise you, there will be a day when I'll find you all by yourself. You won't know where or when...but I'll get you."

The outlaw looked toward young Hawes and said, "When you're done here, Donnie, you know where to find us."

Donnie nodded.

Cold looked down at Stranger one more time and grated, "Remember what I said, pal. I'll get you."

"Do it first, then talk about it," retorted Stranger.

Grinning maliciously, Cold turned away and led his riders down the street and out of town.

Stranger walked to Donnie and said, "Apparently that little talk we had didn't sink in."

Donnie avoided the tall man's probing gaze and mumbled, "Denvil said he needed me. He's my brother. What else could I do?"

"That line won't hold a fish, kid. Your pa's running the farm all by himself. He needs you more than Denvil could ever need you."

Shame tinted the youth's features. Still he would not look Stranger in the eye.

"Do you care anything about your pa?" Stranger asked.

"Of course."

"Would it bother you if the next time you went home, you found out he was dead?"

This time Donnie Hawes's gaze came up to meet Stranger's. "What do you mean? You're not tellin' me pa's dead!"

"No. But when I saw him recently he was at the end of his rope. Only by the Lord's mercy did I happen to be in the right place at the right time. He was about to shoot himself when I arrived at his place."

Donnie's eyes bulged. "He what?"

"That's right. Your pa had already written a suicide note for whoever found his body. He was feeling the shame of how his two sons had turned out, and was going to end his life with a bullet. The muzzle was against his temple when he saw me ride up. Told me so, himself...and I saw the gun lying on the desk next to the note when I entered the house."

Donnie's face went white. He licked his lips, then bit down hard on them. Tears filmed his eyes.

Stranger laid a hand on the youth's shoulder. "Don't you think it's time you let the Lord have His way in your life, Donnie? He wants to save your soul and give you something really worth living for. I told you when we talked before, that you need the Lord for time *and* eternity."

Donnie Hawes stiffened under Stranger's touch and jerked his shoulder free. "Ain't none of your business what I do, Stranger. My time and my eternity are my business, not yours."

"I'm just trying to help you see that you've chosen the wrong way to go in life, kid. It'll take you the wrong way into eternity, too."

"Says you."

"No. Says God. In Proverbs, he says, *There is a way that seemeth right unto a man, but the end thereof are the ways of death.*"

"That's just religious hodge-podge!"

"It's just the plain truth."

"Says you."

"Wrong again. Your brother chose to live outside the law. It seemed right to him, but he'll be at the end of a rope before sundown tomorrow. Like God said in His Word, *the end thereof are the ways of death.* I'm trying to get you to see where you're headed,

Donnie. Outlaws are fools, and that's what you're running with. God's Word is true, kid. You'd better heed it. Don't go back and run with Gavin Cold and the rest of that vermin. Go home to your pa."

"Don't tell me what to do. If I want to run with Gavin, I'll run with Gavin."

"And play the fool."

"I don't have to listen to this!" Donnie snapped, turning toward his horse.

"Where you going?" Stranger asked.

"What's it to you?"

"You're not going to visit Denvil?"

Donnie's shoulders slumped. "I'll go see him right now. But I ain't gonna stick around for the hangin'. I don't want to see that."

Stranger took a couple of long strides, drew up to the youth, and announced, "That's exactly what you're going to do."

"Huh?"

"You're going to watch Denvil hang."

"That's what you think! Ain't nobody gonna make me watch my brother hang!"

Donnie whirled and stomped toward his horse. He had taken four steps when a strong hand gripped his right arm, pulling him to a sudden stop. Stranger's grip was so strong, it felt to Donnie as if his arm was caught in a vise.

Speaking in his usual soft tone, Stranger forced the kid's face close to his and said, "You're going to watch Denvil hang, Donnie. I want you to see what a horrible ordeal it is for a man to climb the steps of the gallows, feel the noose around his neck, and take that final plunge. I want you to get a good look at it, because if you don't go home to your pa and quit running with the likes of your brother and Gavin Cold, you'll end up with your own neck in a noose."

"You can't make me watch the hangin'. I'm gonna see

Denvil, then I'm leavin'."

Stranger reached down, yanked Donnie's gun from its holster, and tightened his grip on the arm. "You're staying for the hanging."

The angry youth tried to free his arm, but to no avail.

"Let's go," said Stranger, pulling him toward the sheriff's office.

The townsmen had gone back to their daily routines, and Sheriff Purdum was standing on the boardwalk, observing the confrontation between Stranger and the youth. When Stranger reached the boardwalk with Donnie in tow, he said, "Sheriff, I want this kid locked up in a cell until hanging time tomorrow."

"On what charge?" demanded Donnie Hawes.

"Don't need a charge," responded Stranger. "This is just something I'm doing for your own good."

Bo Purdum grinned and led the way through the office into the cell block. When Denvil saw his brother being forced down the corridor and into the cell next to his, he rose up from the cot where he was sitting and said to Purdum, "What's been goin' on out there on the street? What's my little brother doin' here? How come he's bein' locked up?"

"You ask too many questions," replied Purdum.

Stranger shoved Donnie down on a cot in the adjacent cell, backed into the corridor, and the sheriff closed and locked the cell door.

While Donnie sat on the cot, jaw set in anger and a sullen look in his eyes, Denvil ran his gaze to the tall, dark man, then said to Purdum, "I want to know what's goin' on!"

The sheriff moved close to the bars and said, "All right, I'll tell you what's goin' on. Remember you told me your boys would come and bust you outta here?"

"Yeah."

"Well, they tried it, but this fella right here put a stop to it."

"I heard a shotgun blast. Who got it?"

"Pal of Cold's. The rest of 'em are headin' back where they came from with their tails between their legs."

"So what's Donnie been arrested for?"

"For being a fool," said John Stranger, pressing close to the bars. "I want him to watch you hang tomorrow. Maybe he'll go home to your pa and straighten up before he ends up like you."

Denvil cocked his head, squinting. "Who are you?"

"A friend of your pa's. And I'm trying to be a friend to Donnie. He's going to spend the night right here with you. Why don't you talk some sense into him, Denvil? Tell him how wrong you've been to live outside the law. Warn him not to end up like you're going to end up."

Denvil glared at the scar-faced man, but had nothing to say.

"Let's give the brothers some time alone, Sheriff," Stranger said.

When Purdum and the man-in-black entered the office, the sheriff closed the corridor door and said, "My friend, I don't know how to thank you for what you did out there. If you hadn't shown up just at the right time and taken control of the situation, I'd be dead right now, and Denvil Hawes would be loose."

"No need to thank me, Sheriff. I just did what I had to do."

"Well, you saved my hide, I'll tell you that much. You also saved this town...and you put some manhood into the men around here. I'm convinced they'll back me next time we have a situation that demands it."

"Good," grinned Stranger.

Purdum lifted his hat, scratched the back of his head, and said, "I...ah...I don't even know who you are. What's your name, stranger?"

The tall man grinned again. "That's good enough."

"Excuse me?"

"Just call me Stranger."

"Just call you *Stranger?* You mean that's your name? Stranger?"

"That's what I'm called."

"You got a first name?"

"John."

"So you're John Stranger?"

"Yep."

"Where you from?"

"Long way from here. I assume Denvil's trial will be in the morning."

"Yeah. Nine o'clock."

"From what I could pick up out there on the street, there's no question he'll be convicted and hanged."

"No question whatsoever. He murdered one of our prominent citizens in front of several witnesses. Trial will only take a few minutes."

"Any idea what time you'll hang him?"

"Probably within an hour after the trial."

"Okay. I'd like to have a few minutes with Denvil after the trial."

"You got it."

"Thank you. Now, I think I'll go deposit my horse at the hostelry, then take a room at the hotel."

"It might be best if you let me put your horse in my barn," said Purdum. "The...ah...man whose head felt your gun muzzle is the hostler. I've got to go have a talk with him. Anyway, my barn's right out back. Plenty of oats, hay, and water. Your horse is more than welcome."

"Fine," nodded Stranger. "I'll take him back there."

"How about lettin' me buy your supper tonight?"

"Okay."

"Good. I'll come by the hotel about six. That be all right?"

"Sure. See you then."

Donnie Hawes was left in his cell the next morning while Denvil was taken to his trial. John Stranger sat in the courtroom and observed as witnesses, judge, and jury had Denvil convicted and sentenced to die in a total of forty minutes.

The hanging was set for 11:00 A.M. While the gallows, which was built on skids, was being pulled to the center of Main Street from behind the jail, Stranger went to the hotel room and picked up his Bible. When he arrived at the sheriff's office, Purdum had just locked Denvil back in his cell and was easing into the chair behind his desk.

Purdum looked up as the tall man entered the office, and his eye fastened immediately on the Bible in his hand. Leaning forward, he put his elbows on the desk and said, "After our talk at supper last night, I figured you had to be a preacher. Now, I see it's true."

"Well, I'm only a preacher at times, Sheriff," grinned Stranger. "This is one of those times."

"Go on back. You can have about twenty minutes."

When Stranger reached the cells, both brothers were seated on their cots. Donnie was weeping, and Denvil was quietly staring at the floor. Both of them looked up through the bars as Stranger said, "Denvil, I'd like to talk to you."

The condemned man jumped to his feet, staring at the Bible in Stranger's hand. "Donnie's been tellin' me all about you, mister! Says you're just like Pa. You been preachin' to him. Well, you ain't preachin' to me! Get outta here!"

"You're about to die, Denvil," Stranger said softly. "You have less than fifty minutes to live. I want to show you from God's Word how to die in peace."

Denvil narrowed his eyes. "I don't want to hear a thing from you! Now, do like I told you, and get outta here!"

"You're making the biggest mistake of your life, Denvil. The Lord will still show you mercy if you'll—"

"I ain't wantin' no mercy! Get out!"

"You'll be begging for mercy an hour from now, Denvil," Stranger said softly. "You'll be begging for water, too. In the

Gospel of Luke, Jesus drew back the curtain and let us see the misery and the torment of a man who died and went to hell. The instant he hit the fire, he was begging for two things—mercy and water."

Denvil went into a tirade, swearing profusely and demanding to be left alone.

Stranger nodded. "All right. As you wish." Looking through the bars at Donnie in the adjacent cell, he said, "The sheriff will bring you out when he comes for Denvil, kid. You and I will attend the hanging together."

Donnie did not reply. He knew there was no way to avoid watching his brother die.

At ten minutes before eleven, John Stranger was on the boardwalk in front of the sheriff's office when Donnie Hawes came out, followed by his brother and Bo Purdum. Denvil's hands were cuffed behind his back and his face was rigid. He looked straight ahead as if the crowd that surrounded the unpainted gallows was not there.

Donnie wanted to run, but he knew it would be foolish to try. Stranger moved up, took him by the arm, and said, "Let's go over here, Donnie. I want you to be able to see Denvil's face."

"Why do I have to see his face? Aren't they gonna put a hood over his head?"

"The answer to your second question is no. As to the first question, I want what you see here to stick in your mind. I hope it'll be shocking enough to make you change course with your life."

As Stranger and Donnie positioned themselves in front of the gallows, the sheriff and the condemned man topped the stairs onto the scaffold. Most of North Platte's citizens were there, including the children. Mayor Harold Smith squeezed his way through the crowd and moved up beside John Stranger just as Donnie looked around and asked, "Why do they allow children to come to a thing like this?"

"They don't allow it," replied Stranger, "they demand it. For the reason I'm making you watch. They want to convey a message to the children that they'll remember. Crime is the wrong way to go."

"Exactly," spoke up Smith, leaning past Stranger to look at Donnie. "When these young people grow up and are deciding what to do with their lives, they'll remember the hangings they attended. When the temptations come to go the wrong way, they'll think twice about it."

"We've got some weak-kneed politicians back East who are trying to sell people a bill of goods that capital punishment is not a deterrent to crime," Stranger said.

"I've been reading about that," commented Smith.

"I'll tell you this," proceeded Stranger, "if we ever come to the place in this country where we coddle lawbreakers, and crime isn't punished like God laid it out in the Bible, there'll be anarchy from coast-to-coast. The cities, especially, will be overrun with killers, and people won't be safe on the streets."

Donnie scrubbed a nervous hand over his mouth and focused on the scene atop the gallows. Sheriff Purdum was cinching the noose tight around Denvil's neck. The condemned man stood rigid, face set in a hard mold.

The eyes of the crowd were fixed on sheriff and condemned man as Purdum took a step toward the stairs and said, "Anything you want to say, Denvil?"

Hawes stared straight ahead without blinking. Lips pressed firm, he shook his head.

Tension mounted amid the throng as Purdum descended the creaky stairs and moved to the lever that controlled the trap door.

John Stranger, still gripping Donnie's arm, said in a low tone, "I wish your brother had let me talk to him."

Donnie saw the sheriff remove the loop that held the lever and grip it with his hand. His brother's life would be snuffed out with one jerk on that lever. A knot tied itself in the pit of Donnie's stomach, and tightened its strings sharply, painfully. A wave of nausea washed over him. He was both fascinated and horrified. The fascination kept his eyes trained on his outlaw brother; the horror urged him to look away.

The crowd stood breathless.

Opening and closing his fingers on the lever, Sheriff Purdum looked up at the condemned man and said solemnly, "Denvil Hawes, you have been duly tried in a court of law and found guilty of the cold-blooded, heartless murder of Clarence Buford. Judge William Blaine has ordered you hanged for your crime, and it is my duty as sheriff of Lincoln County, Nebraska, to carry out this execution. May God have mercy on your soul."

With that, Bo Purdum yanked the lever. The trap door gave way, and Denvil Hawes plunged downward. His fall was broken with a sudden snap as the rope went taut. Mesmerized, the crowd watched as Denvil jerked and spasmed for a few seconds, then went limp, his body sagging against the rope.

Donnie's face was flour-white as he turned to Stranger and said, "Would you let go of my arm, now? I'd like to leave."

Releasing his grip, Stranger asked, "For home...or for wherever Gavin Cold is holed up?"

"I don't have to tell you," Donnie said, and walked hastily away.

Stranger shook his head, then looked back at the body of Donnie's brother swaying beneath the scaffold. "There is a way that seemeth right unto a man, Denvil, but the end thereof are the ways of death."

It was almost one o'clock by the time Sheriff Purdum had turned Denvil's body over to the undertaker and directed the return of the gallows to the alley behind the jail. When he could not locate John Stranger on the street, he stuck his head in the office, thinking he might be waiting for him there. There was no sign of him.

Purdum wanted to buy Stranger's lunch and express his gratitude for what the man had done. When he did not find him in any of North Platte's three cafés, he hastened to the hotel, only to find that Stranger had paid his bill and checked out before the hanging.

Muttering to himself, Purdum ran as hard as he could to the barn behind the jail, hoping to catch Stranger before he rode away. The big black gelding was gone.

Feeling a keen sense of disappointment, Purdum returned to his office. "Strange fella," he said to himself as he passed through the door and headed for his desk. "Sharp as a razor and tough as pig iron, but a strange fella."

Sunlight was coming through a window and shining on the desk. A sharp reflection stabbed his eyes, coming from something shiny on the desktop. As Purdum stood over the desk, he saw that the object was made of polished silver and the size of a silver dollar. Picking it up, he realized it was a medallion. There was a raised five-point star in its center, and words were emblazoned around its edge: *THE STRANGER THAT SHALL COME FROM A FAR LAND—Deuteronomy 29:22.*

Purdum recalled the conversation from the day before when he asked Stranger where he was from. The man had replied casually, "Long way from here," then quickly changed the subject.

"Long way from here, eh?" he said aloud. "Where *are* you from, Mr. John Stranger? And I still wonder what your real name is. But...thank you for showin' up when I needed you. I'll never forget you."

Looking at the medallion in his hand, he smiled, dropped it into his pocket, and sat down to wade into some distasteful paper work.

CHAPTER FOUR

Harry Sturgis stood at one of the windows in his office and let his tired old eyes take in what they could see of Jefferson City, Missouri. It was mid-April. The grass was getting green and the trees were showing new leaves. Sturgis loved Jefferson City. It had been his home for over fifty years. This was where he had met and married beautiful Lily, and this was the birthplace of Jason, his only son.

Lily had been gone over fifteen years, since before the Civil War. And Jason had been killed in the War. Harry had no one left. No one, that is, except his brother Leo who lived down in Arkansas. Both of Leo's sons had been killed in the battle at Pea Ridge. And Marian, Leo's wife, had died of heart failure shortly thereafter. Harry and Leo only had each other now.

The old man swung his gaze to the feed lots and cattle pens that had been his life since just after he had married Lily. The Sturgis Cattle Company had done well.

At seventy-three, Harry Sturgis was beginning to stoop some. He had once stood nearly six feet tall, but the years had taken their toll. He was thin and hollow-cheeked, and his thick mop of hair was completely gray.

Turning from the window, he set his gaze on attorney Lyle

Findlay, who sat at Harry's desk, making notes. Lyle was in his late fifties, and had handled Harry's legal affairs for twenty-five years. They were close friends.

Findlay laid down his pencil, shuffled the papers into a neat stack, and said, "I'll draw these up in final form at my office. You can drop by and sign them tomorrow, or I can bring them here. Either way is fine."

"I'll drop by," smiled Sturgis.

"Fine," Findlay nodded, rising to his feet and stuffing the papers into his valise. "Have you told Jim yet?"

"No. I want to choose the right moment. There's time, yet. Besides, I need him until then."

"That's for sure. From what I've observed, the man's a workhorse."

"There's never been one to match him."

"He's had a pretty heavy load since Vince and Shorty left you. Is Jim handling it all okay?"

"Yep. I've had to work him about fifteen hours a day, but so far, he's getting the job done. However, no man can keep up that pace for long. I've got two new men hired. In fact, I'm expecting them to show up any minute. It'll be a nice surprise and a relief, I'm sure, for Jim."

"Where is he now?"

"Over at the Coats farm getting a load of hay. I buy about half of my hay from Willard Coats."

"You hire anybody I know?"

"You knew them when they were teenagers. Ralph Studdard and Ed Patton."

"Oh, sure. They haven't been around here since before the War."

"They came back right after the War was over. You must not have seen them. Both fought for the Confederacy under Stonewall Jackson. Well, that is, until Jackson was killed at Chancellorsville."

"Right."

"Of course you remember what happened to their kid brothers. When General Lyon brought his Union troops into Jefferson City to drive the Confederate-sympathizing Missouri state troops out of here, Wesley and Gary got caught in a crossfire and were killed."

"I'd forgotten about that. What a tragedy."

"Well, Ralph and Ed didn't know anything about it until they came home after the War. Shook 'em pretty hard. They only stayed a day or so, then left. From what their widowed mothers have told me, all they've done is drift around since. There's no proof, but their mothers think they've gotten into trouble with the law off and on."

"So what are they doing back here?"

"Sponging off their mothers. That's why I offered them jobs. Jim will make sure they earn their money."

"You're a case, my friend. Generous to a fault. I've seen people take advantage of your soft heart and generous soul time and time again."

Sturgis shrugged, embarrassed at the compliment.

"Wasn't Jim a Union soldier under General Lyon?" Findlay asked.

"Yep. He was amongst the troops when Lyon came in here. Young feller did all right for himself in the War. He never told me, but I learned from Merilee that he saw a lot of action. She told me he got a letter from General Ulysses S. Grant, himself, commending him for valor shown under fire."

"I didn't know that. I'm impressed."

Jim's been with me, now, just over a year. Nobody's ever stayed with me more than three months. There's plenty of hard work around here, and most of 'em don't last long. Fine boy. Great family, the Logans. Those children sorta look to me as a granddaddy."

"Well, I gotta get back to the office and go to work on these papers, Harry," said Findlay. "See you tomorrow."

"All right, Lyle," said Sturgis, patting him on the back. "I'll see you then."

Sturgis moved ahead of him and opened the office door. The smell of stock pens assaulted their nostrils, and the sound of bawling cattle met their ears. Sturgis stood on the porch of his small office building, watching the attorney walk away, then turned to go back inside when he saw his newly hired employees coming on foot from a different direction.

The old man waited till Ralph Studdard and Ed Patton drew up, and said with a smile, "'Mornin', boys."

The two returned his greeting, then Studdard said, "We're ready to go to work, Mr. Sturgis."

Both men were in their late twenties, and in Harry Sturgis's opinion, they could use a shave, haircut, and bath. Studdard was a short, beefy man. His head appeared to sit flat on his shoulders where a neck should be. Ed Patton was six-two and quite slender. Their clothing and their broad-brimmed hats were dirty.

"You boys come on inside the office," said Sturgis. "I'm expectin' my other hired man to show up with a load of hay right soon. He'll put you to work helpin' him unload the hay, then he'll show you around and lay your work out for you."

Seemingly eager to go to work, the two men entered the office, which was merely an old shack Sturgis had built within a few yards of the cattle pens many years previously. They had just sat down when the old man noticed his hay wagon turning off the road into the yard.

"Ah," Sturgis grinned, "here's Jim, now. Come on. I'll introduce you to him."

Jim Logan had been told by his employer before pulling out that morning that new help had been hired. The thirty-two-year-old father of four had welcomed the news. For several weeks, feeding all the cattle, cleaning the pens, pumping the water for the stock tanks, hauling the hay, and various other chores had been his alone to handle. Though he needed the extra pay from the fifteen-hour days, he also needed to spend time with his family.

Logan pulled the wagon up to the large hay shed, which stood near the auction barn, and slid to the ground. He saw Harry Sturgis and the new hired help emerge from the office, so he stood beside the heavily-loaded wagon, waiting for them to cross the yard alongside the split-rail fence. He smiled at his employer as he drew up with the two men on his heels. After introductions and handshakes, Sturgis turned Studdard and Patton over to Logan and returned to the office.

"You fellas look like you can do a good day's work," Logan said. "We'll unload this wagon, then I'll show you what to do next."

Putting pitchforks in their hands, Jim told them he would pitch hay from the wagon through the shed door, and they were to stack it at a spot against the back wall that he had cleared off earlier. There was older hay stacked near the door which was to be fed to the cattle first.

Studdard and Patton went to work as Logan stood atop the load on the wagon and began tossing forkfuls down to them. He kept both men busy trying to stay up with him.

"You've got a real knack for handlin' that pitchfork, Jim," Ed Patton said. "You raised on a farm?"

"Yep."

"Where abouts?"

"Near St. Louis."

"On this side of the Mississippi?"

"Yep."

Grinning, Patton looked at his partner, who was coming from the rear of the shed with an empty fork and said, "Jim's a Missourian, too, Ralph."

"Good," grinned the beefy man. "What part?"

"Near St. Louis," replied Logan.

"So what brought you to Jeff City?" queried Patton.

Logan explained that after the Civil War, he had taken a job running a ferry across the Mississippi at St. Louis, but that his real desire was to work with beef cattle. One day a little over a year ago, he had chatted with a male passenger from Jefferson City, and had mentioned that he wanted to get into the cattle business. The man knew that Mr. Sturgis was wanting to hire an additional employee, and told Jim about it.

"So," said Jim, resting for a moment, "I wrote Mr. Sturgis a letter, asking if the job was filled yet. He wrote me right back, saying the job was still open, and that he would like for me to come to Jefferson City and talk to him. I did. It looked plenty good to me, so I went home to St. Louis, packed up my wife and four children, and...here I am."

"Had you ever been to Jeff City before?" asked Studdard.

"Once," nodded Jim, sleeving sweat from his brow. "During the War."

Those words drew both men's attention.

"Oh?" said Studdard. "How was that?"

For Jim Logan, the Civil War was over. He held no hard feelings toward any of the Confederates he had faced in battle. He gave no thought as to whether Studdard and Patton had even fought in the War, much less on which side. "I was here with General Lyon when we came in June of '61 to drive out the Missouri state troops."

Studdard and Patton exchanged glances, then set hard eyes on Logan.

"You were shootin' in that skirmish that took place here on June 12?" Studdard asked.

"Yep. Why?"

Patton threw down his pitchfork and blared, "You killed my kid brother, you bloody Yankee! And Ralph's little brother, too!"

"You're both from right here?" asked Jim, shocked at the outburst.

"Yeah!" gusted Studdard. "We were fightin' in Virginia with

General Stonewall Jackson at the time, but when we came home from the War, we found out what you snake-bellied Yankees did!"

Jim could feel the tension building between himself and the two ex-Confederate soldiers. "Look," he said calmly, "the War's over. We're all just Americans again. I'm sorry about your brothers getting killed, but they were wearing gray and I was wearing blue. Both sides were shooting at each other. Men get killed when bullets fly."

Face flushed, Studdard spat, "Our brothers weren't wearin' gray, Yankee! They were just kids! My brother Wesley was ten years old! And Ed's brother was nine! They were right over there in them woods to the south, squirrel huntin', when the fightin' broke out all around 'em. They got caught in the crossfire and cut down. Between the two of them, they had thirty-two bullets in 'em."

Patton leaned over, picked up his pitchfork, and pointed the sharp tines toward Logan. His hands were shaking, and the fingers around the handle were white. "You killed my little brother, Logan!"

Jim Logan gripped his own fork with both hands and held it waist high. He looked down at Ed from his elevated position and said, "Ralph just said the boys were caught in the crossfire. They no doubt caught bullets from both sides. How can you say I killed your brother?"

"Because there wouldn't have been any skirmish if you slimy Yankees hadn't come in here to attack the Missouri state troops! If you'd left them alone, our brothers would still be alive!"

"Hey! What's goin' on here?" bellowed Harry Sturgis, making a sudden appearance. "What are you boys arguin' about?"

Jim Logan quickly explained.

The old man's brow furrowed as he ran his gaze from Logan to the new men. "You two are sayin' Jim personally killed your brothers? How can you prove such a thing? Wesley and Gary were riddled with bullets from both sides. How can you say Jim killed 'em?"

Studdard and Patton gave their employer a sheepish look, and Patton said weakly, "Well, maybe some of his bullets struck our brothers, and maybe they didn't. But if them filthy Yankees hadn't come here in the first place, there wouldn't have been any shootin', and our brothers wouldn't have been killed."

Sturgis shook his head and eyed the two men narrowly. "Look, fellas, Jim was fightin' under General Lyon like you were fightin' under Stonewall Jackson. He was only doin' his duty in the army of his country like you were doin' in the army of your country. The War's over. We're all one country again. There's no reason for it to be a problem anymore. Now, if you two want to keep your jobs, you'll let the matter drop."

There was stone-cold silence for a long moment while Studdard and Patton eyed each other.

Logan broke the silence by saying, "Well? What's your decision? There's work to be done. If you two are going to quit, then do so. I'll unload the rest of this hay by myself."

"I'm waitin', too," said Sturgis, eyeing them quizzically.

Studdard shifted his weight from one foot to the other, and said, "I can't speak for Ed, but I'll let the matter drop, Mr. Sturgis."

Sturgis nodded, then set his gaze on Patton.

"Okay," sighed Patton. "We'll drop it."

"Fine," said Sturgis, "then I'll get back to my office work, and you gentlemen can get back to pitchin' hay."

Studdard and Patton were silent until all the hay was off the wagon and in the shed. As Logan was closing the shed door, Studdard checked to make sure Sturgis was nowhere in sight, then moved close to Logan and said, "I still hate your guts, Yankee...and I still hold you responsible for Wesley's death."

Jim eyed him coldly. "I thought you told Mr. Sturgis you'd let the matter drop, Ralph."

Studdard looked at him woodenly, his face set in grim lines. "As far as the old man's concerned, I have. But I ain't lettin' you think I'm just gonna forget what you did to my brother."

"Me, neither," growled Patton.

"You guys are acting like fools," Jim said curtly. "I'm not going to argue with you about it. Now, let it go, or—"

"Or what?" Studdard cut him off. "You'll go tattle to the boss?"

Jim Logan felt a storm welling up inside him. He struggled to contain it. Taking a deep breath, he said, "C'mon. We've got pens to clean."

Studdard and Patton did what Logan told them to do for the rest of the day, but openly burned him with their hate-filled eyes. Jim felt the pressure of their malice, but tried to ignore it. He needed help with the work load, and the labors of the two men would give him more time with his family.

Merilee Logan had supper cooking, and took a moment to step into the back yard of their humble four-room house to watch her children at play. The setting sun was throwing long shadows across the yard as eleven-year-old Jeremy was down on all fours, letting little three-year-old Susie ride him like a horse. Susie was giggling and enjoying herself immensely. Darlene and Benjamin, who were nine and six, were swinging on ropes anchored to limbs in the cottonwood trees.

Merilee smiled, thanking the Lord for her wonderful children. She marveled at how much the two boys resembled their father. Darlene was her mother made over. Then, of course, there was little Susie. She resembled no one in the family. She had medium-red hair and freckles, and there was a hint of devilment in her pale-blue eyes. She was also the child with the strongest will and the most out-going personality.

Merilee, who was two years younger than her husband, took

a moment to tidy up the back porch where Susie had left a mess after making mud pies. She was about to return to the kitchen when the door came open and Jim emerged with a smile.

"Hello, darling," Merilee said. She hurried to him and embraced him.

"Something sure smells good in the kitchen," chuckled Jim as he hugged then kissed her.

"Papa!" chorused the children as they beelined for the porch.

When Jim held and kissed their mother for what seemed much too long, Jeremy said, "I'm sure not gonna act like that when I get married. Ugh! All that mush!"

Darlene giggled and said, "I hope I can marry a man just like Papa."

Finally, Jim released Merilee and picked up Susie, saying, "How about some sugar?"

The three-year-old planted a juicy kiss on his cheek, hugged him, and said excitedly, "Papa! Jewemy let me wide him! He's my horsy!"

Jim reached down and messed up Jeremy's hair, saying, "I always thought you'd make a good horse, son! Maybe we'll start feeding you oats."

Jeremy laughed, hugged his father, then stepped back to give Darlene and Benjamin their turns. Little Susie stayed in one arm while Jim hugged Darlene and Benjamin.

While her family was washing up, Merilee worked at the stove, placing hot food into bowls and setting them on the kitchen table. Soon they were all seated. Holding hands around the table, they bowed their heads while the head of the household thanked the Lord for His generous bounties.

During the meal, Merilee detected that something was wrong with her husband. Though he was kind and loving to his family, he wasn't quite himself. Thinking it was because he was tired, she looked at him across the table and asked, "So how late will you have to work by lantern light tonight?"

"I don't have to go back at all tonight."

"You don't?"

"You don't?" echoed the three oldest children.

"Nope," grinned Jim. "Mr. Sturgis hired two men today. I won't have to work nights anymore, and I won't have to go in so early in the mornings."

"Wonderful!" exclaimed Merilee. "I've been concerned that these long hours were wearing you down."

"I was feeling the strain some, but the worst part was all the time I was missing with my family."

"Oh, boy!" piped up Benjamin. "Can we play games tonight, Papa?"

"We sure can," grinned Jim.

There was pure joy in the Logan household for the rest of the evening. Jim played with the boys and Susie while Merilee and Darlene did the dishes and cleaned up the kitchen. When they joined the others, the entire family was involved in happy games. Merilee, however, noted once again that Jim seemed to be bothered by something.

When Bible and prayer time were over and the children were in bed, Jim and Merilee sat together on the couch in the small parlor. Bone tired, Jim was holding her hand while laying his head against the back of the couch.

"I'm so happy Mr. Sturgis finally hired some help," Merilee said.

"Yeah," Jim sighed. "We'll miss the extra pay, but it'll sure be nice to have my time at home again."

Jim closed his eyes, totally satisfied to have Merilee's hand in his. She leaned back and let a few quiet moments pass, then sat up straight and said, "Jim."

Without opening his eyes, he responded, "Mm-hmm?"

"Something's bothering you. What is it?"

Remaining as he was, Jim asked, "What makes you think something's bothering me?"

"I don't think it, I know it. What is it?"

Jim looked at her by the light of the lantern that sat on a table nearby and said, "You sure are beautiful."

Merilee squeezed his hand and said, "Don't change the subject, Mr. Logan. I know you, and I know when something's eating at you. Come on. Out with it."

He sat up straight and looked her in the eye. "You females are a perceptive lot, aren't you?"

"Yes. The Lord made us this way so we could be the helpers to our husbands that He means for us to be."

"Honey, I don't want to weigh you down with my problems," he said softly.

"Your problems are my problems," she countered. "Out with it."

Jim sighed, ran splayed fingers through his thick, dark locks, and said, "Well, it's those two men Mr. Sturgis hired."

"What about them?"

Jim explained to Merilee about the trouble Ralph Studdard and Ed Patton started when they learned he had been in Jefferson City with General Lyon.

Merilee agreed that for Studdard and Patton to blame Jim for the deaths of their little brothers was ridiculous, but she asked him to keep a guard on his temper and not do something that would cost him his job. Jim assured her he would keep his cool.

Merilee kissed her husband warmly, then said, "There's something I want to show you, darling." As she spoke, she went to a nearby table and picked up that day's edition of the Jefferson City News.

"Something happen in town I haven't heard about?"

"No," she smiled, "but there's an article in here concerning what we've been talking about for the past six months."

"Cattle ranching in the West?"

"Mm-hmm," she nodded. She turned up the flame in the lantern, then sat down beside him. "Let me read it to you."

Jim Logan perked up. The subject of cattle ranching was something he thought about often. He and Merilee shared the dream that one day they could move west and have their own ranch. Working with the cattle at the Sturgis Cattle Company had whetted his appetite for raising his own herd. In the past six months, they had talked about it continuously, and had even prayed together, asking the Lord to make a way for them to realize their dream.

At first, Jim had faith that the Lord would come through, but of late his faith was wavering. Merilee had reminded him that sometimes God makes His children wait for prayers to be answered in order to test and strengthen their faith.

Easing back on the couch once more, Jim listened intently while his wife read the article aloud. It was written by a Jefferson City columnist, and told of great opportunities for people who were willing to work hard to make it in the cattle ranching business west of the Mississippi. The columnist gave several examples of men and their families who had gone west and become successful ranchers:

> One outstanding example is Corey McCollister, a rancher in the northwest corner of Nebraska. Now in his early forties, McCollister settled in that area some five years prior to the Civil War, and with a few hundred dollars, bought land and a small herd. Today, McCollister and his wife Emily Grace are quite wealthy. Their ranch, which is some twelve miles west of the small town of Hay Springs, Nebraska, has grown to be the largest spread within a hundred-mile radius.
>
> Once a year Corey McCollister and his ranch hands run a cattle drive south to the railroad at Ogallala, some forty-five miles west of North Platte. Beef buyers are there to make their offers, and McCollister sells them on the hoof to the highest bidders. The buyers then load the cattle on the trains and take them east to market.
>
> Land in that part of Nebraska is going for a very rea-

sonable price. A man can buy enough grassland to start a small herd for less than five hundred dollars.

Merilee finished reading the article and laid the paper in her lap. Jim sat up, sighed, and said, "A little less than five hundred dollars, eh? Plus plenty more to buy the cattle for getting started...and money to build a house and barn, plus money to live on till you sell your first steer. The adventure sounds great, honey, and I'd sure love to be in on it, but it'd take fifteen hundred dollars to do all that. And plenty more than fifteen hundred if we wanted to buy a place big enough to really expand when the herd got bigger. That'd be asking an awful lot of the Lord to come up with, wouldn't it?"

Smiling, Merilee responded, "That depends."

"On what?"

"On how big your God is."

Jim felt his face flush. Merilee had a way of putting him to silence when it came to his little faith in God's capabilities.

Knowing she had hit him in his weak spot, Merilee said, "Jim, you've trusted the Lord to save your soul and take you to heaven when you die, right?"

"Of course."

"Then, darling, if He can do that, why is it so hard for you to believe He can make a way for us to realize our dream of going west and getting into cattle ranching?"

"Well, I—"

"Don't you remember God's words to Abraham when Sarah doubted that He could give them a son in their old age?"

Jim bit his lower lip. Clearing his throat, he said, "Yes. God asked Abraham, 'Is there anything too hard for the Lord?' "

"And what was God implying?"

Jim cleared his throat again. "That there's nothing too hard for Him."

"Right! Well, is there?"

Jim took Merilee in his arms and squeezed her tight. "Okay,

Reverend Merilee. Your sermon has me under conviction. Where's the altar? I've got to repent of my unbelief."

Pulling back far enough to look him in the eye, she chuckled, "The couch will do as an altar. And while your confessing your unbelief to the Lord, why don't you ask Him if He's big enough to handle our dream."

CHAPTER FIVE

The next day was Saturday, which proved to be as busy as most Saturdays. Since the weekly auctions at the Sturgis Cattle Company were held on Monday, the majority of cattlemen all over the area liked to get their herds to the pens on Saturday.

The usual procedure was for Harry Sturgis to make an offer for the cattle as they were brought in. If the sellers felt Sturgis's offer was as good or better than the price they might get at the auction on Monday, they would close the deal immediately. If they decided to gamble and wait for the auction, Sturgis charged a fee for keeping and feeding the animals until they were sold.

Sturgis had made his best money by buying the cattle during the week and selling them at the auction. He had a knack for knowing how to make a good buy.

Under Jim Logan's directions, Ralph Studdard and Ed Patton were helping the cattlemen herd their beasts into the pen while Sturgis looked them over and made his pre-auction offers. All day long, Studdard and Patton gave Logan a hard time, even trying to provoke him into a fight, not realizing that Sturgis was watching.

At the close of the hard day, Sturgis stood at his office window and watched his three employees leaving for home. Again, the ex-Confederate soldiers were vexing Logan, who was struggling to hold his temper. When Logan had turned one direction and his tormentors had gone the other, Sturgis smiled to himself, admiring Jim for taking the abuse without retaliation. The old man knew it wasn't fear that kept Jim from lighting into them. He had seen him in action before. Sturgis had no doubt Jim could whip the two of them.

On Sunday morning, the Logan family sat in their usual pew at the Jefferson City Community Church. The pastor preached on faith, emphasizing that the Almighty God tests the faith of believers by making them wait on answers to prayer. He pointed out that the God who was powerful enough to create the universe and to provide salvation for a world of lost sinners was powerful enough to do great and mighty things for His children. Harry Sturgis sat across the aisle from the Logans, nodding his assent to what the preacher was saying.

After the service, people stood outside the church building talking in groups large and small. The Logans had been in conversation with another couple and were just turning to go to their buggy when Sturgis approached, offering pieces of horehound candy to his "adopted" grandchildren.

As the Logan children were gladly accepting the candy and thanking Grandpa Sturgis for it, Merilee said, "Don't eat that candy now, kids! Save it for after dinner."

The old man grinned at her. "I was about to tell them the same thing, Merilee."

Hands-on-hips, Merilee narrowed her eyes and said, "Mm-hmm. Likely story."

At that instant, Merilee saw Susie pop the piece of candy into her mouth. When told to remove it, the little redhead insisted that she was hungry and could not survive until dinner without it. Jim stood over her like some towering ogre and said, "Susie, didn't your mother tell you not to eat the candy now?"

"Uh-huh, but I was hungry."

"You'll survive, young lady. I want that candy out of your mouth. Now!"

Susie gave her father a supercilious look, shoved the candy over her lower lip with her tongue, and let it fall to the ground.

Jim recognized the show of rebellion. When he picked her up and headed for the far side of the building, she was wailing like a banshee, knowing what was coming.

Harry frowned and said, "Oh, my. I'm afraid I've caused a problem here."

Merilee was glad for the murmur of the crowd. It covered the sounds of spanking and wailing. "Not really, Mr. Sturgis," Merilee replied quietly. "The actual problem is that our fourth child is quite spirited, and needs that spirit bent in the proper direction more often than I care to admit."

Sturgis chuckled hollowly and changed the subject to the sermon they had just heard. They were discussing it when Jim returned carrying Susie, who had been crying.

"Sorry I caused a problem, Jim," the elderly man said. "I'll be more careful about the timing of my candy handouts from now on."

"It's all right, Mr. Sturgis," smiled Jim, looking around at his other three offspring. "It was a good obedience test. Jeremy, Darlene, and Benjamin passed the test. Susie didn't. But then, three out of four isn't too bad."

"I was just commenting to Merilee what a great sermon we just heard," Sturgis said.

"Sure was," nodded Jim. "We really do have a big God. I'm afraid we limit Him too often by our little faith."

"That's for sure," agreed Sturgis. "Changing the subject, Jim, but I want to commend you for the way you've taken the verbal abuse from Studdard and Patton."

"You know about that?"

"Yes. I...ah...I was doing a bit of eavesdropping yesterday

when neither you nor your tormentors knew I was near. I'm amazed at how well you've kept your temper under control."

"Well, sir, it hasn't been easy, but by asking the Lord to help me, so far I've been able to control myself."

"I'd fire them over it, Jim, but as you know, there aren't any men in this town looking for work. Especially such hard work. At least with Studdard and Patton around, the whole load isn't on your shoulders."

"Can't blame you for their fool stupidity, sir," responded Jim. "They'll probably ease off once they've gotten the bitterness out of their systems."

"Well, I hope so. Anyway, I want to tell you how much I appreciate your effort to get along with them. And I also want to thank you for sticking with me. You're the only man who's ever stayed with me over three months."

Jim shrugged. "Why shouldn't I? You've always treated me right and paid me a good wage. I have no reason to seek other employment. Besides, I thoroughly enjoy working with cattle."

Sturgis grinned. "I can see that. Come to think of it, some of the people in town have told me that you have a big dream to one day go west and start your own cattle ranch."

Jim had told a few close friends of his desire, but hadn't realized it might get to his boss. He feared that if Mr. Sturgis knew about it, he might look till he found another hard-working man to take his place. Stammering, he said, "Well, sir, it's...only a dream at best. It would take more money than I ever hope to have to realize it."

"Would take a bundle," nodded the old man, rubbing his chin. "Well, guess I'd better head for home."

"What are you doing about dinner, Mr. Sturgis?" piped up Merilee.

Hoping he might get an invitation for Sunday dinner—as he had many times before—the old man drew his mouth down in a pitiful curve, put a sad look in his eyes, and with a mock quiver in his voice, said, "Well, ma'am, I'll go home and see if I can't find an old crust of dried-up bread and maybe some water to drink with it."

Merilee giggled. "You can come home and eat with us, if you want to."

Reaching toward her, he said, "Well, twist my arm."

She had barely touched it when he said, "Ow! That's enough! Don't torture me! I'll come eat with you!"

The Logan children cheered and asked if they could ride in Grandpa Sturgis's buggy. Granted permission, they ran to the buggy and began climbing in. When the three older ones were seated comfortably, little Susie was still struggling to get aboard. Jeremy jumped down and boosted her in. Quickly, she scrambled into his spot.

Giving her a perturbed look, Jeremy said, "Well, thanks a lot, Susie. I help you in, and what do you do? You take my seat!"

"I s'pose to," reasoned the three-year-old. "Papa say gen'men s'pose to give his seat to a lady."

Jeremy looked toward the sky, shook his head, and said, "Please, Lord. Give me strength."

Harry Sturgis climbed aboard as Jeremy was settling in his second-choice seat. "Everybody ready?" he asked.

When the children said they were, Sturgis put the horse to a trot and headed out of the church yard.

As Jim helped Merilee into the Logan buggy, she said, "Darling, you talked to Mr. Sturgis as if we had never even prayed for the Lord to make a way for us to realize our dream. God owns the whole world. What's a couple of thousand dollars to Him?"

"Well, I—"

"Jim...how big is your God?"

Jim ducked his head in shame, silently climbed into the buggy, and put the horse to a trot.

* * * * *

As the next week progressed, Ralph Studdard and Ed Patton continued to give Jim Logan a hard time. Jim was fully aware that they were trying to press him into a fight. If he struck the first blow, they could tell Mr. Sturgis and possibly get him fired. Jim prayed for the Lord's help, and though it was difficult to do, he held his temper in check day after day.

On Friday, Merilee had been shopping alone and dropped by the feed lots to invite Mr. Sturgis ahead of time for Sunday dinner. Harry was delighted to accept the invitation, and thanked Merilee for her kindness. He stood on the small porch of the office shack and watched her as she headed across the yard toward the road. Jim and his two tormentors were just coming in with a load of hay.

Studdard and Patton were riding on top of the hay, and Jim was in the wagon seat holding the reins. When he saw his wife coming toward him, he pulled rein, smiled, and said, "Hello, sweetheart."

"Hi," she responded, flashing him her own warm smile. "I was just inviting Mr. Sturgis to come to dinner on Sunday."

"Of course he turned you down."

Merilee giggled. "Of course." She could feel the eyes of the ex-Confederate soldiers on her.

"What's for supper tonight?" queried Jim.

"Merilee Logan hash."

"Sounds great. Well, we've got to get this hay in the shed. I should be home on time."

"All right," she nodded. "See you then. I love you."

"I love you, too," he responded, and moved the team forward.

Atop the hay, Ralph Studdard whispered to his friend, "I'll get him, now."

Patton grinned and nodded.

When Jim drew the wagon to a halt in front of the open shed door, Studdard and Patton slid to the ground and approached him as he was climbing down from the seat.

"That's some wife you've got there, Logan," Studdard grinned. "She reminds me of a gal I met once in a cat house. In fact, I think it was her. She looks the type."

Patton's heart was pounding with expectation.

Logan's face turned thunder black. The dam that had been holding back his temper was breaking apart. "You know better than that. Nobody talks that way about my wife."

Studdard was caught flat-footed by a fist that came so fast he didn't even see it. He had barely hit the dust when Logan turned on Patton. The lanky man was bringing up his fists, but he was too slow. Jim gave him a solid right, followed by a stinging left, then dropped him with another right.

Studdard was trying to rise to his knees. Standing over him, Logan growled, "C'mon, Ralph. Get up. You've had this coming, and you're gonna get the whole load while I'm at it."

While Studdard struggled to his feet, Patton was up and preparing to attack. Jim saw him and rushed to meet him. Patton swung a haymaker, but Jim was too agile for him. He dodged the hissing fist and drove a powerful blow to the man's midsection. Patton doubled over and was caught solidly with a chopping blow to the temple that flattened him.

Jim turned to check on Studdard, and found the husky man thundering toward him. Their bodies met with a heavy whump, and they went down with Studdard on top.

Swearing at his opponent, Studdard began pounding him with big, meaty fists. Jim fended many of the blows off, but most of them were getting through. Jim did a quick roll, surprising the big man, and threw him off balance as he rose to his knees. Logan balled his fists and closed in. Studdard could see Patton coming up behind Logan with an ax handle in his hands, but Logan was already in his face, sending a barrage of blows. Studdard went down just as Patton came up behind Logan.

Jim heard Patton's footsteps and wheeled to meet him. The

ax handle missed Jim's head, but caught him on the tip of his left shoulder. Streamers of fire shot through the shoulder and across his back, but he still managed to seize the ax handle with both hands.

For a moment, Logan and Patton wrestled for control of the handle. Logan's upper lip was cut and bleeding from the pounding Studdard had given him, and a bruise was showing on his left cheekbone. Patton also had a cut lip, and there was a purple knot on his temple.

Studdard was gaining his feet a few steps away just as Jim wrested the handle from Patton and drove an elbow against his jaw. Patton staggered, swore, and made a lunge for the handle. Jim sidestepped him and cracked him solidly on the side of the head. Patton went down, unconscious.

Studdard's thick lips were split and bleeding, and there was a crimson flow coming from his nose as he charged the smaller man. A wildness was crawling through Jim Logan, spawned by the pent-up anger he had felt toward the two men. Studdard's vile words about Merilee echoed freshly through his mind as the big man rumbled toward him. Planting his feet, he swung and caught Studdard on the side of the head with a loud crack.

Studdard went down like a dead tree in a high wind and lay still. Standing over the two unconscious men, Jim sucked hard for breath and spit blood. He was wiping a sleeve over his mouth when Harry Sturgis came around the wagon, his wrinkled face set in a grim smile.

"I'm...sorry...Mr. Sturgis," panted Jim, "but they drove me to it. I've put up with their guff about me killing their brothers, but Studdard made a wicked remark about Merilee, and I'm not about to ignore that."

"I saw most of it from behind the wagon, Jim. I'd have done somethin' to stop it, 'cept I saw it was goin' your way. So I just let the river run its course, if you get my drift."

"Yes, sir," nodded Jim, sleeving blood from his mouth once more.

"Soon's they wake up, I'll fire 'em," Sturgis said flatly. "I'm sorry the load'll have to fall on you again till I can find more help, but I've had it with these two. They gotta go."

"I'd rather do the extra work than put up with them," agreed Jim.

Moments later, Studdard and Patton regained consciousness. As they staggered to their feet, rubbing their heads, Sturgis stood with Jim Logan beside him and said sternly, "You two are fired. Get off my property!"

Studdard cursed, wiped blood from under his nose, and said, "Why are we fired? Logan started it!"

"That's a lie and you know it!" blared Logan. "You've been badgering me ever since day one about killing your brothers...trying to push me into a fight. You knew when you insulted my wife I'd take offense. I threw the first punch, yes, but you started it, Studdard!"

"I've observed this badgering, myself," said Sturgis. "You two both told me you'd drop the issue about your brothers, but you didn't do it. You stayed after Jim day after day, but he was able to hold his temper. I'm proud of him for that. I'm also proud of him for bashin' the two of you to defend Merilee's honor. He did the right thing. Now, get off my property this minute, or I'll have the law remove you!"

Ralph Studdard and Ed Patton went to their mothers' homes and washed the blood off their faces, then walked to Jefferson City's business district and entered the Bluebell Tavern. They sat at a table in a back corner with a whiskey bottle between them and sullenly nursed their pride.

"I think Logan needs to feel the sting of our revenge for what he did," said Patton, his face solemn.

Studdard was quiet for a long moment, then said, "I dunno, Ed. If we mess with him anymore, we'll no doubt have to kill him. He's one tough egg. I don't cotton to no murder charge hangin' over my head."

"Yeah, I guess you're right. How about we punish him by burnin' his house down? When he and his family ain't in it, I mean."

"Naw. He don't own it. Ma says he rents it from old Hugh Ferguson. We'd be hurtin' Hugh, not Logan, and I don't want to hurt Hugh. He stood strong for the South durin' the War."

Patton took a swig of whiskey, set the glass on the table, looked around to make sure no one was within earshot, and said, "Well, for sure we oughtta punish Sturgis for firin' us. How about we go over to the cattle yards after midnight, when the whole town's asleep, and let all those cattle out? That'd give him some headaches, tryin' to round up all them beasts. They'd be scattered all over three counties by mornin'."

Ralph grinned wickedly. "Now, I like that idea, my friend. And...why don't we torch his buildings while we're at it? Wouldn't be doin' the old man any bodily harm, but it'd sure hurt his business not to have no barn, or hay shed, or office shack."

"Yeah!" breathed Patton, his eyes lighting up. "That'd put some punishment on Logan, too! Might even cost him his job!"

Studdard chuckled. "Wouldn't that be a shame. Let's do it!"

Pouring more whiskey in his glass, Ed said, "We prob'ly oughtta leave town after we set the fires, though. We'll be suspected because he fired us."

"That's all right with me. This town bores me, anyway. Let's do our little job, then light outta here."

Harry Sturgis had lost his bookkeeper a few months prior to the time Jim Logan came to work for him, and since there was no one to go home to, he often worked on his books at the office in the evenings. There were also many papers to prepare for the big influx of cattle on Saturdays, so Friday nights he always worked late.

This Friday night was no different.

Sturgis kept an old clock on the wall in his office, and had been working steadily since returning after supper. Laying his pencil down, he glanced at the clock and noted that it was almost ten-thirty. Removing his spectacles, he rubbed his eyes, yawned, and told himself it was bedtime. There was still some paperwork to do before the cattlemen showed up with their herds the next morning, so Harry decided he would just sleep on the cot he kept at the office, rise early, and finish it before the cattle began arriving. When Jim reported for work at seven, Harry would be free to go home, shave, freshen up, and eat breakfast. The heaviest influx of cattle wouldn't come until mid-morning, and he would be back at the office by then.

Stretching his weary limbs, the old man blew out the lanterns, laid down on the cot, and soon was in a deep sleep.

The moon was clear-edged and bright against the blackness of the sky as Studdard and Patton led their horses into a patch of woods across the road from the Sturgis Cattle Company. A soft breeze rustled the leaves in the trees. Both men carried a five-gallon can of kerosene as they crossed the road and hastened through the yard to the office shack.

They could hear the cattle moving around restlessly in the nearby pens as they splashed kerosene on the four walls and the door. Striking matches, they ignited the kerosene, then ran toward the auction barn and hay shed while flames snaked around the shack's exterior, spreading quickly with the help of the night breeze.

Moments later, they had the other two buildings burning, then dashed to the gates of the pens, throwing the empty kerosene cans in a patch of weeds. The restless cattle, frightened by the nearby fires, bolted through the open gates, bawling loudly as they ran.

Studdard and Patton hurried across the road, swung into their saddles, and galloped away in the moonlight, heading west.

Brilliant sunshine kissed the rolling plains as vagrant winds toyed with the lush green grass that spread every direction around Jim Logan. The spirited horse beneath him seemed to thrive on galloping back and forth behind the wide-spread herd of fat cattle on their way to market. His ranch hands worked equally as hard, riding their long-legged ponies expertly as they kept the bawling bovines bunched up and moving steadily.

Suddenly above the bellowing and rumble of hooves, Jim heard Merilee's voice calling his name. The distant clanging of a bell punctuated the silent spots between her words.

"Jim! Wake up!" cried Merilee, shaking him vigorously. "There's a fire somewhere in town!"

Jim shook his head and sat bolt upright in the bed. The clanging of the distant bell was clearer now, and meant one thing. Jim was a member of Jefferson City's volunteer fire department, and the bell was calling him to duty.

Bouncing out of the bed, Jim grabbed his pants from a nearby chair, sat down long enough to ram both feet into the pantlegs, then grabbed boots and socks. While he was putting them on, Merilee went to a window and looked outside.

"See anything?" he asked.

"Not from here," she replied, hurrying toward the bedroom door. "I'll go outside and see."

Merilee grabbed her robe from another chair and disappeared. The fire bell continued to shatter the night while Jim slid into a shirt and ran toward the front of the house. He was aware of Susie calling for her mother as he dashed past the children's bedroom.

Merilee was on the front porch as her husband emerged through the door, donning his hat. She pointed westward. "Sky's lit up over there, honey."

Jim saw the flare over the town's west side and said, "I hope it's not somebody's house."

"Me, too," she said.

Jim kissed her quickly and took off running.

It was three blocks to the fire house. Jim saw other men converging there when he turned the last corner onto Main Street. The fire chief was also the town's head constable, Will Denning. Denning and two other men had hitched up the horses to the pump wagon and were bringing it out of the fire house as Jim drew up. The bell in the building's tower was still clanging.

"Have any idea what's burning?" Logan asked Denning.

Denning gave him a grim look. "It's Sturgis Cattle Company."

Minutes later, the pump wagon pulled into the yard with a dozen men clinging to its sides. The office shack was enveloped in flames, and it was evident that it was beyond salvaging. Denning took a good look at the large auction barn and the hay shed and shouted that they'd best work on the barn. The hay shed was almost totally aflame.

After an hour's work, Jefferson City's fire department was able to save part of the barn. The hay shed and office shack were burned to the ground. Having noticed that the pens were completely empty while fighting the fire, the firemen asked who among them had let the cattle out. It appeared that someone had opened the gates, possibly fearing for the safety of the cattle, which were penned up quite near the barn and hay shed.

When no one spoke up to say he had done it, Jim Logan said, "Chief, I have a feeling I know who let the cattle out...and who set the fires."

"You do? Who?"

"Ralph Studdard and Ed Patton. I may be wrong, but Mr. Sturgis fired them yesterday, and they weren't taking it too good."

Denning looked around at the sleepy-eyed crowd that was

gathering. When he could not find the faces of either man, he said, "I'll go to their mothers' houses and see what they've got to say. If they so much as stutter, I'll throw them in jail."

"Good," nodded Logan, also searching the crowd. "I don't see Mr. Sturgis, so I'll go to his house and be the bearer of the bad news."

"All right," agreed Denning. "I'm sure since somebody has to tell him, he'd rather hear it from you."

Arriving at Sturgis's house, Jim was surprised to find no answer to his knock. The old man was an early riser, and though the fire bell might not have awakened him, certainly he should have been awake by now. Jim circled the house to see if Sturgis was out back. When he found no trace of him, he decided to ask the neighbors if they had seen him.

When the neighbors on both sides said they had not seen him since suppertime last evening, Jim became worried. Maybe the old man was sick and unable to answer the door. He decided to break in and find out.

He made a thorough search of the house but still there was no sign of Harry Sturgis. Hastening through the streets, Jim returned to the site of the fire to find Chief Denning standing among the other firemen at the charred ruins of the office shack. The crowd of onlookers had grown larger. Jefferson City's undertaker and one of the firemen were carrying a canvas tarp, with something weighty wrapped in it, from the blackened heap. The undertaker's hearse was parked close by.

When Denning saw Logan approaching, he stepped up to meet him, his face sheet-white. Jim knew what the chief was going to tell him. Before Denning could speak, Jim glanced to where the undertaker and fireman were loading the body into the hearse, and said, "Now I know why I didn't find Mr. Sturgis at home."

"I'm sorry, Jim," Denning said. "I know he was like a father to you."

"He was a wonderful man. I can't believe this has happened."

"Yeah," sighed Denning. Then pointing to two empty five-gallon kerosene cans that lay nearby, he said, "Couple of the men found these in the weeds over there between the barn and the pens. Looks like Studdard and Patton really had it in for the old man."

"Did you find them?"

"No. Both mothers said they pulled out in the middle of the night. Took what belongings they had and left without saying good-bye."

Jim Logan's eyes were misty and his throat was tight as he watched the hearse pull away. Swallowing hard, he asked, "You going after them?"

"You bet. I've already got six of these men ready to ride with me. Two are scouting the area to see if they can discern which direction they went."

"I want to go with you."

"I don't think you have time, Jim."

"What do you mean?"

"Well, somebody's got to round up all those missing cattle."

Logan rubbed his chin. "Yeah, I guess you're right. I'll take care of it. You just run those dirty rats down and bring them in."

"I'll do my best."

Jim wheeled and walked away. He would seek help and go after the cattle once he had gone home and told Merilee the bad news. He felt sick all over. What would the Logans do now? Sturgis Cattle Company no doubt would fold. With no Harry Sturgis to run it, and its buildings all but completely destroyed, it would be out of business. Jim Logan was out of a job.

CHAPTER SIX

"We'll make it, all right, darling," said Merilee, wiping tears as Jim held her in his arms. "I'm so sorry that dear man had to die...and in such a horrible way. But the Lord knows all about our predicament. He'll take care of us."

Jim Logan was wrestling once again with his lack of faith. Doing all he could to mask it, he said, "Sure, honey, I know that. Well, you break it to the kids when they come in from playing. I've got to find a couple of men to stay at the pens and meet the cattlemen who'll be showing up anytime, now, with their herds and turn them back. There's no way we can have an auction on Monday. Then I've got to gather me a crew and go after the cattle. I'll be back as soon as—"

A knock at the front door cut into Jim's words. Releasing Merilee, who was dabbing at her eyes with a hanky, he went to the door and pulled it open. Standing before him with solemn faces were attorney Lyle Findlay and Walter Payne, president of the Jefferson City Bank.

Jim knew both men well because of their close relationship with Harry Sturgis. Findlay's voice quivered as he said, "We both knew there was a fire in town because of the bell, Jim, but only twenty minutes ago did we learn that it was at the cattle pens, and that poor Harry had burned to death. We arrived there just moments after you had headed for home."

Nodding, Logan said, "Come in, gentlemen."

As they moved inside, both men greeted Merilee, then Walter turned to Jim and said, "We know this tragic incident is going to throw a heavy burden on you. We want to help all we can."

Jim sat them down and explained that he had to go after the scattered cattle. He also had to find a couple of men to stay at the pens and meet the cattlemen who would be coming with their herds. "Then I've got to find another job."

Walter Payne said, "Jim, as you know, there are Sturgis Cattle Company funds in my bank. When you round up the missing cattle, they'll need hay and grain. Working with Lyle, here, I can allot the money to pay for that until the buyers come and take the cattle. Lyle and I will be your men to explain to those cattlemen coming in today that there won't be any auctions until the company is in new hands."

"I appreciate that," nodded Logan. "I'll find some men to help me and get after those wandering animals right away."

"Good," said Payne, rising to his feet. "I'll send someone out to the Coats farm and get some hay delivered, and I'll also have some grain brought in."

"See you when you get back, Jim," Lyle Findlay said. "And...ah...how about coming to my office Monday morning? There are some things we need to talk about."

"Sure," nodded Logan. "Any particular time?"

"Ten o'clock okay?"

"Sure. I'll be at your office at ten on Monday."

Since the records had burned up with the office, Jim had no way to know if they had rounded up all the cattle. But by late afternoon, he and his crew of ten men had placed over three hundred head in the pens. When the cattle had been fed and the water tanks filled, Jim thanked the men for their help and let them go home. He was about to leave, himself, when he saw Constable Will Denning and his posse riding in from the west. Denning signaled for his riders to halt, said a few words to them, then veered off the road toward Logan while the others continued on into town.

Jim could tell by the look on Denning's face that they had failed to run down Studdard and Patton. As the constable slid from his saddle, he said dismally, "They gave us the slip, Jim. They headed due west, but after about fifteen miles, we lost their trail. Big country out there, and not enough lawmen to go around. It galls me to know they're going to get away with what they did, but I've got a town to look after, and the men in my posse have jobs and businesses to see to. We can't be chasing Studdard and Patton all over creation."

"I understand, Will. It galls me, too, but I can't see that there's anything more you can do."

The Logan family attended church services as usual on Sunday morning. Harry Sturgis's funeral was held at three o'clock that afternoon. Hundreds of people attended, including many of the cattlemen who had done business with him for years.

When the Logans returned home after the evening service on Sunday night, Jim did his best to show his family that he was trusting the Lord to take care of their needs. He kept up a brave front at Bible reading and prayer time, even suggesting that whoever bought the company might keep him on.

When the children were asleep, and Jim and Merilee lay side-by-side in the darkness, holding each other, Merilee said, "I'm so proud of you, darling. This is the greatest crisis our family has faced, yet you're faith is strong that the Lord is going to see us through."

Jim was silent for a long moment. Inside, he was churning with doubts. But he had to keep up a strong front for his family's sake. Feeling a bit hypocritical, he said, "God can do it, sweetheart. If the new owner of the company doesn't want me, the Lord will give me the job He wants me to have."

"And the Lord will provide for us even in the time between now and when you're being paid again."

Jim Logan hadn't even thought about what he would do for money until he had a job again. A deadness seemed to settle in his chest.

"You believe that, don't you?" asked Merilee.

The darkness seemed to close in on Jim. "Sure," he replied, trying to sound convincing. "Guess we'd better get to sleep, sweetie."

The Logans kissed goodnight and rolled opposite directions. Jim lay staring into the darkness and silently prayed, "Oh, Lord, help me to trust You in all this. I'm scared. Please. I can't bear the thought of my family going hungry, or being without things they need. But my faith is so weak. Like the man in the Bible who came to You, Lord, I'm asking You...*help mine unbelief!*"

The next morning at breakfast, Merilee focused on her husband across the table and asked, "What do you suppose Lyle Findlay wants to talk to you about?"

"I have no idea," said Jim, shrugging his shoulders.

"Maybe he's going to give you a job in his office, Papa," Darlene said.

Jeremy gave her a scornful look. "Doin' *what?*"

"Being a lawyer," came Darlene's quick reply.

Jeremy shook his head slowly. "Girls are so dumb."

"What do you mean, *dumb?*" challenged Darlene. "I got better grades than you on my last report card."

"Prob'ly 'cause you cheated," snorted Jeremy. "Don't you know a man can't be a lawyer unless he's been to college?"

"Hah! Talk about girls being dumb! Abraham Lincoln was a

lawyer, and he never went to college. Papa's as smart as Abraham Lincoln was!"

"Now, that's enough, you two," said Merilee.

"Hey," said Jim, smiling for the first time since the fire, "let her talk! Darlene's making good sense, here!"

"Papa's the smartest man in the world, aren't you, Papa?" Benjamin said.

Jim eyed the youngster lovingly. "Well, Benjamin, I don't think I quite qualify for that position, but—"

"Oh, yes you do!" put in Darlene. "You *are* the smartest man in all the world."

"Mama's smarter!" Susie said.

Merilee broke into a hearty laugh, which spread around the table, until the entire family was laughing together.

A little before ten, Jim Logan entered the law office of Lyle Findlay and found the secretary-receptionist, Fern Tandy, bent over a filing cabinet. She looked up and said, "Good morning, Mr. Logan. Mr. Findlay is in his office. He's expecting you. Just tap on the door."

Logan did as Fern said, and Findlay called for him to enter. Jim stepped inside and pulled the door closed behind him.

The portly attorney stood up, gestured toward a chair in front of the desk, and said, "Take a seat, my friend."

Observing a mixture of curiosity and nervousness in Logan's eyes, Findlay sat down and said, "I'll get right to what I wanted to see you about, Jim. You know I've been Harry Sturgis's attorney for many years."

"Yes."

"He was a sharp man, my friend, but then I don't have to tell you that."

"Right."

"Well, he left a will, and assigned me as executor of his estate. Realizing that a man can die suddenly, he also placed in my hands the power to handle the sale of the Sturgis Cattle Company should something happen to him. I didn't go into this on Saturday because there wasn't time to cover it thoroughly. So you see, I can move ahead immediately on the sale of the company."

"That's good."

The attorney squinted. "You look worried."

"Well, it's just that there's a strong possibility that whoever buys it will have his own workers...and my job will be gone."

"I can appreciate your concern. However, let me continue."

"Certainly."

"What you don't know, Jim, is that Harry Sturgis was already negotiating to sell the company to a cattle dealer in St. Louis."

"He was?"

"Mm-hmm. He was getting on in years and felt it was time to retire. We had the sale almost closed, but with the fire destroying the buildings, I wasn't sure if the St. Louis dealer would still want to go ahead with it. However...we've had the telegraph wires hot since eight o'clock this morning, and the man still wants to buy the company. He's going to send a crew over here to rebuild as soon as the deal is closed, which will be within ten days."

"So if you're this close to closing the sale, you must know whether the man is going to bring his own people over here."

Findlay closed his eyes and nodded. "Yes. He is."

"Then my job is gone."

"Yes."

Jim Logan's mouth went dry. His heart sank within him. Findlay seemed so unfeeling about it. How could the man sit there so calm and relaxed when he had just told a family man that his job was gone?

Why had the Lord let this horrible thing happen? Didn't He care? And...Harry Sturgis. Why hadn't he told him about the sale? Jim could have been looking for another job.

Jim felt betrayed by Sturgis...and deserted by God. Panic was rising up within him.

"However..." said Findlay, opening a desk drawer and pulling out a folder. "I have something else to tell you."

Jim licked his dry lips as the lawyer opened the folder, displaying some official-looking papers.

Smiling, Findlay said, "Knowing the sale would soon go through, and you would be out of a job, Jim, a few days ago Mr. Sturgis made legal arrangements that when the sale of the company was closed, you would be given a check in the amount of sixteen thousand dollars. He knew about your big dream of going west and starting a cattle ranch. This money is to make your dream come true."

James Whitford Logan was overwhelmed. Throat locked with emotion, he felt sudden shame for the thoughts he had just entertained. Fighting tears, he swallowed with difficulty, leaned forward on the chair, and said, "This is all such a shock, Mr. Findlay. I...I can't believe it's true."

Still smiling, Lyle Findlay said, "There's more, Jim. As executor of Mr. Sturgis's estate and controller of his funds, both business and personal, I have decided to meet your wages from company money until the day you receive your sixteen-thousand-dollar check."

Jim wiped tears from his cheeks. "Thank you, sir. Your kindness is appreciated more than I could ever tell you. I also thank you in behalf of Merilee and the children."

"You did Mr. Sturgis a good job, Jim. He spoke so highly of you. I'm sure he would have wanted me to see that you were taken care of until you have the large check."

Jim Logan left the office of Lyle Findlay and headed home. He made it about half a block off Main Street, then went into a small park where there were many trees and bushes. Finding a spot where the brush was heavy, he squeezed in out of sight, fell to his knees, and sobbed, "Dear Lord, please forgive this faithless servant of Yours for his sinful doubting. You put a test before me, and I failed You. I'm sorry, Lord. You're a big God. Much bigger than I gave You credit for. Now I can go home and tell Merilee just how big my God is!"

On Wednesday, May 9, the Jim Logan family rolled into St. Joseph, Missouri, in their brand new covered wagon. Along with the wagon, Jim had bought four spirited horses and brand new harness.

The sun was shining bright in a clear sky, and the town was bustling. Little Susie sat on the seat between her parents, while Jeremy, Darlene, and Benjamin rode behind them, sitting higher inside the wagon, and looking over their heads.

Jim knew of wagon trains that left St. Joseph, embarking for the Wild West. By wire, he had contacted an agent in St. Joseph who put him in contact with wagon master Ward Fleming, who was putting a train together that would pull out at sunrise on May 10. Fleming was leading several wagons to Wyoming Territory, and would pass right by Hay Springs, Nebraska. Jim wanted to go to the Hay Springs area and build a spread near that of Corey McCollister, the rancher written up in the *Jefferson City News.*

Ward Fleming's wire had stated that he wanted all the wagons planning to be part of the train to be on the bank of the Missouri River at St. Joseph by four o'clock on the afternoon of May 9. The guide fee must be paid at that time, and there would be a meeting at four-thirty. Any travelers who were not present for the meeting would not be allowed in the train when it pulled out the next morning.

Asking directions from a man on the street, Jim learned the exact spot on the river bank where Fleming was assembling the wagons. A few minutes later, the Logan family hauled to a stop amid the happy laughter of playing children and men and women who stood about in small groups, talking.

Jim wrapped the reins around the brake handle and said to Merilee, "I'll find Mr. Fleming. You and the kids might as well climb down, stretch your legs, and meet some of these folks."

Jim helped Merilee and the girls down, then headed toward an area which seemed to be the center of activity. Men and women spoke to him in a friendly manner as he moved amongst them. As he drew near a well-worn wagon, he noticed a group of men gathered beside it, talking to two tall, rugged-looking individuals who were unmistakably father and son.

The older one noted Jim's approach, cut off his conversation with the others, and stepped up to meet him. Extending his big, bony hand, he smiled and said, "Howdy. I'm Ward Fleming."

"I thought you might be," grinned Jim. "I'm Jim Logan."

Logan felt the power of Fleming's grip as he was welcomed, then the wagon master introduced him to his son, Gerald, explaining that the two of them worked together.

Ward Fleming was in his early sixties, but his hair and mustache were still dark, with only a fleck of gray. He was tall and muscular. Gerald was a makeover of his father, and in his late thirties.

Ward introduced Logan to the other men who stood around, then Jim pulled out his wallet to pay his fee. When the transaction was done, the wagon master informed him that the meeting of all adults in the wagon train would take place promptly at four-thirty as scheduled.

By four-thirty, Merilee had met every woman in the wagon train, and the Logan children had each found playmates their own age. Some of the older children played about the wagons while the adults gathered for the meeting. The smaller children remained with their parents.

Ward Fleming announced that there were fourteen wagons in the train besides his own. While Gerald stood beside him, he went over some simple rules which, he explained, were for everyone's benefit and safety. Gerald knew his father's speech by heart, and knew just when to reach in the wagon and pull out a large roughly drawn map. While father and son held up the map so all could see, Ward showed them the route they would be taking.

They would cross the Missouri where it was wide and shallow directly in front of them and follow the west bank northward to the Nebraska line. They would head due west from there through Falls City, Nebraska, on to Beatrice and Hastings, then to Fort Kearny, on the south bank of the Platte River. They would follow the south bank for the next hundred miles to the town of North Platte, where they would stock up on supplies, then head for Hay Springs, 150 miles northwest. At Hay Springs, the Logan wagon would pull out of the train, and the rest would continue on toward Wyoming.

Ward then talked about hostile Indians they could encounter on the journey, naming the Kiowa, Blackfoot, Crow, Sioux, and Cheyenne as the tribes who inhabited their route. He explained that they were all a potential threat toward white men, but that the Cheyenne were the most dangerous and most easily riled. Fleming explained precautions that would be taken, and schooled them as to what to do if an attack came. Making sure that every wagon was well supplied with guns and ammunition, he showed them how to quickly form the wagons into a tight circle for the best defense.

When all other questions were answered, Fleming dismissed the apprehensive travelers, saying they would be pulling out at sunrise.

That night, Jim Logan read the Bible to his family and led them in prayer around one of the campfires, asking the Lord to protect the wagon train as it traveled.

Dawn found the travelers up with cookfires going and the smell of breakfast in the air. By the time the sun was peeking over the eastern horizon, Ward and Gerald Fleming had the wagons lined up and ready to cross the Missouri River.

The wagon master then gathered everyone in one spot and said, "Before we move out, I want to ask the Lord God in heaven to watch over us." When Fleming removed his hat, all the other men did the same. Everyone bowed their heads and closed their eyes while Fleming prayed, closing his prayer boldly in the name of Jesus Christ.

Jim and Merilee Logan were pleased at their wagon master's prayer, and expressed their pleasure to him.

While the travelers were climbing into their wagons, Ward mounted his horse. Gerald drove the Fleming wagon. Guiding his horse down the bank, Ward urged it into the water, threw his right hand forward, and shouted, "Wagons, ho!"

Averaging just under fifteen miles per day, the wagon train halted in the early afternoon on June 4 as Ward Fleming pointed north toward the town of North Platte. They were on the bank of the South Platte River a mile west of the spot where the north Platte and the South Platte joined in their southeastern flow to become the Platte River. The town lay inside the fork between the two sun-struck streams.

Fleming led his covered wagons across the South Platte to the outskirts of the town and formed them in a circle. Whenever they camped near a town, Fleming allowed half the families to enter the town at a time, while the other half remained with the wagons to guard them.

The Logans were amongst the first half to enter North Platte. Jeremy and Benjamin flanked their father, who carried little Susie, and Darlene walked beside her mother. The town's business district was two blocks of false-fronted clapboard buildings. Most of them were unpainted and weather-worn. Merilee decided to take the girls to the general store. Jim would take the boys to the gun shop, where he would replenish his ammunition supply. The wagon train families had feasted on wild game, and the Logans had been no exception. Jim had bagged deer, antelope, and jackrabbits in Nebraska's wide open country.

Jim said he and the boys would meet Merilee and the girls at the general store, then he headed for the gun shop, which was several doors down the street.

While Jim and his sons were inside the gun shop, two unkempt men crept up to the window and peered inside. When they saw Jim peeling off bills from a thick wad of money, Ralph Studdard whispered to Ed Patton, "That's him, all right. Wonder where he got his hands on that much money."

"Hard tellin'," replied Patton, "but I'd sure like to take that wad from him."

"I bet he's with that wagon train that pulled up south of town a little while ago."

"S'pose?"

"Yep. Looks like our old pal is a-goin' west to make his fortune."

"Looks to me like he already made it."

"Guess it costs quite a bit to travel in a wagon train," mused Studdard. "I bet the rest of them people have got those kind of wads, too."

"Whoops!" gasped Studdard. "He's comin' out. C'mon, don't let him see us!"

The two men dashed between the gun shop and its neighboring building, and watched while Jim Logan and his boys strolled past within a few feet.

Harry Sturgis's unwitting killers followed at a comfortable distance and observed as Jim, Jeremy, and Benjamin went inside the general store. Moments later, they emerged with Merilee and the girls. Everyone in the family was carrying something, even Susie.

The evil pair kept out of sight as they tagged along behind the Logans all the way to the south edge of town and watched them enter the circle of wagons.

"Yep," said Studdard as they stood behind a huge cottonwood tree, "they're in the wagon train, all right. And I've got an idea."

"I'm listenin'," chuckled Patton, scratching at his ribs.

"We'll follow the wagon train when it leaves here."

"Yeah?"

"When they camp for the night, we'll sneak in and grab that littlest kid...the one Logan called Benjamin. While one of us holds a gun to his head, the other will be obliged to collect all the money in the whole stinkin' wagon train!"

"Hey, Ralph, that's good thinkin'! Ain't nobody gonna refuse to hand over their cash and gold while we threaten the kid's life."

"Exactly. Then once we've got the money, for safety's sake, we'll take the kid with us. We'll tell 'em if somebody gets on a horse and follows us, we'll still kill the kid. But if they cooperate and don't give us no trouble, we'll leave him on the trail ahead of 'em, unharmed."

Laughing, Ed Patton said, "What a stroke of luck, us bein' here in North Platte when that wagon train pulled in. And double luck, us seein' Logan and his brats on the street. We're gonna make us a real haul, ol' pal, a *real* haul!"

At sunrise the next morning, Sheriff Bo Purdum stood at the Fleming wagon, chatting with Ward and Gerald, whom he knew from the many previous times they had stopped in North Platte. "Like I told you at supper last night," said Purdum, "keep a sharp eye. The Indians have been on the prowl lately. Attackin' ranches, stagecoaches, and trains, both railroad and wagon."

"I've already alerted everybody in the train," nodded Ward. Then shaking Purdum's hand, he said, "See you next time, Bo."

Purdum stood on the bank of the North Platte River and watched Ward lead the wagons across to the opposite bank, then headed back into town.

The wagon train had been traveling about three hours when Ward trotted along the line of wagons, reminding everyone to keep a sharp lookout for any sign of Indians. After reaching the last wagon, he galloped his horse to the lead vehicle and pulled alongside, holding his mount to a walk. "So far so good, son," he said to Gerald, who held the reins.

"Long way to go, though. The Lord's been good to us on all these trips, only being attacked three times. I'm not so concerned as long as the Indians run in small packs. If they ever put a whole bunch together to attack us, we're in real trouble."

"Well, we'll keep praying that doesn't happen," Ward said.

The older man noticed his son looking straight ahead and squinting. Following his line of sight, he saw what Gerald was looking at. A lone rider had just topped a gentle rise on the rolling plain and was headed straight for them. "Not too many men ride alone out here," remarked Ward.

"I was thinking the same thing," said Gerald.

Moments later, as the rider drew close, Ward said from the side of his mouth, "Scuzzy-looking dude."

"To put it mildly," Gerald nodded.

Under a sweat-stained hat, the rider had long, greasy carrot-red hair that lay matted on his shoulders. He had a bushy mustache the same color, rust-colored eyes, and a ruddy complexion to match. Above the mustache was a hawk-like nose. He had facial scars and a heavily drooped right eyelid.

Drawing abreast, the rider looked at Ward and said, "Howdy."

"Howdy," Ward nodded.

Seeing that the wagon master was not going to stop, Gavin Cold wheeled his mount so as to ride alongside him.

"Kinda dangerous for a fella to ride these Indian-infested plains by himself," Ward said.

"True," replied Cold. "Reason I'm travelin' alone is that I'm lookin' for a man. Important that I find him. He's tall...real tall. Slender, but well muscled and broad-shouldered."

"That could describe quite a few men," said Ward.

"Yeah, but this one's different. He dresses like a preacher...or maybe a gambler. You know...all in black with a white shirt and string tie. Long-tailed coat, flat-crowned hat, and real shiny boots. Has a pair of white-ridged scars on his right cheek. Medium side-burns, well-trimmed mustache. Fella couldn't miss noticin' him. Folks in these parts have seen him lately. Last report was he seemed to be anglin' southeast. Rides a big shiny, solid-black horse. You seen a man like that in these parts?"

"Nope. Sure haven't."

Sensing that the rider might have an ulterior motive for finding the man-in-black, Gerald Fleming spoke up. "This man a friend of yours?"

"Not exactly. I owe him. Just want to find him and settle with him."

"Sorry we can't help you," said Ward.

"Me, too," nodded Cold. "Much obliged for your time." With that, he spurred his mount, made a wide circle, and galloped southeast.

Gerald looked at his father and remarked, "That ugly dude's up to no good."

"I'm thinking the same thing."

CHAPTER SEVEN

The prairie wind whipped dust across the broad, sun-bleached street of Byers, Colorado, as the Butterfield stagecoach rolled in. The stage was on its regular run between Goodland, Kansas, and Denver.

In the box were driver Ozzie Davis, grizzled and in his early sixties, and shotgunner Walt Green, who was clean-shaven and would soon turn twenty-five.

Wind, rain, snow, sleet, and summer's sun had turned the log stage station a pale gray. Even the sign over the door—Butterfield Stage Lines—was faded and cracked.

It was almost ten o'clock in the morning, and there were many people on the street, along with a few riders, buckboards, buggies, and wagons moving about. Davis drew rein and halted the coach directly in front of the stage office door.

While his shotgunner eased his way down on the coach's right side, Ozzie scrambled down and opened the door on his side, which faced the office. "There you go, folks," he said in an amiable manner. "Water inside, privies out back."

There was an elderly woman aboard, and two businessmen in their early forties. Ozzie took the lady's hand to help her down. "I hope the ride isn't jolting you too bad, Mrs. Matherly. I can't miss all the bad spots in the road."

"You're doing fine, driver," Esther Matherly said warmly, patting his shoulder.

Davis showed a mouthful of false teeth in a broad smile. "You're very nice, ma'am, but I know it's bumpy. At least we're only forty miles from Denver, now. We'll be there before sundown."

"That'll be nice," she replied, and headed around the log building to the back where the privies stood.

Ozzie grinned at Donald Frame and Russell Nelson as they alighted. "Hope you gentlemen are enjoying the trip."

"No robbers and no Indians thus far," commented Frame, "so in that sense it's been enjoyable."

Both men also headed out back.

Walt moved up and said, "Didn't you say we're picking up a passenger here, Ozzie?"

"Yep. Wire said it's a lady. Let's go inside and see if she's here."

A young man about Walt's age emerged smiling from the office. "Howdy, Ozzie...Walt."

"Howdy, Reggie," chorused driver and shotgunner.

"Make it snappy changin' teams, okay?" Ozzie said. "I want to pull out right on schedule...ten-thirty."

"Will do, my friend," grinned Reggie, and quickly made his way to the six-up team.

As Davis and Green entered the office, they saw station agent Roy Hamm sitting on a chair in the middle of the waiting area. The sleeve of his left arm was rolled up, and a young woman with honey-blond hair was examining a swollen and obviously infected gash on his upper arm. Both men noticed a black medical bag sitting on a chair next to Hamm, but their attention was drawn more to the young woman. She gave them a flicking appraisal, then reached in the bag and pulled out a small bottle of iodine.

"Hey, look who's here on time!" Hamm laughed. "Will wonders never cease?"

"Aw, comoffit!" snapped Davis in mock anger. "I've never been late more'n five or six times in the ten years I've been makin' this run, and you know it! And even then, none of 'em was my fault!"

Hamm sent an ornery grin to Green and asked, "Are you listenin' to what's comin' outta your age-old partner's mouth, Walt?"

"No. I have to listen to the old codger all the time when we're up in the box. When we come down to earth, I ignore him as much as possible."

Ozzie looked at the ceiling and guffawed. "Age-old and an old codger, am I? Well, let me tell you two somethin' right now. I'm twice the man either one of you could ever hope to be!" Edging up closer to the young woman, he asked, "Don't you think so, Miss?"

She eyed Davis, smiled, and said, "I think you're cute, grandpa, but *twice* the man these two ever hope to be? That might be stretching it a bit."

"Ma'am, I thank you for setting the old duffer straight," Walt said. "He has a magnificent opinion of himself. If you could buy him for what he's worth, and sell him for what he thinks he's worth, you'd be a millionaire overnight."

The woman stopped her work again, smiled, and said, "If this kind of banter goes on all the time you two are in the box, I'm glad I'll be down below in the coach."

"Oh, are you the one we're picking up at this stop, ma'am?" asked Green.

"Yes," she said cheerfully, "and we're going to be late leaving for Denver if I don't get finished with Mr. Hamm's cut pretty soon."

"Oh. S'cuse us, ma'am," said Ozzie. "I didn't realize we were picking up a nurse."

She smiled again, and returned to her work.

At that moment, Esther Matherly entered the back door and headed for the water pail, located on a small table near the back door.

"Miss Baylor is a C.M.N., fellas," offered Hamm. "Certified Medical Nurse. That means she had to work for a time under the supervision of a qualified doctor before she could earn the certificate."

"How do you know all this, Roy?" Walt asked.

"She told me," grinned Hamm.

"How'd you get that gash?"

"I was workin' in the barn out back a few days ago. Nail was stickin' through a board and I accidentally brushed my arm across it. My missus treated it the best she could, but it got infected. The closest doctor is in Denver. When I found out she was a nurse, I asked her to take a look at it."

The back door opened, and the two male passengers entered, also heading for the water pail. They showed interest in the treatment Roy was getting, so he filled them in on the situation and told them that the nurse would be riding with them to Denver.

"Miss Baylor, these here are your fellow-passengers," Ozzie said. "Mrs. Esther Matherly, Donald Frame, and Russell Nelson."

Each greeted the nurse, then the shotgunner said, "Miss Baylor, I'm Walt Green, and the old codger there is Ozzie Davis."

Smiling, she said, "I'm happy to make everyone's acquaintance."

"Pardon me, ma'am," Walt said, "but we haven't heard your first name. All we know is 'Miss Baylor'."

"It's Breanna."

"Mmm. That's pretty," grinned Walt. "Breanna Baylor. It *is* Miss Breanna Baylor, right?"

"Yes," nodded Breanna. Then she said quickly, "Well, it looks like we'll be able to pull out on time."

Breanna left Roy Hamm with a small supply of iodine, additional bandages, and instructions on further care of the infected cut. She was sure it would heal up fine if he took care of it properly.

The prairie wind was still raising dust on Byers' main thoroughfare as the coach pulled away from the Butterfield office precisely at ten-thirty, heading due west.

The two women talked about the wind and the weather, sharing their concern that the coming summer was going to be a hot one. For the first week of June, it was already quite warm.

Soon the steady beat of the horses' hooves and the drone of the wheels had Donald Frame and Russell Nelson slumped on the seat side-by-side, hats over their faces, snoring.

Breanna smiled at her new acquaintance and said, "I love your first name, Mrs. Matherly. It makes me think of one of my favorite Bible characters."

The elderly woman's eyes lit up. "You're a Christian, Miss Baylor?"

"Yes, ma'am. By the blood of the Lamb."

"Me, too! I'm a pastor's daughter. I'm traveling from Goodland to Denver to visit my older sister. We're both widows."

The coach hit a deep rut and jarred the male passengers awake. Both of them swore as they retrieved their hats from the floor and adjusted themselves on the seat.

Esther caught her breath, eyes widening while color flooded her throat and ran truant through her cheeks. "Such language! There are ladies present, in case you hadn't noticed! And even if there weren't, you shouldn't be using profane words."

Both men quickly apologized.

"Rather than apologize to us, you ought to apologize to God," Breanna said. "He has to listen to it all the time."

Frame and Nelson exchanged glances. Avoiding the hard glares of the women, they slumped back down on the seat, placed their hats over their faces, and tried to go back to sleep.

The elderly woman winked at Breanna, then asked, "Do

you live and work in Byers?"

"Oh, no, ma'am. Are you acquainted with the C.M.N. certificate?"

"Yes."

"Well, I'm a visiting nurse. I just spent five weeks at a ranch about twelve miles north of Byers, caring for the rancher's wife. It was her third child, but she developed some serious problems during the pregnancy. I gave her prenatal care for three weeks, delivered the baby, then stayed another two weeks to make sure mother and child were both all right."

"So Denver is home?"

"Yes. I work out of Dr. Lyle Goodwin's office there. I hope to get a few days' rest before taking on another job."

Esther was quiet for a few moments, then she said, "I know you're not thirty yet, honey...but my curiosity is getting the best of me."

"You're wondering why I'm not married."

"Yes. You're quite lovely, and have such a sweet way about you. I can't imagine why some fortunate man hasn't put a wedding ring on your finger."

Breanna's lower lip quivered, and tears filmed her eyes.

When Esther saw it, she took a sharp breath and said, "Oh, honey, I'm sorry. I didn't mean to—"

"It's all right, Mrs. Matherly," Breanna said, reaching for the purse at her side and pulling out a hanky. "You are no more curious than a thousand other people I've met. I...was jilted once by a man. He cut my heart out. I've never known such pain of mind and soul. When I got over the initial shock of it, I vowed never to fall in love again."

While Breanna dabbed at her eyes, Esther asked cautiously, "Have you kept your vow?"

Stifling what could become sobs, Breanna buried her face in the hanky and fought for control of her emotions.

Esther laid a gentle hand on Breanna's arm and said in a

voice barely audible above the sounds of pounding hooves, spinning wheels, and creaking stagecoach, "I thought so. There *is* a man, isn't there?"

Pulling the hanky from her face, Breanna nodded and whispered, "Yes." She swallowed hard, cleared her throat twice, and said, "Another man did come along, Mrs. Matherly. I did fall in love with him, but complications set in, and I haven't seen him for some time."

Esther was curious again. She wondered what had happened between Breanna and the second man, but she decided to leave well enough alone. She asked some medical questions. When Breanna had answered them, both women went quiet and gazed out their windows.

Soon Esther was asleep. Breanna leaned over, placed the hanky back in her purse, then closed her fingers around a medallion of polished silver the size of a silver dollar. She held it to her heart and fought tears once again. "Oh, John, why was I so foolish? Why did I send you out of my life? I love you, John. I love you so much!"

Taking the hanky again, Breanna wiped tears, then laid her head back. She let her mind drift back to the day she first met the tall, handsome stranger. She was working out of Dr. Myron Hunter's office in Wichita and had spent a week with farmer Will Scott and his wife, nursing him back to health after a bad fall. Though a violent thunderstorm loomed in the west the day she left, she bid Will and his wife good-bye, then climbed into her buggy and headed for home. It was a decision she would regret.

Deafening thunder clapped like a thousand cannons all around, and the frightened horse bolted. Terrified, Breanna screamed at Nellie to slow down and pulled back on the reins with all her might. Suddenly the crazed animal veered off the road and plunged down a grassy slope. Breanna saw a ditch yawning at her and braced herself for the impact. The buggy hit the ditch full-force and came to a sudden stop against the far bank, sending Breanna headlong into a patch of long, thick grass. Nellie bounded across the field dragging reins, harness, and singletree behind.

Breanna was dizzy and bruised, but the soft bed of grass had saved her from serious injury. Slowly she made her way back to the road, the rain pelting her face, when she heard something different than wind, lightning, and thunder. It took her a few seconds to place its source, but when she looked behind her, she found it. It was the sound of rushing hooves. The lightning had frightened a herd of cattle she had passed earlier, and they were stampeding straight toward her.

The herd was no more than two hundred yards away. Frozen with terror, Breanna steeled herself for what was coming. Then something out of the corner of her eye caught her attention. It looked at first like some kind of apparition speeding toward her, but it quickly crystallized into a horse and rider. The horse was jet-black, and the man in the saddle was dressed in black.

The cattle and the rider were closing in fast. Horror and panic stabbed Breanna's heart. She could scarcely breathe.

The herd was no more than fifty yards away when the rider leaned from the saddle and snatched her off the ground, holding her tight against him as they veered to the right and headed south. The black gelding quickly put space between them and the deathly horns and hooves.

"You all right, ma'am?"

"Yes, thanks to you...and to the Lord!"

"That's right! Thank the Lord! No need to thank me. I was just doing my job. We'll be in Wichita shortly. Ebony can run like this for hours."

"How do you know I want to go to Wichita?"

"That's where you live isn't it?"

A strange feeling went over the nurse. How did he know that? Perhaps he had seen her in town. "So you're from Wichita, too."

"No, ma'am."

"Then how do you know I live there?"

The man-in-black did not reply.

Some time later Wichita came into view. When they reached the edge of town, the rider slowed his horse and trotted him onto Broadway.

"I live on Kellogg Street, west of Broadway a block and a half," Breanna said.

Breanna relived in her mind the harrowing events of the afternoon, and she did not notice when they turned onto Kellogg. She did notice when the man who had saved her life hauled up in front of the boarding house where she lived and dismounted. "Well, here you are, ma'am. Safe and sound."

In the worst way, Breanna wanted to ask him how he knew where she lived, but could not work up the courage. Instead, she thanked him for saving her life, then told him her name and that she was a visiting nurse. But something inside told her he already knew her name and her profession. She had never met a man like him.

The stagecoach was rocking along the road to Denver as Breanna Baylor adjusted herself on the padded seat and looked around at her fellow-passengers. The breeze coming through the windows was warm, and all three were still asleep.

She laid her head back against the seat again, closed her eyes, and let her mind return to that day in Wichita when the strange man accepted her invitation to come back the next evening for supper. She had mentioned a moment earlier that he had not told her his name. In his deep, soft voice, he said, "You can call me John."

Swaying with the coach's rhythm, Breanna smiled to herself. John did not volunteer his last name to her that day or in the days that followed as they spent more and more time together. It was some time later when she learned that people who knew him called him John Stranger.

She smiled to herself again as she recalled how John showed up for supper that next night with Nellie, a new buggy, and her medical bag. *Such a wonderful man,* she thought. *And I sent him out of my life.*

Breanna thought of all the times she and John spent together in the next few months, and of how his presence was both comforting and disconcerting. There was a gentleness in him she had never seen in a man, and the indescribable expression in his iron-gray eyes drew her like a magnet.

Yet Breanna had vowed that she would never love another man. She would never allow herself to be so deeply hurt as she had been by Frank Miller. She realized that if she let herself, she would fall in love with John Stranger. She could not let herself be hurt again.

It was a cold, bleak day in November when she finally told John not to come see her anymore. She would never forget the hurt in his eyes nor his last words to her before he rode away.

"Good-bye, lovely lady. I will be out of your life, but you will never be out of my heart. From time to time, I may be looking at you, but you'll not know I'm near. I'll respect your request."

As the stagecoach rocked on, Breanna thumbed tears from her eyes, looked at the medallion in her hand, and said quietly, "I will always love you, my darling. Oh, dear Lord, please bring John back to me."

The other passengers slept on as she looked out the window and thought of the times John had been near her since that cold day she sent him away. He had even saved her life, but without revealing himself to her. Somehow...somehow she felt as if he were near her at that moment. Leaning forward, she stuck her head out the window. The warm breeze kissed her face, but she could see only sagebrush, trees, bushes, and wide open prairie.

Adjusting herself on the seat, she leaned her head back once more and closed her eyes. Her mind ran to Dr. Lyle Goodwin. She wondered what her next nursing job would be after she had a few days of well-deserved rest.

CHAPTER EIGHT

Up in the box, Ozzie Davis and Walt Green let their eyes roam about them as the six-up team pressed into the harness, snorting as they pounded the dusty trail. The prairie's steady undulations were before them, broken by low hills to the north and south. They could barely make out the jagged tips of the snow-capped Rockies on the western horizon.

The sun was reaching its apex in the cloudless sky as the shotgunner said to the driver, "She's a real beauty, isn't she?"

Ozzie grinned and rubbed his bristly chin with one hand while holding the reins with the other. "That she is, my boy. That she is. In fact I've been thinkin' that maybe I could fake some kind of sickness before we get to Denver so's I could have a little personal attention from her."

Walt laughed. "Why, you old codger! I wouldn't put anything past you!"

Ozzie punched him in the ribs with an elbow. Grinning from ear to ear, he said, "Why don't you admit it? You were considerin' fakin' somethin', too, weren't you."

Walt lifted his hat in mock knavery, and said, "Yeah. That I was."

"Well, if both of us put on a sick act, she just might get suspicious."

"So why don't you just forget it and let me be the one to get Miss Baylor's lovely attention?"

"Nuts to that!" Ozzie chortled. "I'm sure the little nurse likes more mature men, anyhow. I'll just develop me a sudden pain somewhere."

"She may like mature men, ol' pal, but not tottering, ancient relics!"

Ozzie elbowed him again, this time harder. "Why, you immature, wet-behind-the-ears little striplin'! I ain't lettin' no runny-nose little kid like you get ahead o' me with the ladies!"

"Hah! Well, I ain't lettin' no grizzled old grandpa get ahead of me, neither!"

"Well, then, I guess we've got us one o' them there Mexican standoffs, kid! 'Cause I ain't budgin'!"

"Well, I ain't either!"

Both men were quiet for several minutes. Then Walt said, "You're a stubborn old coot."

Ozzie regarded him with mock disdain. "Who's stubborn? Me? No, it's you who's stubborn. Why, compared to a mule, you're—"

"Don't look, now, Ozzie," cut in the shotgunner, "but we've got company."

Davis frowned, gripping the reins with both hands. "Indians?"

"No," Walt replied, squaring around on the seat. "It's a lone rider."

"Not an Indian?"

"No. It's a white man."

"Well, what's so strange about that? Lots of people travel this road."

Looking back over the top of the coach once more, Walt said, "He's not ridin' the road, Ozzie. He's followin' at a distance of about two hundred yards at an angle. He's movin' in and out among those rollin' hills to the south."

Curious, Ozzie ventured a glance over his shoulder. He could make out no sign of movement. "Aw, c'mon, kid. You're imaginin' things. I don't see no rider."

Still looking that direction, Walt replied, "He just went behind one of those hills. Keep watchin'. He'll appear in a minute."

Only seconds later, Ozzie saw horse and rider emerge from behind a grassy knoll. The horse was solid black, and the rider sat tall in the saddle. "Well, I doubt he's followin' us, kid."

"He *is* followin' us, Oz."

"Then why's he way over there? Why ain't he on the road behind us?"

"I don't know that, but he's keepin' pace with us and headin' due west, just like we are."

Straightening on the seat, Ozzie said, "Well, keep an eye on 'im."

Walt checked the rest of the prairie for any sign of Indians, while keeping track of the lone rider. After several minutes, he said, "He's still with us, Oz. Same distance. Same angle."

Ozzie took another look. "Guess I can't argue. He's followin' us, all right."

"Sure isn't tryin' to hide the fact, either," Walt said. "What do you make of it?"

Ozzie hesitated before answering. "Well...when I was drivin' for Wells Fargo in Dakota Territory 'bout twelve years ago, there was a rider followin' like that. Me and my shotgunner noticed him, but figured he was harmless. Boy, did we get fooled."

"Yeah?"

"We finally lost sight of him, then about twenty minutes later, we were skirtin' a stand of trees when all of a sudden this gang of robbers comes chargin' out, holdin' guns on us and wantin' a cash box we were carryin' from one bank to another. That guy who'd been followin' us was part of the gang."

Walt took another look at the man on the black horse, then

said, "But we're not carryin' a cash box."

"Maybe that fella and his gang think we are."

"Probably be a good idea if we let the passengers know there could be trouble up ahead," Walt said. "I mean, since Frame and Nelson are wearin' guns, we just as well alert 'em in case we suddenly need their help."

"Good idea," agreed Ozzie, pulling back on the reins.

As the coach slowed to a halt, Walt glanced to the south, but the lone rider was nowhere to be seen.

While driver and shotgunner climbed down from the box, all four passengers stuck their heads out the windows, asking why the coach had stopped.

"Why don't you folks step out and stretch your legs?" Ozzie said. "There's somethin' I need to tell you."

Frame and Nelson alighted first, intending to help the ladies. Walt rushed up to give Breanna a hand, mildly brushing Nelson aside. When Breanna was out, Nelson helped Esther from the coach.

Ozzie checked the prairie for any sign of movement, but saw none. There were no Indians, and the mysterious rider had disappeared. Moving to where the passengers and his shotgunner were collected beside the coach, he said, "Walt spotted a lone rider followin' us several miles back, folks. He's kept off to the south at an angle about two hundred yards distant ever since Walt first saw him. Once in a while, he was out of sight, but soon was where we could see him again. Right now, he's nowhere to be seen."

"So what do you suppose this rider's got planned for us, Mr. Davis?" Donald Frame asked.

Rubbing his grizzled chin, Ozzie said, "Well, I was tellin' Walt about a similar rider followin' a stage I was drivin' up in Dakota Territory a few years back. Turned out he was part of a gang who eventually stopped the coach and robbed us. I'm not sayin' for sure that we're about to be waylaid a piece down the road, but Walt and I agreed we should alert you as to that possibility."

"Oh, dear," whimpered Esther, putting her hand to her mouth.

Breanna laid a hand on the older woman's shoulder and asked, "What color is this rider's horse, Mr. Davis?"

"Coal black, ma'am."

Breanna's heart leaped in her breast. "Could you tell how the rider is dressed?"

"He's been keeping himself at a measured distance, Miss Baylor," Walt said. "There's no way to tell that."

"Do you think you know who this rider might be?" Frame asked.

"Well...I know a man who rides a black horse. He dresses in black like a preacher or a gambler. I just thought—"

"If this rider is your friend, ma'am, why would he follow the stage in such an odd manner?" Frame said. "Or at all, for that matter? I mean...if he somehow knows you're on the stage, and if he needs to see you, wouldn't he just ride alongside and tell Mr. Davis he would like to talk to you?"

Breanna's face tinted. Smiling, she said, "Of course, Mr. Frame. I really wasn't thinking too clearly when I asked about how the rider was dressed. I'm sure Mr. Davis and Mr. Green are correct in wanting us to take caution. I sure hope it won't be a repeat of what happened to Mr. Davis in Dakota Territory."

"Me, too," spoke up the stage driver. Slapping his hands against his hips, he said, "Well, let's get movin' again." Then to Frame and Nelson, "I'd appreciate it if you two would kind of stay prepared just in case we run into trouble."

"We'll do it," replied Frame.

Nelson nodded his assent.

Esther Matherly's features showed the fear she was experiencing. Breanna guided her toward the stagecoach door and spoke in a steady voice, "Don't be afraid, dear. It'll be all right."

As the coach resumed its westward movement, Breanna's heart was in her throat. Her mind went to the mysterious rider. A black horse. *Could it be John?* If so, did he know that danger lurked ahead on the road to Denver? Was he allowing himself to be seen so she would know he was there to look out for her?

Breanna leaned past Esther, who was now resting with her eyes closed, and looked out the window toward the south. There was no rider to be seen. The coach tilted forward as it dropped into a shallow valley. Nelson and Frame were alert, each watching the passing landscape and listening for any alarm from driver or shotgunner. Breanna settled back on the seat, touched the two men with her gaze, then looked out her own window.

About the time the stage came to level ground on the floor of the valley, the sound of distant gunfire met everyone's ears. The two women looked at each other while both men stuck their heads out the windows. "What's that?" Nelson called to the crew.

Keeping the team at a steady trot, Ozzie called back, "It's gunfire, for sure! Maybe we've got cavalry shootin' it out with Injuns somewhere around here."

"Can you tell which direction? Hard to make it out down here."

"Not for sure. This open country does strange things with sound, especially with the wind always blowin'."

"What are you going to do?" asked Frame.

"We'll just keep movin'. No sense stoppin' down here."

Both male passengers settled once again into their seats. Breanna was attempting to calm Esther. The older woman was showing more fear of Indians than she had been showing of robbers a little while earlier.

The sound of gunfire soon dwindled, then died out.

The stage was in the valley for some twenty minutes, then began a long pull up a gentle slope. Up in the box, Walt was twisted around on the seat, shotgun-in-hand, looking for any sign of the mysterious rider or hostile Indians. He was looking directly behind the coach when it reached the crest, and he heard Ozzie say, "It was cavalry and Injuns shootin' it out, all right."

Walt swung around in the seat and followed the driver's line of sight. Up ahead about a hundred yards was a cavalry unit of a dozen men or more. They were off their mounts and collected in a circle, looking down at something on the ground. Nearby stood several riderless painted ponies grouped together. There were two army horses, heads drooped, with dead soldiers draped over their backs.

"Looks like the soldiers came out on top," Walt said.

"Yep," nodded Ozzie. Leaning over the side of the box, he called, "Looks okay, folks. Army up ahead. 'Pears they've killed a bunch of redskins."

The passengers were craning their necks through the windows as Ozzie pulled rein and drew the coach to a halt. Fourteen troopers stood straight-backed in their cavalry blues as every man in the circle turned to look at the coach. From their elevated position in the box, Ozzie and Walt could see the bodies of several dead Indians sprawled on the grass.

Walt did a quick count. "Eleven dead Indians...eleven painted ponies."

One of the soldiers detached himself from the circle and headed toward the stagecoach. The crew was sliding out of the box and the passengers were piling out of the coach. The young officer drew up and said, "I'm Lieutenant Hugh Barstow, Fifth Cavalry out of Fort Morgan."

Ozzie introduced himself and his partner, then without giving names, he said, "These here are my passengers, Lieutenant."

Barstow touched his hat, then looked back at the crew. "These Kiowas you see lying dead, here, attacked a stagecoach on its way from Sterling to Denver yesterday. Killed all five passengers and the crew, stole the horses, and set the coach on fire. Colonel Farrington, our fort commandant, sent me and my patrol out early this morning to track them down. We found them about thirty minutes ago. They were hiding in that draw over there, waiting to attack your stagecoach. The same thing would have happened to you that happened to that stage yesterday if we hadn't come upon them when we did."

Esther gasped and clung to Breanna. "Oh, how awful!"

"It's all right, now," said Breanna, embracing her and patting her back.

Donald Frame moved up to Barstow and said, "Lieutenant, since the Indians were hiding in that draw, how did you know they were there?"

"I was about to tell that part," grinned Barstow. "Actually, we had some help. We were coming in from the west, and all of a sudden, we saw a lone rider galloping our direction from due east. We thought he was intending to meet up with us, but all the time, he was closing in on the Kiowas in the gully. We were still about a hundred yards from the gully when this rider opened fire on the Kiowas, whom we hadn't even seen yet. He kept his repeater rifle hot while the Indians came charging up out of the gully after him.

"We closed in and helped him finish them off. When we talked to him, he said he saw the Indians go into the draw. He knew the stage was on its way, and put two and two together. When he saw us coming, he knew he would have some back-up if he went ahead and charged into the draw."

Breanna's heart was racing. "Lieutenant, did this lone rider tell you his name?"

"No, ma'am, he didn't. But he did tell us he'd been following your stage for awhile, intending to move in and help if you met up with a band of hostiles."

"Lieutenant, can you describe this lone rider?" Breanna asked.

"Sure. He's tall. Very tall. Dark hair and mustache. Has two identical scars on his right cheek. Dresses more or less like a gambler...you know, all black except for a white shirt. Wears a string tie. Handles his rifle expertly, and also wears a tied-down Colt .45 Peacemaker."

"Is this the man you were thinking it was, Miss Baylor?" Donald Frame asked.

"Yes. When Mr. Davis said the man was alone, and was on a black horse, I sure thought it was him."

"A friend of yours, indeed, miss," smiled Barstow, reaching into his pocket and producing a silver medallion the size of a silver dollar. "Your name has to be Breanna Baylor."

"Yes."

Barstow extended the medallion to her and said, "The man didn't tell me his name, ma'am, but he did tell me your name, and asked me to give this to you. He said you would know who it came from, and what it means."

"Yes," she nodded, taking the medallion and closing her fingers around it. Tears surfaced as she said, "I know exactly who it came from, and what it means."

"Pardon me, ma'am," said the lieutenant. "I don't mean to stick my nose in where it doesn't belong, but I couldn't help noticing what's engraved on the medallion. *The stranger that shall come from a far land,* then a reference to a Scripture verse."

"Yes," Breanna said, blinking against the tears. "Deuteronomy 29:22."

"He a preacher?"

"Sometimes."

"What's it mean...this *stranger from a far land?*"

"I can't really tell you, Lieutenant. John is a very mysterious man. He has never told me where he is from."

"John?"

"Yes, he calls himself John Stranger."

Barstow's eyebrows arched. "John *Stranger?* That's his name?"

"The only name by which I know him," nodded Breanna.

Lieutenant Barstow looked off to the east, the direction John Stranger had taken when he rode away, shook his head, and said, "He's a strange one, all right, but he sure can handle a gun." He then turned to the driver. "Mr. Davis, there may be more hostiles between here and Denver. My men and I will escort you there."

A sergeant said, "Lieutenant?"

"Yes?" replied Barstow, turning toward him.

"What about the bodies of Brady and Wilson?"

Barstow glanced at the corpses of the two soldiers draped over their horses' backs. Grimly, he said, "We'll leave them over here in the draw and pick them up on the way back to the fort after we escort this stage to Denver."

"Yes, sir," responded the sergeant, then turned and gave orders for two corporals to lead the horses bearing the bodies down into the draw.

"I'm sorry about those two men, Lieutenant," said Ozzie.

"Me, too," Barstow nodded. "They were good soldiers." He took a deep breath, then said, "Well, let's get you people safely to Denver."

When the stagecoach was once again rocking its way westward, Breanna Baylor sat in silence, clutching the medallion the lieutenant had given her. A lump lodged in her throat and she bit down on her lower lip. Sick at heart that she had not been able to see John and talk to him, Breanna closed her eyes, and laid her head back against the seat. *Oh, John, I want to talk to you. I must tell you how very much I love you. And I must tell you how sorry I am that I sent you out of my life.*

It was mid-afternoon when the stage pulled into Denver and rolled to a stop in front of the Butterfield Stage Lines office on Glenarm Street. The passengers alighted, and along with the crew, thanked Lieutenant Barstow and his men for their protection.

As the cavalry unit rode away, Myron Kurtz, the Butterfield agent, emerged from the office and approached Breanna.

"Hello, Mr. Kurtz," she smiled.

"Howdy, Miss Baylor," he said, returning the smile. "Dr.

Goodwin came by the office this morning and asked me to tell you that he needs to see you immediately upon your arrival."

"All right. Thank you."

There were wagons for hire at the hostelry adjacent to the Butterfield office. Breanna quickly engaged a driver and wagon to take her to Dr. Goodwin's office. While the driver was placing her luggage in his wagon, Breanna bid Ozzie Davis and Walt Green good-bye, then embraced Esther Matherly, saying she hoped they would see each other again.

When they reached the doctor's office, the wagon driver carried Breanna's luggage inside and set it down. She greeted Mary Sheldon, the receptionist, paid the driver, then said to Mary, "Dr. Goodwin left a message that I was to come here as soon as I arrived in town."

"Yes," replied the receptionist, rising from her desk. "We have an emergency, and Dr. Goodwin has already volunteered you to fill the need."

"Oh? Where and what is it?"

"I'll let him tell you," said Mary, heading for the closed door that led to the clinic. "He'll want to give you the information himself. He's with a patient, but I'll let him know you're here."

Mary disappeared through the clinic door just as a frantic young mother came in from the street, carrying her five-year-old son. The boy was purple. He was gagging, eyes bulging with terror, trying to get a breath.

"I need to see the doctor, ma'am!" gasped the mother. "Lennie was with me over in the dress shop. He picked up a button and put it in his mouth. It's lodged in his throat!"

"I'm a nurse, ma'am," Breanna said quickly. "Let me have him."

Handing the child to Breanna, the mother pled, "Hurry! He'll die!"

Breanna quickly stood the child on the floor, facing away from her, grabbed her right wrist with her left hand, and gave a quick thrust to his midsection. The button popped out of his mouth. Lennie took a big gulp of air as Breanna held him in her arms.

The young mother broke into tears. Lennie was gagging a bit, but the purple was leaving his features, and it was evident the danger was over. Breanna handed the boy to his mother, saying, "He'll be all right, now, ma'am."

"Oh, thank you!" exclaimed the tearful woman. "You saved Lennie's life!"

Dr. Goodwin came through the clinic door, followed by Mary. Breanna explained what had just happened, and Goodwin commended her for her fast thinking. The mother praised Breanna to the doctor, then asked what the cost would be.

Goodwin smiled and said, "Well, if there's any charge, Mrs. Gerhardt, it'll come from Nurse Baylor, here."

"No charge," Breanna smiled. Then leaning close to the child, whose head rested on his mother's shoulder, she said, "No more buttons in the mouth, Lennie. Understand?"

The boy nodded.

Mrs. Gerhardt thanked Breanna again and left, carrying Lennie.

Dr. Goodwin said to Breanna, "I've got Nurse Jenkins finishing up with the patient in the clinic. Let's go into my office."

Breanna followed the good doctor to his office, where he sat her down in front of his desk, then eased into his chair. "Thank you for coming right over," he said warmly.

"Mary says there's some kind of emergency?"

"Yes. Do you know where Hay Springs, Nebraska, is?"

"No, sir."

"Well, it's about two hundred and fifty miles northeast of Denver. Right up in Nebraska's northwest corner. Wells Fargo runs stages into that country. Several towns between here and there."

"I see. And there's some reason that you want me to go to Hay Springs."

"Yes. I received a wire from Dr. Gerald Getz, the town's physician, yesterday afternoon. They've got a typhoid epidemic in Hay Springs. Bad water. One-fourth of the people in the town are down with it. Six have already died—four children and two older adults. Dr. Getz is all by himself. He has no nurse, and needs help in the worst way. Since the town's whole water system is polluted, he's sure many people drank the water before they knew there was a problem. He's expecting a great deal more to come down with typhoid."

Breanna leaned forward. "Mary says you've already volunteered my services."

"Yes. Knowing you were to be in here today, I wired Dr. Getz back immediately and told him I'd put you on the next available stage as soon as you arrived."

"And when does it leave?"

"In about forty minutes."

Breanna's bones ached at the thought of climbing on another stagecoach so soon, but she smiled and said, "All right. I'll go."

CHAPTER

NINE

Ward Fleming's wagon train had made good time the first day out from North Platte. They had covered nearly seventeen miles when the sun touched the western horizon, turning the prairie a fiery orange-red.

Fleming trotted his horse along the wagon line, telling the drivers that there was a small creek about a half-mile ahead. When they reached the creek, they were to form their usual protective circle and make camp for the night.

By the time the wagons reached the creek and began forming the circle, the sun disappeared over the earth's western rim. The sky was still aflame, but steadily gave way to a purple dusk that spread its soft beauty over the land. Soon twilight settled on the prairie, and campfires began to flicker against the thickening shadows. While the weary travelers ate their evening meals family-by-family, stars broke through the enamel black of the sky overhead.

The Logan family sat around their campfire, enjoying juicy pheasant Jim had shot earlier that day. Little Benjamin looked at his father and said, "Papa, are we almost to Hay Springs?"

"Not yet, son. We've still got a ways to go."

"How long will it take us?"

"About another ten days or so."

"That's a long time," Benjamin said dully.

"Aren't you enjoying the trip?" his older sister asked.

"I'm just tired of travelin', that's all."

"Are you bored, son?" asked Merilee.

"Guess you might say that. Nothin' exciting happens. It's just the same thing every day. Travel, travel, travel."

"Well, little brother," spoke up Jeremy, "when we get our ranch goin', you won't get bored. There'll be chickens to feed, and barns to clean, and wood to chop, and plenty more chores to do."

Benjamin looked at his father, "Won't there be any time to play?"

"Of course there will be, son. But Jeremy is right. You won't get bored on our ranch. We're going to have a wonderful life together."

"Of course that'll only last a few years for us kids," put in Darlene. "Won't be too many more years and we'll get married and have our own homes."

"Well, I don't know about you, Darlene," said Jeremy, "but I won't be livin' far from Mama and Papa. I'm gonna have me a ranch real close by."

"That depends on who I marry," clipped Darlene. "Maybe I'll marry some real rich man who lives in New York City."

"That's dumb," said Benjamin. "Why would you do that? New York City don't have no ranches."

"Doesn't have any ranches," corrected Merilee.

Benjamin smiled at Darlene. "See what I told you? Mama knows everything, and she says they don't have no ranches there, neither."

Jim and Merilee had to hide their smiles.

"Maybe I won't want to live on a ranch all my life," Darlene said. "Maybe I'll be one of those high society ladies I saw in a magazine at Mrs. Weatherton's house. Maybe I'll have big diamond rings and fancy necklaces and wear my hair piled up high.

Ranchers' wives don't live like that."

"So you really want to move away from Mama and Papa, huh?" asked Benjamin.

"I only said maybe."

Little Susie had been taking it all in. Seated beside her father, she took hold of his arm and announced, "I'm not leavin' Papa. I'm gonna marry him an' stay wif him a thousan' years!"

This time Jim and Merilee laughed aloud.

When supper was over and the plates and cups had been washed, the adults gathered in small groups to talk while the children ran about the camp.

Gerald Fleming sat on the ground, leaned against a wagon wheel, and played his harmonica. Soon the moon appeared in the eastern sky.

In the darkness outside the circle of wagons, Ralph Studdard and Ed Patton crept close. Going to their hands and knees, they crawled under a wagon and ran evil eyes over the camp. It took only a few seconds for Studdard to spot Benjamin Logan. The boy was playing hide-and-seek with several other children.

Studdard whispered, "This is gonna be a cinch, Ed. Nobody's payin' any attention to them kids. You be ready. I'll grab Benjamin and move right into the center of the circle by the biggest fire. Soon's I have everybody's attention, you come in and start takin' their money. Them women will have some kind of sack you can put the money in."

"Okay," nodded Patton.

"Some of those folks are gonna try to hold back the bulk of their money. I'm gonna scare the livin' daylights out of 'em so's they don't do any such thing. You just go along with me."

"Will do," grinned Patton.

"Okay," said Studdard. "Soon's I see my best bet for grabbin' the kid, I'll move."

Less than a minute had passed when Benjamin came within thirty feet of the wagon where the two men were hiding. Studdard sprang forward and grabbed Benjamin in his left arm. Thinking one of the men in the wagon train had grabbed him in fun, Benjamin squealed and laughed.

Suddenly the adults who were collected in small groups heard a loud, piercing shout, "Hey, everybody! Look over here!"

Everyone looked at the man who stood near the central fire, holding six-year-old Benjamin tightly in his arm with the muzzle of his Colt .44 pressed to Benjamin's head. Benjamin's breathing was fast and irregular, and his innocent little face showed stark terror.

Jim and Merilee froze.

"Studdard!" breathed Jim, eyes wide.

Ralph Studdard waited till the noise around him began to subside. The children soon realized what was happening, and their playful sounds died out. They scurried to their parents. Gerald Fleming's harmonica went suddenly silent. Every man and woman looked on, standing like statues.

When all that could be heard was the crackling of the fires, Studdard slowly cocked the hammer of his .44, letting the metallic sound cut through the night.

"Now, listen up, everybody!" he blared. "This here is what's known as a robbery!"

The sound of the hammer being cocked, and the sight of the deadly muzzle pressed against her little son's head stabbed Merilee's heart with a dagger of ice-cold fear. Her hands covered her mouth and horror widened her eyes. Her other children pressed close between her and their father. Jim drew in a deep breath, and his fingertips began to tingle.

Ralph Studdard barked, "Logan! I mean business! If anybody in this camp tries to run away or move against me or my pal, here, I swear...I'll scatter this kid's brains all over Nebraska! You understand?"

"Yes," Jim nodded. There was nothing to do but give the man whatever he wanted. "Don't hurt my boy. Tell us what you want."

"Money and gold!" blurted Studdard. "All of it! If I find out anybody held some back, this kid dies!"

A deep voice came from near the lead wagon. "Mister, I'm Ward Fleming, wagon master. I'm asking you to put the child down. I'll come over there and you can put your gun to my head."

"You stay right where you are, wagon master! This is my show, and it'll go accordin' to my script! Now, my partner here needs a nice big sack of some kind to put all the money and gold in. Let's have one of you nice ladies get him one pronto."

"I have a flour sack," spoke up one of the women.

"Fine. Ed, go with her and get it."

Merilee whispered to Jim, "Did I hear you say *Studdard?*"

"Yes," Jim whispered back. "These are the two who burned out the feed lot and killed Mr. Sturgis."

Patton returned to the center of the circle, carrying the flour sack. "All right, now listen up," Studdard said. "My pal's gonna come to you one wagon at a time. I know you're all carryin' plenty of money, and some of you are packin' gold, too. So don't hold out on us if you don't wanna see this kid get hurt. Okay, Ed. Start with the Logans."

Merilee saw the fury in her husband's eyes as Patton headed their direction. Husbands and wives exchanged dismayed glances.

When Patton drew up, his face was an evil thing to see by the flickering firelight. He showed crooked yellow teeth in a malicious grin and said, "Okay, Jim, lead me to your wagon. I want that big wad we saw you with in North Platte, and all the other wads, too."

The thought of what Studdard and Patton were doing to Benjamin, and what they were doing to the Logan family's future, unleashed a savage temper within Jim. Yet he knew he must control himself for Benjamin's sake. Jim gave Patton a withering glance and headed for his wagon.

"Hurry it up, Logan!" hollered Studdard. "We gotta clean out these other wealthy folks, too!" Noting that the fires were dwindling, he bawled, "Hey! Some of you men put some more wood on the fires! I want plenty of light around here!"

While the men obeyed, the women and children looked on, terrified at what was happening. Some of the smaller children started whimpering and were quickly quieted by their mothers.

At the Logan wagon, Jim handed Patton the fifteen thousand dollars they had left for starting their new life in Nebraska. His body trembled as he fought off the emotions welling up within him.

"Thank you," Patton grinned as he dropped the money in the flour sack. "Now, get back over there with your wife."

Studdard laughed insolently when he saw Logan return from the wagon with Patton behind him, and asked, "Get it all, Ed?"

"I'd say so, Ralph. Pretty good wad."

"Okay, get busy on the others. Just take whoever owns the wagon this side of Logans and work your way around the circle."

One by one, Ed Patton forced the men to their wagons, grinning evilly as they gave him their life savings. Each time, Studdard asked his partner if he was sure he was getting everything. When Patton said he was, Studdard sounded a warning to the next man that he had better not hold anything back.

Vann Simmell, the seventh man to be forced to his wagon, climbed up and opened his cash box. Patton was on the ground and couldn't see in the box. Along with Simmell's life savings in the cash box was a loaded Derringer.

Simmell's hands trembled as he eyed the Derringer, then glanced at Studdard. The thought entered his mind that if he could get the drop on Patton and put the Derringer to his head, they would have a standoff. Studdard's partner would be in as much danger as little Benjamin Logan was.

A cold chill washed over Simmell. He wondered if Patton's life would mean that much to Studdard. He decided it would not. A foolish move on his part could cost the boy his life. It wasn't worth it. Vann Simmell took out the money, closed the lid on the cash box, and climbed down.

Patton snatched the money from his hand and looked at it. Eyeing Simmell with suspicion, he said, "This ain't all of it."

"It *is* all of it," insisted Simmell.

"Don't lie to me! Ain't enough money here for buyin' no property and startin' a ranch. I want the rest of it!"

"I tell you, that's all there is!"

"You're lyin'!" spat Patton.

"Hey!" Studdard blared. "You wanna get this kid killed, mister?"

"I'm telling the truth!" responded Simmell, setting pained eyes on Studdard.

"He's lyin'!" grunted Patton. "Ain't enough money here!"

Studdard had already planned what to do in a case like this. He whirled about, lowered the boy, took the muzzle from his head, and fired a shot into the grass. To the people, it looked as though he had shot Benjamin.

Merilee screamed, and Jim's pent-up temper put springs in his legs. He bolted toward Studdard as fast as he could run. He was within twenty feet when Studdard abruptly stood straight with Benjamin in his arms and put the smoking muzzle to his head once again.

"Hold it!" shouted Studdard.

When Jim saw that his son was alive and unharmed, he skidded to a halt. Benjamin was too frightened to cry out. His eyes stared hollowly at his father.

"Get on back there with your wife, Logan!" commanded Studdard.

Jim stood still for a moment, filled with wrath and breathing hard.

"Now!" bellowed Studdard. "Or I *will* kill him!"

"Do you realize what you're doing to my little boy, Studdard? What has he done to be terrorized by you?"

"Shut up! He won't get hurt if everybody cooperates! Now tell that dude who's holdin' out on Ed to fork over the rest of his money."

Jim could hear Merilee whimpering behind him as Simmell said, "I'm telling you the truth, mister. I gave him all the money I have."

"You liar!" Patton hissed. "Like I said, there ain't enough money here to buy no property and start a ranch!"

"That's just it," retorted Simmell. "I'm not going to buy property and start a ranch. My wife and I are going to Wyoming to join her brother, who already has a ranch. He and I are going to become partners. That's why I'm not carrying the amount of money you think I should be."

"Okay, okay," grumbled Studdard. "Move on, Ed. This is takin' too long."

Jim Logan stepped back to his wife and children. He put an arm around Merilee and pulled the others close. In a low voice, he said, "It'll be all right. These men will be gone soon."

Merilee clung to her husband, wondering how he was going to handle the loss of their money. Beyond her fear for Benjamin's life was a deep concern that the loss of their money would crush Jim's faith, which had begun to grow stronger. She stopped whimpering and started praying.

The ordeal had lasted for a half hour when Patton took cash and gold from the owner of the last wagon. "Okay, Ralph," he said. "We can go."

Merilee was ready to dash to Benjamin and take him in her arms once Studdard set him down.

Running his hard eyes over the fire-lit crowd, Studdard said, "We're leavin', now. Don't anybody try followin' us, either."

"Go on, Studdard," Jim said. "Just put Benjamin down and

leave. Nobody's going to follow you."

"You don't really expect me to believe that, do you, Logan?"

Ward Fleming boomed, "You got what you wanted, mister! Give the Logans their boy and be on your way!"

Shaking his head, Studdard grinned maliciously. "Oh, no. Oh, no! The kid goes with us. I ain't takin' no chances on the bunch of you comin' after us."

Merilee cried, "No! Please! Don't take our son! Please!"

Jim's face was stricken. "Studdard! What kind of animal are you?"

"Shut up, Logan! Ain't nothin' gonna happen to this kid 'less somebody follows us. We see anybody comin' after us, I guarantee you, I'll put a slug in his head! If nobody follows us, we'll leave him unharmed on the trail ahead."

"Studdard! If you've got to have a hostage, take me!" Jim said.

"I ain't makin' no deals. The kid goes with us. And like I said...if nobody follows, you'll find him on the trail ahead, unharmed."

Merilee's body was rigid. Clenching her hands into fists, she shook them at her sides and cried, "There are wild animals on this prairie! And hostile Indians! You can't leave my child alone out there!"

Ignoring her, Studdard jerked his head toward the dark edge of the wagon circle and said, "Let's go, Ed."

Seconds later, the ex-Rebel soldiers and little Benjamin Logan were past the wagons and out of sight. Merilee's heart froze when she heard his pitiful wail: "Mama-a-a! Papa-a-a!"

Jim took her in his arms and held her while Jeremy, Darlene, and Susie clung to both of them, confused and terrified.

The crowd of travelers stood in shock. A moment later, galloping hooves were heard heading north, and soon faded away.

Ward Fleming hurried to the Logans and said, "I'm calling a prayer meeting right now. We're going to ask God to keep

Benjamin safe till we find him on the trail."

Jim stood like a post, gazing northward, and mumbled, "God didn't have to let them take Benjamin in the first place."

Merilee looked at her husband and said, "Oh, Jim, I understand how you feel. I've been battling some of those same thoughts. But don't blame the Lord for this. He didn't make those two men evil. They did it themselves...with the devil's help."

Jim's face was like granite. "God still could have kept them from taking Benjamin. He could have kept them from even seeing us in North Platte and learning that we are in this wagon train. Now, not only do we have Benjamin's life on the line, but our money's gone. We have no reason to go to Hay Springs. All our dreams are up in smoke."

The people were gathering close, their faces showing deep concern for Benjamin and their own financial losses. One of the older men said, "Jim, don't give up on God. The Lord's let a lot of unpleasant things come my way, and tested me sorely, but He's never forsaken me. My wife can tell you how I've reacted in some of my trials, got angry at God and all, but every time He's come through for me and showed me quite plainly that His ways are best. The Lord's put a test on you, now. Let it draw you closer to Him."

Merilee watched her husband's face as the older man spoke. She wished Jim could overcome the see-saw experience in his walk with the Lord. He seemed to find it difficult to trust the Lord in any and all circumstances.

"I appreciate what you're trying to do, Mr. Armand," Jim finally said. "I'm just having a real hard time right now."

"We're about to have a prayer meeting, son. Are you going to join us?"

Jim glanced at Merilee, then at Armand and nodded. "Yes. Of course."

Merilee looked at the others and said, "While we're asking the Lord to return Benjamin to us safely, let's ask Him to return all of our money, too. We've got a great big wonderful God. Nothing is too hard for Him."

Ward Fleming managed a faint smile. "Mrs. Logan is right, folks. Nothing is too hard for the God of heaven."

"Amen," came a voice from the group.

Fleming's smile broadened. "I realize this may sound strange to those of you who don't know the Lord, but here's your chance to see what He can do. Mrs. Logan and I are going to pray for the safe return of little Benjamin and the return of all our money. All of those who will join us in prayer, gather around right here."

Jim removed his hat and knelt on the grass beside Merilee. Jeremy and Darlene joined them, and little Susie squeezed into her father's arms.

Some of the men who thought religion was for weaklings and women remained aloof from the prayer meeting. They would, however, accept their stolen money back if somehow God could get it returned.

Merilee touched Jeremy and Darlene with one hand as the praying began, and laid her other hand on Jim's arm. Though his voice was shaky, Jim asked the Lord to protect little Benjamin, not only from harm at the hands of Studdard and Patton, but from Indians and wild animals. Hesitantly, he also pleaded with God to perform a miracle and let them have their money back.

Many tears were shed during the prayer time, and afterward, most of the travelers in the wagon train approached the Logan family to speak words of encouragement.

Later, when Merilee was bedding her children down, Jim was at the creek filling the family water barrel. He looked up in the pale moonlight to see the shadowed form of Ward Fleming walking toward him.

"Mrs. Logan said I'd find you here, Jim," Fleming said softly.

Jim was kneeling on the bank, dipping a bucket into the shallow rush of water and pouring it into the barrel. "Something I can do for you, Ward?"

"No. I just wanted to tell you that it's going to be all right. I believe you'll have your little son back tomorrow, safe and sound. And the money, too."

"I hope you're right, Mr. Fleming," Jim said with a sigh. "I'm having a battle with it, though. I'd be lying if I said I wasn't."

"Has the Lord ever tested your faith before?" queried the wagon master.

"Yes, sir. Many times."

"And how many of those times did He fail you?"

Jim swallowed hard. "None. I've failed Him countless times, but He's never let me down."

"Keep that in mind when you pillow your head tonight. You'll get some sleep if you will."

With that, the wagon master walked away and disappeared in the shadows. Jim capped the water barrel, hoisted it onto his shoulder, and sighed as he headed for his wagon.

CHAPTER TEN

Ralph Studdard and Ed Patton rode at a steady trot for an hour, then dismounted in a dense stand of trees next to the trail.

Benjamin Logan sat on a fallen tree in a small clearing, trying not to cry. While riding on Studdard's horse with him, Benjamin had started to cry once, but the man railed at him, telling him if he cried, he would pound him senseless. Fear gripped the small boy as he sat biting his lips.

Benjamin's captors built a fire, set a coffee pot in it, then began laying out their bedrolls.

"So where's the kid gonna sleep?" asked Patton.

"In your bedroll," grunted Studdard.

"Why mine?"

"I don't trust this kid's old man. He's liable to try sneakin' up on us durin' the night."

"You really think so? I don't. I doubt Logan will jeopardize the kid's life by doin' a dumb thing like that."

"I hope you're right, ol' pal," Studdard said, "but just in case you ain't, we'll trade off keepin' watch. You can go first, and the kid can sleep in your bedroll. When we switch in the middle of the night, you can use my bedroll."

Patton looked like he had just swallowed a dill pickle, whole. Noticing the look on his face, Studdard said, "What's the problem?"

Glancing toward Benjamin, then back at his partner, Patton replied, "Kids his age wet the bed."

"Aw, they don't either."

"Yes, they do! Especially if they're scared!"

"That's poppycock."

"Ain't neither!"

Looking at the boy, Studdard said, "Hey, Benjamin! How old are you?"

"Six."

"You still wet the bed?"

"No, sir."

Studdard smirked at Patton. "See there? He don't wet the bed."

Patton knew that arguing would get him nowhere. The six-year-old was going to sleep in his bedroll. Turning and setting hard eyes on the boy, he said with iron in his voice, "You better not moisten my bedroll. Got that?"

"Yes, sir," came a small tremulous voice.

"You hungry, kid?" Studdard said gruffly.

"A little bit."

"How about some hardtack, beef jerky, and coffee?"

"My mama won't let me drink coffee," came the timid reply.

The frightened lad was given hardtack, beef jerky, and water. Patton made sure Benjamin visited the shadows at the edge of the clearing before he slipped into his bedroll for the night.

The long hours were uneventful for both men as they took turns keeping watch. When dawn lightened the eastern horizon, Studdard did a careful check of the surrounding terrain, looking for any sign of movement. When he saw none, he built a fire, then awakened his partner.

As soon as Benjamin was rousted out of the bedroll, Patton

checked it to make sure it was dry. When he found that it was, he rolled it up and tied it behind his saddle. While the men ate their breakfast and drank hot coffee, Benjamin devoured his share of hardtack and beef jerky.

With his mouth full, Studdard smacked his lips and said, "We're gonna do like I told your pa, kid. We'll leave you here amongst these trees so's you can hide from any Indians that come by, but you can easily see back down the trail and watch for the wagon train. Best you don't go runnin' back that way to meet them. Could be dangerous. Understand?"

"Yes, sir."

"So you'll stay right here and hide till the wagons arrive, right?"

"Yes, sir."

Satisfied that Benjamin would do as he said, Studdard and Patton finished breakfast, packed the utensils in their saddlebags, and made ready to leave. They took a couple of minutes to check their loot in the flour sack, and laughed together. They had hit it big. It would be counted and divided between them equally when they were at a safer spot.

Benjamin stood beside a tall cottonwood and observed as Studdard tightened up his cinch while Patton tied the flour sack to his saddlehorn. Both were about to mount up when a bold voice seemed to come from out of nowhere. "Hold it right there!"

Startled, Benjamin jumped. He turned to see a tall man dressed in black standing at the edge of the clearing about ten feet to his left. He was holding a cocked Colt .45, and it was pointed toward Studdard and Patton, who were some forty feet away.

Both men turned to face the owner of the voice that had startled them. He wore a black broadcloth coat with white shirt, black string tie, shiny black boots, and a black flat-crowned hat. He was square-jawed and had a pair of identical white-ridged scars on his right cheekbone. His eyes were pools of gray that seemed to look through them, rather than at them.

Patton felt his pulse throbbing in his temples, and his face turned the color of weather-beaten stone. His glance shifted from the man-in-black to his partner.

Studdard's features were set in a snarl as he met the man's cool gaze and said, "Who are you, and what do you want?"

"Who I am is of no consequence. But what I want is for the two of you to step away from your horses, then lift your guns from their holsters with your fingertips and drop them on the ground."

"What's this all about?" Studdard asked.

"Kidnapping and robbery," came the level, ragged-edged reply.

"What are you talkin' about?" Studdard blurted.

The tall man fixed him with piercing eyes. Nodding his head in Benjamin's direction, he pressed, "One of you this boy's father?"

Studdard and Patton exchanged nervous glances. When they didn't answer, the tall man said, "Son, is one of these men your father?"

"No, sir."

"Where is your father, son?"

"In a wagon train back that way. My mama and brother and sisters are there, too."

"That flour sack on your saddle, there, Slim...what's in it?"

Patton licked his lips and glanced at his partner, but did not reply.

"Money, right? Money you two stole from the people in the wagon train. You kidnapped this boy as a hostage, didn't you? A little insurance to make sure you got away?"

When the guilty pair remained mute, the tall man said, "Enough talk. Do like I told you. Move away from those horses and take your guns out with your fingertips and drop them on the ground. You two are going to Sheriff Purdum's jail in North Platte."

"Okay," mumbled Studdard, moving slowly. "You got us."

Patton kept step with his partner, with some twelve feet between them. Patton would go for his gun when Studdard did.

As Studdard walked away from his horse, his stubby fingers twitched above the butt of his gun. Patton stealthily eased his hand down toward his weapon.

The man-in-black spoke with a soft voice that carried a heavy weight of authority. "Stop right there and do as I told you. Don't play fools and try anything—"

The tall man's words were cut off as Studdard suddenly threw himself on the ground, clawing for his gun. The tall man's .45 roared, and the slug laid a white-hot iron across Studdard's gun arm. Studdard howled, swore, and went for his gun again.

The man-in-black swung his Peacemaker on Patton, who had his gun in hand, and was about to fire. The Peacemaker boomed and Patton took the .45 bullet dead-center in the chest. For a short, breathless instant, Patton held himself rigid, his eyes bulging, then pitched face-first to the ground.

The tall man unleashed a second shot on Studdard, who was on his knees, cocking and aiming his revolver. The slug ripped through his heart, toppling him backward. He hit the ground with a heavy whump, dropped the revolver, coughed once, and died.

Holstering his gun, the tall man turned to Benjamin, who still stood next to the cottonwood tree, and bent over, opening his arms. Benjamin rushed to him, breaking into heavy sobs. The man's strong arms enclosed him, and while Benjamin trembled and wept, he talked to him in soft tones, soothing him and assuring him that everything was going to be all right.

When the boy's weeping subsided, the man asked, "What's your name, son?"

"B-Benjamin," came the shaky reply.

"Benjamin who?"

"Logan."

"My name is John Stranger, Benjamin. But since we're friends, you can call me John."

"Oh, no, sir. My papa told me I'm not to call a big person by their first name."

Stranger smiled, tousled Benjamin's curly hair and said, "Your papa is right, Benjamin. I'm sorry. You can call me Mr. Stranger."

"Yes, sir."

Glancing toward the lifeless forms of Studdard and Patton, Stranger said, "I'll stay with you till we see the wagon train coming, Benjamin, then I'll have to go. Will you ask your father to see that those two are buried?"

"Yes, sir. But why can't you stay till the wagon train gets here? My papa and mama will want to thank you for keeping those bad men from getting away with our money."

"I've got somewhere else I have to be, my friend," replied Stranger. "But while I'm still here, let's take the sack that has the money it, and put it over by these trees."

Benjamin walked to Patton's horse with John Stranger, eyeing the bodies of his kidnappers warily. Stranger laid the flour sack next to the cottonwood where he had first found Benjamin, then looked southward through the trees and pointed. "Look out there, Benjamin. What do you see?"

Following John Stranger's finger, the child soon focused on the wagon train as it wended its way toward them on the grassy plains. "Oh! It's my mama and papa!"

The lead wagon was no more than a mile away. When Stranger saw the wagon master riding out front, he reached into his pocket and pulled out a silver medallion the size of a silver dollar. Kneeling down, he said, "Open your hand, son."

Benjamin gave him a speculative look, then showed the man his right palm.

Placing the coin in Benjamin's hand, he said, "I want you to give this to your papa. His name is Jim, isn't it?"

Benjamin's eyes widened. "Yes, sir. How did you know papa's name?"

"Tell your papa John Stranger killed those two bad men, won't you?"

"Yes, sir, but how—"

"You're a fine boy, Benjamin," said Stranger, rising to his full height. "We're friends, right?"

"Yes, sir, Mr. Stranger, but how did you know my papa's name?"

"Maybe we'll meet again someday." Walking toward the north edge of the trees, Stranger made a half-turn, smiled, and said, "Don't forget to give that medallion to your father."

"I won't," Benjamin said. He watched until John Stranger was deep in the trees, then lost sight of him. Moments later, he heard galloping hooves, then caught a tiny glimpse of a huge black horse loping northward. Horse and rider soon vanished among the grassy knolls.

Benjamin grasped the medallion tightly and ran to the edge of the stand of trees. Ward Fleming was riding about a half-mile in front of the lead wagon, which put him no more than three hundred yards from where Benjamin appeared from the patch of woods.

Benjamin waved his arms wildly, and broke into a run. He saw the wagon master draw rein, stand up in the stirrups, and peer at him. Suddenly Fleming sat down and put the horse to a gallop.

Quickly the space between man and boy closed, and the wagon master was out of the saddle, gathering Benjamin into his arms. "You all right, Benjamin?" asked Fleming, putting him down and looking him over.

"Yes, sir," responded the boy, looking southward to see the Logan family wagon barreling past Gerald Fleming, bounding over the grassy plain at full speed. Benjamin started to tell Ward Fleming about John Stranger, but since his family was so close, he decided to wait till they got there.

Moments later the Logan wagon skidded to a halt and Benjamin was being hugged and made over by his parents and siblings. As the rest of the train was drawing up, Merilee looked her son over and asked, "Did those bad men hurt you, honey?"

"No, ma'am. The short one said he'd bash me good if I cried, so I didn't."

Bending low over Benjamin, Jim laid a hand on his head and asked, "How long ago did those men leave?"

"They didn't leave, Papa. They're still there."

"What?" gasped Jim. "Still there?"

Fleming laid his hand on his sidearm, swinging his gaze back to the spot where he had seen the boy emerge from the trees.

"They're dead, Papa," said Benjamin. "And the sack of money is still there."

Jim and Merilee exchanged glances and looked at Fleming. Jim took Benjamin gently by the shoulders and said, "Son, this is no time to make up stories."

Shaking his head vigorously, the boy said, "I'm not making up a story, Papa. A man named John Stranger shot both those bad men and killed 'em, and told me to give you this."

Jim's eyes widened as he accepted the silver medallion from his son's hand. The light of the early morning sun flashed off it as he turned it between his fingers and silently read the inscription.

Curious, the others squeezed in close to see it. Jeremy and Darlene could read the inscription, but Susie wanted to know what it said. She still didn't understand when Merilee told her, but acted as if she did.

Letting Fleming take it and get a better look at it, Jim said, "Benjamin, did you say the man who gave you this told you his name was John Stranger?"

"Yes, Papa. And he killed those two bad men."

The other wagons were pulling up one by one. Amidst the hubbub, Ward Fleming told the people the brief story Benjamin had given and showed them the medallion.

Everyone agreed they should hasten to the wooded area. Jim placed Benjamin in the wagon with the rest of the family, asked Merilee to drive, and hopped on Ward Fleming's horse.

Fleming put the horse to a full gallop, and moments later, the two men dismounted and stared at the corpses of Ralph Studdard and Ed Patton. Jim rushed to the cottonwood where the flour sack lay against its trunk, opened it, and whooped, "Mr. Fleming! It's all here! The money's all here!"

There was elation in the wagon train when the people saw for themselves that the kidnappers were indeed dead, and their money was safe.

While the currency and gold were being returned to their owners by Ward Fleming and his son, Jim Logan held the medallion in his hand with Merilee and the children present and said to Benjamin, "What did this man look like?"

"Oh, Papa," the boy said, suddenly recalling what the stranger had asked him to do. "Mr. Stranger wants you to see that those two bad men are buried."

"We'll take care of that in a little while, son. Now, what did Mr. Stranger look like?"

"Well-l-l, he was tall. Really tall. And...and he had scars on his face. And sorta dark skin—not real dark, just sorta. His hair was black and his clothes, too. 'Cept his shirt was white. His horse was black, too. I saw him ridin' away on his black horse."

At that instant, Ward Fleming interrupted. "You said fifteen thousand, didn't you, Jim?"

"Yes. A little more. Maybe fifteen thousand and a couple hundred. If it doesn't tally out for everyone else, just the fifteen thousand will be all right."

Smiling warmly, Fleming handed Jim three rolls of currency. "Appears they didn't even touch it. Most everybody's money is in wads and rolls just like before. I thought these were yours. There's fifteen thousand two hundred and twenty-nine dollars, here.

Seems intact. Must all be yours."

"That's the exact amount, Mr. Fleming," spoke up Merilee. "I watch it a little closer than Jim does."

Both men laughed, then Jim said, "Females! Just like 'em to track every penny!"

As Ward walked away, Merilee said, "I'll put the money back in the wagon, my love."

While Merilee was walking to the wagon, she prayed. "Thank you, Lord. You indeed are a wonderful God. I give You all the glory for such a wonderful and complete answer to prayer. Not only did You spare our little boy from harm, but You also gave us our money back. Please...help Jim to see how precisely You answered our prayers. And that man, John Stranger. Lord, I don't know who he is, or how he happened to come along at just the right time, but I have no doubt that You sent him. Bless him for being Your obedient servant."

When Merilee returned to her family, Jim was kidding Benjamin, asking him if the trip was still boring.

"I'd rather have it borin' than to go through that again, Papa!"

Everyone in the wagon train had their money back and stowed where it belonged. Jim then approached the wagon master and suggested that he ask for volunteer grave diggers. Fleming called for attention, and explained that they needed men to dig graves for the two dead outlaws. Every man in the train volunteered, and by noon the bodies of Ralph Studdard and Ed Patton were six feet in the ground.

Fires were built in the clearing, and women began preparing the midday meals. It was one-thirty by the time the food had been devoured, and the tin cups, tin plates, and utensils washed and put away.

Ward Fleming called for attention again and said, "I've decided that we'll just make a day of it right here. We'll rest our animals and ourselves, and get a good early start in the mornin'."

There were sighs of relief among the adults and wild cheers among the children. Raising his hands to settle everyone down, Fleming said, "I think it would be fittin' to take time right now and thank the Lord for the way He answered our prayers.

"Amen!" someone shouted. Others followed suit.

Turning to his son, who stood at the lead wagon, Fleming said, "Gerald, bring me my Bible, would you please?"

Parents gathered their children to them and commanded them to be quiet while Mr. Fleming spoke. Taking the Bible from Gerald's hand, he opened its well-worn pages to the book of Jeremiah. Removing his hat and dropping it on the grass at his feet, he licked his thumb and flipped pages till he found the place he wanted.

The afternoon breeze began to flutter the Bible's pages, so the wagon master spread one hand over them while holding the Bible flat in the other. Lifting his voice, he said, "Last evening after those two men we just buried took off with little Benjamin and all our money, I called for a prayer meeting. I wanted us to pray for Benjamin's safe return to his parents. You will recall that it was Mrs. Logan who suggested that we also ask the Lord to return all of our money, too. She reminded us that nothing was too hard for our God. Well, believers and unbelievers alike in this wagon train learned a good lesson today on the power of God, didn't we? Not only did the Lord deliver the little Logan boy, but every one of you got your money back. Now, is that somethin' great, or is that somethin' great?"

There were several "Amens" again.

"I heard some of you men talkin' while we were diggin' those graves. One of you asked, 'Who do you suppose this fella John Stranger is?' Well, I can't tell you *who* he is, but I can sure tell you *what* he is. He's a livin', breathin', gun-totin' answer to prayer!"

There was a rousing cheer, mingled with "Amens".

Looking down at his Bible, Fleming said, "I want to read

you somethin'. Listen real close. Comes from Jeremiah 33:2 and 3. *'Thus saith the LORD the maker thereof, the LORD that formed it, to establish it; the LORD is his name; Call unto me, and I will answer thee, and shew thee great and mighty things, which thou knowest not.'"*

Fleming's voice broke momentarily. Swallowing hard, he blinked at the moisture filming his eyes. "Last...last night I quoted Mark 11:24 to you, where Jesus said, *'What things soever ye desire, when ye pray, believe that ye receive them, and ye shall have them.'* Can anyone here doubt that we have seen the Lord keep His Word?"

Some of the men who had avoided the prayer meeting looked at each other with a tinge of shame while many voices were speaking up, agreeing with Fleming's words.

Jim Logan was feeling the familiar guilt of having doubted the Lord, then having seen Him come through magnificently.

"I want us all to bow before the Lord," Ward Fleming went on. "I want us to praise and thank Him for the great and mighty things we've seen Him do here today."

With that, Fleming began his prayer of praise and thanksgiving for the way God had watched over little Benjamin Logan, and for sending the strange man-in-black to stop the robbers from making off with the life savings of so many people.

Suddenly the dam within Jim Logan broke. Merilee's eyes were closed, but when she heard him dart away, she opened them, whispered for the children to stay put, and followed him.

Jim was deep in the dense woods, on his knees, when Merilee caught up with him. He was sobbing with his hands over his face, and his entire body was quaking as she knelt beside him and laid a tender hand on his shoulder.

He uncovered his face and looked at her through a wall of tears. "Oh, Merilee, I'm such a wicked sinner! I prayed aloud last night, making everybody think I was believing the Lord would answer...but I didn't really believe He would do it."

Merilee kissed his cheek softly, and said, "I think this moment is a private one between you and your Lord, darling. I'll go back to the children." She kissed his cheek again, and hurried away.

Jim Logan poured out his heart in contrition over his lack of faith, asking the Lord to forgive him and to help him never to doubt His power and willingness to answer prayer again.

When Jim returned to the clearing, he found that the wagons had been formed in a circle beside the wooded area. The children were still playing in the clearing, but most of the adults were within the circle of wagons. A few mothers stayed to watch over the children.

Just as Jim was about to enter the circle, he saw a lone rider coming from the south. At first his mind went to John Stranger, but it took only a few seconds to tell that the horse was not black, nor was the rider as well-dressed as Benjamin had described Stranger. Jim entered the circle and joined Merilee, who was washing clothes at their wagon.

Ward Fleming was at the lead wagon, sharpening his hunting knife on a slab of whetstone, when he looked up to see a man emerge from between two wagons and head toward him. It took a moment to remember when and where he had seen the man before. This was the man who had met them on the trail a few miles outside North Platte, and inquired if they had seen a tall, dark man dressed in black. Fleming thought of little Benjamin's description of John Stranger and knew that it was Stranger the unkempt, long-haired man was hunting.

"Howdy, again," said Gavin Cold, drawing up to Ward Fleming.

Without smiling, Ward said, "Howdy."

"Remember me?"

"Reckon I do."

"My friend I told you I was lookin' for?"

"Yeah."

"Well, word is that he's in this area, now. I was just wonderin' if you'd seen him."

Fleming's instincts warned him that the man was up to no good. He would not do anything to help the man find John Stranger. "Nope. Still haven't seen him. Guess you'll have to keep lookin'."

Gavin Cold pulled his mouth tight, nodded, and turned away.

When Cold was gone, Gerald Fleming approached his father and said, "I hope that dude never finds John Stranger."

"Even if he does," Ward said, "from what I know about Stranger, I have a feeling he can handle the likes of him."

CHAPTER ELEVEN

The promise of summer was in the air as the Wells Fargo stage rolled into Hay Springs, Nebraska, in the heat of the afternoon, surrounded by a cavalry escort from Fort Sidney. The recent Indian uprising had forced the army to put a uniformed patrol with every stagecoach in northeast Colorado, southeast Wyoming, and the western two-thirds of Nebraska.

Breanna Baylor had ridden a stage the sixty-five miles from Denver to Fort Morgan, Colorado, in relative safety. At Fort Morgan, a fifteen-man patrol joined the stage and escorted it on the hundred-mile journey to the North Platte River at Broadwater, Nebraska. There, she boarded another stage, which was escorted by a similar unit from Fort Sidney the entire seventy-mile trip from Broadwater due north to Hay Springs.

By the time the stage reached Hay Springs, Breanna was its only passenger. Word of the typhoid epidemic had spread far and wide, and no one wanted to enter the town.

When the stage pulled up to the Wells Fargo office, Breanna noticed two men with badges on their chests standing on the boardwalk. The younger lawman stepped up and opened the door of the stage while the crew was climbing down. The older lawman was on his heels.

"Miss Baylor?" said the younger lawman, smiling warmly.

"Yes," replied Breanna, smiling in return.

"I'm Deputy Marshal Bob Osborne. May I help you down?"

"Thank you," said Breanna, taking his hand.

As Breanna's feet touched the boardwalk, Osborne gestured toward the older man and said, "Miss Baylor, this is Marshal Jed Luskin."

Luskin was a tall, slender man with graying hair and mustache. Smiling, he touched his hat brim. "Welcome to Hay Springs, ma'am. I'm sorry your first visit to our fair town has to be under these circumstances. Bob and I are here to meet you because Hal Robinson, the Fargo agent, is down with the typhoid."

"I'm sorry to hear that, Marshal. I can well imagine that Dr. Getz has his hands full."

Luskin cleared his throat. "Well, ma'am, it's worse than that. I hate to tell you this, but Dr. Getz has come down with the typhoid, too."

"Oh, no. Who's caring for the patients?"

"Some of the local ranch wives and their daughters are working with them, ma'am...and a few of the women who live here in town."

"Where are they? I assume they're isolated from the rest of the people."

"Yes, ma'am. Dr. Getz did that right away. They're all at the town hall."

"All right. I'd like to get there right away, if you'll see that my luggage is taken to the hotel."

"Bob will take care of that," nodded Luskin.

Breanna smiled at Osborne, who was young and a bit on the beefy side. "Just tell the hotel clerk I'll be there sometime later. If he'll go ahead and assign me a room, you can put the luggage in the room."

"Won't be any problem with that, ma'am," said Osborne.

"Right now, you'll be the only guest in the hotel."

"You do understand, Miss Baylor," spoke up Luskin, "that the town is picking up your food and hotel bill."

"I was not aware of it, Marshal, but it certainly is appreciated."

"We appreciate your coming to help us, ma'am. Let's get you to the town hall."

Breanna took her medical bag from the stage's boot, told the stage crew good-bye, and walked briskly down the street with Marshal Luskin.

As they walked, Breanna said, "Do I understand correctly that the typhoid is in the town's water supply?"

"Yes, ma'am. Dr. Getz determined that almost immediately. None of the surrounding ranchers are having any trouble with their water. In fact, they're hauling barrels of their well water into town for us."

"That's good. Have there been any more deaths? The message I received in Denver was that there had been six so far."

"I'm sorry to say that there have been five more, ma'am...a total now of seven children and four adults."

Breanna was silent for a few seconds, then she asked, "Is Dr. Getz able to talk?"

"He hasn't been for about twenty-four hours, ma'am. His fever has been terribly high, and Mrs. McCollister—that's a ranch wife—says he's been delirious."

Breanna shook her head sadly. She had dealt with typhoid many times in her medical career and knew its symptoms well. The infected person would first develop a headache, followed by a fever. Red blotches would appear on the chest and abdomen. Within a few hours would come nausea, chills, and cold sweat. The fever would continue to rise each day for about a week. The only way to reduce the fever was to continually bathe the patient in cool water. If the patient lived past the crisis that came on the seventh or eighth day, they were usually out of danger. Depending on the survivor's physical stamina, the recuperation period could be anywhere from ten days to three months.

Water barrels were evident all along Main Street, and were attended by men and women who assured anyone who took the water that it was from neighboring ranches. When they reached the town hall, Breanna noted several water barrels on the boardwalk. Teenage girls were filling pails and carrying them inside.

"Mrs. McCollister has sort of taken charge since Dr. Getz got sick, ma'am," Luskin said as they drew up. "The McCollisters are the wealthiest ranchers in the territory, and of course have the biggest spread."

Breanna followed the marshal inside the town hall and found some patients lying on beds and cots, though the majority were on the wooden floor. There were about fifty to sixty patients, and most were either quite young or past sixty.

There were some fifteen to twenty women and teenage girls busily attending to the patients' needs, especially bathing their fevered bodies with cool water. A few were delirious with fever, and were moaning or wailing.

Marshal Luskin led Breanna to a tall, slender woman in her late thirties. Emily Grace McCollister was standing over a cot, speaking soothing words to an elderly man, when she saw Luskin and Breanna coming toward her. Eyeing the black medical bag in Breanna's hand, she knew the nurse they'd all been waiting for had arrived.

Leaving her patient, Emily Grace greeted Luskin and smiled warmly at Breanna. "You must be Nurse Breanna Baylor."

"Yes," smiled Breanna.

"Miss Baylor," said Luskin, "this is the lady I told you about. Meet Emily Grace McCollister."

"Happy to meet you," smiled Breanna. "I appreciate what you're doing here."

"Oh, I'm so glad you've arrived, Miss Baylor," sighed Emily Grace. "I'm sure Marshal Luskin told you about Dr. Getz."

"Yes. How is he doing?"

"This is his third day. He's quite delirious with fever, but he's always been a strong man. I'm trusting the Lord to bring him through."

"I like that kind of talk, ma'am," said Breanna. "We would see more done in our own lives and the lives of others if we'd put more faith in Jesus. Are you a Christian?"

"Yes, indeed, Miss Baylor. I became a Christian when I was twelve years old. I won't tell a young lady like you how long that's been." Glancing at the marshal, she added, "Some of us are still working on our chief lawman, here."

Luskin cleared his throat and said, "Religion just isn't my cup of tea."

"Mine either, Marshal," Breanna said.

"Pardon me?"

"There's a difference between religion and salvation."

"Corey and I have tried to tell him the same thing, Miss Baylor," put in Emily Grace, "but so far, he goes deaf on us."

Luskin's back straightened. "Well, I'll leave you ladies to your patients. Got work to do."

As Luskin walked away, Breanna called after him, "Thanks for your help, Marshal."

Luskin waved over his shoulder, and was gone.

"I'd like to see Dr. Getz first, if I may," Breanna told her new Christian friend.

"Certainly. He's over here in the corner. My daughter is trying to keep his temperature down."

Emily Grace's skirt and petticoats made a swishing sound as she weaved her way among patients and workers to the far corner of the town hall. Through an open window, Breanna could see benches and other items of furniture sitting outside. The furniture had been moved to make room for the cots, beds, and patients on the floor.

Dr. Gerald Getz was lying on the floor with a blanket

underneath him. Kneeling beside him with a water pail at her side was a pretty young woman who strongly resembled Emily Grace. She was holding a wet cloth to the doctor's fevered brow and talking to him in low, soothing tones as he moaned in his delirium.

The girl stood up when she saw her mother coming. There was a ready smile on her lips as Emily Grace touched the nurse's arm and said, "Honey, this is Nurse Breanna Baylor. Miss Baylor, this is my daughter, Taylor Ann. She's eighteen, going on twenty-two."

Taylor Ann McCollister was slender like her mother though shorter, about an inch taller than Breanna. She had pale blue eyes and long, blond hair.

Doing a mannerly curtsy, Taylor Ann maintained her smile and said, "I'm very happy to meet you, Miss Baylor." Looking around at the room full of sick people, she added, "And I'm very happy you're here."

"Thank you. It's a pleasure to meet you, Taylor Ann. How's Dr. Getz?"

"Not much change. Perhaps you should have a look."

Brushing gently past Taylor Ann, Breanna knelt beside the fevered, delirious physician and laid an experienced palm on his brow. Looking up at Emily Grace, she said, "His temperature is very high. Isn't there a bed or cot for him?"

Emily Grace folded her hands. "I tried to get him to take one, but he wouldn't hear to it. You'd have to know him to fully understand, but you're looking at one of the most humble and caring men in all the world, Miss Baylor."

"Like so many in the medical profession," put in Taylor Ann, laying appreciative eyes on Breanna.

Rising, Breanna said, "Don't let me keep you from working on him, Taylor Ann. He needs all the cool water you can put on him. I know the natural tendency is to keep water on the brow, and that's good, but also keep water on the sides of his neck where the jugular veins are and on his wrists. That will help cool the blood."

"I didn't know that," replied the teenager.

"I didn't either," said Emily Grace.

Breanna smiled. "I guess that's what nurses are for, hmm?"

Breanna took the next hour to look at every patient, then discussed what hygienic measures had been taken to ward off spread of the disease. She was pleased to learn that Dr. Getz had taken the precaution to see to it that the body wastes of all patients and possible carriers were buried outside of town. The women and teenage girls who had been helping him had been instructed on how to sterilize their own clothing, and how to safeguard themselves as much as possible against contacting the highly contagious disease.

As soon as she could take them away from their patients, Breanna met with the workers in groups of three and four to answer questions and give instructions so the afflicted could have the best care possible. She worked with them steadily, meeting new workers as they came to relieve the others.

She fell into the hotel bed at 2:00 A.M., and was up at 6:00 to eat breakfast, bathe, and return to the town hall for another full day.

A week to the day after the ordeal with the robbers, wagon master Ward Fleming was riding his mount a half-mile ahead of the wagon train through dry country that resembled some of the desert area he had seen in north central Wyoming.

The land heaved away in irregular monotony, but as the day wore on, he soon saw the rounded crests of Nebraska's Sand Bluffs off to his left, standing boldly against the western sky. The lowering sun was throwing long shadows of the bluffs eastward. Out of those shadows, a small herd of antelope bounded, angling northeast into the sunlight. Fleming had to smile at the young antelope as they struggled to keep up with the others. It took the herd only a couple of minutes to vanish as they reached a rounded sandy crest and darted down the other side.

Fleming's wagon train was soon skirting the Sand Bluffs and moving across patches of strewn slab rock and wind-tufted sagebrush. The shade cast by the bluffs brought cooler air to the wagon train, and was appreciated by all. Wagon wheels squeaked in rhythm, and the gentle sound of hoof falls ran forward through the afternoon's drowse.

There was no security in this land, especially in daylight. Hostile Indians could pop up at anytime, and from just about anyplace. Fleming twisted in the saddle to give his train the once-over. Gerald held a steady course behind him, and the rest of the wagons were in a perfect line. All was calm and serene. Ward Fleming liked it that way.

Straightening in the saddle, he let his gaze touch the Sand Bluffs to the west, then run northward, all the way to his extreme right. No half-naked savages on painted ponies.

Fleming knew the bluffs ran almost twenty miles, and beyond them would be Soda Lake off to his right. When they reached the white-ringed lake, they would be just fifty miles from Hay Springs, where the Logan family would leave the train. Fleming would miss the Logans, especially Benjamin. *Brave little squirt,* he thought. *Most kids would have been nervous wrecks after going through what he did. Little guy was back to normal almost in no time.*

Fleming's thoughts settled on Jim Logan. Jim was a fine man. Diligent. Honest. Straightforward. Good husband and father. He no doubt would work hard and make a go of it as a rancher. Jim's one drawback seemed to be his wavering faith in God's willingness and ability to see him through difficult situations. Fleming had met a few Christians like that. He hoped this latest experience with Benjamin and the money would put some fiber into Jim's spiritual life.

The sun was soon gone, and purple shadows began to flow along the sandy slopes across the plains and into all the pockets and rock-spined gullies of the broken country. Fleming signaled Gerald to begin making a circle. They would camp for the night at the base of the Sand Bluffs.

During supper that night, Jim talked to his wife and children about God's marvelous answer to their prayers. It had taken him several days to come to it, but he asked Merilee and the children to forgive him for not being a better example to them. He admitted his weak faith, but assured them it would be different from now on. The Lord had taught him a significant lesson.

"Papa," Jeremy asked, "was John Stranger really sent to us from God? Ever since that day, when you pray, you always thank God for sending that man to take care of Benjamin and keep us from losin' our money."

"Of course he was," nodded Jim.

"You mean, like from heaven?"

"Well, not from heaven, son. He just sent him from some place around here to answer our prayers."

"Then what's it mean on that medallion when it says he's from a far country?"

Merilee eyed her husband thoughtfully by the firelight, waiting for his reply.

"Well, Jeremy, there's really no way to know. Maybe he's from some other part of the world."

"Must be, if he's a stranger here," concluded Jeremy.

Jim looked at Merilee and rolled his eyes as if to say, *Whew! I'm glad that satisfied him!*

Then Darlene said, "Papa, do you really think his last name is Stranger? I mean...I can believe John, all right, but who ever heard of anybody's last name being Stranger?"

"Well, honey, there are no doubt lots of peculiar last names you've never heard of."

"Yeah, but not Stranger. Have you ever heard of anybody with that last name?"

"Well, no, but—"

"Why would anybody's last name be Stranger?"

Abruptly, the redheaded three-year-old spoke up. "I know."

Every eye fell on Susie.

"His mama's name is *Mrs.* Stranger!"

Everyone around the Logan fire had a good laugh. Then it was time to wash the cups and plates and get to bed.

Tendrils of smoke lifted lazily from the charred timbers of the house, barn, and outbuildings as Ward Fleming rode through the gate of the small ranch at the northern tip of the Sand Bluffs. The sun was going down, and some of the families in the wagons were running short of water. Fleming had been this way before, and recalled visiting the Collins ranch. He had ridden ahead of the wagon train some three miles, intending to ask Harvey Collins if they could fill their barrels from his well.

Fleming noted that the windmill was still intact. The blades were turning slowly in the breeze. At least they would get their water.

Fleming estimated the buildings had been torched, probably by the Cheyenne, about an hour to an hour-and-a-half earlier. The black, smoking rubble of what was left of the Collins buildings still emanated some heat. The split-rail corral fence remained intact, but the gate was open and the corral was empty. The saddle horses had been stolen.

Wanda Collins lay in a lifeless heap in the yard, only a few feet from her dead husband. There were two arrows in her upper body. One had pierced her heart.

Sixty-year-old Harvey Collins lay sprawled face-down on the sandy ground. There was a spear centered in his back, and the feathers in spear and arrows identified them as Cheyenne. Harvey Collins was unarmed.

Ward dismounted slowly, feeling sick inside. Casting a glance southward, he could barely make out the wagon train wending its way toward him on the sun-bleached prairie.

Placing a foot on the dead man's back next to the spear, he gave it a yank, and it came free. Throwing the spear aside, he went to the woman's body and removed the arrows, tossing them next to the spear.

Tenderly, he picked Wanda's body up and laid it next to her husband's. Standing over them, he said softly, "I'm sorry, folks. You didn't deserve to die like this. We'll at least give you a decent burial."

As Fleming stood in the yard and watched the wagon train draw closer, he felt a sick dread come over him. The Cheyenne were somewhere near, and they were thirsty for white men's blood.

The people in the wagon train were appalled at what they found when they caught up to their leader. Fear ran through them, and Ward Fleming used the fear to help them see that they needed to stay alert at all times, and be ready to fight.

Harvey and Wanda Collins were buried near the blackened heap that was once their house. Ward read Scripture over the mounds of dirt, prayed for the safety of the wagon train, and put the men to work filling the water barrels.

Fleming moved the train on another mile before stopping for the night. When the wagons were in a circle, he gathered everyone and told them they would reach Soda Lake sometime in the morning. From there, it was fifty miles to Hay Springs. This would put them in Hay Springs in about four days. They would take a day to rest themselves and the animals at that time, then move on toward Wyoming.

After the evening meal, Fleming called another meeting. Standing before the group by firelight, he said, "Since we know we're in hostile territory, instead of two men on watch at intervals during the night like we've been doing, I want four. We're not taking any chances."

One of the men spoke up. "Mr. Fleming, I've been told that

Indians won't attack at night. Something about their superstitions. Do we really have that much to worry about during the night?"

"That depends on the tribe," said Fleming. "You can't put a blanket on it. The Cheyenne religion teaches that if they die fighting between sunset and sunrise, their souls will be locked forever in some nocturnal state, floating in the spirit world, and never reach the happy hunting ground."

"Then what do we have to fear?" asked the same man. "Certainly they're not going to attack us before sunrise."

"There's only one problem," Fleming said flatly. "As with every tribal religion on earth, the Cheyenne have their infidels who don't believe the accepted superstitions. The problem we face is, are the Cheyenne warriors who lurk in these parts infidels or believers? Since we don't know, we'll double our watch force tonight."

There was little sleep amongst the adults in the wagon train that night. Having seen the work of the Cheyenne first-hand, the travelers were on edge, upset, and nervous. Some gathered for prayer while the men assigned to watch walked the inside of the circle, eyes searching the darkness, ready to shoot any infidel Cheyenne who would risk attacking by night.

Morning came with the travelers as weary as they had been when the train stopped the evening before. Ward Fleming remained close to the wagons as wheels rolled northward, riding up and down the line, making sure every man had his gun ready, and that the mothers had a plan in mind for getting their children to a relatively safe place in the wagon if an attack came.

It was nearly nine o'clock in the morning when the sun's reflection off the surface of Soda Lake caught Gerald Fleming's eye. Standing up in the wagon, he looked back to find his father. Ward was riding alongside the Logan wagon, talking to Benjamin, who was sitting on the seat between his parents. Susie was in the back with Jeremy and Darlene.

"Hey, Pa!" shouted Gerald. "Soda Lake in sight!"

Some seventy yards to the west was a huge rock formation. It was not tall or towering, but it was nearly two hundred feet square, and averaged eight feet in height. Suddenly a shot pierced the morning air, and Gerald Fleming toppled from the wagon.

The bark of the rifle was still echoing across the prairie when two dozen whooping and yelping Cheyenne warriors galloped around the end of the rock formation.

While the lead wagon moved on without a driver, the other wagons began to form a circle. Though there were only twenty-four warriors on horseback, to the frightened occupants of the covered wagons, the heavy beat of the galloping hooves was like a thousand death-drums beating out an ominous rhythm.

CHAPTER TWELVE

While the anxious drivers completed the circle, terrified mothers flattened their children on the floors of the wagon beds. Cheyenne bullets tore through the canvas covers, chewed into the wooden sides and tailgates, and buzzed through the air like angry bees.

Quickly, the men and the teenage boys were on their bellies under the wagons, firing. Hot lead plowed into the ground, scattering dirt and tossing sandy particles into their eyes.

Ward Fleming was off his horse, bellied down under Dexter Armand's wagon, firing his revolver at the Indians. He had no idea whether Gerald was lying out there alive or dead.

Armand, who lay beside him, lined a bronze body in the sights of his rifle, and squeezed the trigger. The Indian stiffened on his pony's back, ejected a wild screech, and fell to the ground. At the same time, Fleming dropped his hammer. The revolver bucked in his hand, and another Indian peeled off his pinto.

It was bedlam all around the wagon train as guns boomed and barked. Horses in the harnesses were nickering and dancing fearfully, and the terror-edged screams of children could be heard above the din. Men in the wagon train were being hit, and their horrified wives were wailing their husbands' names from inside the wagons.

The fierce charge lasted about five minutes, then the Cheyenne—as if on signal—wheeled about and disappeared around the edge of the rock formation.

The sudden silence seemed to fall over the wagon train like a blanket. The screaming of the children subsided, and women whose husbands had been shot were out of their wagons, kneeling over them. Some of the men were dead.

Ward Fleming scooted from under the Armand wagon, leaped to his feet, and shouted, "Everybody stay put! Those savages will be back right quick!"

At the Logan wagon, Jim called from underneath, "Everybody all right up there?"

"Yes!" responded Merilee. "We're fine, so far!"

"Papa," came Jeremy's voice, "I want to come down there and help you. My gun's loaded. Can I come down?"

"No, son. I want you up there with Mama and your brother and sisters."

"But, I can shoot straight, Papa. You know I can."

"I know, and if there weren't so many Indians, I might let you. But it's just too dangerous out here."

"Jim," Merilee called, "the children and I are praying for God's protection, but don't you take any chances."

"I won't, honey," Jim answered. "I'm staying right here, trying to make myself as small a target as possible."

"How about the others, Jim? Can you tell how bad it is?"

Jim twisted around and gave a quick sweep of the inside of the wagon circle. His heart sank to see five wives bending over their husbands. "Looks like we've got five down, honey. All we can do is—"

Jim's words were cut off as the screeching, howling Cheyenne rounded the rock formation, coming for another charge. Squaring around, he saw that six had flaming, smoking arrows notched in bows. "Stay low, Merilee!" he shouted. "And watch for flaming arrows! Here they come!"

It was bedlam once again, with horses whinnying, children wailing, and guns roaring like a string of giant firecrackers.

Ward Fleming was running across the inner circle, shouting at the women who were kneeling over their husbands to get back in the wagons. Suddenly a Cheyenne slug centered his back, and he went down, face-first. His body twitched a few times, then went still. Ward Fleming was dead.

Flaming arrows hissed through the air, each leaving a trail of blue-gray smoke. All six thunked into canvas covers, igniting the fabric. Women and children came spilling out of the burning wagons.

Jim caught sight of an Indian hanging on the outside of his pony and firing a carbine underneath the horse's neck. Jim knew the warrior would be too hard to hit, so he shot the horse instead. The stricken pinto shrieked as it went down. The hapless rider hit the ground hard. When he stopped rolling, he had lost his carbine. He yanked his knife from its sheath and let out a wild, primal scream as he charged. Jim drew a bead on the center of the man's chest and squeezed the trigger. The impact of the slug flopped the Indian to his back. He lay there, his breast pulseless, vacant eyes staring toward the cloudless sky.

Three more Cheyenne were galloping near, and unleashed their carbines on the Logan wagon. One bullet chewed through its side, another ripped through canvas, and the third furrowed dirt in front of Jim's face, spraying him with stinging particles.

While he wiped his eyes, he heard Merilee cry, "Jim! Jeremy's hit!"

Jim was about to crawl out from under the wagon to see about his oldest son when more savages galloped by, unleashing their guns on him. He rolled to one side in time to evade two slugs, fired once, missing his target, and took another shot. That one missed, too.

The wild-eyed Cheyenne were making havoc of the wagon train. More women and children who fled from burning wagons were cut down. Three teenage boys who had fired from underneath wagons lay dead. Six wagons had become blazing infernos. There were moans and cries from all over. The frightened horses were champing at their bits, stomping, and rearing. Suddenly one team bolted and thundered away across the flat land with the wagon behind them aflame and billowing smoke.

Jim Logan wanted to get to Jeremy, but the determined Indians were keeping him busy. When he stopped to reload his rifle, he shouted upward, asking Merilee how bad Jeremy was wounded, but the din of battle drowned out his voice. While thumbing cartridges into his rifle, he took a quick look behind him. There were bodies of men, women, and children sprawled all over the place. Burning wagons sent billows of smoke skyward.

The Cheyenne were coming in waves, yelping and screeching to intimidate their foes. Firing as fast as he could, Jim prayed for Jeremy and feared for everyone in the wagon train. There had to be at least fifteen or sixteen Cheyenne warriors still aboard their mounts, closing in for the kill. So many white men had been taken out of the fight that only intermittent rifle fire was coming from under the wagons.

Soon Jim's rifle was empty again. It seemed the Indians would soon wipe out the train as he nervously reloaded the Henry. They didn't have a chance.

Inside the Logan wagon, Merilee was trying to stay the flow of blood coming from Jeremy's shoulder. The Cheyenne slug was embedded deep, and Jeremy was unconscious. Susie was weeping, and Darlene was trying to quiet her with encouraging words. Benjamin lay frozen in fear, his eyes fixed on Jeremy's wound and the blood that flowed from it, staining his mother's frantic hands.

Beneath the wagon, Jim drew a ragged breath and took aim as another wave of Indians galloped toward him. He fired his first shot, then was amazed as he saw warriors peeling off their mounts. They were going down as if four or five marksmen were unleashing their guns on them.

Jim squeezed off a few shots, then scooted forward to see if he could tell where the rapid gunfire was coming from. To his surprise, a lone rifleman was nestled atop the rock formation. Jim was amazed at how fast and accurately the man could fire. The shots kept coming, and the Indians kept toppling off their horses. Jim wondered when the rifleman had time to reload. It seemed that he had fired twenty-five or thirty times without stopping.

Some of the Indians turned to shoot at the man up in the rocks. At the same time, what few men were left in the wagon train pumped hot lead at them. One of the Indians gave a sharp command, and the others wheeled their pintos, goaded them with their moccasined heels, and galloped away. Jim counted seven of them. The man in the rocks blasted away at them, and two more fell to the earth before the rest of them were out of range. They topped a rise to the north and disappeared.

Jim saw the rifleman stand up, and noted that except for his white shirt, he was dressed in black. He wheeled about and quickly passed from Jim's sight. Jim crawled backwards from under the wagon and dashed to the rear where he found Merilee holding a towel to Jeremy's shoulder. The boy was barely conscious. Susie was whimpering as Darlene held her in her arms, and Benjamin was still lying on the floor of the wagon.

"It's okay, now," breathed Jim. "The Indians are gone. Some sharpshooter over there in the rocks took out a bunch of them, and the others hightailed it out of here. How is Jeremy?"

"He's got a bullet in his left shoulder," Merilee told him. "I've got the bleeding under control, but the bullet will have to come out."

"I don't know how close the nearest doctor is, honey," said Jim, "but it's probably Hay Springs. That's fifty miles. Four days."

"He can't wait that long," she sighed. "If nothing else, I'll have to try taking it out, myself."

"Maybe there's somebody left here who knows something about it, honey. You keep him as comfortable as you can, and I'll check. It's pretty bad out here. Lots of people dead, others wounded. I'll be back in a few minutes."

"I want to get out of the wagon, Papa," said Benjamin. "Please?"

"Sure, son. Come on."

Jim Logan took his youngest son from the wagon, stood him on the ground, and led him by the hand as they made their way across the circle. Bodies were strewn everywhere. Some of the women were in hysterics as they knelt beside dead husbands and children. There were men weeping whose families were wiped out. Children were crying, and a tiny baby inside a wagon was wailing shrilly.

The wagons that had been hit with flaming arrows were still burning. Jim's eyes fell on the lifeless form of wagon master Ward Fleming. Dexter Armand and his wife were working on one of the wounded men, who had taken an arrow in his left leg.

Amid all the sorrow and confusion, some of the people were talking about the rifleman in the rocks. One man, who was wrapping a torn piece of petticoat around his wife's bleeding arm, eyed Logan and said, "You see that fella in the rocks, Jim?"

"Yeah. I don't know what kind of rifle he's got, but that was some kind of shooting."

Looking toward the rock formation, the man said, "I sure hope he comes in here so we can thank him."

"Me, too," nodded Jim. "Say, Eric, do you know anything about removing bullets?"

"Nope. Somebody in your family take a bullet?"

"Yeah. Jeremy's got one in his shoulder. It's got to come out right away."

"Too bad there ain't a town close so we could find us a doctor," Eric said.

Suddenly Benjamin pointed toward the gap in the circle

where the missing wagon once stood. "Papa! It's Mr. John Stranger!"

Jim turned and looked at the tall man-in-black who was leading a big black gelding inside the circle. He noted the repeater rifle in his hand, and saw the butt of another protruding from his saddleboot.

Many eyes turned to look as Benjamin pulled loose from his father's grasp and ran toward John Stranger.

Bending low as the boy drew up, Stranger smiled and said, "Hello, Benjamin Logan. I'm glad to see you again." He wrapped an arm around him and hoisted him up.

Benjamin hugged his neck, and said, "We had lotsa Indians shootin' at us, and they shot my brother!" Looking over his shoulder, he added, "This is my papa."

Stranger extended his right hand, saying, "Glad to meet you, Jim Logan."

Jim met his strong grip and said, "Not as glad as I am to meet you, sir. We had plenty to thank you for prior to this situation, but we've really got a lot to thank you for now. If it hadn't been for you, those savages would have killed us all."

"No need to thank me, Jim," said Stranger. "I was just doing my job."

"As you can see, Mr. Stranger," Jim said, gesturing in an arc about the circle, "we're in pretty bad shape here."

"Indeed you are. I have a small amount of medical supplies in my saddlebags and some experience at patching up wounds. Let's see what I can do to help. Benjamin said his brother's been shot."

"Yes, my eleven-year-old son, Jeremy. He took a bullet in the shoulder. Do you know anything about removing bullets?"

"I've had some experience, yes. Wish I had more medical supplies."

Dexter Armand had heard the conversation. Drawing up, he said to Logan, "Jim, it just dawned on me. I heard Ward talking to Gerald a couple of days ago about some medical supplies in the wagon Gerald was driving. I noticed that wagon is stopped about a half-mile further north. Horses must have decided to halt once they were far enough away from all the shooting."

"I'll go get it, then," said Jim. "Hopefully there'll be enough medical supplies to help us."

"Good," said Stranger. "While you're bringing the wagon, I'll take a look at Jeremy's wound, then check on all these others."

Looking at Benjamin, Jim said, "Son, take Mr. Stranger to our wagon and tell Mama who he is, okay?"

"Yes, sir."

To Stranger, Jim said, "My wife's name is Merilee. Tell her that I'm going after the lead wagon, will you?"

"Sure. I'm just glad there's a possibility of more supplies. From what I see here, I'm going to need them."

Jim hurried away, and Benjamin pointed out the Logan wagon. Before they reached it, a few people took time to step up to the tall, dark man and thank him for coming to their aid against the Cheyenne. They also thanked him for what he did in saving their money from Ralph Studdard and Ed Patton. Others picked up that he had some medical experience and were eager to get him to tend to their wounded. Stranger explained that he would be with them momentarily, but wanted to look at Jeremy Logan's wound first.

Stepping up to the rear of the Logan wagon with Benjamin in his arms, Stranger looked at Merilee and said, "Mrs. Logan, I'm John Stranger."

Merilee's eyes widened when she saw her youngest son in the tall man's arms. "John Stranger?"

"He's the man who killed those bad men that took me and the money, Mama!" Benjamin exclaimed. "He's my friend!"

Darlene and Susie eyed the twin scars on the man's right cheek as their mother said, "You're the sharpshooter who took out a bunch of the Indians and drove them off?"

"Well, I had help," Stranger said modestly. "Benjamin told me about Jeremy being shot. Your husband is going after the lead wagon right now because reportedly there are medical supplies in it. I carry some in my saddlebags, but there are a lot of wounded people out here. I'll need plenty of bandages, alcohol, salve, and iodine, I'm sure. Laudanum, too."

"You know how to treat wounds?" asked Merilee.

"I've had a little experience, ma'am. Right now, I'd like to take a look at Jeremy. I'll check on the others in a moment. I'll make an assessment as to who's in the worst shape, and act accordingly."

Jeremy was still barely conscious, for which Merilee was thankful. As Stranger examined the wound, she said, "How we thank God for you, Mr. Stranger. You took care of our Benjamin and kept us from losing our money. And now..." She choked slightly, cleared her throat, blinked at the tears that were surfacing, and said, "And now, here you are driving the hostiles away to save our lives, and tending to Jeremy's wound. God bless you!"

"He does that, all right, ma'am," nodded Stranger. Setting Benjamin down, he said, "Now, let me take a look, here."

Merilee removed the blood-soaked towel from Jeremy's wound. She had already torn his shirt so she could examine the wound for herself. Stranger scrutinized it for a few seconds, then said, "Doesn't look like it splintered any bone, ma'am. I see a bullet hole here in the side of the bed. Is that the one that got him?"

"Yes."

"Well, you can thank the Lord that while the slug was chewing through the wood, it lost some of its power. If he'd taken the slug directly, it would have shattered bone, no question about it."

"Thank You, Lord," Merilee breathed.

"You did right, putting that compress on the wound," said Stranger. "Keep it there till I get back. I won't be long."

Jim Logan pulled in with the lead wagon, announcing to the survivors that Gerald Fleming had been killed by the bullet that knocked him from the wagon. John Stranger had five wounded to check, and ascertained that only one was worse off than Jeremy. One of the women had taken a bullet in the stomach, and was hemorrhaging internally. She was losing blood fast. Stranger knew there was nothing he could do for her. She would be dead in a matter of minutes. Her husband had been killed, and two of the women were doing what they could to make her as comfortable as possible.

Besides Jim Logan and Dexter Armand, four men had survived the Cheyenne attack unscathed—Frank Prosser, Randall Sykes, Ted Wymore, and Eric Bowman. Eight women and eleven children were unhurt. Prosser's wife had been killed, and Sykes's wife and teenage son had also died of gunshots. Dexter Armand's wife was unhurt. She was busy taking care of some of the children who had been suddenly orphaned. Ted Wymore's wife and four children were all unscathed, and Eric Bowman's wife had sustained a slight arm wound.

While Prosser and Sykes knelt beside their dead in deep mourning, John Stranger approached Jim Logan, telling him that he was going to remove the bullet from Jeremy's shoulder once he inspected the lead wagon for supplies.

While Stranger was inside the lead wagon, Bowman, Wymore, and Armand discussed the need to bury the dead in a common grave. When Jim said he would join them in digging the grave, they told him he could help dig once Jeremy was patched up. Taking shovels from their wagons, the three men found an acceptable spot and began digging.

John Stranger was pleased to find ample medical supplies in a wooden box in the Fleming wagon. He asked Jim to carry Jeremy to the wagon and place him on the tailgate, which was suspended by small chains anchored to the wagon.

Stranger gave the semiconscious lad a proper amount of laudanum, and while it was taking effect, he said to the family, who stood close by, "I work best alone. Why don't all of you wait over by your wagon? This won't take more than an hour or so."

While John Stranger went to work on Jeremy, the Logans returned to their wagon. Keeping her eyes on her son and the tall, dark man, Merilee said, "What do you make of him, Jim? The way he's dressed, I'd say he's a circuit-riding preacher. Doesn't he look like a preacher to you?"

"Or a gambler," offered Jim.

"He's no gambler, honey. Talks about the Lord like he knows Him."

"I wonder if maybe he's a doctor, and for some reason he just doesn't come out and say it. He carries medical supplies in his saddlebags."

"Could be. Seems to be a very humble man. Sure acts like he knows what he's doing over there."

"I sure hope so. We're trustin' our son to him." Jim was quiet a moment, then said, "Somethin' else, honey."

"What's that?"

"That tied-down hogleg with the bone handles on his right hip. You don't suppose he's a gunhawk? I mean, he looks like he'd be real good with it. And he sure is good with a rifle. He was pickin' those Indians off like it was somethin' he does every day."

"I wouldn't think he's a gunfighter," said Merilee. "They're always calloused and hard-edged. This man has compassion and heart. And like I said, he talks about the Lord in the same way we do."

"Well, he sure knows how to handle himself. He took out both of those men who kidnapped Benjamin and stole our money."

"That he did," she said, letting a faint smile curve her lips. "The man is simply a walking answer to prayer."

"No argument there," Jim replied.

Some fifty minutes after he had started on Jeremy, Stranger finished bandaging the wound and placed the boy's arm into a sling he had made with a piece of bedsheet from the Fleming wagon. Turning toward the anxious parents, he said, "You can come over, now. I'm done."

Jim and Merilee stood over their son and saw that he was resting peacefully under the influence of the laudanum. The wound was bandaged expertly, and the sling was well-made.

"He's going to be fine," smiled the tall man. "You'll want to change the bandage tomorrow, then every other day till there's no more bleeding. It'll be stiff for a while, but Jeremy's young and healthy. In six months he won't even know it happened, except for the scars."

Merilee focused on the scars that rode Stranger's right cheekbone and wondered how he got them. "Thank you so much. How can we ever repay you?"

"We have money, Mr. Stranger," said Jim. "We'll be glad to pay you."

"No. I want no pay. I was just doing my job." He paused, then said, "Well, I've got to wash up and get to my other patients."

John Stranger found that the woman with the bullet in her stomach had died. While he tended to the others, the able-bodied men worked on digging the common grave. Finishing up with his patients before the grave was completed, Stranger found a shovel and helped the other men with the digging.

The sun was slanting downward in the afternoon sky when the grave was ready. Bodies were wrapped in blankets and tenderly lowered into the cold, unfeeling ground. While the survivors who were able stood beside the grave, the seven men shoveled the dirt back into the hole, leaving a mound some two feet high.

Mopping tears, Frank Prosser looked around at the others and said, "One of us ought to read from the Bible and say a few words, don't you think?"

Jim Logan spoke up, "I'll get my Bible from the wagon."

"I'll take care of it if you'd like, Jim," said John Stranger.

All eyes were suddenly fixed on the tall man with the Colt

.45 on his hip.

"Are you a preacher, sir?" asked a teary-eyed Randall Sykes.

"Sometimes."

"It sure would be nice if you'd read us something."

"I'll get my Bible," nodded Stranger.

Everyone stood silent while Stranger went to his horse and pulled a well-worn Bible from one of the saddlebags. While the prairie breeze toyed with Stranger's thick, dark locks, he read a portion of 1 Corinthians 15. He spoke of how all who put their trust in Jesus and Him alone for salvation will one day come forth from the graves in glorious resurrection. He then explained the gospel, urging those who had never put their faith in Jesus for the forgiveness of their sins and the salvation of their souls to do so.

John Stranger closed his Bible and prayed. All were weeping when he reached his "Amen," for the prayer was both soul-searching and heart-touching.

Everyone thanked him for conducting the graveside service. Some remained to talk to him about salvation, while others headed for the wagons.

Soon the sun settled on the horizon, then dipped out of sight. Daylight struggled against the oncoming night, but soon succumbed, and darkness flooded the land.

CHAPTER THIRTEEN

The women prepared a meal, and the wounded were fed first. Afterward, the rest of the wagon train's survivors sat around the fire in the darkness and ate together. John Stranger sat amongst them, beside the Logan family.

Dexter Armand and Frank Prosser led the group in a discussion about whether they should turn back or go on. Without Ward Fleming, they had no guide. The widows wanted to turn back, while the widowers and families who were still intact felt they should push on and try to salvage their dreams.

"Seems to me all of you should go as far as Hay Springs, where my family and I will be settling," Jim Logan said. "Those of you who want to go back east will have to wait till you can come up with someone to escort you. Those of you who are going on to Wyoming shouldn't try it until the Indian trouble settles down. You certainly don't need anymore of what we faced today. And the children who have been orphaned—they must be placed in adoptive homes."

"Far as I'm concerned," spoke up Dexter Armand, "those of us who're going on to Wyoming can take the children with us."

Those who would push west all agreed that they would divide the children up and provide homes for them.

"I want to commend you people for taking the children in," John Stranger said. "Jim is right about all of you going on to Hay Springs until the Indian situation gets better. Or if you can get army escorts for going either direction, you'll be all right."

With that, they all agreed to go on to Hay Springs. Soon the people were talking in small groups on different subjects. Stranger noticed Jim and Merilee whispering to each other, then Jim looked at him and said, "Sir, Merilee and I can never thank you sufficiently for all you've done for us. If it weren't for you, Jeremy would probably have died. In fact, if you hadn't cut down so many of those Indians, we'd all be dead. Merilee and I have been talking, and...well, you've really got us curious."

"How's that?" Stranger said softly.

Jim cleared his throat nervously. "Well...do you mind if I ask you somethin' personal?"

Stranger grinned. "Of course not."

"Well, sir...are you a doctor, a gunfighter, or a preacher?"

"I guess you could say I'm all three."

"But are you actually trained? I mean as a doctor or preacher. Nobody takes formal training as a gunfighter."

"Not in the sense of which you speak, Jim. I've just gained a lot of valuable experience in my work."

Rubbing his chin, Jim said, "Which brings up something else that has our curiosity up. Twice today you said you were only doing your job. Pardon me if I'm pushin' this too far, but exactly what is your job?"

Stranger smiled. "Taking care of people who get in trouble."

"But you go beyond that. You preached salvation today as clear as any preacher I've ever heard."

"Well, aren't people without Christ in trouble?"

Jim looked at Merilee, grinned, then looked back at the tall man and said, "You are a wonder, Mr. Stranger. That's all I can say."

"You're a living answer to prayer, Mr. Stranger," Merilee said. "God sent you to us exactly when we needed you."

Stranger's eyes leveled on Merilee. "Mm-hmm. That's my job. Sometimes my missions crisscross each other and I'm a little late showing up. Like today. I wish I could have been here a little earlier."

"I'm just glad you got here when you did," said Jim. "A few more minutes, and we'd have been goners."

"I hope the army can get the Indians settled down soon," Stranger said. "They've really been on the rampage lately. Not that I can really blame them. After all, they had this country first."

"Speaking of countries, sir," said Jim, who was growing bolder, "that silver medallion you gave Benjamin to pass on to me..."

"Yes?"

"I'm intrigued by the Scripture used on it—The stranger from a far land. Just where are you from?"

Merilee was glad her husband had worked up the courage to ask. She was dying to know.

Stranger lifted his flat-crowned hat, ran splayed fingers through his thick hair, and said, "Well, Jim, I'm afraid that's one subject I'll have to close the gate on."

"Oh, sure. I was just, you know...curious," Jim said, feeling the same disappointment he was reading in Merilee's eyes.

At that moment, Dexter Armand and Frank Prosser appeared. "Frank and I have been talking, Jim," said Dexter. "We figure to take all the wagons and animals with us. Except for the wagons that burned, of course. We'll just tie the horses from them onto the backs of other wagons. Some of the women can help us drive."

"Merilee can drive real good," said Jim, rising to his feet. "I'll let her drive ours, and I can drive another one."

"Good enough," said Armand. "We'll work on the situation at dawn. Should be ready to pull out about an hour after sunup."

"We'll plan on it," agreed Jim.

When Armand and Prosser were gone, Jim said, "Mr. Stranger, we can probably find room for you to sleep in one of the wagons."

"Won't be necessary. I have my bedroll. I'm used to sleeping on the ground."

"Whatever you say. Do you suppose we ought to put somebody on watch? Those Indians might come back and bring some of their pals with them."

"I was about to suggest it," said Stranger. "Couple men at a time. I can guarantee you they'll be back, and that they'll bring more with them...but I doubt it'll be tonight. They're still licking their wounds. But they've got dead men lying around here, and several pintos running loose. They'll be back to get them, probably tomorrow night. Won't hurt to be careful, though. I'll help with first watch."

"Okay, I'll take first watch with you. Let me go work out the other watches with the men. See you in a few minutes."

Jim Logan and John Stranger did their part for two hours, then awakened two more to take their place. They told each other good-night, then Jim went to his wagon and Stranger went to his horse. He took off his bedroll, rolled it out on the ground, and went to sleep.

Dawn was turning the eastern sky a pale gray when Jim Logan slid out of his wagon, stretched, and yawned. While yawning, he gazed to the spot where John Stranger's horse had been tied.

The big black was gone.

This snapped him fully awake. He moved briskly around the camp, looking for the horse or its owner. He found neither.

Ted Wymore and Eric Bowman had volunteered for the last watch. Jim dashed up to Wymore.

"Mornin', Jim," said Wymore. "Up kinda early, aren't you?"

"You see John Stranger leave?" pressed Logan.

"Nope. He gone?"

"Yes."

Jim dashed to the other side of the camp. "Eric, did you see

John Stranger leave?"

"No. I didn't know he was gone."

"He must move quieter than an Indian."

"His horse, too," suggested Bowman.

"I guess. Of course, he may have left during another watch. Might have already been gone when you and Ted took over. I'm sure if any of the other fellas saw him go, they'd have told somebody."

"Too bad," sighed Bowman. "I figured he'd stay with us all the way to Hay Springs. Those redskins might decide to attack us again between here and there. Would have been good to have a marksman like him along. On top of that, he just makes you feel safer with him around."

"I agree," nodded Jim. "Kind of surprises me that he'd just ride off without sayin' good-bye."

Breakfast was over and the wagons were almost ready to go when the sun had been up for just over an hour. Dexter Armand would be driving the lead wagon, with his wife at the reins in his own wagon directly behind. Women drivers were alternated with the men so as to give the maximum amount of protection in case they came under attack again.

Randall Sykes was standing in the seat of his wagon, mending a torn spot in the canvas, when his eye caught movement at the edge of the rock formation, the same place the Cheyenne had attacked from the day before. His heart jumped in his throat, then quickly settled down when he saw that it was a cavalry patrol.

Calling to the others, Sykes shouted, "Hey! We got the army here!"

The travelers who could walk quickly assembled on the west side of the wagon train to greet the men-in-blue. There were many smiles to welcome the fifteen-man patrol as they drew up and halted at their lieutenant's hand signal.

"Good morning. I'm Lieutenant Bryce Keffer. We're from Fort Sidney, which is about twenty miles or so due west of here.

We've been sent to escort you to Hay Springs."

Dexter stepped forward and said, "We're mighty glad to have you, lieutenant, but who sent you? How did they know about us?"

"Colonel Lloyd Adams sent us, sir. He is our fort commandant. About four o'clock this morning, a tall man on a black horse rode up to the fort and told the sentries it was urgent that he see our commandant. He convinced the sentries that his message for Colonel Adams was sufficiently urgent to roust him out of bed, so they did. The man told Colonel Adams about the Cheyenne attack you underwent yesterday, and that the survivors needed army protection from Soda Lake to Hay Springs. So...here we are."

"God bless John Stranger!" shouted Merilee Logan.

There was instant agreement among the travelers.

"Well, Lieutenant," Dexter said, "we were about to pull out."

"Good," smiled Keffer, "then let's go!"

Guns blazed in the street in front of the bank of Merriman, Nebraska, as the gang once led by Denvil Hawes shot it out with the townsmen. A man on the street had recognized one of the gang when they dismounted in front of the bank, and he alerted the town marshal.

Young Donnie Hawes had stood at the bank door to watch for any sign of lawmen, while the other six outlaws were emptying the safe and forcing tellers to clean out their cash drawers.

Marshal Efram Lackore had quickly recruited a dozen townsmen to help him meet the robbers as they came out of the bank. Donnie had seen them coming at the same time the rest of the gang was heading for the door, carrying heavily stuffed money bags. When Donnie shouted to Max Worley and the others that the marshal was coming with a group of armed men, Worley—who was in charge due to the absence of Gavin Cold—blurted,

"We don't want to get holed up in here! Let's go out shootin'!"

And shoot they did. Dust and gunsmoke filled the street as the outlaws shot it out with the marshal and townsmen.

Worley knew his only hope of surviving was to get in the saddle and ride. As he swung aboard his horse with bullets cutting the air all around him, he saw Marshal Lackore go down with a slug in the chest. Gang members were taking lead, too, and falling in the dusty street.

Worley gouged his horse's flanks and galloped westward. Looking behind, he saw the townsmen closing in on the rest of the gang. They didn't have a chance. Suddenly from out of the cloud of dust and smoke, came Donnie Hawes on his horse, thundering westward behind Worley.

Holding onto the money bag he had carried out of the bank, Max shouted, "C'mon, kid! C'mon!"

One townsman swung his gun on the escaping Hawes and fired twice. Worley saw Donnie stiffen in the saddle. He was hit, but he was gamely trying to stay on his horse.

"You can make it, kid! Hang on!" Worley shouted.

Soon they were out of town and out of gun range. Worley slowed his mount enough to allow Donnie to draw up beside him. Staying abreast of Donnie's horse, he saw that the kid had been hit in the upper left arm at the tip of the shoulder. He was gripping the wound with his right hand while holding the reins with his left.

"Is it bad, kid?"

"Can't tell!" replied Donnie through clenched teeth.

"We'll stop in a couple more miles. Gotta get farther outta town!"

Donnie hung on, pain evident in his face, and nodded.

They had ridden for about twenty minutes when Max pointed to a deep ravine off to the right. "Let's pull down in there!"

Hooves dug into sandy dirt as the horses were reined to a

halt at the bottom of the ravine. Worley dismounted and helped the nineteen-year-old from his saddle. Donnie stumbled to where the grassy slope met the bottom of the ravine and sat down, gripping his wound. Blood was running through his fingers.

Kneeling beside him, Worley said, "Let me take a look at it."

He tore the shirt a little so as to examine the wound. "Ain't too bad, kid. Bullet only creased you. Wound ain't deep. Let me see if I can tie it up some way so's the bleedin' will stop."

Using Donnie's bandanna and one of his own, Worley was able to bind the wound and stay the bleeding. He took Donnie's belt from around his slim waist and made a sling.

"There you go, kid," he breathed, easing back and sitting beside him on the slope. "That'll hold you till we can get you to a doc. The wound really needs to be stitched up. You'll have to be real careful about movin' the arm. You could start it bleedin' again real easy."

Fear was on young Hawes's face. "Where we gonna find a doctor, Max? We can't go back to Merriman."

"Closest town is Hay Springs, kid, about fifty miles straight west. I've been there before. They've got a doc."

As he spoke, Worley pulled a cigar out of his shirt pocket, bit the tip off it, and lit it with a match from his pocket. Puffing it into life, he said, "We'll let you rest a few more minutes, then we'll mount up and keep movin'. We'll ride till dark, then make camp. By then we oughtta be within fifteen miles or so of Hay Springs. If we ride out at sunrise, you'll be seein' the doc by about eight o'clock."

Donnie gritted his teeth and fought tears. "You think any of the guys got away, Max?"

"Doubt it. They were goin' down like flies...and the townsmen were closin' in. At least I've got my money bag. I'll share some of it with you."

Donnie stared at the ground. "I don't want it, Max. You keep it all."

"I guess you're still mad at me, eh?" Worley mumbled.

"Yeah. Especially now. If you'd let me go home and see my pa like I wanted, I wouldn't have got shot."

"I told you, kid," Worley snapped, "Gavin would have my hide if I'd let you leave. By what he said to you when we rode away from North Platte, you know he was expectin' you to come back to the hideout."

"Which I did."

"Yeah. Good thing. You don't want Gavin sore at you. And I don't want him sore at me, either. That's why I ain't lettin' you go home. Once Gavin runs that fancy-dressed dude down and kills him, he'll find us. When he does, I want you with me. Gavin's just like your big brother was...nobody rides away unless the boss says so."

"All I want to do is go see if my pa's all right."

Worley fixed the youth with hard eyes. "Yeah? I don't think so. You don't seem the same since you seen your brother hang. I'm thinkin' you want outta this business."

"So what if I do?"

"When you're in a gang like your brother put together, kid, nobody ups and quits. Its like bein' a deserter in the army. Besides, if you wanted out, why'd you come back to the hideout?"

Donnie paused for a long moment. "I didn't decide I wanted to quit bein' an outlaw till after I came back. I'd been thinkin' on it all the way from North Platte."

"'Cause you saw Denvil hang and decided the same thing might happen to you."

Donnie did not reply.

"I want to ask you somethin'," said Max.

"What?"

"That fancy dude in black—he plant some do-goodie thoughts in your head?"

Donnie thought of the time John Stranger had talked to him at home, then of the incident in North Platte. He knew

Stranger was right in forcing him to observe Denvil's hanging...and he was right in what he had preached to him from the Bible. His parents had been right in the way they had raised him, too. Donnie Hawes wanted out, but he didn't want Max Worley or Gavin Cold to kill him for what they would deem as desertion.

"I asked you a question, kid! That dude try to steer you onto the do-goodie road?"

"You might say that. Same as my pa has."

Chewing on the cigar, Worley extended his open hand. "Lemme see your gun."

"Why?"

"Lemme see your gun!"

Slowly, Donnie took the .45 revolver from his holster and handed it to Worley.

Breaking it open Worley swore. "Just as I thought. No spent cartridges! You didn't fire a shot back there in town. The rest of us was fightin' off them townsmen and that marshal, and you didn't even try to help us!"

"I...I've never shot anybody, Max, and I wasn't about to do it in Merriman."

Worley jerked the cigar from his mouth, spit into the grass, and swore vehemently. Jamming the .45 back in Donnie's hand, he gusted, "You're a do-goodie, all right." He stuck the cigar back in his mouth, pushed his face within inches of Donnie's, and blew smoke into his eyes. "I oughtta shoot you down like a mangy coyote, kid! That's what I oughtta do!"

Donnie coughed, blinking against the stinging smoke. He had seen Max do this same thing to other men who had riled him and to women who had refused his advances. He seemed to enjoy burning people's eyes with cigar smoke.

Worley drew back, stood up, and said to the coughing youth, "All right, let's ride. Much as I'd like to work you over, I'll refrain myself. When Gavin finds us, I want you all patched up.

Between the two of us, we'll make an outlaw of you yet. First thing we'll do is make you kill a couple guys, then you'll get a taste for the good life. You're Denvil's brother, so you gotta have it in you to be a good outlaw."

It was a bright sunny morning in Hay Springs. Breanna Baylor had been there for nearly two weeks, and though five more people had died from the typhoid fever, the rest of her patients were on the road to recovery. The use of pure ranch water and the hygienic precautions had curbed the spread of the disease. There had not been a new case of the fever for several days.

Breanna was able to send most of her patients home, along with instructions to family members on how to care for them, and was now nursing only eight of them in Dr. Getz's clinic, including the good doctor himself. The women and girls were separated from the men and boys by blankets that hung on cords from wall to wall. She was happy that she had been able to let all the women go home who had been helping her.

News of the disease tapering off in Hay Springs had spread, and life in the town was just about back to normal. Stagecoaches were coming and going as usual, once again carrying the customary number of passengers. One thing remained unusual, however. Every stage was accompanied by an army escort.

Leaving her patients at the clinic, Breanna angled across the wide dusty street toward Rudd's General Store. She noted a ruckus in front of the Mulehead Saloon. Deputy Marshal Bob Osborne was breaking up a fight between two drunk men.

Breanna met two women coming out of the store, who greeted her and spoke their appreciation for the wonderful work she had done for the typhoid patients. They commended her, also, for the way she was handling Dr. Getz's normal run of patients.

Entering the store, Breanna saw a man and wife at the

counter, being waited on by elderly Wilson Rudd, the proprietor. All three spoke to her. She returned the greeting with a sweet smile, and made her way to the rear of the store. The store was L-shaped, and the items Breanna was after were around the corner, out of sight from the counter.

Picking up what she wanted, she rounded the corner to find the couple gone and Mr. Rudd unpacking a crate of goods and placing the items on shelves. Grinning at her, he hurried behind the counter and asked, "How's everybody's favorite nurse this mornin'?"

"I don't know," giggled Breanna, "but whenever I see her, I'll ask her."

Rudd cackled, shook his bald head, and said, "You can be modest if you want, honey, but you've won the hearts of this whole town, I can tell you that."

"That's nice to hear. It's been my joy to help out."

"You've done more than help out, little lady. You've saved lives here. That's what you've done."

Breanna's countenance fell. "I only wish I could have kept so many from dying."

"There'd be a lot more dead if you hadn't come to Hay Springs, honey. We just thank God for you."

"You're very kind, Mr. Rudd."

Eyeing what Breanna had laid on the counter, he asked, "This it?"

"For now, yes."

Placing the items in a sack, Rudd grinned and said, "No charge."

"Now, look, Mr. Rudd, you keep saying 'no charge' when I come in here and buy personal items. I insist on paying you."

"You're money's no good here," replied the old man. "Whatever you need is on the house."

"But, Mr. Rudd, I—"

"Ah ah ah," he said, throwing up his palms. "No arguments.

While you're here in this town, Rudd's General Store will donate everything you need."

Shaking her head, Breanna said, "Thank you. You're a generous man."

"How much longer you gonna be with us, honey?"

"Well, it's hard to say for sure. Dr. Getz is still awfully weak. He's up three or four times a day, walking around the clinic, but he wears out pretty fast. It'll be a few more days before he can take over the clinic again."

"I'll tell you somethin'. This whole town's havin' mixed emotions, missy."

"How's that?"

"We want Doc to get all better, but we don't want you to leave. Couldn't you just stay here and be his nurse? Whole area's growin' in population, especially with new ranchers movin' in. I'm sure you'd stay busy."

"Without a doubt. But my work is as a visiting nurse, which means I must move on once I've done my job in a certain place. By the time I get back to Denver, there'll be any number of places I'm needed."

Suddenly the front door came open and a teenage boy entered. Setting adoring eyes on Breanna, he said, "Miss Baylor, there's a couple strangers on the boardwalk over at the clinic. One of 'em's been shot. They found the card Doc Getz puts in the window when he's out of the office and asked me if I knew where the doctor was. I told 'em he was sick, but that we had a purty nurse who'd take care of 'em. How soon will you be comin' back to the clinic?"

Picking up the paper sack, Breanna said, "I'll come right now."

Thanking Rudd once more for his generosity, she followed the boy through the door.

CHAPTER FOURTEEN

Donnie Hawes was feeling weak and dizzy, and was leaning against the wall by the clinic door as the teenage boy came running across the street, shouting, "I found the nurse, mister! She's comin'."

Max Worley grunted, "Thanks, kid," and set lascivious eyes on Breanna Baylor as she stepped off the boardwalk in front of the general store. Turning to Donnie, he smacked his lips and said, "Take a look at that. Think I'll shoot myself in the foot or somep'n so's I can get her to take care of me!"

Donnie did not comment. His wound had opened up shortly after they had left the ravine the day before and had bled steadily the rest of the day. He had been able to stay the bleeding for the night, but once they started riding at sunrise, the blood began to flow once again. He was feeling too weak to comment. Besides, he was sick of Max's continual eye for the women, his ribald remarks about them, and the way he acted around them.

Breanna weaved her way across the street between buggies and wagons that moved both ways, and finally mounted the boardwalk. She approached the youth who leaned against the wall with blood running down his arm, and said, "I understand you've been shot."

"Yes, ma'am."

Opening the door, she gestured for him to enter ahead of her. "Go on in and sit down on that bench against the wall."

Worley followed as Donnie sagged onto the bench, gripping his wound. Breanna set her sack on the desk, placed her purse in a drawer, then turned to Donnie and said, "I'll take you back to the examining room, and we'll get you taken care of."

As Donnie slowly rose to his feet, she guided him across the waiting room, opened the door, and led him to the examining table. "Can you get up there by yourself?" she asked.

Max was on their heels. "I'll help him," he grunted.

Breanna set peevish eyes on Worley. "All right. Then I'll ask you to take a seat in the waiting room."

"You might need me in here, nursie," Max retorted, giving her a wide grin. "Donnie might fall off the table or somep'n."

Breanna had dealt with all kinds. She smelled trouble from this crude, unshaven man. "Well, then you'll have to take a seat over there," she said, pointing to a straight-backed chair across the room.

Max nodded, grinned at her again, and made his way toward the chair. As he did, he noted the blankets that hung in the next room between several beds and asked, "This a hospital, too?"

"Sort of," replied Breanna, picking up a pair of shears from the nearby counter. "We've had a typhoid epidemic in Hay Springs. Many people died. The epidemic is in check, now. Those are the last of my most seriously ill patients."

"The boy that came after you said the doc is sick. He get the typhoid, too?"

"Yes. Right now, he is one of my patients."

Worley chuckled. "Well, I'm sure the kid here would rather have you takin' care of him, anyhow. No doubt you're a whole lot purtier than the doc."

Donnie was sitting up on the examining table and getting

whiter by the minute. Breanna said, "I've got to cut the sleeve off so I can get to the wound—Donnie, is it?"

"Yes, ma'am."

"Donnie who?"

The bleeding youth glanced at the older outlaw. Max shrugged his wide shoulders as if to say there was no reason to withhold his name from her.

"Hawes," came the weak reply.

"Hoss?"

"No, ma'am. H-a-w-e-s. Hawes."

Breanna was cutting through blood-soaked cloth. "How'd you get shot, Donnie?"

Again, young Hawes glanced at Worley. They had already rehearsed this part. "Max and I were huntin' south of here yesterday afternoon. He accidentally shot me. It was my fault. I got in the way."

"Must have been quite a ways south," remarked Breanna. "That is, unless you just plain took your time getting here."

"Was quite a ways."

"So where are you from?"

"Prairie Centre."

"Is that in Nebraska?"

"Yes, ma'am. Southeastern part of the state."

Breanna had a feeling Donnie was lying about how he got shot, but chose not to push it.

"All right," she said, tossing the severed sleeve into a trash receptacle. "I want you to lie down and let me see what we've got here."

Worley watched intently as Breanna worked on Donnie. Within half an hour, the wound had been cleaned and sutured. Breanna bandaged it, then said, "You've lost a lot of blood, Donnie. I mean a lot of blood. I don't know if you and your friend are planning to ride out of here soon or not, but I advise you not to. You'd better stay in Hay Springs for a few days. Drink lots of water. You're going to have to let your body build up some more blood, and that will take some time. Be sure to drink only the water that's in barrels out on the street. If you're going to stay at the hotel, they have barrel water that's safe."

Max rose from his chair and came close. "We appreciate your advice, nursie. But we can't stay around this town very long. Won't he be all right in another day or so?"

"No, he won't. You should plan on staying for at least a week. He shouldn't even think of riding for at least seven days."

"Well, we'll see about that," grunted Max. Looking down at Donnie, he said, "Let's go over to the hotel. We'll decide how long to stay a little later."

Donnie pushed himself to a sitting position, took a deep breath, and lost what little color he had gained. His eyes rolled back, and Breanna grabbed him to keep him from falling. He had passed out. Adjusting him on the table, she looked at Worley and said, "See what I mean? You'll have to keep him in town till he gets some strength back."

"I guess he's worse off than I thought. Shall I carry him over to the hotel?"

"Why don't you go get a room, give it an hour, then come back? I've got to tend to my patients in the back room. I'll keep an eye on him."

Max took a step closer to her and grinned. "Okay, nursie. I'll do that."

Breanna did not like the way the man looked at her, nor did she appreciate him calling her "nursie." She felt a flush of anger and whetted the edge of her words as she said, "That's enough of the 'nursie' stuff, mister. My name is Miss Baylor to you."

Max threw his head back and guffawed. "Hey! Little nursie's got spunk!" Leaning close, he said, "I've got a sore lip. How about kissin' it and makin' it all better?"

"Get out of here right now!" Breanna said with fire in her eyes.

Worley jumped back and threw up his hands in mock fear. "Oh! The little nursie is gonna throw me out!" Moving toward the door, he said, "I like you, honey. You and me could become real good friends."

Deputy Marshal Bob Osborne came from the cell block into the marshal's office and hung the key ring on a peg. "Well, they'll sober up now, I'll guarantee you."

Sitting at his desk, Marshal Jed Luskin chuckled, "Yeah. We don't provide whiskey in our jail cells."

Heading toward the door that faced the street, Osborne said, "Well, Marshal, I'll get back out amongst 'em."

"You're a good boy, Bob," smiled Luskin. "Keep up the excellent work."

"I plan to, sir. Check with you later."

With that, the deputy moved out onto the boardwalk and ran his gaze up and down the street. A thick-bodied, unshaven, unkempt man was walking toward him, puffing on a big cigar. As he drew abreast, he said, "Mornin', deputy."

"Good mornin'," nodded Osborne. "New in town?"

Pausing, Max Worley replied, "Not really. I've been here before. Left my partner at the doc's office for that purty little nurse to take care of. Gotta stay in town a couple days, so I'm headin' for the hotel to get us a room."

Osborne smiled weakly. "Have a nice stay in Hay Springs."

"Plan to," grinned Worley, his face in a cloud of smoke.

As Worley moved on down the boardwalk, Osborne's attention was drawn to a wagon rattling up the street toward him. He recognized it as a Circle M wagon, and observed the eight Circle M riders who accompanied it. The deputy knew the eight-man escort was for protection against a potential Indian assault.

Seeing that the wagon was going to haul up in front of the general store, Osborne stepped off the boardwalk and angled in that direction, weaving amongst the traffic. The deputy was delighted to see wealthy rancher Corey McCollister's pretty blond daughter on the wagon seat. He was not delighted to see that young ranch hand Zachary Adams was holding the reins and sitting next to her.

Osborne stepped up to the wagon, ignoring Adams, and smiled from ear to ear. "Good mornin', Taylor Ann."

"Good morning," Taylor Ann said, smiling in return.

"You going to be in town long?"

"Just long enough to pick up some things here at the general store for my mother." Turning to Zachary, she said, "I'll be about twenty minutes, Zach."

Adams knew Osborne would want to help Taylor Ann from the wagon, so he moved past the girl, hopped down from the wagon on her side, and offered her his hand. "I'll give it twenty minutes," Adams said, "then I'll come inside to carry the stuff out for you."

Taylor Ann gave the deputy an amiable smile, then hurried inside the store.

Adams and Osborne were the same height, but the deputy was about sixty pounds heavier. He scowled at the smaller man and said, "How come it's always you who drives the wagon when Taylor Ann comes into town? If you have to come in when she does, why ain't you one of the riders in the saddle?"

Zach Adams was a warm and likable person, but he also had a bulldog quality to him. Meeting Osborne's steady gaze head-on, he said, "I drive the wagon every time Taylor Ann comes to town because she asks me to. She wants to be near me."

The deputy's face flushed. "Aw, baloney! It ain't Taylor Ann askin' for your company. It's the sway you have with her dad. You lick Corey's boots and shine up to him all the time, so when Taylor Ann's comin' to town, you ask Corey if you can drive, and he lets you."

"Hah! Tell you what, chubby, let's just go in there and ask

the little lady about that! Okay?"

"Who you callin' chubby? Better watch your mouth!"

"You don't scare me, Osborne! You hide behind that badge and act the tough hombre. Without that badge, you're just a greasy tub o' lard."

People were looking on as they passed by on the street. They had observed such scenes before. Everyone in town knew that both young men were vying for the hand of Taylor Ann McCollister.

"This badge can come off, Adams!" blared Osborne, red-faced. "And when it does, you'll find out about the lard!"

"Take it off and let's see!"

Osborne took a sharp breath, licked his lips, and said, "I can't take it off right now. I'm on duty."

"Yeah. Sure. Even if you were man enough to take me on, and even if you *could* whip me—which you can't—it wouldn't make any difference. Taylor Ann loves me!"

A few interested spectators had stopped to watch.

Osborne shook his head in disgust. "Whatever put that in your head? Has she told you she loves you?"

"Well, not in so many words, but I see it in her eyes and in special little things she does and says."

"Well, until she puts it in words, don't assume it!"

The two young men continued the argument. They were still at it hot and heavy when Taylor Ann interrupted by saying, "Zach! Did you hear me?"

There was a sudden silence. Neither man had noticed that she was standing there, nor had they heard her voice.

Looking at her, Zachary said, "Sorry, Taylor Ann. What did you say?"

Hands-on-hips, she said, "I'm ready to go. You said you'd come in and carry out the goods for me."

"Oh, you're right! I'll get right on it."

When Adams returned, carrying two heavily loaded

cardboard boxes, he saw the deputy helping Taylor Ann into the wagon. Fire welled up within him, but for the girl's sake, he remained silent.

When the boxes were in the wagon bed, Zach climbed up beside Taylor Ann and looked at the deputy, who was leaning on the wagon, peering dreamily into her eyes. "So long, Bob. Now you can get back to chasin' bad guys, or whatever it is you do."

Zach snapped the reins, causing the team to leap into the harness. The wagon sprang forward, almost toppling Osborne.

Adams drove the wagon two blocks and pulled up in front of the Great Plains Gun Shop. Taylor Ann had said nothing during the short time it took to drive the two blocks. Zach hopped down and asked, "You want to go in the shop with me?"

"Might as well," she nodded.

As Zach helped her down, he noted that she avoided looking him in the eye.

"Howdy, Miss Taylor Ann...Zach," smiled Wesley Bond, who stood behind the glassed-in counter. "What do you need today?"

"Ammunition, Mr. Bond. Mr. McCollister wants a case of .45s and a case of 44s."

"Cases! Corey gonna start a war?"

"Might come to that," Adams replied flatly.

"Indians, you mean?"

"Yes, sir. They're stealing Circle M cattle right and left. Other ranches are losin' cattle to the thievin' savages, too."

While the gun shop proprietor was out of the room, Taylor Ann moved around, idly gazing at rifles and shotguns in the racks on the walls. Zach knew he was being ignored.

Wesley Bond returned, carrying the cases of cartridges, and expressed his hopes that the ranchers wouldn't have to fight the Indians. When Zach and Taylor Ann returned to the street, the Circle M riders were waiting for them.

They were about two miles out of town when Zach could

stand the wall of silence no longer. Turning to Taylor Ann, who was staring straight ahead, he said, "Are...ah...are you mad at me?"

Giving him a level stare, she replied, "Not mad. Just a bit miffed."

"About what?"

"You and Bob have embarrassed me. That's what."

"Embarrassed you?"

"Yes. While I was in the store, people came in, telling me that I was the subject of a hot argument between you and Bob. Sure enough, when I came out of the store, there you were, arguing over which one of you I'm in love with. Really, Zach. Does the whole town have to hear it? I haven't told you I'm in love with you, and I haven't told him any such thing, either. Don't you think I should be consulted before you two make me a spectacle in front of the whole town?"

Zach gave her a half-grin. "You sure are beautiful when you're mad."

"I'm not mad," she snipped, giving him a hard glare.

"Oh. Excuse me. I mean, you sure are beautiful when you're miffed."

Taylor Ann held her hard glare on him a few seconds, then it began to soften, followed by a tiny smile. "You're impossible, Zach."

Zachary Adams smiled back. "I work at it."

They rode for a few moments without speaking, then Zach said, "Taylor Ann, I might as well come out with it. I've never put it in words before, but...well, I'm head-over-heels in love with you. I think you're the most wonderful girl in all the world. I can't stand the thought of you being in love with that chubby deputy."

Taylor Ann was touched by Zach's confession. Laying a hand on his arm, she said softly, "Zach, you are one of the nicest young men I have ever met. I like you a lot. I can even say that I am very fond of you. Bob's nice, and I like him, too. I want to be friends with both of you, but I'm not ready to fall in love yet."

Zach nodded and stared straight ahead. He had hoped Taylor Ann was feeling stronger toward him than she had just expressed. His plan had been to ask her to marry him, but he knew he could not support her on his present wages. As he drove the wagon over the rolling hills westward toward the ranch, he determined to win Taylor Ann's heart, to become Circle M foreman, and to make the lovely girl his bride.

Curly Ford, the Circle M foreman, was getting too old for the job, and was planning to retire soon. Though Zach was younger than many of the ranch hands, Corey McCollister had given evidence that he liked his work and liked him as a person. Curly had been off work twice in the past six months, once because of an injury and the other time because of a serious bout with influenza. Both times, Corey had used Zach to substitute for Curly. Zach felt he had a good chance of becoming foreman of the Circle M when Curly retired.

The Circle M was a huge spread, with thousands of acres of lush, green grass. Two streams ran across the ranch, giving ample water for irrigating the rich pastures, and the uneven land was blessed with many thick stands of brush, cottonwoods, and junipers. The eastern border of the Circle M stretched for over five miles from the large log ranch house and outbuildings, which lay in a shallow valley. One of the streams ran near the huge barn and corral.

As Zachary drove silently over the Circle M range, heading for the ranch buildings, he let his eyes roam the peaceful setting. Innumerable cattle dotted the land, grazing lazily in the sun. Zach hoped the peacefulness of it all would not be disturbed by gunfire and whooping Indians.

When the wagon and eight-man escort neared the ranch house, the riders veered off toward the corral and bunkhouse, and Zach aimed the wagon for the back porch of the house. As they drew up to the porch, the back door flew open, revealing a bright-eyed five-year-old boy with hair as blond as Taylor Ann's. Tyler

O'Brien McCollister had been watching for his sister, and was excitedly charging across the porch to meet her.

Taylor Ann thought of how much Tyler looked like Corey McCollister, Jr., who had died at the age of six of pneumonia. Corey, Jr. had been four years younger than Taylor Ann. Though it had been eight years since he died, she still missed him very much. Tyler was born three years after Corey, Jr.'s death, and ever since, had been a tremendous source of joy to Taylor Ann and the rest of the family.

The boy jumped off the porch and dashed up to the side of the wagon, smiling from ear to ear. He was making hand signals, asking Taylor Ann if she had brought him a surprise. When she nodded that she had, he jumped up and down, clapping his hands and laughing with glee.

When her little brother was three, Taylor Ann had worked out the hand-signal system on her own, then taught it to Tyler. Soon Corey and Emily Grace caught on, and it had worked well ever since.

Zach slid to the ground, rounded the vehicle at the rear, and moved up to help Taylor Ann down. First he had to hug Tyler, who adored the rangy cowhand. Zach held a special love for the little boy, and the two of them had become good friends.

Taylor Ann was besieged by her little brother, who was making hand signs fast and furiously, asking what she had brought him. She signed back that it was a surprise. He couldn't know until Zach had carried the boxes inside.

Squealing with excitement, Tyler signaled for Zach to hurry and carry the boxes in. Zach laughed and said, "Whatever it is, Ty, you'll have to share it with me!"

Ty had read Zach's lips, but still did not grasp what he had said. He looked to his sister for help.

Taylor Ann made hand signals, working her mouth at the same time. When Tyler understood, he giggled and signaled he would share it with Zach if he would hurry up.

When Taylor Ann interpreted it for Zach, he laughed, picked up the boxes, and said, "Let's go!"

Entering the kitchen with sister and brother ahead of him, Zach smiled at Emily Grace, who was busy at the cupboard, kneading dough.

She smiled in return and said, "Back already? No Indian trouble, I assume."

"Didn't even see a feather," replied Zach, setting the boxes on the large kitchen table.

"Thank the Lord," breathed Emily Grace.

Looking at her mother as Tyler was eagerly awaiting his surprise, Taylor Ann asked, "All right if I give Ty his peppermint sticks?"

"Just show him the sticks," the mother replied, "and give him *one*. It's almost lunch time."

Emily Grace looked on with a pleasant smile as her little son squealed with joy at the sight of his peppermint sticks. When given one stick by his sister, he handed it to Zach, then signaled for one for himself. Zach thanked Tyler for sharing, then played tag with him around the kitchen table while Taylor Ann began emptying the boxes.

Continuing to knead the dough, Emily Grace smiled at the two playing tag. She adored Zach in a motherly way, and secretly wanted him for a son-in-law. Though she had never heard Zach say he was in love with her daughter, it was evident in his eyes when he looked at Taylor Ann. She knew Taylor Ann was fond of Zach, and unknown to anyone but the Lord and herself, had been praying for nearly a year that her daughter would fall in love with him.

Zach held the boy in his arms and talked to mother and daughter, while finishing his peppermint stick. When he was done, he put Tyler down, messed up his hair, and said, "See you later, little pal."

Tyler responded with a squeal.

Zach then told mother and daughter good-bye and left to return the wagon to the barn.

Tyler tried to persuade his mother to let him have another stick of candy, but she sent him outside to play, then went back to her bread-making. Taylor Ann was finishing putting grocery items away.

"He's so nice, isn't he, honey?" said the mother.

"Hmm?" responded the daughter.

"Zach. He's such a nice young man."

"Yes. Yes, he is."

"The kind I hope the Lord has picked out for you."

Taylor Ann gave her mother a sweet smile, but did not comment.

It was high noon when Corey McCollister crossed the yard from the corral and watched the little boy riding a stick horse near the back porch of the house. When Tyler saw him, he galloped toward his father, squealing with excitement. Tyler dropped the stick horse and raised his arms. It was customary that whenever Corey returned to the house, he would swing Tyler upward and place him on his shoulders.

Tyler was used to ducking when the two of them passed through the door and entered the house. He was still on his father's shoulders when they moved into the kitchen. Greeting his daughter, Corey put Tyler down, took his wife into his arms, and breathed, "Hello, world's most luscious and beautiful woman."

Emily Grace smiled, kissed him, and said, "Hello, yourself. Hungry?"

"I could eat a bear. Been a long time since breakfast."

"Almost seven hours. A hard-working man will work up quite an appetite in that amount of time."

At forty-three, Corey McCollister was successful and wealthy. He was six-two, slender, and handsome in a rugged way. His hair was medium-blond, he had pale blue eyes, and was clean shaven. His jawline was square and his chin jutted forward.

Corey led his family in prayer, thanking God for the meal, and began devouring his food. Between bites, he said, "I hate to bring this up, but the Indians have stolen more of our cattle. Boys say we're missing a couple dozen head from the bunch over by the gulch. Eight months this has been going on. It's got to stop."

"What are you going to do, Daddy?" Taylor Ann asked.

"Well, since we don't have an army fort close by, I guess the boys and I will have to handle the thieving savages ourselves."

"You had Zach buy two cases of ammunition today. Is that because you're planning on a big fight with whatever Indians are stealing our cattle?"

Her daughter's words jolted Emily Grace. Wide-eyed, she looked at Corey and gasped, "Two cases! Oh, Corey, our men aren't capable of going up against Indian warriors!"

"Some of them are. They fought in the Civil War."

"I know, but we'll be greatly outnumbered. Darling, is the loss of a few cattle now and then worth bringing on wholesale bloodshed?"

"Doesn't have to be like that, honey," parried Corey. "I've got a plan. I'm going to send some of the boys out every day to scout the entire spread. If they catch any of the Indians in the act, they'll try simply shooting over their heads to scare them away."

"What if that doesn't work?" asked Emily Grace.

"Then the next time we catch them stealing Circle M stock, we'll shoot to kill. I've got a right to protect what's mine."

Emily Grace's features showed her fear.

"You know I've said before," continued Corey, "that I wouldn't care if the Indians took a steer now and then in the winter time when game is hard to come by, but summer's on us now, and they're taking anywhere from two or three dozen at a time. I know those are insignificant numbers when we run over five thousand head, but to me its a principle. The Indians should be hunting their own meat now, not stealing it from us."

"Daddy," interjected Taylor Ann, "how do you know it's

Indians? Couldn't it be rustlers?"

"Rustlers don't bother with taking a few here and there, honey. They always go for big numbers. The thieves are Indians, all right."

"Corey," Emily Grace said cautiously, "I know what the Indians are doing is wrong, but if you start shooting them—or even at them—you could start a war. We've got fifty-three ranch hands, but any one of the three tribes around us have plenty more warriors who could attack the ranch and kill us all. I fear the Crow and the Blackfoot...but I fear the Cheyenne the most. We've been told about that new young chief of theirs. What's his name?"

"Iron Hand."

"Yes. Iron Hand. You know the army has passed the word to be wary of him...that he's hard and brutal. And Marshal Luskin told us that day—remember?—that the village Iron Hand rules has over a hundred and fifty warriors."

Corey sighed, and said, "E.G., I know things could get rough, but I can't just stand idly by and let those savages steal us blind. I've got to put a stop to it."

"Daddy," said Taylor Ann, "have you any idea whether it's one tribe that's doing the stealing, or whether two or maybe all three are guilty?"

"Well, in the past eight months since it started, oftentimes our men have seen Crow and Cheyenne on our land, and after some of these sightings, we've discovered cattle missing within a day or two. No one has ever reported seeing any Blackfoot on our land, but other ranchers have suspected Blackfoot of stealing their cattle, though as of yet, they have no proof."

Emily Grace dabbed at her lips with a napkin, set fearful eyes on her husband, and said with a tremor in her voice, "Corey, please...a few stolen cattle aren't worth getting our men or ourselves killed over."

Corey got that familiar stubborn look in his eyes that she had seen countless times before. His voice was inflexible.

"Nobody's going to get killed but thieving Indians, E.G. The Circle M patrols will begin their scouting missions tomorrow."

CHAPTER FIFTEEN

Breanna Baylor was seated at the desk in the waiting room with Dr. Gerald Getz, showing him the paper work she had done while he was laid up. They both looked toward the door when it came open, and young Donnie Hawes stepped in. Breanna was hoping he would be alone, but Max Worley was behind him like a shadow. Worley had a lighted cigar clenched between his teeth.

Rising from her chair, Breanna looked past Donnie and said, "There is no smoking allowed in here, Mr. Worley."

Worley leered at Breanna with hungry eyes, showing her a yellow-toothed grin. Glancing at the man sitting at the desk, he stepped back through the door into the mid-morning sunlight, flipped the cigar onto the boardwalk, and returned.

"Well, it's been four days since I first stitched you up, Donnie, and two days since I changed the bandage," Breanna said. "The wound was looking better two days ago. How is it feeling now?"

"It's hurtin' some today," replied Donnie, touching fingers to the bandage.

Turning to Getz, Breanna said, "Doctor, I'll take care of Donnie and be right back with you. Just rest a moment, okay?"

"Oh, is this the doc?" blurted Worley. "How ya doin', Doc? Feelin' better, eh?"

"I'm doing much better, thank you," said Getz.

"Gonna be back sawin' bones purty soon, eh?"

"Let's go, Donnie," said Breanna, guiding him toward the clinic door.

When Worley started to follow, Breanna said, "You can wait out here. This won't take very long."

"Nope. I wanna see what the wound looks like."

Breanna was in no mood for a fuss, and she didn't want Dr. Getz upset, so she let it go. Max Worley followed them into the examining room.

Worley stood over Breanna while Donnie sat on the examining table and she removed the two-day-old bandage. The wound was still swollen, and there was fresh blood oozing through the stitches.

"Have you been riding a horse?" Breanna asked.

"No, ma'am," Donnie replied quickly.

"Well, what have you been doing, then? You've put a strain on these stitches."

Young Hawes glanced at his friend, then looked at the nurse and said, "I was just doin' a little fast-drawin' and target practice yesterday afternoon. Since I'm right-handed, and the wound is on my left arm, I didn't think it would hurt it none."

"Well, it did," she sighed. "Honestly, couldn't that part of your life wait a couple of weeks?"

"Man's gotta keep up his fast-draw these days, nursie," interjected Worley. "Kid's plenty good, too. Not only is he quick on the draw, but while he's doin' it, he can shoot the bill off a woodpecker at thirty paces and never harm his head. Kid's good, I tell you."

Breanna felt her temper flare. Dabbing at the wound with a ball of cotton she had just soaked with alcohol, she said, "Mr. Worley, I'm not, 'nursie.'"

"You are to me, honey," he chuckled. "Too bad you ain't twins. You got enough good looks for two women. I think 'nursie' fits you fine."

Praying for strength to subdue her anger, Breanna ignored Worley and said, "Donnie, I know you're anxious to ride, but I'm telling you for your own good—wait at least another six days. And *don't* be practicing your fast-draw."

Donnie looked at his friend. Worley shrugged. "Guess we'll have to obey nursie's orders. Won't hurt nothin', I guess, since we don't know where Gavin is. Gonna take him and us a while to find each other anyway."

"Yes, sir," said the rancher, "the man you describe stopped here to fill his canteen two days ago."

"And he was ridin' a big black?"

"Sure was. Beautiful animal."

"He didn't perchance say where he was goin', did he?"

"Sure did. Hay Springs."

Gavin Cold grinned with deep satisfaction. If he made a hard ride, he could be in Hay Springs within a day. If the man-in-black had enough business in Hay Springs to detain him a couple of days, he would die there.

John Stranger topped a gentle rise, looked across the rolling plains ahead of him, and let his gaze take in the uneven rooftops of Hay Springs.

"Well, Ebony, we'll look in on her and make sure everything's all right."

The big black nickered as if it understood.

Stranger pictured beautiful Breanna in his mind and thought of that cold, wintry day in Wichita when she had sent him out of her life. He recalled the pain in his heart, and the words he spoke from the saddle before riding away: *Good-bye, lovely lady. I will be out of your life, but you will never be out of my heart. From time to time, I may be looking at you, but you'll not know I'm near. I'll respect your request.*

It was coming up on ten o'clock when horse and rider entered Hay Springs. Stranger rode Ebony slowly down Main Street, noting the water barrels that lined the boardwalks on both sides of the street, spaced some thirty to forty feet apart. Noting a couple of old-timers who were sitting on a bench, soaking up the warmth of the mid-morning sunlight, Stranger veered toward them and hauled up. "Morning, gentlemen," he said.

Both elderly men returned the greeting.

"I understand you've had a water problem here."

"That's right, mister," one of them responded. "We've had a real epidemic of the typhoid because of it, too. If you're gonna drink any water while you're here, be sure to get it outta one o' them barrels."

"Thanks for the information. I also understand there's been a young visiting nurse from Denver here to help out during the crisis."

"Keerect. Purty as a picture, too. Doc Getz's been mighty sick, hisself. She took care of him, too. 'Bout got him to where he can pick up his practice again."

"That's good. She'd be at the doctor's office, then, eh?"

"Yep. She a friend of your'n?"

"That's right. Well, much obliged for the information."

"You're welcome, young feller."

Stranger looked up the street and saw Dr. Gerald Getz's shingle. Beyond it a block was the Hay Springs Hotel. Not far past the hotel was the hostelry. Guiding Ebony to the first intersection, he turned off Main Street and rode to Second Street so there was no chance of Breanna seeing him from the doctor's office. When he had passed that block, he returned to Main Street and left Ebony at the hostelry for a good feeding and a rubdown.

Stranger walked down the boardwalk and halted between two buildings almost directly across the street from the clinic. He had been there only a few minutes when the office door came open and a thick-bodied man emerged. Stranger recognized him immediately as a member of Denvil Hawes's gang. He had been with Gavin Cold and the others that day in North Platte.

Directly behind Max Worley came Donnie Hawes. Stranger's heart quickened pace when he saw Breanna Baylor standing at the door, talking to Donnie. Donnie nodded while she spoke and said something in return. Breanna disappeared and Donnie turned to Worley, put a hand to his head indicating that he was not feeling well, and said something. Worley nodded and headed across the street. Donnie lifted his hat, sleeved sweat from his brow, and moved in the direction from which Stranger had just come.

Stranger decided to follow Donnie. He wanted to talk to him again. He was about to leave the shaded space between the buildings when he saw an elderly man wearing a green visor hasten toward the clinic door, carrying a telegram. When the Western Union man entered the clinic, Stranger moved out and started up the boardwalk after Donnie. Looking over his shoulder, he saw Worley entering one of the town's four saloons.

Staying a half-block behind young Hawes, Stranger followed and watched him enter the hotel. Two minutes later, Stranger stepped up to the desk in the hotel lobby and smiled at the clerk. "I'd like a room, please."

While leaving the clerk to wonder at the name he had signed in the register, the man-in-black mounted the stairs, dropping the key to room 10 in his pocket. The register had shown him that there had been few guests at the hotel since the typhoid epidemic had hit the town. Breanna was in room 7, and Donnie Hawes and Max Worley were in room 4. Moving up to room 4, Stranger tapped on the door.

Footsteps were heard from within, then the door came

open. Donnie Hawes's mouth gaped open in surprise. "Mr. Stranger! What are you doin' here?"

"I came to town on other business and saw you come out of the doctor's office. Thought I'd talk to you, if you'd let me."

Donnie sighed with obvious relief. "You bet. Come in."

Stepping into the room, Stranger saw an ashtray loaded with cigar butts on the bedstand next to the bed near the window. The bed near the door had its own bedstand, and next to the lantern on it lay an open Bible.

Gesturing toward the room's only chair, Donnie said, "Sit down, Mr. Stranger. I'll sit here on the bed."

Donnie sighed again as he sat down on his bed, and said, "You'll never know how glad I am to see you."

"Oh?"

"Yes. Our gang got shot to pieces over at Merriman durin' a bank robbery. Max Worley—that's the guy you saw me talkin' to—and I were the only ones to get away. As you can see, I got shot in the arm."

"Is it doing all right?"

"Yeah. It'll be fine if I take care of it properly."

"Gavin Cold get it, too?"

"No. He's been tryin' to hunt you down and kill you, like he told you that day in North Platte. I'm glad to see he hasn't found you."

Stranger's gray gaze swerved to the open Bible on the bedstand. "I see you've been reading God's Book."

"Yeah," nodded the youth, tears welling up in his eyes. "I know the Lord sent you here, 'cause I need help. You and Pa have talked to me about it before, but I've been a stubborn fool. Will you show me from the Bible how to repent and be saved? I'm sick of my life the way it is. I want Jesus in my heart, and I want to go home to Pa."

* * * * *

Breanna accepted the telegram from the hand of the Western Union agent, thanking him for bringing it to her.

"You're welcome, Miss Baylor," said the agent, giving her an almost toothless smile. "It'll require an answer, m'um. Would you like me to wait?"

"No, that's all right. I see it's from my sponsoring physician in Denver. When I'm ready to send the reply, I'll come over and do it."

The little man made a hasty exit, and while Dr. Gerald Getz sat at the desk, Breanna read the lengthy telegram. When she finished, she looked at Getz and said, "Dr. Goodwin says there's been a coal mine cave-in in the foothills of the Rockies southwest of Denver. Several miners are trapped deep in the mine, but are alive. They've sent up messages that most of them are seriously injured. It'll take several days to get them out, and Dr. Goodwin will need my help when they do."

Dr. Getz put a hand to his brow. "Let's see...next stage in and out of here will be tomorrow morning."

"Yes. He's already made reservations for me to be on the stage when it leaves Hay Springs at nine-thirty in the morning. He leaves me an out, though, if you're still not able to resume your work. I'm to wire him back immediately."

Getz nodded slowly. "I can handle it now, Breanna. You're needed worse at that cave-in. By taking tomorrow's stage, you can be back in Denver by Sunday. That should put you there before they get the miners out."

"You're sure you can handle it?"

"Yes. Go send the wire and tell Dr. Goodwin you'll be on the stage in the morning."

When Breanna reached the telegraph office, the agent was receiving a second message from Dr. Goodwin. It stated that the mine tragedy was worse than he had thought at first. There were more miners trapped than initially reported. Unless Dr. Getz was bedridden, Breanna was to be on tomorrow's stage. Breanna sent a return message assuring Goodwin that he could depend on her. Nurse Baylor would be on the stage and in Denver by Sunday.

In room 4 at the Hay Springs Hotel, Donnie Hawes rose from his knees beside the bed, wiping tears. "Thank you, Mr. Stranger," he said, drawing a shuddering breath. "As soon as this arm's where I can ride, I'm goin' home to Pa."

Stranger grinned and closed the Bible. Laying it on the bedstand, he said, "When you walk in and tell your pa you've become a Christian and are going to stay and work the farm with him, he'll be the happiest man on earth, Donnie."

"Yeah, I know," sniffed the youth. "I've sure given him some sleepless nights."

"He'll forgive you, believe me."

Donnie nodded, wiped more tears, and said, "Now, I've got one problem. Max Worley."

"He'll try to keep you from going home?"

"Yes. He told me that when a man joins up with a gang, the only way out is death. He's got plans for Gavin and himself to make a hard-cased outlaw out of me."

"How many days till you can ride?"

"Nurse said six."

"I've taken room 10 down the hall. Was only going to stay a day or two, but I'll hang around sort of out of sight till the day you're ready to ride. I'll work out a plan to detain Worley so he doesn't get in your way."

Donnie reached out with his good arm and gripped Stranger's shoulder. "You're a real friend, Mr. Stranger," he said with feeling.

"You'll find out now, Donnie, that your best friend is Jesus."

"I already know that, sir. Boy, is my pa gonna be happy!"

At 9:15 the next morning, Breanna Baylor—totally unaware that the man she loved had slept two doors down and across the hall from her—left the hotel, carrying her purse and overnight bag. Her luggage had already been taken to the stage office.

Having peeked at Breanna from his hotel room door, John Stranger had seen the Wells Fargo agent take the luggage from her door at 8:45. By their conversation, Stranger learned that she was taking the 9:30 stage, and why.

Max Worley had gone to the Lazy Bull Saloon at 8:30, leaving Donnie Hawes in the room. The Lazy Bull was on the same side of Main Street as the hotel, and stood between the hotel and the Wells Fargo office. The hotel and the Fargo office were a little more than a block apart.

Donnie had also heard the conversation in the hall, and having learned that Breanna was leaving on the 9:30 stage, wanted to express his appreciation for the way she had cared for him. Some ten minutes before she left the hotel to walk to the stage office, Donnie joined the crowd that had gathered to bid the beloved nurse good-bye.

As she moved along the boardwalk, Breanna was unaware that John Stranger was watching her from between the Hay Springs Mercantile building and the Northwest Nebraska Land Office. The Lazy Bull Saloon was directly across the street from where Stranger stood in the shadows.

Riding in from the other end of town was Gavin Cold. As the outlaw urged his horse along the street, he noted the stagecoach standing in front of the Wells Fargo office, and the fifteen-man cavalry unit waiting to escort the stage southward. Cold wondered why the crowd was gathered around the stage, and as he rode by, he did not see young Donnie Hawes amongst them. Donnie was busy talking to someone in the crowd, and he did not see Cold.

As she neared the Lazy Bull Saloon, Breanna's attention was drawn to the crowd at the Fargo office. Never dreaming that they were there to see her off, she wondered what the attraction might be. The sight of the men in blue uniforms was comforting. She was glad for the cavalry escort.

Breanna was almost to the saloon when a stocky figure moved out in front of her. Max Worley had a live cigar in his mouth as he grinned and blocked her way. "Hello, nursie. Somebody inside just told me you're leavin' town."

Breanna stopped abruptly and burned him with hot eyes. "I'm not 'nursie'! Now get out of my way!"

"Aw now, honey, you hadn't oughtta be that way. I think since we've become good friends, you really owe me a good-bye kiss."

"Get out of my way, you sorry excuse for a human being!"

Worley grabbed Breanna's arms and backed her up against the wall of the saloon. Pressing close, he put the tip of the smoking cigar an inch from her nose, blew smoke in her face, and growled, "Ain't no filly nowhere gonna talk to me like that!"

The smoke made Breanna's eyes water. Coughing, she cried, "Let me go, you filthy pig!"

Worley swore and slapped her. The sting of it took Breanna's breath.

"Let me go!"

"Not till you apologize for callin' me a filthy pig!"

"You're worse than a filthy pig!" came a booming voice from behind Worley.

Worley pivoted to face a tall, dark man whose gray eyes seemed to look right through him.

"John!" Breanna gasped.

John Stranger had not meant for Breanna to see him while he was in Hay Springs, but the sight of Worley pinning her against the wall and blowing smoke in her face was more than he could stomach. The slap had come after Stranger was already headed toward them.

It took Worley a couple of seconds to realize who the man

was. "You!" he choked, suddenly recognizing him from the incident in North Platte.

While Stranger was taking a step closer to Worley, people were aware that something was going on and were hastening down the street from the Wells Fargo office to have a look.

Directly across the street, Gavin Cold was off his horse, eyes fixed on John Stranger's back. He had noticed him while Stranger was crossing the street. Now was Cold's chance to gun down the hated man. He was ready to pull his revolver and shoot him in the back, when he saw the crowd rushing down the street toward him.

Cold wasn't about to get himself in a situation he couldn't control. If he shot Stranger from where he stood, the crowd would see him, and the cavalry patrol would be on him instantly. Thinking fast, he led his horse between the Hay Springs Mercantile building and the Northwest Nebraska Land Office. When he reached the alley, he stationed his horse in a spot where he could leap into the saddle from the back porch of the land office, and gallop away.

Slipping his Winchester .44 carbine from the saddleboot, he looked around to see if anyone was watching. There was no one in sight. Scrambling up a pile of wooden boxes next to the back porch, he was quickly on the porch roof, working his way to the flat roof of the land office.

On Main Street, Donnie Hawes was hurrying along with the crowd when he caught a glimpse of Gavin Cold dismounting from his horse. A couple of riders crossed in front of Donnie, blocking his view. When they were out of his way, Cold had disappeared.

While all of this was going on, John Stranger took a step closer to Max Worley, looking down at him with vengeful eyes. There was frost in his voice as he said in a flat tone, "Pretty good at slapping women, are you? Why don't you slap me?"

Worley uttered a profane word and started an open-handed

swing toward Stranger's face. Without taking his piercing eyes off Worley, Stranger caught the wrist in a steel grip in midair.

Worley's eyes bulged. Stranger then slapped and backhanded Worley repeatedly with stinging blows. The smoking cigar flew out of his mouth on the second blow. Stranger did not stop slapping Worley till his knees buckled and he went down.

By this time, the crowd had arrived and formed a semicircle in the street. Donnie looked anxiously back and forth, trying to locate Gavin Cold. Donnie knew Cold would shoot Stranger the instant he had the opportunity to do it with the prospect of a safe getaway.

Breanna stood with her back against the wall of the saloon, watching the man she loved batter the bully senseless. When this was over, she would finally have her long-awaited opportunity to talk to John and tell him that she was in love with him...and how foolish she had been to send him out of her life that wintry day in Wichita.

Worley lay on his back on the boardwalk, trying to clear his head. Stranger leaned over and picked up the smoking cigar. Straddling Worley, he jammed the burning end of the cigar into Worley's mouth, then clamped it shut and held it closed.

Worley's eyes bulged and his face turned purple. A nasal whine came from the outlaw while his eyes watered, smoke came out his nostrils, and he gagged and twisted in agony.

"So you like to blow smoke in a lady's face, huh?" gusted Stranger, pinning him with his weight and holding him in hands that felt like spring steel. "Well, here's some of your own medicine!"

Breanna knew that John Stranger was rough on bullies. She had seen the evidence when he had unleashed his fury on them before, but this was the first time she had seen him in action. She was pleased to know he had been looking in on her as he said he would do. She knew the incident would be over in minutes, then she could get him alone and tell him of her love.

Atop the land office, Gavin Cold bent low and crept across the flat roof to the false front that rose above the roof some four feet. Taking off his hat, he went to his knees and peered over the edge. The press of the crowd was so tight that Cold could barely make out the top of Stranger's flat-crowned hat. He could hear Worley's high-pitched whine. It was evident that the tall man had Worley down, and was putting some kind of punishment on him.

Cold glanced up the street to the Fargo office. The cavalry unit had remained there, mounted and ready to ride out with the stage. Cold knew his horse. The animal could outrun the army horses. All he had to do was shoot the man-in-black, dash to the rear of the building, hop onto the porch roof, and leap from there into the saddle. By the time the cavalry could figure out where he was, he would have all the head start he needed.

Licking his lips, Gavin Cold bent low, wiped the sweat from his hands and took a fresh grip on his carbine. Raising up for another look, he found that the crowd had shifted slightly, giving him a clear shot at Stranger's head.

Steadying himself against the false front, he cradled the carbine butt against his shoulder. He drew in a deep breath and put the sights on Stranger's head.

Donnie Hawes was still looking for Gavin Cold when his eye caught movement atop the Northwest Nebraska Land Office. Donnie's heart froze when he saw the outlaw drawing a bead at the center of attention. *He had his sights on John Stranger!*

Donnie pulled out his revolver and cocked it in one smooth, swift move.

Gavin Cold was about to squeeze the trigger when a beefy man on the inner edge of the circle moved and blocked his view. Swearing under his breath, he stood up to give himself the angle he needed to get a clear shot at Stranger.

A split second before Cold pressed the trigger, Donnie Hawes's gun roared from below. Cold's hammer dropped and the carbine fired the same instant Donnie's bullet tore through his head.

The crowd gasped as John Stranger's hat flew off and he dropped on top of Max Worley like a sack of grain. Blood appeared instantly at his temple.

The cavalrymen up the street heard the gunfire and looked up in time to see Gavin Cold's body peel over the false front, bounce like a rag doll on the boardwalk overhang, and drop to the street.

Marshal Luskin and Deputy Osborne had been out of town, and were just riding in from the east when they saw the crowd in front of the Lazy Bull Saloon and heard the gunshots. They, too, caught sight of Cold taking a dive from the roof of the land office.

Both men put their horses to a gallop and charged toward the scene.

Donnie glanced at Cold's lifeless form on the ground and tried to push through the crowd to see if John Stranger had been hit. He found it virtually impossible.

With her heart in her mouth, Breanna Baylor fell to her knees beside the man she loved and with shaky hands, examined his head wound. The bullet had run a crease along the right side of his head at the temple, leaving a furrow in his hair. Blood seeped from the wound. The concussion of the .44 slug had knocked him unconscious.

While Breanna held John's head in her lap and spoke soft words to him, Max Worley was getting up, gagging and spitting cigar fragments from his mouth. He was crazed with wrath. Before anyone could stop him, he whipped out his gun to empty it into John Stranger.

Marshal Luskin remained in the saddle, pushing his way through the crowd. From his elevated perch, he saw Breanna holding the man-in-black on the ground, and Max Worley bringing his gun to bear on him.

There was no time to ask questions, and no time to call out a warning. Luskin's gun was out of the holster and spitting fire in less than a second.

Worley went down with the marshal's bullet in his heart. He twitched a couple times, and lay still.

The crowd was pushed back with the help of the soldiers, and Dr. Gerald Getz hurried to the spot on shaky legs. Breanna's face was white as she watched Getz make his examination. Stranger was still unconscious.

The doctor asked a couple of men to carry the wounded man to the clinic, where he was laid out on the examining table. Marshal Luskin went inside while Deputy Osborne stood guard at the door to keep anyone else from entering. Donnie Hawes stayed close to the office door, eager for word about John Stranger's condition.

While the doctor did a thorough examination, checking Stranger's heavy-lidded eyes, Breanna hovered close. Standing nearby, Marshal Luskin asked, "You know this man, Miss Baylor?"

"Yes, I do. We're...we're good friends."

Within another minute, Dr. Getz looked at Breanna and said, "He's got a severe concussion. No telling how long he'll be out. Far as I can tell, there's no other damage except for the crease in his temple and hairline. I'll patch up the wound and get the bleeding stopped."

Deputy Osborne stepped in and said, "Miss Baylor, Lieutenant Vernon Beemer of the cavalry patrol is at the door. He says to tell you that the stage must pull out immediately. It is already past departure time, and the army insists they keep the stages running on schedule. If you don't board the stage within one minute, it'll leave without you."

Breanna looked at Dr. Getz. "I can't leave till I know John's all right."

"He'll be fine, Breanna. You must go. Dr. Goodwin's depending on you for the lives of those men in the mine."

Tears filmed Breanna's eyes. She knew the doctor was right. Duty called.

"All right," she sighed, blinking back her tears. "Tell him...tell him when he can to come to Denver, I want to see him."

"I will," nodded Getz. "Now, hurry, or you'll miss your stage."

Breanna bent over and kissed the lips of the unconscious man and moved her mouth in a silent, "I love you, my darling." Wheeling, she walked to the door, paused to look back at John Stranger, then was gone.

CHAPTER SIXTEEN

"Look, Papa!" exclaimed little Susie Logan. "So'diers an' a stagecoach!" The wagon train had Hay Springs in sight, and Susie—sitting between her parents on the wagon seat—was first in the Logan vehicle to spot the Wells Fargo stage with its army escort moving out of the town, heading due south. Soon the stage and escort were lost on the southern horizon in a cloud of dust, and the wagons reached the outskirts of the town.

"Is this where we gonna live, Mama?" queried Susie.

"We won't be living in town, honey," replied Merilee, "but our ranch will be somewhere near here."

Lieutenant Bryce Keffer came riding along the line and drew up beside the Logan wagon. "We'll leave you now, Mr. Logan. We've got to report back to Fort Sidney as soon as possible."

"Appreciate the escort, Lieutenant," replied Jim.

"Our pleasure. I told Mr. Armand we'll be sending another patrol to take him and the rest who want to go on to Wyoming within a couple of days. I think the widows who want to go back East will be able to join some commercial wagons that run across these parts periodically. Any of the merchants in Hay Springs will know when the wagons will be coming through again. Hope you have great success in your new venture."

"Thank you, Lieutenant," smiled Jim.

When the wagons veered toward Hay Spring's main thoroughfare, the cavalry escort galloped away. Susie looked up at her mother and asked, "Wif the so'diers gone bye-bye Mama, will the In'ians get us?"

"No, honey," said Merilee, putting an arm around Susie and pulling her close. "The Indians won't bother us here."

Merilee gave her husband a worried glance. Both parents had discussed privately their fears that the Indian attack on the wagon train might leave their children with emotional scars that would affect them for a long time. Jeremy and Darlene had said little about it since it happened, but Jim and Merilee wondered what might be going on in their minds. They were praying for wisdom to handle the situation correctly.

People on Main Street eyed the wagon train with curiosity as it rolled into town. Jim said to Merilee, "We'll get our hotel room, then I'll park the wagon in the alley and take the team to the stable. After I talk to them at the land office about ranch property available for sale, I'll rent a horse and go talk to Mr. McCollister about buying some cattle from him to get our herd started."

Donnie Hawes paced the floor in the waiting room at the clinic. Dr. Getz had assured him Stranger would be all right, but Donnie wanted to see for himself, once his friend had regained consciousness. Abruptly the examining room door came open and Dr. Getz said softly, "He's conscious now, son."

Getz led Donnie to the examining table where John Stranger lay with a bandage around his head. Stranger focused his iron gray eyes on the youth, smiled weakly, and said, "Dr. Getz tells me I owe my life to you."

Donnie's face tinted. "Well, I—"

"I saw the whole thing, son," spoke up Getz. "If you hadn't shot that guy on the roof when you did, his bullet would no doubt have split this man's skull."

"Thanks, Donnie," said Stranger.

"Just did what I had to do," grinned young Hawes, modestly.

The doctor excused himself, saying he had to see to his typhoid patients in the back room.

Stranger looked up at Donnie and asked, "So when are you going home?"

"Soon as I'm sure you're okay."

"Doctor says I'm fine," smiled Stranger. "Got a pretty bad headache and a bit of a wound on the side of my cranium here, but no real damage done. I'll be up and on my way by tomorrow morning. Bandage can come off in a few days, and I'll be good as new." Glancing at his flat-crowned hat that hung on a wall peg next to the waiting room door, he added, "Real damage was to my hat. Cold's bullet chewed up part of the brim."

"Guess that's better than chewin' up part of your head."

"Fella might say that," grinned Stranger. "Hats are cheaper and easier to come by."

Donnie was quiet for a moment, then said, "Well, I guess I'd better get goin'. I'm eager to get home and tell Pa you led me to the Lord. I'm sure beholdin' to you."

"My pleasure, Donnie. I only wish I could have led Denvil to Christ before he went to the gallows."

"Wasn't your fault he wouldn't let you talk to him."

"Yeah. Well, at least your pa's going to have something to really rejoice about now." Extending his right hand, Stranger said, "Give him my best, and tell him I'll stop and say hello next time I'm in the area."

"Do that, Mr. Stranger," said Donnie warmly, meeting the tall man's grip. "We'd both love to see you again. Good-bye till then."

As Donnie started to walk away, Stranger said, "Stay close to the Lord, Donnie. Get in the Bible and spend time in prayer daily."

Pausing halfway to the door, young Hawes smiled. "You can count on it. And by the way...if you and that pretty little nurse Baylor end up at the altar, let me know and I'll send a wedding present."

"We're just good friends, Donnie. Nothing more than that."

"Sounds more serious than just friends from what I could pick up out there on the street when she was holdin' your head in her lap."

"She's...she's a nurse, kid. They're supposed to be concerned when somebody's hurt."

"Mm-hmm. But it's pretty plain you're more than just *somebody* to Miss Baylor. I was at the door out there when the lieutenant was pressuring her to hurry so the stage could leave. She came out crying. She didn't want to leave you."

"Dr. Getz told me she had a commitment in Denver...a mine cave-in, I believe."

"I figured there was somethin' that was makin' her go. She sure didn't want to leave you."

"Like I told you, we're friends."

When Donnie was gone, John Stranger's thoughts fastened on Breanna. He was pleased that she showed so much concern for him, and that she was reluctant to leave until she knew he was all right. But still he would honor the request she had made that day in Wichita.

John Stranger's heart longed for Breanna. Though she had spurned his love and sent him out of her life, he would continue to look in on her from time to time. He wanted to be sure all was well with her...and it helped just to set eyes on her.

Carrying a crude map drawn on a piece of paper by the hostler in Hay Springs, Jim Logan rode west over the rolling hills and finally found himself on Circle M land. He was amazed at the size of it as he trotted the rented saddle horse across the grassy fields dotted with cattle. Seeing the cattle stirred his desire to get into the business as soon as possible. His thoughts ran to Harry Sturgis, who had made it all possible, and to John Stranger who had recovered the money when it looked like it was gone.

Jim was nearing a wide wooded area, which he would skirt along its south edge. The ranch house and outbuildings had not yet come into view.

At the same time Jim Logan was approaching the southeast side of the wooded area, six Circle M men were riding patrol on its northeast side some four hundred yards away. Riding three abreast in the lead were Ed Harris, Norm Shea, and Drew Voss. Behind them some twenty feet were Harley Metcalf, J.T. Woodard, and Ray Premro. Woodard and Premro were the rookies in the group, having been employed at the Circle M only eight months.

Suddenly Voss raised up in his stirrups, looking south, and gusted, "You boys see what I see?"

Every eye turned that direction and focused on four Indians riding their pinto ponies slowly across Circle M land.

Shea swore and said, "Suppose they're gonna steal some cattle right here in broad daylight?"

Harris, who was leader of the group, pulled his gun, spit a brown stream of tobacco, and growled, "We ain't gonna give 'em a chance. Boss said to put some hot lead over their heads. Let's go!"

Thundering across the fields of lush grass, the Circle M riders began firing over the heads of the Indians. Frightened cattle scattered every direction at the sight of the galloping riders and the sharp sound of their guns. The Indians instantly galloped away, heading southwest around the wooded area.

The cowboys pursued until their guns were empty, then Harris signaled for them to haul up. All six noticed the Indians race past a lone rider, then disappear amongst the hills.

"Let's see who that is," Harris said.

When they had all reloaded, the Circle M men trotted toward the lone rider, who had now halted and was waiting for them. As they drew up, he threw a thumb over his shoulder and said, "They went behind those hills, fellas."

"We know," nodded Harris. "All we're supposed to do is scare 'em. We're Circle M men. I'm Ed Harris. By the direction you're headed, I assume you're wantin' to see somebody at the ranch house or the bunkhouse."

"My name's Jim Logan. Just arrived in Hay Springs. Wagon train my family and I were traveling with was attacked by Cheyenne down by Soda Lake. Lost a bunch of people and several wagons. Those were Cheyenne, weren't they?"

"Yeah," nodded Harris. "Iron Hand's cattle-stealin' thieves."

"Iron Hand?"

"New chief of a village not far from here. Meaner'n a rattler with the seven-year itch. You didn't say who you were wantin' to see."

"Oh, excuse me," said Jim. "We've come here to buy land and go into the ranchin' business. I wanted to talk to Mr. McCollister about buyin' some cattle so I can get my herd started."

"Well, I'm sure he'll be happy to talk to you, Jim," said Harris. "Have any idea where you'll buy land?"

"I'm gonna take a ride with Mr. Bolton of the Northwest Nebraska Land Office tomorrow. He said there's plenty of good land for sale. Can't tell you any more than that right now."

Nudging his horse close to Logan's, Harris extended his hand. "Welcome to the area, Logan." When they had shaken hands, Harris introduced Jim to the other men.

As they rode toward the ranch buildings, Ed Harris explained to Jim Logan about the trouble the Circle M was having with Indians stealing cattle. Logan asked if it might be rustlers instead of Indians. Echoing his boss's words, Harris said, "Rustlers don't bother with stealing a few cattle at a time. They only go for big numbers. There's no doubt the thieves are Indians."

Pulling his tobacco plug from a shirt pocket, Harris bit off a chaw and said, "Anyway, this is the first time we've shot at any redskins on Circle M property. Maybe this little incident you just witnessed will be enough to bring an end to the thievin'."

The sun was lowering toward the horizon when the six Circle M men rode up to the front porch of the ranch house where Corey McCollister was sitting with his family. McCollister rose from a wicker chair, smiled, and said to Harris, "What'd you do, Ed? Hire me a new man?"

"I think he'd make a good one, sir, but looks like he's gonna be givin' you some competition. Name's Jim Logan. He's new to the area and wants to talk to you about buyin' some cattle to get his herd started."

Smiling broadly, Corey McCollister said, "Competition in this area is no problem, Mr. Logan. The ranchers around here can sell everything they raise to the eastern beef buyers. Slide out of that saddle and come up here and sit a spell."

While Jim was dismounting, Harris told McCollister of seeing the four Cheyenne braves on Circle M land, and of firing over their heads.

Emily Grace's brow creased and she bit her lower lip. Taylor Ann noticed her mother's reaction, but said nothing. Little Ty sat beside his sister on the porch swing, trying to figure out what was being said.

A tall, gangly man with silver hair and deep lines in his face came ambling toward the house from the barn as Corey said, "I hope Iron Hand will get the message and stop sending his thieves over here to steal our cattle."

"Me, too," said Harris. "I hope this'll be the end of it."

The six riders wheeled their mounts and headed toward the corral as Jim Logan mounted the porch steps. Corey shook his hand, then gestured toward his wife and children and said,

"Come meet my family."

Emily Grace rose from her wicker chair, and Taylor Ann slid off the swing. Tyler followed suit, setting his inquisitive eyes on Jim.

"Mr. Logan," said Corey, "this is my wife, Emily Grace."

The stately woman warmed the newcomer with a smile and offered her hand. "Happy to meet you, Mr. Logan."

Logan took her hand and replied, "The pleasure is mine, ma'am. You can call me Jim, though."

"All right, Jim," she smiled, looking toward her children.

Corey led Jim to his daughter and said, "This is Taylor Ann."

The lovely nineteen-year-old offered her hand, welcoming Jim to the Hay Springs area. Jim took her hand and said, "Thank you, Taylor Ann." Then looking down at the bright-eyed little boy, he asked, "And what's your name, partner?"

Tyler squinted, cocked his head, then looked at his sister.

Jim knew something was wrong. He was trying to think of something to say when Taylor Ann offered, "My little brother is deaf and dumb, Mr. Logan. His name is Tyler."

"Oh," said Jim, embarrassed. "I'm sorry. I—"

"No need to be," cut in Emily Grace. "Tyler can read lips if you speak slowly."

Corey was looking at the silver-haired man who was mounting the porch steps as Jim Logan knelt down to Tyler's level and shook his hand, saying slowly, "Hello, Tyler. My name is Jim Logan. How old are you?"

Grinning, the towheaded lad pumped Jim's hand and made a friendly squeal.

"He didn't get that last part, Mr. Logan," said Taylor Ann. Tapping her little brother's shoulder to get his attention, she made hand signals, telling him that Mr. Logan had asked his age.

Ty held up four fingers and a thumb.

Jim liked the boy instantly. Using Taylor Ann to interpret

his words with hand signals, Jim told Ty he had four children, and that his son Benjamin was six years old. Ty seemed pleased to know about Benjamin, and was more pleased when Jim suggested that maybe soon Tyler and Benjamin could play together.

"That would be nice," spoke up Emily Grace, signing so Ty would understand. Then to Logan she said, "I'll look forward to meeting your wife and children, Jim."

At that moment, Corey ushered the lanky cowboy toward Jim and introduced him as Curly Ford, his ranch foreman. As the two shook hands, Corey told Ford about Ed Harris and his group firing over the heads of the four Cheyenne braves.

"I sure hope that'll be the end of it," Ford said.

"I'm taking no chances," Corey said. "I want you to send out another patrol tomorrow. If they see any redskinned trespassers, I want bullets to fly over their heads. I'll give Iron Hand one more chance to back off."

"Of course tomorrow it could be Crow or Blackfoot, boss," said Ford. "Indians cross Circle M land quite often, but that doesn't mean they're all here to steal our cattle."

"Maybe not, but let them use another route to come and go from their camps and villages. Just do like I say, and tell your patrol to put hot lead over the heads of any Indians they see on my land."

"Will do, boss," said Curly.

Emily Grace could read Curly Ford like a book. He didn't like the idea of shooting over the Indians' heads any more than she did. The trouble it could bring on wasn't worth the loss of a few head now and then.

Curly was barely on his way back toward the corral when Jim Logan heard Tyler squeal and saw a rider coming toward the house leading a saddled horse without a rider.

The handsome young cowhand was smiling as he reined in and set admiring eyes on the rancher's daughter. "Riding time, Taylor Ann."

Taylor Ann stepped to the swing, picked up her hat, and said, "You're right on schedule, Zach."

"Zach," said Corey, "I want you to meet Jim Logan. He and his family just arrived in Hay Springs by wagon train. The Logans are going to settle here and go to cattle ranching. Jim, this is Zachary Adams, one of my best men."

Zach liked Corey's compliment. Smiling amiably at Logan, he said, "Welcome to northwest Nebraska, Mr. Logan. Where you from?"

"Missouri. Jefferson City. I worked for the Sturgis Cattle Company there. Decided I wanted to come west and get into ranching."

"Sure hope you'll be happy here," Zach said.

"Well, if everyone else is as friendly as the people of the Circle M, I'm sure I will be, Zach."

Zach slid from the saddle and helped Taylor Ann mount her horse.

"I'll be back for supper," Taylor Ann said to her mother. Then to Zach, "Race you to Split Rock."

"You're on," laughed Zach, and both riders galloped away.

Jim Logan then got down to business with Corey McCollister about purchasing cattle. After a brief discussion, McCollister quoted Logan a reasonable price for two bulls and a hundred head of cows and heifers. Jim knew the rancher was being quite fair with him, and shook hands on the deal. Jim would buy them as soon as he was settled on his land.

Making over Tyler once more, Jim bid Emily Grace goodbye, thanked Corey for the good price on the cattle, and rode away. Tyler squealed and waved. Jim Logan had a new young friend.

Taylor Ann and Zach raced all the way to Split Rock, a huge boulder that had broken in half by some shaking of the earth centuries before. The boulder was situated on the bank of one of the ranch's two creeks, and was shaded by a few cottonwoods.

Zach had let the girl win the race, and Taylor Ann was laughing gleefully as she drew rein beside the creek. "Now we know who's the best rider!" she said as Zach skidded his horse to a stop and slid from the saddle.

"Oh," he chuckled, moving toward her. "The horse doesn't get any credit?"

"Of course. But you put an excellent rider on an excellent horse, and they'll beat a plain ol' cow pony and its substandard rider every time!"

"Oh, is that so?" he laughed, helping her to the ground.

Zach held her close, looking into her eyes with deep yearning. Taylor Ann's giggling faded, and for a moment she felt the warmth of Zachary Adams's love pulsating like a heartbeat between them. "Zach," she said, taking in a quick breath, "please let go of me."

Releasing her, Zach continued to adore her with his eyes and said, "I'm still in love with you, Taylor Ann. Only more than I was when I told you before on the way back from town."

After a brief moment, she said softly, "I like you, Zach. I like you a lot, but please don't expect me to tell you something I don't feel honestly in my heart. I'm just not ready to fall in love yet."

"I understand. But I'm serving notice, young lady. I'm stickin' close so when you're ready to fall, it'll be for me."

Reaching up and patting his cheek, she said, "You're sweet, Zach. Let's let the horses get a drink, then sit on the bank for a while."

Unknown to Zachary and Taylor Ann, dark eyes were watching them from behind a heavily bushed grassy knoll some forty yards away. A half-dozen Cheyenne warriors were off their horses, peering through the thick foliage. One of them was Chief Iron Hand, who had become chief in place of his father, Tall Bear, who had died two months earlier.

Iron Hand, who had proven himself a brave and skilled warrior, had been planning to choose a squaw soon from the young women in the village. As he set his deep, black eyes on Taylor Ann, he said, "I have seen her before, but never this close. She is most beautiful. And her hair. It is like sunshine. Would not my people be surprised if I brought her to the village to become my squaw?"

"A white woman?" said one of the warriors.

Eyeing him with care, the Cheyenne leader grunted, "Iron Hand would not be the first Cheyenne chief to take a white woman as his squaw. Chiefs of other plains tribes have done so, too."

The warrior said no more.

Another, eager to please his leader, said, "If Iron Hand wants the white maiden, we will kill the man and take her."

"No," came Iron Hand's deep voice. "It is not time yet. My mother is still in mourning for my father. She is not ready to see her son take a bride. A few more moons, and Iron Hand will take the young woman with sunshine hair for his bride."

Upon returning to the village, Iron Hand found his people in an uproar. Four of his young braves had crossed the McCollister ranch on their way home from an errand to a Crow village, and had been fired upon by Circle M ranch hands.

At first, the young chief was ready to retaliate, but upon talking to the four braves, he learned that the Circle M men had not tried to hit them, but had purposely fired over their heads.

The message was clear. Though Iron Hand was irritated that his people were no longer welcome to ride across McCollister land, he decided not to retaliate. Sooner or later, he and his people would need to ride across Circle M property again. He would see what the white men would do then.

It was 9:30 at night when J.T. Woodard and Ray Premro rode through the trees a few miles southeast of Hay Springs and hauled up in front of a low-roofed log cabin. They could see lantern light flickering in the windows, and the dappled moonlight showed them two men standing on the porch.

From the porch it was difficult to make out any faces. One of the men called out, "That you, Willis?"

"No," answered Woodard. "It's J.T. and Ray."

"Okay, c'mon in. Sy'll be glad to see you." Turning toward the door, he raised his voice, "Hey, Sy! J.T. and Ray are here!"

Heavy footsteps were heard, and the door swung open. The leader of the rustler gang was silhouetted against the yellow light behind him. "Glad you could make it, boys," said Sy Mixler. "I'm expectin' Willis to show up with a new man any minute. C'mon in."

"A new man?" said Ray Premro. "Extra weight, or did somebody leave us?"

Mixler, who was a beefy man, snickered. "Manny left us."

"Manny? How come?"

"Get in here and siddown. I'll explain it."

Mixler told the two men on the porch to keep watching for Willis Day and the new gang member, then followed Woodard and Premro inside where another rustler sat at a rough-hewn table drinking from a whiskey bottle.

Hank Linza belched and said, "Howdy, boys."

Woodard and Premro returned the greeting and sat down at the table. As Mixler eased onto his usual chair at the head of the table, Premro asked, "Now, what happened with Manny?"

"I had to kill 'im. He suddenly decided his cut wasn't enough. We had...ah...a little dispute that got him so mad he went for his gun. Slower'n molasses in January. I drilled him twice while he was huntin' for his gun butt."

"He wasn't that slow," argued Linza. "You're just fast, Sy. How many guys work at bein' a gunfighter for seven years, killin' how many dudes?"

"Twenty-two."

"Killin' twenty-two dudes at quick-draw, then retire still unscathed to become a successful cattle rustler? How many, I ask ya?"

"Hey, boss!" came a voice from the porch. "Willis's here with the new man."

Moments later, Willis Day entered the cabin, followed by the man he had hired, and the two men from the porch, Barry Winkler and Jake Dill.

Day introduced Nate Bishop around, explaining for Woodard and Premro's benefit that Bishop had been a cellmate of his in a Texas jail a few years previously. Day had run onto Bishop while on a trip to North Platte a couple of weeks earlier. When Mixler killed Manny Kline a few days ago, Day had suggested that he ride to North Platte and see if Bishop wanted the job.

Whiskey bottles were passed around, and while everybody but Woodard and Premro imbibed, Mixler looked at Bishop and said, "I assume Willis has filled you in on our operation."

"Yeah," nodded Bishop, "but I wanna know why these two guys ain't drinkin' with us. They unsocial?"

"Nope," Willis Day said. "I told you we had two men workin' as ranch hands on the biggest spread hereabouts."

"Yeah. Circle M."

"Well, J.T. and Ray are the two who work on that spread. Dude that owns it is Corey McCollister. He's one o' them teetotalers. Won't let any of his ranch hands touch liquor. If J.T. and Ray smelled of this whiskey in the mornin', they'd get fired on the spot."

Mixler said, "Okay, Nate, let's see if you were listenin' when Willis told you about this operation. Tell me about it."

Nate Bishop tilted his hat to the back of his head and said, "You rustle cattle a few at a time to make the ranchers think the Indians are doin' it. Because this McCollister's spread is so big, you got Woodard and Premro to hire on a few months ago so they can cut a few head out of the main herd at sundown on certain days, and stash 'em in some gully in a makeshift corral so's the rest of the gang can come along and steal 'em after midnight."

Mixler smiled. "You're doin' fine. Proceed."

"Okay. The stolen cattle are driven by night to an obscure spot east of Hay Springs on the bank of the Niobrara River. You place the cattle on rafts, then float 'em east on the Niobrara to where it empties into the Missouri River, and market 'em to crooked cattle dealers at Yankton on the north bank of the Missouri."

Sy Mixler grinned at Willis. "Looks like you taught him well, my friend." Then to Bishop. "So you ready to go to work?"

"Yep. Percentage Willis quoted is fine by me."

"Good," grinned Mixler. "And you ain't above killin' somebody if we get backed in a corner."

"Not in the least."

Woodard and Premro filled the gang in on what part of the ranch they would be working in the next few days, then established when they would cut out part of the herd and where they would stash them. With that settled, the two stood to their feet to head back for the Circle M.

Mixler took a swig from his bottle and said, "You boys are doin' a great job. Keep it up."

"We plan to, boss," said Woodard. "And you know what's makin' it real fun?"

"What's that?"

"Them stinkin' Indians are gettin' the blame for all this thievin'!"

There was a round of laughter, then Corey McCollister's two newest hired hands rode away into the night.

CHAPTER SEVENTEEN

Jim Logan purchased five hundred acres of choice grassland some eight miles northwest of Hay Springs, putting his ranch but a few miles north of the Circle M. Since it was summer, he moved his family onto the property where they lived in a tent while neighboring ranchers helped him dig a well, and build a log house, barn, corral, tool shed, and privy. It was completed by the last week of July.

Among those to volunteer help were Corey McCollister, Curly Ford, Zachary Adams, and several other men from the Circle M ranch. When it was time for Merilee to move her family into the newly constructed house, some of the ranchers' wives and daughters came to help Merilee set up her home. Among them were Emily Grace and Taylor Ann McCollister. While the women hung curtains and arranged cupboards, the children enjoyed playing together.

Tyler McCollister and a boy his age named Danny Owens soon became fast friends with Benjamin Logan. They had a good time teasing the girls and finding ways to make them scream.

During that same six-week period, the Circle M lost another five dozen head of cattle. Corey McCollister was amazed that no Indians had been spotted riding on Circle M property during that time. He concluded they were doing their thievery at night.

Once the corral and barn were completed on the new Box L ranch, Jim Logan purchased a few saddle horses from a nearby horse dealer, then bought the cattle from Corey McCollister as planned. The cows and heifers were already bred and would calve in early spring. The cost of the land, buildings, tools, and livestock had run the Logan family funds low. There would be no cash coming in until they sold some of the young calves in mid-spring.

Wilson Rudd, the elderly proprietor of Hay Springs' general store, looked up to see Jim Logan enter the store with little Benjamin hanging onto his hand. Rudd was behind the counter, and at the moment there were no other customers.

"Afternoon, Jim," smiled the silver-haired man, then beckoned with a finger toward the dark-haired lad and said, "Come here, pal."

Benjamin was well-acquainted with the storekeeper, and had captured the old man's heart. Rudd knew the boy loved horehound candy, and always let him fill his pockets with it when he came into the store.

Benjamin rushed to Rudd, gave him a customary hug, and was allowed to begin stuffing his pockets. Jim, of course, would make sure his son did not eat all the candy at once.

While Benjamin loaded up on horehound, Rudd asked, "What can I get for you, Jim?"

Nervously, Jim cleared his throat and said, "Ah...I need a few things, Mr. Rudd, but I have to talk to you first."

Wilson Rudd had a warm and winning way about him. Smiling amiably, he said, "All right. What is it?"

"Well, sir...I...well, getting set up on the ranch has cost more than I anticipated, and...well, we're a little short of cash. It's goin' to be a long winter, but I'll have a good calf crop to sell come May. It's too late to plant a vegetable garden, and—"

"I'll grant you the credit, son," cut in Rudd.

"Thank you, sir. We'll get by on as little as possible during the winter, and I promise I'll pay my bill in full in May."

"Don't scrimp on food, now, Jim," said Rudd. "The Lord's been good to the likes o' me, and I can get by without the money till you sell your calf crop."

Tears were in Jim's eyes as he thanked the old man for his kindness, then handed him Merilee's list of items.

A half hour later, Jim and Benjamin arrived home with the groceries and the good news that Mr. Rudd had granted them credit until they sold off a portion of their young calves. There was rejoicing in the Logan household, and Jim's faith in the Lord's ability to provide was deepening.

Early in August, one of Corey McCollister's patrols sighted a small band of Cheyenne braves riding across Circle M property, and gave chase. Since no Indians had been seen on the ranch for a few weeks, Corey's orders were still to shoot over their heads if they were spotted.

Although the ranch hands were firing high, one bullet struck a brave in the shoulder. The brave fell from his horse, and the Circle M men held their fire while the other Indians picked him up.

It was close to sundown the following day when one of the Circle M hands spotted a band of two dozen Cheyenne warriors topping a rise and heading for the ranch house. One riding in the lead beside Chief Iron Hand was carrying a pole topped with a white flag.

Men in the bunkhouse and around the barn and corral were alerted, and soon were on the run toward the house, guns-in-hand.

It was customary in the McCollister household for the family to sit together on the porch in the warm weather and watch the sun go down. Corey and his family were on the porch when they heard Zachary Adams shouting that Indians were coming.

The McCollisters were on their feet, looking in the direction Zach was pointing. The Cheyenne were riding their pintos at a slow walk.

Shakily, Emily Grace said, "Taylor Ann, take your brother inside."

"No, E.G.," Corey said. "Let them stay. I want them to get a good look at these redskins up close...and I want Iron Hand to see that we don't fear him."

Emily Grace tried to erase the fear from her features as she gathered her children close to her, signaling for Tyler to remain absolutely still and quiet. Zach Adams bounded onto the porch, set anxious eyes on Taylor Ann, then sided Corey, who was standing on the top step, eyes glued on the Indians. The other ranch hands collected near the porch.

Corey read their uneasiness and said, "Easy, men. That white flag means they don't want trouble. Let's not give them any."

Curly Ford stood at the corner of the steps and said, "We'll remain cool as long as they remain peaceful, boss. But we're here just in case things get out of hand."

Chief Iron Hand sat his horse regally, his back straight as an arrow. He drew up with the flag carrier beside him, the others flanking him. The warriors were clad only in breechcloths, and the flare of the setting sun magnified the deep-bronze color of their skin. Each man wore a single eagle feather under a thin headband, a knife in a sheath on his waist, moccasins on his feet, and carried a repeater rifle.

Iron Hand wore a chieftain's multi-feathered headdress and a bead-studded leather vest. The headband that held the headdress on his head also held back from his dark, angular face the long black hair that dangled to his broad shoulders. He had a powerful upper body.

Iron Hand looked intently at Corey McCollister, lifted a

hand in a sign of peace, and spoke English with a deep guttural sound. "Though you and I have never met, Corey McCollister, I have heard enough to recognize you. I am Chief Iron Hand of the Cheyenne."

Raising his hand in the same gesture of peace, the rancher replied, "I also recognize you by description, Chief Iron Hand."

The air was tense as ranch hands and warriors eyed each other warily.

"You are great cattleman among the whites, Corey McCollister," Iron Hand said. "One does not need the eyes of an eagle to see that you are a noble leader of ranchers. One does not need the ears of a wolf to hear your name in this part of the world. I come to you, therefore, as one leader to another."

"I'm listening," nodded Corey, holding the chief's hard gaze with his own.

"It has come to my ears that you believe my braves steal your cattle. A few moons ago, your men shot at four of my braves as they rode on your property. Yesterday, they did this again, but this time, they wounded one of my braves. I am come to say that we do not steal your cattle, and to ask why we are not welcome to cross your land. We do it no harm."

"If your braves do not steal my cattle, why do they come up missing?"

"Maybe Crow steal your cattle, or maybe Blackfoot, but not Cheyenne."

At Emily Grace's side, Tyler felt the strain in the air and let out a squeal. All eyes turned that direction as Emily Grace attempted to calm the boy. Iron Hand stole a furtive glance at Taylor Ann, taking in the long shower of blond hair that fell over her shoulders and down her back almost to her hips.

"Is there some reason I should believe that it is not Cheyenne who are stealing my cattle?" Corey asked.

"Yes. Because Iron Hand says so! I am a man of my word, Corey McCollister. When I say it is not my people who are stealing your cattle, my honor is at stake. We do not steal your cattle. Because this is true, Iron Hand demands an apology for his brave being shot yesterday."

Bristling, Corey McCollister snapped, "I'm not about to apologize! Your men were trespassing on my property!"

The ranch hands tensed up, as did the warriors. On the porch, Emily Grace's heart was pounding. Tyler felt it, and ejected a tiny squeak. Taylor Ann motioned for him to keep still.

Eyes blazing, Iron Hand retorted, "What you call your property was Cheyenne property before white man came and took it from us!"

Emily Grace brushed up beside Corey and whispered, "Their honor means everything to them, Corey. Iron Hand is telling the truth. It is not his braves who are stealing our cattle. This conversation is getting you nowhere. It won't hurt for peace's sake to apologize for our men shooting his brave."

Corey's anger was kindled. He stubbornly replied so Iron Hand could hear, "This land is ours now! That's what counts! I'm not about to apologize. That Cheyenne wouldn't have been shot if he hadn't been trespassing. If the Cheyenne don't want to get shot, they should stay off our property!"

"I came in peace, white man!" Iron Hand said. "You greet me with the threat of being shot if I set foot on your land. If there is bloodshed, the grass will taste white man's blood as well as Indian's!"

Wheeling his pinto, the chief rode away.

While the ranch hands watched the Indians ride away, Emily Grace gripped her husband's arm and said with a shudder in her voice, "Corey, you saw the look in Iron Hand's eyes. There is going to be trouble. We don't have enough men to fight a hundred and fifty Cheyenne warriors!"

Corey patted her hand and said, "It'll be all right, honey. It'll be all right."

* * * * *

Several days passed with no Indian trouble. The Logan family arrived at the Circle M ranch house in their wagon at suppertime on August 11. Emily Grace had suggested to her husband that they invite the Logans for supper, and Corey agreed.

Meeting the Logans on the porch, Emily Grace welcomed their new neighbors and embraced Merilee. Jeremy and Darlene were all eyes, taking in the house, barn, bunkhouse, and other outbuildings. Emily Grace explained that Taylor Ann and Corey had gone into town with the usual Circle M escorts, and were due back momentarily. Merilee asked if she could help in the kitchen, and Jim volunteered to stay outside and play games with Tyler and Benjamin.

Corey and Taylor Ann arrived just before meal time and sadly announced that Wilson Rudd, proprietor of the general store, had suffered heart failure and died on August 6.

Jim asked if Corey knew who was going to take the store. Corey said that Mr. Rudd's daughter and son-in-law, George Nelson, had inherited it. The Nelsons were from some small town near the North Platte River, and were already in Hay Springs running the store. George knew the business well, having managed a general store in their home town for several years.

During the meal, Corey and Jim discussed the Indian problem, but Jim kept thinking about the death of Mr. Rudd. He wondered if the store's new owner would continue to extend credit until spring as Mr. Rudd had agreed to do.

It was nearly ten o'clock when the Logans climbed in their wagon and headed home by the light of a half-moon. As they drove, Jim told Merilee his concern. True to her nature, Merilee reminded her husband that the Lord had his hand on the Logan family. He had never failed them in the past, and He would not fail them now. Jim agreed, but inside was having another battle with his faith.

* * * * *

While the Logan family was on their way home, Sy Mixler and his gang of rustlers were on Box L land, stealing cattle. J.T. Woodard and Ray Premro had suggested to Mixler that since there was Indian trouble in the air, there was no time like the present to rustle greater numbers of cattle. Every ranch in the area was aware of Corey McCollister's unpleasant confrontation with Iron Hand. The blame for any rustling now would definitely fall on the Cheyenne.

That night, a hundred head of Circle M cattle were stolen from a wooded gully where Woodard and Premro had stashed them just after sundown. Three other ranches suffered a like loss. Jim Logan's Box L lost a hundred and two—all the cows and heifers, and both bulls.

Early the next morning, Jim and Jeremy Logan left the house with Jim carrying a bucket. They had bought a milk cow a few days earlier, and Jim was teaching his oldest son how to milk.

While father and son walked toward the barn, they were aware of the milk cow and the horses watching them from behind the pole fence in the corral. Jim let his eyes stray to the green fields that were now his property, and he felt uneasy. What was wrong? Something was definitely wrong. The cattle! Where were the cattle? There were always some within view from the house and barn, but not one was in sight.

Dashing thirty yards to the edge of the yard, Jim searched the rich grassland for any sign of his herd. Nothing. Running the same distance the opposite direction, he still could see no cattle. Hurrying back to Jeremy, he handed him the bucket, telling him to go ahead and milk the cow. He was going to saddle a horse and see if he could locate the cattle. Jeremy watched his father gallop away, then ushered the cow inside the barn.

Merilee and the three younger children stood with Jeremy on the front porch of their log house and watched for Jim to come home. He had been gone over two hours when little Susie pointed a finger off to the southeast and exclaimed, "There come Papa!"

A wagon was rambling toward the house with one person on the seat. "That's not Papa, Susie," corrected Darlene. "Jeremy said Papa's riding one of the horses."

The wagon was within two hundred yards when Jim came galloping in from the north. He hated to tell his family the bad news, but there was no choice. Sliding slowly from the saddle, he moved up to the porch, pale as a ghost, and said, "Merilee...kids...our cattle are gone. All of them. I talked to the neighbors east, west, and north of here. Three of them had cattle stolen last night...a hundred head each. That's not so bad for them. They've got plenty more. But for us, it's the loss of everything."

Merilee rushed to him and threw her arms around his neck. There were tears in her eyes. They were both silent for some time, then Merilee said softly, "The Lord knows all about this, Jim. He'll take care of us. Maybe we can get the army to come and help us find the herd."

"Not a chance. The army's too busy protecting humans to worry about animals."

"Well, we'll take this to the Lord. He cares about us, and he has allowed this to happen for a reason. We just have to—"

"What possible reason could there be for this? Why doesn't God quit pickin' on us?"

"Jim Logan!" Merilee gasped. "After the way He has come through for us so many times, how can you say such a thing?"

The wagon was drawing up, which took Jim's attention. He did not recognize the heavy-set, middle-aged man on the seat.

"Mr. Logan?" asked the man as he set the brake.

"Yes. What can I do for you?"

The man touched ground and stepped up to Jim. "I'm George Nelson, the new proprietor of the general store in town. I'm son-in-law to Wilson Rudd. I presume you know of his death."

"Yes, we know about it."

Producing a folded sheet of paper from his hip pocket, Nelson said, "I've come to talk to you about this bill at the store. It's almost sixty dollars!"

"I'm aware of that, Mr. Nelson. Your father-in-law and I had a gentleman's agreement. I can charge whatever my family and I need from now till next May, then when I sell—"

It struck Jim like a bolt of lightning. His cattle were gone. There would be no calf sale next spring.

Nelson cocked his head. "You were saying?"

A sick dread settled in Jim Logan's stomach. "I...uh...Mr. Nelson, your father-in-law had agreed to carry us on credit until our calf crop came in next spring. I was planning to sell off about half of them, but—"

"Yes?"

"Our entire herd was rustled by Cheyenne last night. We aren't the only ones. Three other ranches that I know of were hit for a hundred head apiece last night, also. There are probably others."

"Well, you and the other ranchers will be going after your cattle, won't you?"

"No, sir."

"Why not?"

"Because there are more Indians than there are white men, that's why. We would only get scalped for our effort."

Nelson rubbed his chin and let his features settle like stone. "Well, I'm sorry about your problem, Mr. Logan, but I must insist that this bill be paid in full immediately."

"Mr. Nelson, I—"

"Even if your cattle hadn't been stolen, Mr. Logan, I would still demand payment immediately. I don't believe in credit. My philosophy is if you can't afford it, don't buy it on credit. Man only gets himself deep in debt using credit." Turning toward his wagon, he said over his shoulder, "I want the money in my hands by noon."

Jim started toward him. "Mr. Nelson, there's no way I can come up with the money by noon! You've got to give me time to—"

"Time is what you need?" blared Nelson.

"Yes. I've got to—"

"All right. I'll give you a week. If I don't have fifty-nine dollars and thirteen cents in my hand by a week from today, you're in real trouble!"

Jim stood there with a pounding of hammers inside his skull. A scream came up from somewhere deep within him, but he stifled it. He wanted to run away, but it was like a nightmare in which his legs had turned to lead. He couldn't move.

George Nelson settled in the wagon seat, set hard, uncompromising eyes on the devastated man, pointed a stiff forefinger at him, and thundered, "One week! One week, or else!"

As the wagon pulled away, the dam burst inside Jim Logan. He stomped forward, a look of sheer rage on his face. He screamed at the top of his lungs, *"You heartless beast! My wife and children won't have anything to eat! Don't you care, you vile devil!"*

George Nelson drove away without looking back.

"Jim," Merilee said, squeezing his arm to get his attention. "We'll be all right. Haven't we seen the Lord come through for us before?"

Jim pulled his gaze from the bounding wagon and looked down into Merilee's eyes. "What?"

"I said haven't we seen the Lord come through for us before? Like when Mr. Sturgis died, then we learned he had left us sixteen thousand dollars? And when those men kidnapped Benjamin and took all our money, the Lord sent John Stranger to get them both back for us? And when He sent John Stranger when we were under Cheyenne attack?"

Jim Logan clenched his teeth and silently nodded.

Pressing him for his own good, Merilee said, "Need I remind you how utterly ashamed you are when the Lord comes through and you look back and remember how you doubted him? Don't doubt him now, darling. Your children are watching."

Jim clenched his fists, fought the bitterness that was trying to claim him, and looked at his four offspring, who stood in a row, eyeing him carefully. Swallowing hard, he moved to them and said with choked voice, "I'm sorry, kids. I love you and your mama very much, and I can't stand the thought of you going hungry."

"We love you, too, Papa," said Darlene.

"Thank you, sweetheart. That means a lot to me right now."

"Papa," Jeremy said, "Jesus said He'd never leave us nor forsake us. Do you think He'll keep His Word?"

"You're right, son, He did make us that promise, didn't He. I think maybe we should talk to Him about that right now."

Then the distraught husband and father led his family in prayer, asking the Lord to help him to provide for them, and to strengthen his faith that he might be the proper example to his wife and children.

In the next couple of days word spread among the ranchers that other herds had been hit for a hundred head of cattle, including the Circle M. The ranchers got together and talked about what to do. They could bring Iron Hand to a showdown and demand their cattle back, but to do so would no doubt bring on a bloody battle with the Cheyenne. There was a chance that the Crow and the Blackfoot would join with Iron Hand. If that happened, many if not all of their families would be massacred. All they could do was hope the Indians were satisfied, and would leave off stealing their cattle.

Jim Logan attended the meeting, but no one mentioned his total loss. He saw no reason to bring it up.

During the next few days, Logan hunted game, large and small, to provide meat for his family, but he was keenly aware that their staples were running low, and that they had no fruits or vegetables.

The pressure mounted as George Nelson's deadline drew near. He had three days to go.

The Logans prayed together daily, and Jim rode to ranch after ranch in search of work, but no one needed an extra hand, not even the Circle M.

When he was down to two days, Jim returned to the Circle M with something else in mind. As he dismounted in front of the ranch house, a couple of cowpokes were passing by on range ponies and told him they had heard of his plight. They spoke encouraging words, then rode on.

Emily Grace answered Jim's knock and welcomed him. When he told her he was back to talk to Corey again, she led him to the den where Corey was doing some paper work at his desk. Remaining at the door, Emily Grace observed as Jim Logan asked her husband to let him have more cattle on a loan basis. He explained the pressure he was under from George Nelson, saying that if he had another herd that could give him calves next spring, he could possibly talk Nelson into waiting till then for his money. Once Jim was on his feet, he would pay Corey for the cattle.

Corey McCollister refused. It was too shaky. Such a venture was not good business practice. He would suggest that Jim take his problem to the Hay Springs Bank, but with only five hundred acres and a few buildings, they would surely turn him down. The bankers in town were known for being hard to deal with. Jim had already asked another rancher about that possibility, and had been told the same thing. The bank was out.

Jim then asked McCollister if he would loan him the amount he needed to pay the bill at the general store. As soon as he found work, he would begin paying him back. Corey turned him down on that, also, saying such a deal was too shaky.

Jim thanked the wealthy rancher for his time and headed for the door, dejected and angry. Emily Grace walked with him, then hurried back to the den. Giving her husband a hot look, she said, "Corey, we have so much, and the Logans are hard against it.

Besides, Jim is your Christian brother. Why didn't you let him have the cattle? And if you've got a good reason for turning him down on that, why couldn't you at least have loaned him the money to get George Nelson off his back?"

Corey rose to his feet, took hold of his wife's hands, and said, "Nobody helped us when we came here, sweetheart. But we trusted the Lord and put some blood, sweat, and tears into this place and made a go of it. If I met either of Jim's requests, I'd be doing him a disservice. When he trusts the Lord and sweats it out, then makes it, he'll be a stronger Christian and a better man for it."

Emily Grace looked him square in the eye and said in a steady voice, "Corey McCollister, you know I seldom disagree with you. But this time you're wrong. Jim's desperate and desperate men do desperate things. I hope you don't live to regret your decision."

Jim Logan was about to mount his horse when he saw Zachary Adams trotting toward him, waving his hat. "Wait up, Jim!" he called.

"What can I do for you, my friend?" Jim asked.

"It's not what you can do for me. It's what I can do for you."

"Oh?"

"Everybody on the ranch knows about the loss of your herd. I've been thinking that you're probably low on cash. So...I'd like to help a little."

As he spoke, Zach produced a thin wad of green bills from his pocket. "Here's thirty dollars."

Jim felt his mouth go dry. Shaking his head, he said, "Zach, that's a month's wages for you! I can't let you do this."

"I want to be sure you and your family have food on the table. Take it."

"Zach, I can't. You worked hard for—"

"If I was the Lord Jesus standing here offering you this money, would you take it?"

"Well...sure."

"Then take it. Everything that's mine belongs to Him. So you see, in a sense it *is* Him offering it to you. It's His money."

Jim Logan had no answer for this argument. Tears filled his eyes as he took the money. "Thank you, Zach," he said, lips trembling.

"Don't thank me. Thank Jesus. Like I said, it's His money."

As Jim Logan galloped toward home, he indeed was thanking the Lord for the thirty dollars that would put food on the table. With tears running down his cheeks, he asked for forgiveness, saying once more how ashamed he was that he had doubted the veracity and the ability of his God to keep His promises and meet the needs of His own.

"And Lord, I know that somehow You will provide the money to pay Mr. Nelson...or make him willing to wait till I can find work and pay him."

There was joy in the Logan household when Jim entered the house and showed them the thirty dollars. Jim would go into town the next day and load up on groceries. While he was out, he would stop at more ranches and see if anyone was hiring.

CHAPTER EIGHTEEN

After breakfast the next morning, Taylor Ann McCollister hoisted her little brother onto the seat of a Circle M wagon in front of the house, then allowed Zach Adams to help her up.

Zach didn't like having even Tyler McCollister between himself and the woman he loved, but he smiled at the boy as he settled in the seat and mouthed slowly, "Good mornin', Ty. Goin' to town with big sister, huh?"

Tyler clapped his hands and squealed.

As the wagon pulled away, young Adams turned around on the seat to check the eight riders loping toward them from the corral. "Looks like we've got our escort," he said, squaring around.

"I hope we don't need them," Taylor Ann said. "I'm still nervous about Iron Hand."

"Yeah. Me, too," admitted Zach.

Ty pointed at a large jackrabbit as it bounded across the wagon's path. Tapping his sister's knee to get her attention, he made long ears with his fingers next to his head and laughed. Zach and Taylor Ann laughed with him.

They rode silently for a few minutes, then Zach asked, "So what are we going to town for today?"

"Oh, I'm to pick up some staples and some new dress material for Mother that she ordered from back East. Sure hope it's in. She's eager to get started on it."

"You suppose the general store will do as well with Mr. Rudd's daughter and son-in-law running it?"

"I would think so. Mr. Nelson is well-experienced in the business, I understand."

Again they rode in silence, then Taylor Ann looked at him and said, "Zach, I appreciate what you did for Jim Logan yesterday."

Zach's eyebrows arched as he looked at her past Tyler and asked, "What do you mean?"

"You know what I mean, silly. I was watching out the window and I saw you give him some money. That was very generous and thoughtful of you."

Shrugging, the young cowhand said, "It was really the Lord's money. Everything I have is His."

"You're sweet," she said softly. "If Tyler wasn't between us, I'd kiss your cheek."

Zach surprised Ty by quickly picking him up and putting him on his lap. Without looking at her, he said, "He isn't between us anymore."

Sliding over and planting a tender kiss on his cheek, Taylor Ann said, "There. That's for giving some of the Lord's money to a family that really needs it."

Zach replaced Ty between them, then touched the spot on his cheek and said, "I'll never wash this side of my face again."

"Oh, Zach, you're impossible!"

"I work at it," he chuckled.

Riding quietly again, Taylor Ann stole a secret glance at the man who held the reins. His kindness toward Jim Logan had raised him a notch in her eyes. She wished her father was more kind and generous, and found herself silently praying to that end.

When they reached Hay Springs, the eight riders scattered,

saying they would meet Zach and Taylor Ann at the general store in an hour. Zach said he would do some errands, too. After helping Taylor Ann out of the wagon and setting Ty on the ground, he headed down the street.

Intending to take Tyler inside the store with her, Taylor Ann took him by the hand and headed for the door. Ty's little friend Danny Owens came running up, making hand signals at Ty. The two boys greeted each other in their own way, then Danny looked up at Taylor Ann and said, "Hi. Are you goin' in the gen'ral store?"

"Yes, I am," she nodded.

"Can Ty stay out here and play with me? My mommy's over there."

Taylor Ann saw Letha Owens sitting on a bench a few yards down the boardwalk. She was in conversation with another young woman who sat beside her. "Well, let's ask her if she minds," said Taylor Ann, moving that direction.

Greeting both women, Taylor Ann said, "Danny wants to know if Ty can play out here with him while I'm in the general store, Letha. I won't be too long. Is that all right with you?"

"By all means," smiled Danny's mother. "I'll be here an hour or so. It'll be nice to have Danny occupied for a while."

"All right. I'll see you in a little while." Then getting Tyler's attention, Taylor Ann signed that he must be good and do what Mrs. Owens says.

Ty agreed, and hugged his sister.

The boys were already laughing and chasing each other up and down the boardwalk and into the shadowed space between buildings when Taylor Ann turned to head for the general store. She stopped abruptly, finding herself face-to-face with a smiling Deputy Marshal Bob Osborne.

"Oh, hello!" she gasped. "Nice to see you, Bob."

"Nicer to see you, pretty lady. I was hoping to see you today. Wanted to ask if we could go ridin' this comin' Sunday afternoon."

"Oh," she said, putting a hand to her cheek. "I've already got a riding date for this Sunday with Zach."

"How about the next Sunday, then?"

"All right," she said cheerfully. "It's a date."

"Good," he responded, smiling broadly. "I'll look forward to it."

Bob and Taylor Ann were unaware that Zach Adams was watching them from inside one of the stores.

Taylor Ann and the deputy discussed the Indian problem for a moment. While they talked, she noticed Jim Logan pull his wagon up beside the Circle M vehicle and go into the general store.

Inside the store, Jim approached George Nelson, who stood behind the counter, and said, "Good morning, Mr. Nelson. A friend of mine gave me thirty dollars to buy some groceries for my family."

"What about my fifty-nine dollars and thirteen cents?"

With his faith running high, Jim replied, "I've still got another day. You'll get your money. Right now, my family needs some groceries."

"Too bad you have to buy 'em from a heartless beast," clipped Nelson, scowling. "I couldn't make out the other thing you called me, but I think it was a devil or somethin' like it."

Jim's features tinted. "I was upset, Mr. Nelson. I'm sorry."

"Before I haul out the thirty dollars worth of groceries, I want to see the money."

Pulling the bills from his pocket, Jim fanned them out so the man could see the full amount."

"Okay," mumbled Nelson. "What do you want?"

Reading from Merilee's list, Jim made his order and Nelson began placing the items on the counter.

While this was going on, Taylor Ann followed two male customers into the store and made her way quietly around the L-shaped corner, looking to see if the material her mother had ordered was in. George Nelson placed the last article on the counter and set heavy eyes on Logan. "Comes to twenty-eight dollars and seventy-six cents."

Jim handed him the thirty dollars and said, "I'll use the change to buy my children some candy, Mr. Nelson."

"You ain't gettin' no change, and you ain't gettin' these groceries, either. I'm puttin' this thirty dollars on your bill. Now you only owe me twenty-nine dollars and thirteen cents."

Jim looked at him in disbelief. "You're not serious."

"Serious as I know how to be," muttered Nelson.

"But...my wife and children are home waiting for me to bring them something to eat. You can't do this."

"Whattya mean I can't? I own this store, and you have a delinquent bill of fifty-nine dollars and thirteen cents. You just paid me thirty dollars on the bill. You'll get no groceries from this establishment until the rest of it is paid."

Jim Logan's features went rigid. "I'm takin' these groceries home to my family!"

"You try it and I'll call the marshal!" boomed Nelson.

Jim's temper went out of control. He lunged for Nelson, seizing him by the shirt with both hands. With one powerful, quick jerk, he brought him over the counter, scattering grocery items every direction.

George Nelson found himself on the floor with an enraged father of four pounding him with his fists.

Taylor Ann McCollister observed the incident by peeking around the corner.

The two male customers were all over Logan, wrestling him to the floor. A woman started to enter the store, but froze when she saw what was going on.

One of the men who was wrestling with Logan shouted for her to summon the marshal. In less than fifteen seconds, Deputy Osborne bolted through the door. When he saw Logan still fighting, he pulled his gun, cocked the hammer, and pointed it at him.

"That's it, Logan! Give it up! Now!"

Jim ceased struggling and slowly rose to his feet. The two men were helping George Nelson up.

"Now, what's goin' on here?" demanded Osborne, easing the hammer down and holding the revolver loosely.

The proprietor was bloodied and shaking his head in an attempt to clear it.

Jim Logan explained his desperate situation, told about Zach Adams giving him the thirty dollars, and described how Nelson had tricked him to get his hands on the money.

Dabbing at his bloody nose, Nelson stumbled to the counter, opened a drawer, and pulled out Logan's bill. Jim started to explain about his gentlemen's agreement with Mr. Rudd, but Osborne snapped at him, telling him to shut up.

Still unnoticed at the back of the store, Taylor Ann bit her lips.

Osborne looked at the bill and set hard eyes on Logan. "Here's proof you owe the money. Mr. Nelson had every right to take the thirty dollars and apply it to your bill."

"But my family needs food," spoke up Jim. "I have to—"

"Shut up!" rasped Osborne. Turning to the proprietor, he asked, "You want to press charges?"

George Nelson wanted a good image in Hay Springs. This story would get out. Holding the bloody handkerchief so it was clearly visible, he said, "No. Mr. Logan just lost control for a few minutes. If he will leave quietly, I'll not press charges."

"Consider yourself lucky, mister," Osborne said. "You could've done a stint in jail. Go on. Get out."

There was still fire in Jim Logan's bones. Without a word, he headed for the door.

Nelson called after him, "Twenty-nine dollars and thirteen cents tomorrow, Logan!"

Jim did not look back. The anger inside him was thunder in his ears.

Taylor Ann had found three bolts of material her mother had ordered. She rounded the corner carrying one of them. Bob Osborne's face blanched when he saw her. Burning him with her eyes, she stomped to the counter and slammed the bolt down. George Nelson had met Corey McCollister, but had not yet laid eyes on his daughter.

Osborne started to speak when Taylor Ann's voice stung him like a hornet. "Don't say it, Bob! I saw and heard it all. That poor man has been stolen blind by the Cheyenne. All he's trying to do is keep food on the table for his wife and four children!"

While Osborne was still searching for the right words, the angry young woman put her attention on the proprietor, who was standing behind the counter, dabbing at his bleeding nose. "And *you*, sir, are despicable! I heard enough from Jim to know that he and Mr. Rudd had some kind of agreement about his bill. Where's your sense of decency? What is that in your chest that's supposed to be a heart? A chunk of ice?"

Bristling, Nelson said, "Now, see here, young lady, you have no business coming in here and—"

"Speaking of business, my father could open up a general store in this town any day he wanted to. When he finds out the way you treat your customers, he's just liable to do it! He's known and respected in this area, mister. He'd get all of the business, and you'd be out of business!"

Nelson looked at Osborne, who's face was sheet-white, then back at the nineteen-year-old and asked, "Just who is your father?"

"Corey McCollister," she replied proudly.

Nelson's jaw slacked. "Oh."

"That was an awful mean thing to do, Mr. Nelson," she proceeded. "Letting poor Jim think he was going to get the groceries until you got your claws on his money."

"But Taylor Ann," Osborne said, "Mr. Nelson showed me the bill. It's right there on the counter. Take a look at it. You didn't hear Jim deny he owed it, did you?"

"No, but I heard you tell him to shut up when he tried to explain that he and Mr. Rudd had some kind of agreement about it! You're as despicable as this sorry excuse for a human being behind the counter!"

"But, Taylor Ann, I had to take Mr. Nelson's part in this. I saw the bill."

Ignoring him, she turned to Nelson and asked, "Do you want to sell me this bolt of material my mother ordered, or should I go home and tell my parents you don't want their business anymore?"

Nelson swallowed with difficulty. "Of course I'll sell it to you, Miss McCollister. Is...is there anything else?"

"Yes," she replied, pulling a small slip of paper from her purse. "I also need these items."

"I'll get them for you right away," said Nelson, giving her a faint smile.

While the nervous proprietor was filling the order, Bob Osborne moved close to her and said, "Taylor Ann, I had to stand for Mr. Nelson. When I saw the bill, I—"

"Get away from me! You were totally unreasonable with Jim. That badge on your chest isn't a license to mistreat people."

"But, I—"

"Don't say anymore, Deputy Osborne. This ends it. Our riding date is off, and so is anything else that might have developed between us. As far as I'm concerned, the next time I see you it'll be too soon."

Bob Osborne stood dumbfounded, wishing he could undo what he had done.

Jim Logan left the general store in a half-crazed state of mind. The cupboards in the Logan household were almost bare, and he had to go home without any groceries. Bitterness welled up within him.

Forgotten were the times God had come through for him and his family when it seemed all hope was gone. Forgotten was the shame he had felt for doubting each time. Forgotten was the faith he had that the Lord was going to work out the problem in His own wise and wonderful way.

Jim Logan was mad at Corey McCollister for refusing to help him. He was mad at George Nelson for tricking him out of his money. He was mad at Bob Osborne for refusing to hear his side of the story. He couldn't stand the thought of having to look at the hungry faces of his children. Jim was mad at the whole world, and felt that God had let him down.

In the grip of despair and blind with rage, he headed for his wagon. His eye fell on the Hay Springs Bank up the street. For an instant, he considered going in there and making a withdrawal at gunpoint, then shook his head. It wasn't right, and he would never get away with it anyway.

What was he going to do? Where would he get the money to feed his family?

He climbed into the wagon and took hold of the reins. His hands were shaking. Gritting his teeth, he snapped the reins and put the wagon into motion. Suddenly his eye caught sight of little Tyler McCollister playing with Danny Owens. A grotesque thought flashed into his clouded mind.

Jim Logan drove to the next intersection and quickly turned the corner.

Danny Owens, laughing with glee, came running to his mother where she sat on the bench, talking now to two women. "Mommy! Ty's chasing me! He's gonna get me!"

"That's nice, honey," said Letha Owens, hardly paying him any mind.

Danny looked back, expecting his little friend to come darting from the shadowed space between the buildings. When Ty did not appear, Danny ran back to find him. Reaching the corner of the closest building, he giggled, expecting Ty to lunge from the shadows and squeal at him.

Peering around the corner into the deep shade, he could see all the way to the sunlit alley. There was no sign of his friend.

Danny ran the length of the frame structures and into the sunlight. He looked up and down the alley. There was some activity behind one of the stores where two men were unloading a wagon load of goods, but there was no sign of Ty McCollister.

Was Ty hiding from him? *That's it,* he thought. *He wants me to come find him.*

Danny hopped and skipped down the alley all the way to the street, but Ty didn't leap out at him. Turning around, he went up the alley the opposite way, expecting to have his friend jump out at him from behind a wooden crate or trash receptacle. When he reached the men who were unloading the wagon, they spoke to him, asking if he was looking for something.

"I'm looking for my friend," he told them. "Did you see a little boy about my size with yellow hair come this way?"

"Sure didn't," said one of the men. "We've been here for a half hour, but we haven't seen him."

"Maybe my friend came by when you were carrying those boxes inside."

"I suppose you're right about that, kid. Guess he could've done that."

Danny ran to the street at that end of the alley, but still there was no Ty. Worried, he dashed to the corner, jumped on the boardwalk, and ran past the stores and shops to his mother, who was on her feet, talking to Ty's big sister.

"There you are, Danny," said Letha Owens with relief. "Where's Ty? Taylor Ann is ready to go home."

"I don't know where he is, Mommy. I've been trying to find him. I looked in the alley all the way to both streets, but he isn't there."

Taylor Ann bent down to Danny's level and asked, "Where did you see him last?"

Pointing to the shadowed opening between the buildings, Danny said, "Back there. He was in the alley, an' I came running this way, thinking he was chasing me. When I went back, he was gone."

Panic gripped Taylor Ann. Without a word, she hoisted her skirt, dashed to the open space between the buildings, and disappeared. Letha and the two women hurried to the dark space in time to see the worried sister turn up the sunlit alley. By the time the women and Danny reached the alley, Taylor Ann was coming toward them, an anxious look on her face.

Taylor Ann's breathing was heavy, like a frightened animal, as she said, "I can't find him! Something's happened to my little brother! I'm going to Marshal Luskin!"

Within minutes Taylor Ann had the marshal, the deputy, the Circle M riders, Zach Adams, and a number of townspeople in search of her little brother.

In his world of silence, Tyler McCollister bounced on the seat of the wagon, laughing with glee. To him, the abduction was merely a fun ride with his friend, Jim Logan. He liked the warm wind in his face. Looking up at Jim, who drove the team at full speed, Tyler made a hand signal. Jim did not know what Ty was telling him, but by the happy look on his face, he knew the boy was anything but frightened.

Rapid thoughts raced through Jim Logan's mind. He would write an anonymous note, demanding a ransom for Tyler's safe return. Not that he would harm a hair of the boy's head, but he must convince Corey McCollister to fear Ty's abductor. No longer would Jim Logan's family live under the threat of hunger and need.

Jim would stash Tyler in the tool shed, which was a safe distance from the house. Merilee and the children never went to the tool shed. Jim would find a way to supply the boy with food and water. Once Corey McCollister had delivered the ransom money to a designated spot and Jim had picked it up, he would—

Suddenly the fog in Jim Logan's brain was gone.

What had he done?

Terror replaced the cloud that had been in his brain. What kind of lunacy had overtaken him? Jim Logan, a Christian man, had done a horrible, unthinkable thing!

A wave of nausea swept over him. He sagged on the seat, letting the reins go limp in his clammy hands. The horses slowed to a walk, then came to a stop. Ty McCollister studied his friend with quizzical eyes, knowing something was wrong, but helpless to even say a comforting word.

Jim Logan slumped forward with his hands pressed against the front board of the wagon box. Exhaustion claimed him. He exhaled a shaky, sighing breath. He felt Tyler's eyes on him.

Jim couldn't find the courage to turn and look at the boy. He lashed himself mentally. What a stupid, foolish thing he had done. Even if he could have pulled the abduction off and not been caught, there was no way he could have spent the money anywhere in Hay Springs. Nor could he have moved away without arousing suspicion. Marshal Jed Luskin would have caught on and had him behind bars. He would be the shame of the community.

And Merilee...what would she think of him? And what would his children think? And what did his God think of him now?

Jim Logan wept, begging the Lord to forgive him. When he brought his emotions under control, he felt a small hand on his shoulder. Ty was looking at him with compassion, trying to comfort him by patting his shoulder.

Jim took the child in his arms, held him close, and wept again. The deed was done, and it couldn't be undone. He thought of Taylor Ann back in town. The girl must be terrified, and no doubt had reported Tyler missing to the marshal. There would be dozens of people searching for him.

Jim was against a blank wall. What should he do? There was forest land ahead of him. He would drive into the forest and try to collect his thoughts.

Moments later, Jim parked the wagon beside a gurgling stream deep in the woods. Sliding from the seat, he lifted little Ty down. The boy spotted several squirrels nearby and ran after them, squealing as they skittered up the trunk of a huge cottonwood.

Jim sank down by the edge of the stream and buried his face in his hands.

CHAPTER NINETEEN

Chief Iron Hand and a dozen braves were riding over the rolling green hills a few miles north of Hay Springs. A hundred yards ahead of them lay a heavily wooded area, which was bisected by a stream as it wended its way through the rich grassland.

The chief was telling his braves that his mother had now passed her time of mourning over the death of his father. She would be open to his plans for marriage.

A brave named Spotted Coyote, who was a close friend of Iron Hand, asked, "Is Iron Hand going to choose his bride from among our maidens, or is he still interested in the white rancher's daughter?"

Iron Hand set dark eyes on his friend. Giving him a half-smile, he responded, "I cannot get the young woman with sunshine hair out of my mind. I must have her for my squaw."

Another brave said, "You will have to steal her, my chief. Her father will never give her to you."

Iron Hand nodded. "Yes. I will find a way to take her from her father. No white man dares set foot inside a Cheyenne village. Once I have her in our village, Corey McCollister can never get her back."

Standing Antelope pointed past the forest southward. "There's a wagon coming."

Not wanting to be seen, the Cheyenne quickly galloped their pintos into the deep shadows of the forest, then watched as the wagon came closer. Soon it was evident that the wagon was headed for the woods, also.

The Indians waited in their secluded spot, eyes fixed on the approaching vehicle. It would pass into the woods barely twenty yards from where they sat their horses.

Suddenly Iron Hand recognized Tyler McCollister on the wagon seat with the driver, whom he assumed was a Circle M man. The chief smiled to himself and said to Spotted Coyote, "That's Corey McCollister's son—the boy with ears that do not hear and mouth that does not speak. My problem is solved. We will kill the driver and take the boy. Once the boy is secure in our village, I will send braves to Corey McCollister with this message: If Corey McCollister will send his daughter to be Iron Hand's bride, the boy will be returned unharmed. If Corey McCollister refuses...the boy will die.

The wagon headed into the woods, and the Indians followed.

With his emotions strung tight, Jim Logan was sitting on the bank of the shallow stream watching Tyler McCollister chase squirrels and birds a few yards away. *As if things weren't bad enough, James Logan, you had to go and pull a stupid thing like this!*

Distasteful as the thought was, Jim knew there was only one thing to do. He would take Ty back to Taylor Ann in town, confess his foolish deed, and suffer the consequences. He knew the Lord had forgiven him, but the law and Corey McCollister might find forgiveness more difficult.

Jim dreaded what Merilee and his children would think of him...and worse yet what would happen to them if he went to prison. It might even mean execution. He knew of kidnappers who had been hanged.

Sick with what he knew he had to do, Jim rose to his feet. Tyler was on the bank upstream a few yards. When the boy looked at him, he motioned and pointed to the wagon, signifying that it was time to go. Ty squealed and clapped his hands, darting toward the wagon.

At the same instant, Logan's skin crawled as he saw the Indians come out of the surrounding shadows. One of them snatched up the boy. Jim went for the revolver on his hip, but before he could grab it, an arrow hissed through the air and struck him in the chest. He fell flat on his back in the four-inch depth of the stream.

There was only numbness where the arrow was buried in his chest, but Jim couldn't move. He heard Ty's screams of terror fading away as the Cheyenne put their horses to a gallop.

"Oh, dear Lord, no," he gasped. "No...no...no!"

A black curtain descended over him.

There was turmoil in Hay Springs. Corey and Emily Grace McCollister had been summoned to town with the news that their son was missing. The town and the immediate area had been thoroughly searched. This ruled out the possibility that the boy had simply wandered off to play by himself. There was no question that he had been abducted.

Forty of the Circle M's hands were scouring the hills in every direction, along with over a hundred men from Hay Springs.

Emily Grace sat in the marshal's office, arms around her daughter, as Corey paced back and forth, telling Marshal Jed Luskin there had to be something else they could do.

"Corey," said Luskin, who was seated behind his desk, "I'm telling you...there is nothing else we can do! We've got nearly a hundred and fifty men out there looking for Ty. They'll look behind every bush and search every ranch house and outbuilding. Now, I'll repeat what I said a few minutes ago. I want you to think, and think hard. Who would want to kidnap your son?"

Wringing his hands as he paced, Corey said, "I can't think of anybody, Jed. As far as I know, we don't have any enemies."

"What about ransom?" offered Luskin.

Corey stopped. With searching eyes, he looked at the marshal and said, "Jed, this isn't back East. I mean, scoundrels in the big cities kidnap wealthy people's children for ransom...but this is Nebraska! This is cattle country!"

"Well, in case you haven't noticed," said Luskin, "we've got some scoundrels in these parts, too."

"Like who?"

"Like the scoundrels who've been stealing cattle from you and the other ranchers around here."

"The Cheyenne? They don't want money! Why would they kidnap my boy? Besides, if Indians had come in here and grabbed Ty from an alley, people would've seen them. You know that, and I know that. No, Jed, it wasn't Indians. It's white men...and you're probably right. Somebody'll be showing up pretty soon with a ransom note."

Corey went to his wife and daughter, and embraced them both at the same time. "Don't worry," he said. "We'll get Ty back. If we have to pay a ransom, then we'll pay it. But we'll get him back. And once we do, I'll hound the dirty kidnappers till I find them. They'll pay dearly for putting us through this!"

Jim Logan felt the piercing rays of the sun assault his eyelids. Opening his eyes, he blinked against the sun's light. It was high noon.

Suddenly it all came back. Tyler! The Indians riding away with him. The arrow in his chest. The cool water flowing over his body.

Jim was abruptly aware that he was no longer in the water. He was lying on the bank of the stream. And there was no arrow in his chest. Was this the tail end of some kind of nightmare? He tried to sit up, but felt a sharp stab of pain where the arrow had been.

The pain was high in his upper right chest. With his left hand, he probed the area of the wound and found it to be covered with cloth. A bandage? Who—

"So you're back amongst the living?" came a familiar voice. At the same time, a shadow passed over Jim's face, blocking the sun.

Jim Logan was shocked to see the dark, angular features of the man who had come to his rescue twice before. "John Stranger!" he gasped. "How did you find me?"

"Good thing I did," John said, hunkering down beside him. "If I hadn't, you'd have bled to death by now."

"You took the arrow out."

"Mm-hmm."

"Bandaged me up."

"Well, sort of temporarily. Soon as you can get in that wagon, I'll drive you into town. Doc Getz can do it up professionally. The arrow hit you high enough that it didn't puncture the lung. No bone broken. Give it a few weeks, and you'll be back to normal."

Jim's thoughts went to little Tyler McCollister, and he was about to tell Stranger what had happened when the tall man asked, "Why'd the Cheyenne attack you?"

"How did you know they were Cheyenne?"

"The arrow. Every tribe has its own way of feathering arrows and spears."

"Of course. Let me see if I can sit up, and I'll tell you what this is all about."

Stranger helped the wounded man to a sitting position. Then Jim told his mysterious friend his story, beginning with the loss of his cattle and concluding with his abduction of Tyler McCollister. He confessed to Stranger how foolish he had been, then explained how he and Tyler ended up in the forest. The last thing he remembered before passing out was the sound of the little deaf mute's pitiful wail as the Indians took him away.

"Why would they want the boy?" asked Stranger.

"I have no idea. But we'd better get into town so I can confess this thing to Marshal Luskin. Ty's parents may even be there by now. I'll have to face Corey sooner or later. Just as well get it over with."

Corey McCollister was pacing the floor of the marshal's office, waiting for some contact from Ty's kidnaper, when he looked through the open door and saw Jim Logan's wagon roll by with Jim sitting in the bed and a stranger on the seat holding the reins.

He moved to the door and said over his shoulder, "Something's happened to Jim Logan."

"What do you mean?" queried Emily Grace, dashing to the door.

"Some man I don't know is driving Jim's wagon. Jim's sitting in the bed, and there's a big black horse tied on behind. Looked like Jim's shoulder was bandaged, and they're stopping in front of Doc Getz's clinic."

"I'll go see what's goin' on," said Luskin.

"I'll go with you," Corey said, moving through the door.

"Let's all go," spoke up Emily Grace.

The McCollisters and Marshal Luskin arrived at the clinic just as John Stranger was helping the wounded Jim Logan into the examining room. They crowded at the examining room door. Dr. Gerald Getz was standing by the table, ready to examine the wound.

"Wait here," said Luskin to the McCollisters. "I'll see what I can find out."

The McCollisters backed away from the door, and Luskin closed it as he moved into the examining room.

"All right if I talk to Jim, Doc?" asked the marshal.

"He seems well enough," nodded Getz.

Moving closer, Luskin said, "Howdy, Mr. Stranger. Didn't think we'd see you around here any more."

"Never know," the tall man said softly.

Logan was flat on his back as Dr. Getz began to remove the bandage.

"What happened, Jim?" Luskin asked.

"Took a Cheyenne arrow."

"They just attack you for no reason?"

"Not exactly," replied Jim, his mouth going dry. "Did I see Corey McCollister out there in the waiting room?"

"Yeah. Why?"

"I have something I need to tell him about Tyler's disappearance."

Luskin's eyes widened. "You know about that?"

Looking up at the physician, Jim asked, "Can you work on me while I talk to Corey, Doc?"

"Of course," nodded Dr. Getz. "There's nothing to do here but put on another bandage. John did as good a job as I could do, stitching up the wound."

"You want me outta the room, Jim?" Luskin asked.

"No, Marshal. It's best that you be in here, too."

"Mrs. McCollister and Taylor Ann are out there. You want them to come in?"

"Might as well. They need to hear what I have to say, too."

As Luskin left to bring the McCollisters in, Jim looked up at Stranger and said shakily, "I wouldn't be upset at you if you'd pray for me. This is going to be rough."

Stranger nodded and gave him a slight smile. "The Lord can make order of out chaos, Jim. He may not do it as fast as you'd like, but trust Him."

Jim bit his lip. "This will give Him a challenge. I've really made a mess of things this time."

The McCollisters gathered around the table with Marshal Luskin. Emily Grace and Taylor Ann noted the stranger, but Corey ignored him as he bent over Logan and said, "The marshal said you know about Ty missing, Jim."

Jim's apprehension was savage, tearing at his innermost being like a wild beast. Swallowing hard, he choked, "Yes. It...it was me who took him."

Jim's words were like a bolt of lightning. Emily Grace gasped, Taylor Ann gave a tiny mew, and Corey stared at Jim incredulously, mouth agape.

Clearing his throat and struggling to get the words out, Jim told the whole story, beginning with his plea for Corey's help. As he told of the incident at the general store and what it led to, Emily Grace thought of her words to Corey: *Jim's desperate and desperate men do desperate things. I hope you don't live to regret your decision.*

When Jim told of the Cheyenne riding away with Ty, Corey railed at him and demanded that Marshal Luskin arrest him. Corey then spoke of his conflict with Iron Hand, saying that the chief had seen Tyler that day he came to the ranch. Slamming a fist into a palm, he hissed, "This is that savage's way of punishing me for the shooting of his brave. He'll pay for this! I'll take my men and storm his village! Whoever gets in the way will die, but my son *will* be rescued!"

The soft voice of John Stranger captured everyone's attention as he said, "Mr. McCollister, how many men do you have?"

"Fifty-three, besides myself."

Stranger pushed his hat back from his brow and gave McCollister a solemn look. "It'd be suicide for you to go riding into that village. You'd be outnumbered more than three to one and going up against fierce fighters who are well-trained for battle.

I advise you, don't do it."

"And who are you to advise me, mister?"

"Just a stranger."

"His name's John Stranger, Corey," put in Luskin. "And he's right. It'd be suicide, all right."

"He's definitely right, Corey," said Dr. Getz. "You go storming into Iron Hand's village and every one of you will lose your scalp."

Emily Grace took hold of her husband's arm. "Corey, you're angry right now, and you're not thinking clearly. There's no way you and our ranch hands could ever go in there and come out alive...much less rescue Ty. We've got to take this situation to the Lord. He'll—"

"The Lord doesn't expect me to just stand here, E.G. Those bloody beasts have our son. I've got to do *something!*"

"You're right, you do," said John Stranger. "Give me permission to go after your son. I've dealt a lot with Indians. Let me go talk to Iron Hand. I can get Ty out."

Corey gave him a caustic look. "I don't know you, fella. I'm skeptical of a man named *John Stranger,* and I don't know what your game is. How do I know I can trust you? And besides, if it would be suicide for me and my men to go riding into Iron Hand's village, why wouldn't it be the same for you?"

"To answer your first question...you don't know that you can trust me. But what possible ulterior motive could I have for offering to attempt to rescue your son? And to answer your second question...I would be one man, alone. I would go in unarmed so that I obviously offer no threat to them. I know Indians, and—"

"No! No!" Corey cut him off, throwing up his hands. "I appreciate your offer, Mr. Stranger, but that kind of approach will never work with Iron Hand. He hates white men with a passion. I'm going to send a couple of men on my fastest horses to Fort Sidney for help. The army can go in there much better prepared than my ranch hands and I can."

"Corey," Emily Grace said, "I don't mean to be a contentious wife, but Ty is my son, too...and we don't know what Iron Hand plans to do with him, or when. Fort Sidney is fifty miles from here...even farther from the Cheyenne village. It will take better than two days to send riders to the fort and get the cavalry back here. That is, if they have enough available men to come right away. There isn't time for all that."

"Have you got a better idea?" Corey snapped.

"Yes. I like this man, and for some reason I trust him. He very well could be the Lord's means of getting our son back alive."

"I know my name is a dirty word to you now, Corey," spoke up Jim Logan, "but I've had some experience with Mr. Stranger. Believe me, if he says he can get Ty back for you, he can do it."

"You're right, you're name is a dirty word!" Corey blared, his voice as shrill as the scrape of a file. "If it weren't for your lame-brain deed, none of this would be happening!"

Corey set hard eyes on Luskin. "I meant what I said, Jed. I want this kidnapper arrested and prosecuted to the full extent of the law!"

"I'll jail him for now, and he'll face trial later if you'll sign that you want him charged," Luskin replied, meeting his glare.

"Then let's go to your office and get it signed!"

"And leave him here so he can escape?"

"Oh, all right, I'll sign later," growled McCollister. "Come on, ladies, let's go."

"Jim is where?" exclaimed Merilee Logan. "In jail! What on earth for?"

"I'll explain as we ride, ma'am," John Stranger said quietly. "I'm here to take you and the children to him. He needs you real bad right now."

Putting Merilee and the children in the Logan wagon,

Stranger aimed the team back toward Hay Springs. While they rode over the rolling countryside, he told them the whole story. Merilee was both angry and shocked. Angry because of the way Jim had been treated by George Nelson, and shocked that Jim would go to such desperate measures as to kidnap Tyler McCollister for ransom. Jeremy and Darlene understood what had happened, and Benjamin grasped most of it. But little Susie was confused and wanted to know why her father wouldn't be coming home with them.

As Hay Springs came into view under the late afternoon sun, Merilee assured her children that everything would be all right. Jesus would help them.

John Stranger led Merilee and the children into the town jail where they found Jim in a cell. Stranger stayed in the office with Marshal Luskin, allowing the Logan family privacy in their moment of calamity and sorrow.

There was much emotion in the cell block as Jim asked his wife and children to forgive him for his foolish deed. Merilee kissed him through the bars and assured him that she understood why he had snapped under such pressure. Though he had done wrong in abducting little Ty, she felt that part of the guilt lay on Corey McCollister's shoulders for refusing to help Jim when he had the means to do it. Jeremy, Darlene, and Benjamin made sure their father knew they loved him. And little Susie cried because he wasn't going home with them.

When the weeping was done, and it was time for Merilee and the children to go home, Jim sent Jeremy to the office, asking John Stranger to come to the cell block.

When John and Jeremy returned, Jim said, "Mr. Stranger, I don't know how to thank you for taking the time to go after my family and bring them in to see me."

"Just part of my job. And to relieve your mind, there's a wagon load of groceries parked outside."

Jim and Merilee exchanged quizzical glances.

"I don't understand, Mr. Stranger," said Merilee.

"Well," grinned Stranger, "while you've been in here talking to Jim, I thought I'd mosey over to the general store and give that nice Mr. Nelson some business. So happened there were a couple of ladies with children in the store, so I got their advice on what to buy. I even bought some candy against their advice, but I figured these kids'd like me for it."

As heavy as the moment was, everyone in the cellblock laughed at that.

"I haven't asked if it'd be okay," said Stranger, "but if it is, I'll stay at your ranch for the next several nights to sort of keep watch. Barn's got a hayloft, doesn't it?"

"Sure does," said Jim. "You're plenty welcome to sleep up there. And thank you for the groceries. I'll find a way to pay you back."

Throwing palms up, the man-in-black shook his head. "Nope. Buying those groceries was my pleasure. You owe me nothing."

John Stranger prayed with the Logan family, then followed Merilee and her brood out the door. As they climbed into the wagon, the men who had been searching for Ty McCollister came riding in to learn from people on the street that the boy was in the hands of the Cheyenne.

Tyler McCollister's fears subsided once he reached the Cheyenne village, for he had been placed in the custody of Bear Fang and his squaw, Running Fawn. The squaw's heart went out to the frightened little boy. It took her only moments to realize he was deaf and dumb, but by taking him in her arms and showing him that he was in tender hands, he soon settled down. Tyler assumed the strange surroundings were only temporary, and because of Running Fawn's kindness and gentle care, the fear faded from his countenance.

Indians have a sign language of their own, and Running Fawn decided to use it to see if she could better communicate with the boy. Tyler recognized some of the hand signals, which correlated with those adopted by his sister. This made him feel more comfortable.

When Running Fawn saw that Tyler was warming up to her, she had Bear Fang bring their daughter, Starflower, from a neighboring tepee. Starflower was about Tyler's age. Running Fawn was able to get the message across to him that Starflower was her daughter. By sundown of the day he was abducted, Ty and Starflower had become good friends.

The little Cheyenne girl had a hard time understanding, at first, that her new friend could not hear nor speak, but the handicap did not hinder their having a good time together.

Suppertime was difficult for Ty. He had never eaten the kind of food that was placed before him at the campfire, but he was hungry enough that he cleaned up his plate and signaled for more. When Ty was given a mat to sleep on and a blanket for a cover in the family tepee, a great loneliness came over him. He missed his family, and almost cried. But assuming his situation was temporary, he decided not to be afraid. He looked forward to a good time with his new playmate the next day.

CHAPTER TWENTY

The sun peeked over the eastern plains to find Corey, Emily Grace, and Taylor Ann McCollister sitting around the kitchen table after a sleepless night. Each had an open Bible in front of them, and Emily Grace was using hers to persuade her angry husband that he must get a handle on his temper. His anger, she told him, was keeping him from thinking clearly.

"I *am* thinking clearly," insisted Corey, "and I still say that this man-from-nowhere will get himself *and* Tyler killed if he goes into that village unarmed and alone."

"We've already discussed every other alternative, darling," said Emily Grace, reaching out to touch his hand. "Ty's life will be in more danger if our men or cavalrymen try to storm the village. Your daughter can understand that...and when we talked to Curly about it last night, he agreed. Seems to me John Stranger is our best chance."

"I'm going to kill that Iron Hand with my bare hands!" Corey blared. "How dare he take my son! The dirty—"

"Mr. McCollister!" broke in Zach Adams from the front of the house. "Cheyenne coming under a white flag!"

The McCollisters raced through the house and onto the front porch with Corey in the lead. Zach was standing at the top of the steps. Zach had already summoned the ranch hands, who were coming from the bunkhouse and corral on the run.

Four Cheyenne warriors were riding toward them at a leisurely pace. One carried a staff that bore a white flag.

Zach then pointed north and said, "Someone else is comin'."

The McCollisters turned to see a lone rider dressed in black trotting toward them.

"John Stranger!" breathed Taylor Ann.

By the time the Indians drew up to the porch, John Stranger was dismounting just outside the cluster of ranch hands. The men eyed him with caution, but none bothered him when he pushed his way close to the porch steps.

J.T. Woodard and Ray Premro stood in the group, wondering what was in the offing with the Indians and thinking about the money that was lining their pockets from the last big theft of cattle.

Corey did a courteous nod to Stranger, then eyed the Indians as Spotted Coyote set black eyes on him and said, "We come as messengers of Chief Iron Hand."

"You tell your chief I want my son back, and I want him back *now!*" Corey spat.

"You had best listen to Chief Iron Hand, Corey McCollister," grunted Spotted Coyote.

"All right, I'm listening."

Taylor Ann stood beside her mother on the porch, clinging to her arm. Emily Grace was rigid, nerves on edge, waiting to hear Iron Hand's message. Zach Adam's was close beside his boss.

The morning breeze toyed with the Indians' head feathers as Spotted Coyote spoke in a deep monotone. "Chief Iron Hand says to tell you he will return the boy to you unharmed in trade for the young woman with sunshine hair. He wants her for his squaw." As he spoke, Spotted Coyote pointed toward Taylor Ann.

Taylor Ann gasped, a sudden intake of breath high in her

chest. Emily Grace put an arm around her, pulling her snug.

Corey McCollister was a storm about to break.

Spotted Coyote saw it, and said, "If the young woman comes with us now, we will return the boy before sundown. If she needs more time before she goes to Iron Hand, we will be back at sunrise tomorrow. If she does not come with us then...the boy will die."

"If Iron Hand harms one hair on my son's head, I'll kill him!" Corey raged. "You tell that barbarian I'm not about to let him have my daughter!"

Spotted Coyote stiffened. Eyes blazing, he warned, "Do not come to our village with armed men, Corey McCollister! If you do, the boy will die, the men will die, and *you* will die!"

Corey's passion had stolen his reason. Whipping out his revolver, he pointed it at Spotted Coyote and bellowed, "How about we make it *you* that dies, redskin!"

Spotted Coyote flinched, and the other three Indians raised their carbines. By that time, all the Circle M men had their guns out, cocked, and aimed at the Indians.

Emily Grace and Taylor Ann clung to each other, both silently praying.

Corey's hand trembled as he held the gun on Spotted Coyote. "I think we'll hold you as hostage, savage. You other three get out of here. Tell Iron Hand I'll trade this one for my son. I want Tyler delivered here immediately, or this man dies!"

John Stranger moved up the steps and sided McCollister. "It won't work. Iron Hand has the advantage, and if you'd cool down, you'd see that."

Corey's breathing was shallow and raspy as he kept the muzzle trained on Spotted Coyote's face. "Then I'll keep three and send one with the message."

"That won't work, either," Stranger said levelly. "You're going to get Tyler killed if you keep this up. These men are not Iron Hand's sons. Tyler *is* your son. Iron Hand knows that blood is thicker than water, Corey. Don't make him prove it."

Without taking his burning eyes off Spotted Coyote, Corey gusted, "I'm not giving that feather-headed heathen my daughter to be his squaw, Stranger! I have no alternative but to fight fire with fire! The lives of these three for the life of my son!"

"You're not listening, Corey," pressed Stranger. "Your son means more to you than all three of these braves mean to Iron Hand. He's got the upper hand, and he knows it. Don't kill Tyler by losing your head."

Corey licked his lips. "I'm not giving him my daughter."

"I'm not telling you to do that. What I'm telling you is to back off and let these men go. Let's talk after they're gone."

Finally, Corey McCollister relaxed his hold on the gun, lowered it, and said, "All right. Get them out of here."

Stranger looked at Spotted Coyote, whose features were stolid. "You can go now."

Iron Hand's spokesman wheeled his mount. The others followed suit. Before goading his pinto into a gallop, Spotted Coyote looked over his shoulder at the rancher and said, "We will be back at rise of the sun. If the young woman will not go with us...the boy dies!"

When the Indians had galloped out of sight, Corey looked at Curly Ford and said, "Every man here gets a bonus in his next pay envelope for standing with me both times the Cheyenne have shown up here. I'll set the amount later. You can all go, now."

While the Circle M hands slowly made their way toward the barn and bunkhouse, Zach Adams stayed. He looked on while the McCollisters embraced each other.

John Stranger moved close and said, "We need to remind ourselves that Tyler is actually in God's hands. He can take care of your son and deliver him to you unharmed."

Mother and daughter looked at the tall man, gaining comfort from his words and nodding. Corey began to pace back and forth on the porch, speaking his hatred for Iron Hand. "I don't understand how he could possibly think I would make such a trade...much less that I would let Taylor Ann become the bride of an uncivilized, barbaric heathen under *any* circumstance!"

"That's exactly what I want to talk to you about," said Stranger, stepping in front of Corey to stop his pacing.

Zach Adams moved close to Taylor Ann. He didn't touch her, but gave her an assuring look and a tight-lipped smile. Showing him tear-dimmed eyes, she made an attempt to smile back.

"Okay, talk." Corey said.

"You said you don't understand how Iron Hand could possibly think you would make such a trade. That's just it. You don't understand the Indian mind. To Iron Hand, what he is proposing is quite reasonable...but he has taken these measures to get Taylor Ann for his bride because he *does* understand white man's thinking. He figures this is the only course he can take to make your daughter his squaw. You will give her up to keep Tyler from dying. You would rather have your daughter alive and married to him than have your son dead."

"I will have neither!"

"As it stands, what choice have you got? Iron Hand has made no idle threat. If you don't send Taylor Ann with those braves tomorrow morning, Tyler will die. If you try to go in there by force with your men, they will kill the boy before you can set foot in the village. Same thing would happen if the army tried to go in."

"I've got to do *something!*"

Emily Grace stepped to her husband and put her arms around him. "There's only one thing you can do, darling. If Mr. Stranger is still willing to go after Ty alone, we've got to let him do it."

Corey wrapped his arms around his wife and closed his eyes.

"I'll go in there if you'll give me the go-ahead, Corey," Stranger said. "Ty is your son, and I won't venture it unless you give me your permission. If you'll do so, I must have your full cooperation and your guarantee that you will not interfere in any way. You must give me your word that you'll let me handle it alone."

Corey opened his eyes. Emily Grace looked into them, yearning to hear him tell John Stranger to go after Ty.

Corey set his jaw and shook his head. "How do I know you can pull it off? Iron Hand is just as likely to kill Tyler when he sees you coming as he would if it was me, my men, or the army. What special power do you have that makes you think you can just ride in there, have a nice little chat with Iron Hand, and ride out with my boy, unharmed?"

"I claim no special power, but I know how Cheyenne think. I'm confident I can handle it."

"You're no Indian. You live with them once or something?"

"Maybe."

Breaking away from Emily Grace, Corey pounded fist into palm, shook his head, and said, "I can't let you try it! Those savages might kill Tyler the instant they see you riding toward the village. There has to be some other solution!"

Stranger sighed, adjusted the gunbelt on his slender waist, and said, "Corey, I'm asking you to let me do it."

"No," came the quick reply. "There has to be some other way."

Stranger sighed again and headed for the steps. Silence prevailed while he descended them, walked to the big black, and swung into the saddle. Looking at Corey, he said, "You've got till sunup to invent this other solution. I sure hope you come up with it." Then he touched his hatbrim and said, "Mrs. McCollister...Taylor Ann. I'm sorry. I tried."

With that, he galloped away.

Zach turned to Corey. "Got any ideas, boss?"

Corey shook his head, staring at the porch floor.

"We've asked the Lord to spare Ty and bring him back to us,

Corey," Emily Grace said. "I believe with all my heart He wants to use Mr. Stranger to do it." Turning to her daughter, she said, "Don't you think so, honey?"

Taylor Ann seemed preoccupied. When no reply came, Emily Grace said, "Taylor Ann..."

Blinking, Taylor Ann looked at her mother and said, "Pardon me?"

"I asked if you agree that Mr. Stranger is the Lord's answer to our prayers for Tyler's deliverance."

"Oh. Yes, I...I believe he is. But Daddy doesn't, so there will have to be another solution."

Emily Grace set her eyes on Corey and said, "Well, he's got about twenty-two hours to come up with it."

Corey McCollister crossed the porch and entered the house without another word.

"I guess I ought to get to work," Zach said.

"Why don't you just come over here and sit down?" said Emily Grace. "Taylor Ann and I need your company right now."

Nearly an hour had passed when Corey emerged from the house and approached his wife and daughter, who were in conversation with Zach. As they looked up, he asked, "What have you been doing?"

"We've been praying that you would walk out here and tell us that you'd changed your mind...that you were going to let Mr. Stranger go rescue Ty."

A broad grin spread over the rancher's face. "Well, what do you know? That's exactly what I came out here to tell you."

"Wonderful!" Emily Grace exclaimed, jumping up from her chair and embracing him.

Looking at his hired hand, Corey said, "How about riding with me, Zach? Let's find the man and send him on his way."

"Let's do it!" grinned Zach.

* * * * *

Having learned of the rustling activities in the area from Jim Logan, John Stranger decided to ride the range in late afternoon and stay at it after dark. Maybe he would stumble onto the culprits. Since the Circle M was the biggest spread, he would concentrate his attention there.

The sky was alive with orange and red at sunset as J.T. Woodard and Ray Premro cut twenty head from Corey McCollister's herd and drove them into a tree-lined ravine. While they were rope-fencing the cattle within a circle of trees, Premro said to his partner, "Sy was smart to go back to cuttin' out small amounts again. Keep the suspicion on the Indians."

"Yep," chuckled Woodard. "Sy's a pretty smart cookie."

When the cattle were secure behind the rope fence, Woodard dusted his hands off and said, "Well, let's head for the barn."

"How about the Hay Springs jail instead?" came a cold voice from the shadows.

Both men whirled about to see the tall man-in-black some twenty yards away, holding his Colt .45 on them. They remembered seeing him at the ranch house that morning when the four Cheyenne came with Iron Hand's message.

"Reach down real careful-like and drop those gunbelts," Stranger said sternly. "So you lowdown rustlers are employees of Corey McCollister, eh?"

Woodard and Premro knew the whole operation was doomed if they let this stranger take them to Marshal Luskin. Woodard whispered, "Make like you're gonna do it. When I go left, you go right. We'll plug 'im good."

As the rustlers moved their hands toward the buckles of their gunbelts, Stranger said, "Nice and easy, now."

Suddenly both men leaped to the side, rolling on the ground, and whipping out their guns. Stranger's .45 roared four times in rapid succession.

* * * * *

Marshal Jed Luskin was a widower and lived upstairs above his office and jail. There was a staircase outside the building that led up to his apartment. He was jarred rudely from a deep sleep by someone pounding on his apartment door.

Luskin picked up his revolver from the dresser and headed for the door. The knocking resumed as he stood at the door and shouted, "Who is it?"

"John Stranger!" came the muffled reply.

"What do you want this time of night, John?"

"I've got some marshal business for you to tend to. Get dressed and come on down."

"Can't it wait till mornin'?"

"No. Hurry up."

Stranger was still on the landing when a grumpy Luskin opened the door and eyed the tall man by the dim light of a nearby street lamp. "Are you aware that it's three-thirty in the mornin', Stranger?" he groaned.

"Of course," grinned Stranger, "but sometimes the lawman business ignores the clock. Come on down. I've got some presents for you."

When he was halfway down the stairs, Luskin saw eight horses by the street lamp, tied at the hitch rail. Each horse was laden with a man bellied over its back, his wrists lashed to his ankles.

"What th—"

"Rustlers," said Stranger. "Caught them red-handed stealing Corey McCollister's cattle."

"You mean—"

"The Indians haven't been doing it at all. These gentlemen were quite cooperative. They confessed the whole thing. Been doing it to the Circle M and other ranches for eight months."

One of the rustlers moaned, "Please, Marshal. Make him take us off these horses."

"Presently," said Stranger. "Marshal, I'd like to introduce you to Jake Dill, Nate Bishop, Willis Day, Barry Winkler, and Hank Linza."

The marshal blinked, pointed to the remaining three, and said, "And what about these boys over here?"

"Well, since they're dead and won't be guests in your jail, I didn't think it was necessary to introduce them. However, this one's Sy Mixler. He was boss of the gang. Used to be a gunfighter, but rustling slowed his draw. Other two are J.T. Woodard and Ray Premro."

Luskin's mouth fell open like a trap. "Why, they were on Corey's payroll. I know—*knew* them."

"Mm-hmm. These boys'll tell you the whole story like they did for me."

"Corey's gonna be mighty surprised to find out it wasn't Iron Hand's pack doin' the rustlin' after all," said Luskin, rubbing his mustache.

"Well, let's take them in and lock them up. They've already agreed to sign this confession I wrote up for them. I thought it best to have them sign it in front of you. Your deputy can be a witness to it."

"Okay," said Luskin. "But one other question."

"Yes?"

"How did you hog-tie these five live ones over their horses' backs and hold a gun on 'em at the same time?"

"Simple. I made them hog-tie each other under my close supervision until we were down to Jake Dill, here. Then I took care of Jake myself."

Shaking his head, Luskin said, "Tell me, Stranger...are you a lawman? A U.S. marshal, maybe?"

Stranger grinned and said, "Sometimes."

Corey McCollister and Zachary Adams arrived back at the Circle M just after ten o'clock. They had ridden to Hay Springs, but had been unable to find John Stranger or anyone that had seen him.

Weary and dejected, Zach went to the bunkhouse, and Corey headed to the ranch house.

Emily Grace and Taylor Ann were waiting by lantern light in the parlor. Gloom settled over them like a shroud when Corey told them he had been unable to find John Stranger.

Corey saw an open Bible on the couch where mother and daughter had been sitting. When Emily Grace saw him eye the Bible, she broke down and started crying. Corey took her in his arms as she sobbed, "I was so sure you'd come home and tell me Mr. Stranger was already on his way to the village. Oh, Corey, I'm trying so hard to hold onto God's promises, but my faith is weakening. Those Indians will be here at sunrise to take Taylor Ann!"

Emily Grace felt a shudder go through her husband's body as he wept and said, "This is all my fault! If I had treated Jim Logan like a Christian ought to treat his brother, none of this nightmare would be happening. And if I'd listened to you the first time you said John Stranger was sent here by the Lord, he would have already been to the village. And if he truly *was* sent by the Lord, our prayers would have been answered and we would have our son safely with us at this minute. Oh, what a stubborn fool I've been!"

Clinging to her husband with all her might, Emily Grace choked, swallowed hard, and said, "There's no way we would ever let that man have our daughter. It...it will take a miracle from God to save Tyler, now."

The heart-torn mother felt a tender hand on her shoulder. Turning, she looked at Taylor Ann through a wall of tears, noting again the strange look that had been in her eyes for several hours.

"You're right, Mother," the girl said softly. "It *will* take a miracle from God to save Tyler's life. And I believe that miracle will happen." Taking a deep breath, she added, "I'm going to my room."

Both parents kissed their daughter good-night and watched her move down the hall and disappear into her room.

Corey sighed. "I wish I had the assurance she's got."

"Me, too," nodded Emily Grace. "And the peace. It's in her eyes. Did you notice?"

"I saw that look there, but didn't know what it was. But that's it, honey. Our girl has more peace in this awful situation than her parents do."

Corey and Emily Grace walked to the kitchen together arm-in-arm, and sat down at the table, ready to spend another sleepless night.

Dawn's early light filtered through the kitchen windows. Two tear-stained Bibles lay on the table. Corey was holding his head in his hands and Emily Grace was wiping tears from the table top with her hanky. Rising, she sighed and said, "Think I'll look in on Taylor Ann...make sure she's all right."

Dog-tired and wobbly on her feet, Emily Grace made her way down the hall to her daughter's room. Turning the knob slowly, she inched the door open, wincing when the hinges protested with a squeak. Taylor Ann's room was on the west side of the house, but there was enough light to reveal that the bed was empty and had not been slept in. A light breeze was toying with the curtains at an open window.

Emily Grace rushed into the room, her eyes searching from wall to wall. Suddenly they fell on a sheet of paper that lay on the dresser with a candlestick sitting on one corner to keep it from being blown off. The room was too dark for her to read it. With trembling fingers, she picked up a wooden match from a small dish, struck it on the dresser top, and held it above the paper.

Dearest Mother and Daddy,

The Lord has given you your miracle. I have gone to the Cheyenne village to offer myself to Iron Hand as his bride. Tyler will be home safely soon. I would rather live the horrible life ahead of me than to let my little brother die. I love you.

Your daughter,
Taylor Ann

CHAPTER TWENTY-ONE

Corey McCollister read the note in the kitchen, nerves tingling, breath held in check. Mouth dry, he gasped, "If she left shortly after she went to her room, she's already at the village!"

Emily Grace was sobbing.

Corey's heart beat wildly, and he had to steady himself with one hand on the table top. Choking on his words, he said "This is all my fault. Now that savage has both our children!"

Emily Grace wanted to say that perhaps Iron Hand would keep his word and send Tyler home, but her words were stolen away by a knock at the back door.

Corey stumbled to the door and found Zach Adams standing there. Immediately Zach knew there was some new development. "What's happened?" he gasped.

"Come in," said Corey, and turned to the table. Picking up Taylor Ann's note, he handed it to him.

Emily Grace was stifling her sobs, watching Zach's features tighten as he read the note.

Zach ran his gaze from one to the other. "How long ago did she leave?"

"We don't know for sure," replied Corey. "If she left right

after she went to her room, she's easily been there a couple of hours. If it was later, she could still be on her way."

Adams bolted out the door.

"Zach!" Corey called after him. "Come back here!"

Zach was already halfway to the barn when Corey reached the edge of the back porch and hollered at him again. Emily Grace drew up beside him, watching Zach cut across the yard. "Corey, the Cheyenne will kill him if she's already in the village!"

"He'll be saddled and gone before I can stop him, honey. If she's not there yet, maybe he'll find her and bring her back."

"Oh, dear Lord, what next?" she said, looking heavenward.

There was a knock at the front door. Corey dashed through the house with his wife on his heels. Opening the door, he saw John Stranger and Marshal Jed Luskin standing before him.

The sun was peeping over the horizon.

"Mr. Stranger!" Corey said. "I tried to find you last night, but failed. I realized how foolish I'd been, and wanted to ask if you'd still try to rescue Ty."

Stranger swung his gaze toward the rising sun. "Of course. It may be more difficult with his braves about to show up here, but I'll try."

"Wait a minute, there's more."

"Yes?"

Corey told Stranger about Taylor Ann's note.

"Do you have any idea if she's been gone long enough to have reached the village?"

"I don't know for sure, but it's quite possible."

Pounding hoofbeats were heard, coming from the direction of the corral. Stranger and Luskin turned to see Zach Adams bent low over his saddlehorn, lashing the horse.

"He just learned about the note, too," said Corey.

"He's a dead man if she's already in Cheyenne hands," Stranger said. "I've got to stop him."

"Please!" begged Emily Grace.

Setting his eyes on Corey, Stranger said, "The marshal has something to tell you, my friend. He's got solid proof that the Cheyenne are not the ones who have been stealing your cattle. It involves Woodard and Premro. He'll fill you in."

With that, Stranger was off the porch, in the saddle, and galloping after Zachary Adams.

Taylor Ann McCollister sat in the center of the village, surrounded by Cheyenne women who were carefully dressing her in Indian wedding garb and styling her hair like their own. Her heart was filled with an icy dread.

Iron Hand stood close by, muscular arms folded across his chest. Things had turned out better than he had planned. The beautiful young woman with sunshine hair had walked into the village at dawn and willingly offered herself as his bride.

True to his word, Iron Hand assured her that Tyler would be taken home that very day. The wedding ceremony was to take place when the sun reached its highest point in the sky. Immediately after the ceremony, Taylor Ann could kiss her little brother good-bye, and Spotted Coyote would take him home.

Tyler was happy to awaken and find his sister in the village. Signing by the dull light of dawn, he had asked if their parents would be coming, too. Taylor Ann had signed back a reply, saying that the Indians would be taking him home soon.

As the bride sat with nerves knotting her stomach, she could see Ty playing at the edge of the village with the Indian children.

Happy that his temporary stay at the village was about to come to an end, Ty had decided to have as much fun as possible with his new friends. He especially liked Starflower, and soon the two of them were playing alone some distance from the village on the rolling plains.

From her place in the center of the village, Taylor Ann noticed that she could no longer see her brother. The occupants of the village were caught up in the excitement of the upcoming ceremony, and were unaware that the two children had ventured outside the boundaries permitted for play.

Ty and Starflower were laughing and chasing butterflies some fifty yards from the village when Starflower unwittingly stepped on a rattlesnake. Deadly fangs shot out and struck her on the right thigh, penetrating the skin through her dress.

Screaming in terror, she ran toward Ty, who thought she was playing until he saw the look on her face. He caught a glimpse of the rattler slithering over some large flat rocks, then noted the two dark holes on her dress. His father had taught him about diamondbacks, and he knew that to be bitten by one could mean death.

Taking Starflower by the hand, Ty pointed toward the village and led her as fast as they could run.

Ebony proved to be much faster than the animal Zach Adams was riding. Stranger guided his black steed over the rolling hills, the space between them diminishing. Zach looked over his shoulder, knowing that Stranger was determined to keep him from entering the Cheyenne village if he did not find Taylor Ann before he got there.

Both horses were puffing hard as Stranger pulled alongside. "Give it up, Zach!" shouted Stranger. "If she's already in the village, there's no way you can rescue her!"

"I've got to try! I've got a revolver on my hip and one in my saddlebag. If I have to go in there with both guns blazing, I'll do it! Taylor Ann isn't going to marry that savage! I love her, Mr. Stranger. Don't try to stop me!"

"I understand how it is for a man to love a woman, Zach, but you'll only get yourself killed. Let me do it!"

"Sorry! I've got to do it myself!"

They were already more than halfway to the village. Stranger had to act fast. Letting his gaze run over the terrain ahead, he chose his spot...a level area with a carpet of thick grass. They reached the place in a matter of seconds, and Stranger made his move. He surprised Zach by leaping from Ebony's back, wrapping his arms around him, and using his weight to force him from the saddle.

Both men hit the ground hard. The impact broke Stranger's hold, and they both rolled and cartwheeled, hats flying. When they came to a stop, Stranger was on his feet first. As Zach was getting up, the tall man closed in. The look on young Adams's face told Stranger he was still full of resistance.

Stranger would give him no quarter. For Zach's own sake, he had to be stopped. Just as Zach came to his feet, Stranger caught him with a solid punch to the jaw that staggered him. Zach tried to fight back, but a second blow laid him flat and unconscious.

Stranger tied Zach to a nearby tree, tied his horse close by, vaulted onto Ebony's back, and raced like the wind for the Cheyenne village. When he was within half a mile of the village, he drew rein and took off his gunbelt, placing it in a saddlebag.

The sentries at the edge of the village were impressed when the man on the black horse greeted them in their own language. Using his savvy of Cheyenne ways and showing them he was unarmed, John Stranger persuaded them to allow him in the village for a powwow with Chief Iron Hand. The sentries explained that he might have to wait for some time before Iron Hand could see him. This was to be the chief's wedding day, but there was an emergency in the village, and until it was over, Iron Hand would not be available.

The sentries put two other braves in charge of Stranger, having him sit down on a tree stump amid the tepees while they stood beside him. From where he sat, Stranger could see Taylor Ann, encircled by the Cheyenne women. There was a space of some seventy to eighty feet between them, but their eyes met, and Stranger could see the trepidation on her face. He smiled and nodded, trying to tell her with his eyes that everything would be all right. He couldn't tell whether she got the message. The mask of fear remained.

Stranger's attention was drawn from Taylor Ann to the tepee a few feet away. A crowd of Cheyenne men was gathered near the open flap. The women and children remained farther back. Stranger caught a glimpse of Tyler McCollister. He was seated on the ground with two Indian boys, who were being watched by their mothers. Ty had not seen Stranger.

Inquiring of the braves who stood beside him, Stranger was told that Bear Fang's five-year-old daughter, Starflower, had been bitten by a rattlesnake. Bear Fang and his squaw, Running Fawn, were in the tepee with her. The villages medicine man was working on her.

As time dragged slowly by, Stranger could see Iron Hand appear intermittently at the opening of the tepee, conversing with the men clustered near. It was past mid-morning when the chief finally stepped out of the tepee and spoke sadly to all who could hear, saying in the Cheyenne language that the medicine man had done his best, but little Starflower was dying. There was a deathly silence among the people as Iron Hand turned back into the tepee.

Stranger spoke to the braves beside him and asked if he might speak to Iron Hand. They refused to even consider it until he explained that he knew about snakebites and could possibly help. Quickly they ushered him near the opening of the tepee, and while one stayed with him, the other went inside. In less than a minute, Iron Hand appeared with the brave on his heels.

As the chief drew up, Stranger saw recognition in his eyes. In English, Iron Hand said, "You were at Circle M when I talked to Corey McCollister."

Stranger surprised him by answering in perfect Cheyenne. "Yes, I am a friend of his and happened to be there at the same time you were."

"Your name is?"

"John Stranger."

Iron Hand blinked. "You are a physician?"

"No, but I know a great deal about snakebites, and I have been able to save the lives of several who have been bitten. I actually came here to speak to you on another matter, but that can wait. May I take a look at the child?"

"I will ask her parents," Iron Hand told him.

It took only a moment for the chief to enter the tepee and return, saying Bear Fang and Running Fawn would be most grateful if the white man would see if he could help little Starflower.

Inside, Stranger introduced himself to the parents, then knelt beside the girl. The heavily painted medicine man gave him a wary scowl, but moved back. Stranger laid a palm on her fevered brow and spoke softly to her, saying he was there to help her. Starflower opened languid eyes, but was unable to focus them on him.

Examining the bite, Stranger found that it had been properly lanced and that the poison had been sucked from the wound. He pressed experienced fingers against the side of her neck, feeling for her pulse, then turned to the parents and asked if Starflower had exerted herself after being bitten. When they told him the distance she had run, he knew her bloodstream was loaded with the deadly venom. She was in grave danger. Turning to Iron Hand, he asked that he and the medicine man leave him alone with Starflower and her parents.

The chief complied.

While Bear Fang and Running Fawn looked on, the mysterious man turned his back to them, bent over the child, and went to work. The parents waited with bated breath, clinging to each other.

There were whispers among the crowd outside the tepee. Taylor Ann had seen Stranger go inside, and though she could not understand the chatter of the women around her, she knew the matter with the little snakebitten girl was serious.

When nearly three hours had passed, Bear Fang and Running Fawn heard their daughter call for her mother. Stranger turned, smiled, and said, "She's past the crisis. She will live."

Running Fawn broke into tears, took Starflower in her arms, and held her to her breast. Bear Fang thanked Stranger, smiling from ear to ear. Excited, he stepped outside the tepee and announced that his daughter's life had been saved. Little Starflower would live.

There was much elation among the people. They whooped and shouted for joy. Iron Hand was grateful that the Sky Father had sent the man named John Stranger to their village.

Presently Running Fawn appeared, carrying Starflower out into the sunlight that all might see her. John Stranger stood beside her and in the Cheyenne language announced that the child's fever was gone, she had no more nausea, and she had no pain.

The Indians marveled at the powers of the tall white man. Though the medicine man was envious, still he rejoiced that the little girl's life had been saved.

Iron Hand shook hands with Stranger Indian-style and said, "Truly the Sky Father has sent you, John Stranger. It is with deep appreciation that I say thank you for giving Starflower back to us."

"Just doing my job," Stranger said modestly.

"I ask now, what other matter did John Stranger come to speak to Iron Hand about?"

"I came here to take Taylor Ann and her little brother home."

These words put a scowl on Iron Hand's face. "I am grateful for what you did to save Starflower's life, and I am pleased to allow you to take the boy to his parents. But I will not allow you to take Sunshine Hair with you."

The village people stood close, listening as Stranger said evenly, "I came here to take her back to her parents, Chief. This I must do."

"No! She came to my village of her own free will. She has offered herself to be my squaw."

"Only because you threatened to kill her little brother if she did not return this morning with your braves."

"No! She did not say that!"

"She's a noble young lady, Iron Hand. She wouldn't do or say a thing that might hinder Ty from being taken home unharmed."

The chief cast a glance at his promised bride, who sat amongst the women, looking on fearfully. "No, John Stranger," he gusted, black eyes flashing fire, "she cannot go with you!"

Speaking loud so that all might hear, Stranger said, "You leave me no choice, Chief Iron Hand. I came here as a friend of Corey McCollister to bring his daughter and son home. You have said I could take the son, but I cannot take the daughter. I must take Sunshine Hair also, or I have completed only half of my mission. Therefore...I challenge you as a Cheyenne warrior to meet me on the field of battle for a fight to the death!"

Iron Hand's eyes widened and his face turned to stone. There was an instant murmur amongst the crowd of dark faces.

"I know because of your honor that you will accept my challenge, Chief," said Stranger. "And as challenger, we will fight on my terms—knives. If the great warrior Iron Hand can kill John Stranger, he keeps Sunshine Hair for his bride and will return Tyler McCollister unharmed to his parents. If, however, John Stranger kills Iron Hand, the Cheyenne are to allow John Stranger to ride away with Sunshine Hair and Tyler McCollister unharmed."

Iron Hand felt the pressure of his honor as hundreds of probing eyes looked on. He would not, he *could* not turn down the challenge. Mouth set hard, he said, "Your challenge is accepted, John Stranger, and so are your terms. If I die, sub-chief Bear Fang will allow you to ride away unharmed with Sunshine Hair and Tyler McCollister."

Stranger set his gray gaze on Bear Fang, who nodded his assent.

While the chief discarded his headdress and chose his favorite knife for the battle, John Stranger went to his horse and pulled a long-bladed knife from a saddlebag and slipped it under his belt. He removed his hat and hung it on the saddlehorn. He also took off the string tie and loosened his shirt collar.

The crowd was forming a large circle at the edge of the village as Stranger made his way to Taylor Ann, who now had Ty sitting beside her. The tow-headed boy smiled as Stranger patted him on the head. To Taylor Ann, he said, "Don't worry, honey. The Lord didn't send me here to fail. You and Ty will be riding out of here with me shortly."

Taylor Ann wanted desperately to believe it, but her misty eyes showed doubt.

Touching her cheek tenderly, he said, "Be back in a little while."

The Cheyenne people looked on with pride as their handsome young chief stood in the center of the circle, arms folded. The chosen knife was in a scabbard on his hip. As John Stranger slipped into the circle, his eyes met those of Running Fawn, who still held Starflower in her arms. He smiled at her, and ducking her head, she smiled back. She would ever be grateful for what the white man had done.

Stranger halted a few feet from his opponent and lanced him with piercing gray eyes. Iron Hand did not flinch.

Stranger pulled the knife from under his belt and rolled his broad shoulders to loosen them. Iron Hand jerked his knife out of its scabbard, its blade flashing in the sun. The proud warrior's muscles rippled under his bronze skin, a display of strength and power designed to intimidate his opponent.

It didn't.

Iron Hand ejected a wild whoop and bolted toward John Stranger, knife poised for the kill. Stranger shifted slightly sideways and struck out with his left fist. It connected solidly with the Indian's jaw, staggering him. Stranger did not follow up with the knife.

Iron Hand quickly gained his balance, whirled, and lunged for his enemy. Stranger avoided it, popped him on the jaw again, and danced backward. Once more the chief staggered. He was amazed at the power in Stranger's fist.

Changing tactics, the chief darted for Stranger as before, then suddenly flung himself on the ground, smashing into the white man's legs and knocking him down. The wild-eyed warrior leaped on top of his man and raised his knife to plunge it into his heart.

Stranger's hand shot up and gripped Iron Hand's wrist before he could bring it down. They struggled, meeting strength for strength. Then Stranger brought his knees up solidly against the warrior, sending him sailing head-first into the dirt.

Before Iron Hand could react, Stranger was on his feet, standing over him. The Indian marveled at Stranger's fighting ability, and at his reluctance to go for the kill. Nonetheless, Iron Hand was determined to kill his challenger and keep Sunshine Hair for his squaw.

Taylor Ann looked on as the two men did battle. She knew that sooner or later one of them would die. Ty was mystified by what was happening, but Taylor Ann couldn't take her eyes off the combatants long enough to sign to him.

Red man and challenger were facing off, dancing in a circle, deadly weapons glistening in the sun.

Iron Hand saw what he thought was an opening and lunged in. The tall man, however, had suckered him. Sidestepping, Stranger chopped him with a savage blow on the temple. Iron Hand felt his knees turn watery, but gamely lunged in again. The tip of the knife ripped a thin slit in Stranger's shirt.

Stranger's fist lashed out again. Iron Hand's brain fogged for an instant, but he swung the knife blindly in a deadly arc to keep his opponent at bay. Stranger waited till the arc was almost complete, then stepped in. He nicked the skin on Iron Hand's chest just enough to let him know that he could have killed him, then danced away again.

Bewildered at the man's restraint, Iron Hand determined to take advantage of it and end his life first. The stinging pain of the cut on his chest and the sight of his own blood trickling from the wound served to intensify his desire to finish off his challenger.

Stranger feinted with his knife as Iron Hand came for him again, dodged the warrior's deadly blade, then unleashed a left hook. Fist met jaw, and Iron Hand was down. There was a fearful murmur amongst the Indians as John Stranger leaped on top of the bleeding warrior, snatched the knife from his limp fingers, and tossed it at the feet of Bear Fang.

Dazed and shaking his head, Iron Hand felt the weight of his opponent on him. Blinking as his head cleared, he felt the pressure of Stranger's elbow at the base of his throat, and saw the knife in his hand. The deadly tip of the blade was touching his throat just under his chin. One quick thrust, and Iron Hand was a dead man. Gritting his teeth, the conquered warrior expected to die.

The Cheyenne people looked on in horror.

Keeping the knife where it was, Stranger said, "I will spare your life if you ask, Iron Hand."

The proud warrior wrestled in his mind. Did he want to live and face the dishonor of being defeated by a white man? Was it not best to die an honorable death and leave a memory for his people of a chief who died bravely, rather than to live and face the disgrace of a conquered coward?

Bear Fang knew what was going on in Iron Hand's mind. Standing over his chief, Bear Fang said, "Iron Hand, my beloved leader, do not make this white man kill you. He is offering you your life. Take it. We need you. We see no shame. This man...this man who saved the life of my daughter is a messenger from the

Sky Father. There is no shame that you have been beaten by him. Please. Choose life and lead us."

While Iron Hand stared into Bear Fang's pleading eyes, the people began a chant, telling their chief they saw no shame if he asked the man sent by the Sky Father to spare his life. It started in a low tone, and increased in volume. Their chief must live and lead them.

Iron Hand looked into steel-gray eyes. "John Stranger," he choked, "must you go from here and tell that Iron Hand has been conquered by you?"

"Neither I nor Sunshine Hair will ever tell what happened here today. We will go in peace and tell only that Iron Hand deemed it so. I only ask that the McCollister family never be bothered or harmed by Cheyenne."

"You have my word on it, John Stranger."

"Good. Then live a long life, my friend, and lead your people wisely."

At Hay Springs, Dr. Gerald Getz was about to leave his office to deliver a baby for a rancher's wife several miles to the west. He might be gone overnight, and it had come to his mind that he had forgotten to tell John Stranger that Nurse Baylor had said she wanted him to come to Denver...that she wanted to see him.

Knowing from Marshal Luskin that Stranger was expected back in town soon, he wrote a hasty note:

> Mr. Stranger—
>
> Before Nurse Breanna Baylor left town, she asked me to tell you to come to Denver as soon as you can. She wants to see you. I think by the tone of her voice, it must be important. Sorry I forgot to give you her message.
>
> Best regards,
> Gerald Getz, M.D.

Folding the note and placing it in an envelope, Getz climbed in his buggy, drove down the street, and parked in front of the marshal's office. Dashing in, he found Marshal Luskin behind his desk.

"Howdy, Doc," said Luskin, looking up.

"Mornin', Marshal. I'm on my way out to the Spencer ranch to deliver Olivia's baby. Might be gone till this time tomorrow, so if John Stranger should show up in the meantime, would you give him this? It's important."

"Sure, Doc."

On his way to the door, Getz called over his shoulder, "The man pops in and out so much, I don't want him to do that again and miss that message."

"Got it, Doc. See you when you get back."

CHAPTER TWENTY-TWO

It was mid-afternoon when Corey and Emily Grace McCollister dashed through the door onto their front porch, having heard the Circle M cowhands whooping it up near the bunkhouse. They were overjoyed to see John Stranger riding in with Ty sitting in front of him and Taylor Ann riding behind Zach Adams with her arms around his waist.

Corey took his wife by the hand. They bounded off the porch and ran to meet them.

Both horses stopped. Stranger lowered Ty to the ground, and he ran with extended arms to meet his parents. Because of her long skirt and petticoats, it took Taylor Ann a little longer to get down.

Seconds later, however, they were embracing each other, laughing and crying at the same time. When the two men rode up and dismounted, the McCollisters rushed to them. Emily Grace saw the bruises on Zach's face and asked what happened. At the same time, Corey pumped John Stranger for information, and Taylor Ann was trying to tell her part of the story above it all.

"Hold it! Hold it!" said Stranger, throwing his palms up. "Let's go take a seat on the porch, and we'll give you a few details."

"How about us?" asked Curly Ford, who was among the happy ranch hands.

"Come on," said Corey. "You guys might as well hear it firsthand so you don't spread rumors."

There was joyous laughter as everyone headed for the porch.

The cowhands gathered around while the others mounted the steps and sat down. Taylor Ann took Zach by the hand and sat him on the porch swing beside her.

Stranger said, "You're all wondering about the bruises on Zach's face. Well, the young whippersnapper was so eager to rescue the woman he loves that he wasn't thinking too clearly. I had to take him off his horse. He'd be a dead man if I hadn't knocked him out and tied him to a tree."

Taylor Ann looked at Zach, smiled, and squeezed his hand.

Zach's face tinted as he sent a glance to his boss.

Corey smiled. "It's no surprise to me to hear Mr. Stranger say that you love my daughter, Zach. I've seen it in your eyes for a long time. And even if I hadn't, your heroic attempt to save her life at the risk of your own tells me how you feel about her."

"I've seen it for a long time, too, Zach," spoke up Emily Grace. "And I can never thank you enough for what you did today."

Taylor Ann looked around at the group and said, "I already told Zach this on our way home, but so you all will know...I'm in love with him, too."

The cowhands cheered, whistled, and applauded.

Emily Grace's face beamed. Her prayers were answered.

"Well," said Corey, "it looks like this might be serious."

"It is, Mr. McCollister," said Zach. "I had really planned to do this a little differently, but I can't wait. On the way home, after Taylor Ann told me how she felt about me, I asked her to marry me. This, of course, after a proper courtship and when I'm making enough money to support her. I...ah...I would like to ask you and Mrs. McCollister for her hand in marriage."

"Why am I not surprised at this?" Corey chuckled. "I believe I can speak for both Emily Grace and myself. You have our permission to marry Taylor Ann."

The cowhands whooped it up again. Emily Grace hurried to her daughter, embraced her, then embraced Zach Adams. Taylor Ann embraced her father, and Tyler—who hadn't the faintest idea what was going on—was jumping up and down, squealing, and clapping his hands.

Corey and Zach shook hands, then the happy young couple returned to the swing, and Taylor Ann kissed her future husband's cheek.

Corey cleared his throat, glanced at his wife, then looked at Zach and said, "About this making enough money, Zach..."

"Yes, sir?"

"Curly told me just an hour ago that he'll be retiring and leaving us in three weeks. My mind had been made up some time ago that when Curly retired, I'd offer you his job. You want it?"

"Yes, sir!"

The cowhands whooped it up again, and Corey and Zach both received kisses from Taylor Ann.

Corey took a deep breath, let it out slowly, and said, "Now, John Stranger, we all want to hear how you rescued Ty and Taylor Ann."

Stranger adjusted himself on his wicker seat, grinned at Taylor Ann, and said, "That is forever our secret."

"What?" gasped Corey. "We all want to know!"

"Sorry," said Stranger. "I made a promise to someone that Taylor Ann and I would never tell. Now, you wouldn't want a man to break his promise, would you?"

Corey scratched an ear. "No, I guess not. But I'll always wonder how you did it."

"The important thing, darling," spoke up Emily Grace, "is that we have our daughter and son home unharmed."

All agreed, then Emily Grace said to her daughter,

"Sweetheart, there's something else that needs to be said here. That was a very unselfish and heroic deed you performed, too. One day when Ty is old enough to understand, I'll tell him about it. Then he'll know just how much his big sister loves him."

Tears filled Taylor Ann's eyes. She motioned for Ty to come to her, and folded him in her arms.

John Stranger turned to the rancher and said, "I have some good news concerning Iron Hand, Corey."

"Oh?"

"He gave me his word that you and your family would never be harmed or bothered by the Cheyenne."

"That is good news."

Stranger then told Corey there were a couple of other things he wanted to discuss with him in the presence of just the family. Corey dismissed the ranch hands. When Zach started to leave, Corey told him he could stay, since he was practically family.

When the Circle M crew was out of earshot, Stranger said, "Corey, I assume Marshal Luskin filled you in about Woodard and Premro."

"Yeah, the dirty crooks. I sure appreciate you're clearing this rustling thing up...and putting that gang behind bars."

"This brings up a serious matter," Stranger said.

"Yes?"

"It wasn't the Cheyenne who stole your cattle."

"Oh," nodded Corey, looking sheepish. "I do owe Iron Hand an apology. He'll get that apology tomorrow. I'll ride out to the village in the morning, and I'll also tell him that his people can ride across Circle M land all they want. And from now on, I'll give his people beef enough to see them through the winters."

"There's one other thing, Corey," said Stranger.

"Yes?"

"Jim Logan."

Corey looked at the porch floor and scratched at an ear again.

Stranger proceeded. "Remember when Peter asked Jesus in Matthew 18 how many times he should forgive a brother who had sinned against him?"

"Yes," nodded Corey, his voice breaking. "Seventy times seven."

"I think when you take into consideration the pressure the man was under, he's got forgiveness coming, don't you?"

"He sure does," agreed Corey.

When Emily Grace saw the tears well up in her husband's eyes, she started crying too. Closing her eyes, she whispered, "Thank you, Lord."

"My dear wife has tried to talk sense to me time and time again...but my foolish bullheadedness caused this whole mess." Looking to his wife and daughter, he asked for their forgiveness.

After tearful embraces and words of forgiveness, Corey took out a bandanna, blew his nose, and said to his future foreman and son-in-law, "Zach, would you hitch up a team to the wagon, please? We're going to town. I'm going to square things with Jim Logan."

Darkness was settling over northwest Nebraska when the McCollister wagon pulled into Hay Springs with Zach Adams at the reins. John Stranger rode Ebony.

As Zach veered the wagon toward the marshal's office and jail, Stranger said, "I'll catch up to you in a few minutes. There's something I have to do."

At the same time the wagon creaked to a halt, Zach looked down the street and grinned. Taylor Ann studied him a moment, then followed his line of sight and asked, "What are you grinning about?"

"You didn't see him?"

"Who?"

"Bob Osborne."

"No."

"He was going into the Buttercup Café with Sally Barton on his arm."

"Good. I'm glad it's her and not me."

"Me, too."

Marshal Jed Luskin was just entering the office from the cellblock as the McCollisters and Zach Adams filed in. Tyler was sticking close to his mother.

"Howdy, folks," grinned the marshal.

"We'd like to see Jim Logan, Marshal," said Corey.

"Well, his family's back there with him right now. Jail's pretty well loaded since Mr. Stranger hauled in those rustlers."

"I'd like to see him out here," Corey said quickly.

Luskin studied him a moment. "Well, I can't let him out of the cell unless—"

"That's exactly what I want. I'm dropping the charges. Let him out."

Merilee Logan was crying happy tears when the marshal ushered the Logan family into the office. The children had sparkling eyes, and Jim Logan, face pale, looked at Corey McCollister.

"I don't know what to say, Corey," Jim's voice came in a strained tone.

"You don't have to say a thing," smiled the rancher. "I'm the one with something to say. I'm asking you to forgive me for being such a stubborn, bullheaded fool, Jim. If I'd given you the help you asked for, none of this would have happened. I'm sorry."

"I appreciate you feeling that way, Corey, but there's no excuse for what I did. Marshal Luskin told us Ty was out here with you. Boy, am I glad! How did you get him back?"

"Long story, my friend," grinned Corey. "We'll fill you in on it later. I'll say this much, though. We owe a great debt of thanks to John Stranger."

"Did I hear my name?" came a soft, low voice.

All eyes turned to the tall man with the rip in his shirt as he came through the door from the street. Corey and Emily Grace had assumed the shirt was torn when Stranger and Zach had their tussle. Zach knew better, but still was in the dark about how it happened.

Jim smiled at Corey and said, "My family and I sure owe a lot to this man."

"We sure do," Merilee said.

Stranger looked at Corey, then Jim. "You two get things patched up?"

"Not exactly," replied Corey. "I've dropped the charges, of course, but Jim hasn't actually said he forgives me."

"Oh, didn't I? Well, then I'll say it. I forgive you, Corey. And again, I'm sorry about abducting Ty."

The two men hugged each other. Jim winced slightly because of his chest wound, but there was joy in the marshal's office. The women also traded embraces.

George Nelson stepped into the crowded office and looked at Jim Logan. "I heard there might be some rejoicing going on over here, Jim, and I wanted to get in on it."

Logan didn't know what to say.

Moving in a little further, Nelson said, "Jim, I want to tell you that I've canceled your bill, and I'd like to return the thirty dollars I tricked you out of."

Jim accepted the three ten-dollar bills and smiled at Zach Adams. He then turned to the general store proprietor. "Thank you, Mr. Nelson."

"I have something else to tell you, too. Someone came into the store a little while ago and put five hundred dollars on account for you. When you make your purchases, we'll deduct the amounts from the money held in the account."

Merilee was staring at Nelson, wide-eyed. "That will get us through the winter, Jim," she breathed.

"Who was that someone, Mr. Nelson?" Merilee asked.

The general store proprietor put on a crooked grin, rubbed the back of his neck, and said, "Well, ma'am...I wasn't supposed to identify the person, but I'm gonna break my word. It was a big tall fella with dark hair. He wears a bone-handled Colt .45 Peacemaker, talks in a low tone, and I just can't bring myself to tell you any more than that."

"Oh, Mr. Stranger, how can we ever repay you?" Merilee said.

"No need, Merilee," grinned Stranger. "Just tell your husband it came from the Lord...and that he should never doubt Him."

"Believe me, I won't, Mr. Stranger," Jim said. "How could I ever forget what the Lord's done here tonight."

Corey laid a hand on Jim's shoulder. "Well, my brother, you'll have even more to remember about tonight." As he spoke, Corey pulled a folded check from his pocket and stuffed it into Jim's hand. Jim blinked, eyed his benefactor, and opened the check. Biting his lips, he handed it to Merilee.

"Five hundred dollars!" she exclaimed, and broke down completely.

While her parents were holding each other and weeping, little Susie tapped her mother on the leg and said, "Mommy, if you an' Daddy don' want the five hunnerd dollars, I'll take it!"

There was a round of laughter.

Corey looked at Emily Grace, then at Jim and said, "Guess we'd better get this thing over before we're flooded out of here. Jim...Emily Grace and I talked something over while Zach was driving us into town. We want to give you—I said *give* you—another hundred head of cows and a couple of bulls for a new start. You'll accept them, won't you?"

Jim sniffed, shook his head, and said, "Is there snow in the North Pole?"

There was more laughter.

Emily Grace kissed her husband for his generosity. George

Nelson and Jed Luskin were having their own trouble with extra moisture in their eyes.

Emily Grace said, "We all owe our unspeakable gratitude to Mr. Stranger, and I think we should—"

Every eye turned to the spot by the door where John Stranger had been standing...but he was gone. They dashed out onto the lantern-lit street, but could see no sign of him.

Jim Logan sighed, "That's just the way he works. He's there when you need him, then he vanishes."

"Oh, no!" said Luskin. "I've got a message in my desk drawer that Doc Getz wanted me to give him. I guess it's too late, now."

Something shiny at her feet caught Taylor Ann's eye. Looking down, she saw a silver medallion the size of a silver dollar. Picking it up, she said, "Look at this. A silver piece with an inscription on it: *THE STRANGER THAT SHALL COME FROM A FAR LAND—Deuteronomy 29:22.*"

"Mommy," said Benjamin, "that's just like the one Mr. Stranger gave to me."

"Yes, honey. I have an idea a lot of people get one of these."

Gripping the medallion in her hand, Taylor Ann stepped into the dimly lit street and walked to its center. Looking off into the darkness at the north end of the street, she said softly, "Stranger from a far land...who are you? Who are you *really?*"

OTHER COMPELLING STORIES BY
AL LACY

Books in the Battles of Destiny series:

☛ *A Promise Unbroken*

Two couples battle jealousy and racial hatred amidst a war that would cripple America. From a prosperous Virginia plantation to a grim jail cell outside Lynchburg, follow the dramatic story of a love that could not be destroyed.

☛ *A Heart Divided*

Ryan McGraw—leader of the Confederate Sharpshooters—is nursed back to health by beautiful army nurse Dixie Quade. Their romance would survive the perils of war, but can it withstand the reappearance of a past love?

☛ *Beloved Enemy*

Young Jenny Jordan covers for her father's Confederate spy missions. But as she grows closer to Union soldier Buck Brownell, Jenny finds herself torn between devotion to the South and her feelings for the man she is forbidden to love.

☛ *Shadowed Memories*

Critically wounded on the field of battle and haunted by amnesia, one man struggles to regain his strength and the memories that have slipped away from him.

Books in the Journeys of the Stranger series:

☞ *Legacy*

Can John Stranger, a mysterious hero who brings truth, honor, and justice to the Old West, bring Clay Austin back to the right side of the law...and restore the code of honor shared by the woman he loves?

Available at your local Christian bookstore